The Buffalo Gun
Book Two in the Walking Y Saga

The Buffalo Gun

Book Two in The Walking Y Saga
Jeter Isely

Copyright c 2023 by Jeter Isely
All Rights Reserved.

The characters and events portrayed in this book are fictitious. Any similarity to real persons, living or dead is coincidental and not intended by the author.

No part of this book may be reproduced, or stored in a retrieval system, or transmitted in any form or by any means, electronic, mechanical, photocopying, recording, or otherwise, without express written permission of the author.

ISBN – 13: 979-8-851886-79-9
ISBN – 10: 8-851886-79-9

Cover design by Amanda Hansen and Jeter Isely
Cover Design and contents are property of Jeter A. F Isely

Printed in the United States of America
If you have questions and would like to reach the author, please reach out through e-mail at "yknotfarmandranch@gmail.com"

Dedication

The Buffalo Gun is dedicated to our four-legged friends, with a bias for horses such as the matched Belgians, Nip and Blue. Also, cowponies, Sacramenta, Harley, Ginny, Princess, Nitro and many more.
Also, our canine friends Ozzie, Bijou, Remy (Remington), Patches, Rue (Ruger), Fawkes, Finny and more among a long list.
They have all been good friends while being true to their nature.

Horse Harness Diagram

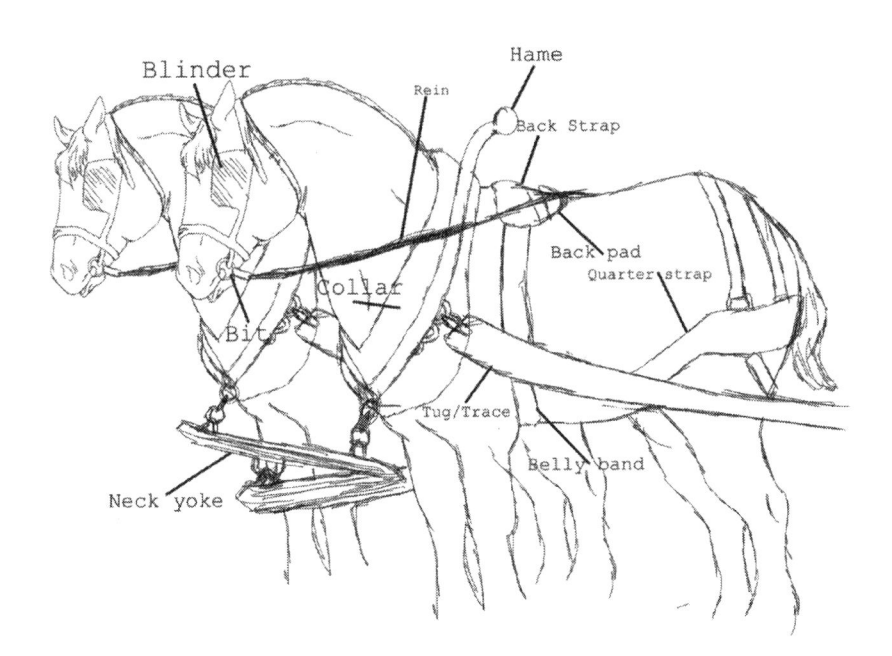

Wagon Diagram

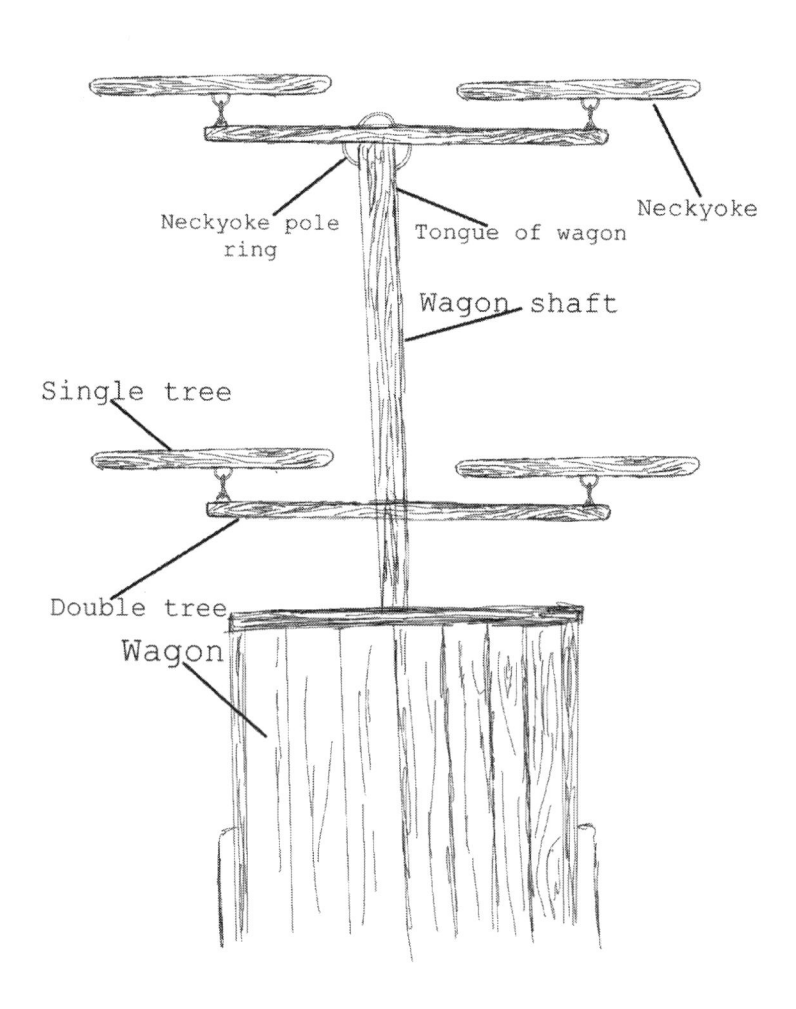

- Neckyoke pole ring
- Tongue of wagon
- Neckyoke
- Wagon shaft
- Single tree
- Double tree
- Wagon

Chapter 1

<u>New Year's Party</u>

    The Christmas wreath shows the cumulative impact of very cold nights, as the hard frost withers the holly woven with the pine boughs. Bright ribbons, and expensive glass balls wage a forlorn fight against the muting delicate ice crystals. The glow from the lanterns by the door casts a glimmering light on the frigid decoration while nature garnishes the neighboring trees with intricate ice constructions. Senator William Howard Bell the Third does not note the beauty of the denuded trees, nor that of the decorations as he shows the last of his guests out of his grand Greek Revival house on what is now New Year's Day.

    It is well past two in the morning, and this party is finally closing. Like all such events hosted by him and his wife Gabrielle on their Ringing Bell Ranch, it is another success with the promise of future profits. His wife made the evening glow, clad in her close-fitting sheer white dress adorned with her gold and diamond studded necklace. Her charm and revealing figure are good attributes and will be the talk of most guests in the coming days. As to the Senator, standing tall, he carefully closes the door dusting off his immaculately tailored three-piece suit, and ignores the serving girls who are now cleaning the debris which they must do before they can call it a night in their cold cramped rooms.

    He walks upstairs to his spacious master bedroom, where he knows that his wife awaits by the marble fireplace. As he enters their large private suite, Gabrielle is seated in a divan in the glass enclosed sunroom. The fire's dancing light reflects on the immaculate windowpanes, many of which have a growing lattice of ice forming due to the cold. As to his wife, she smiles and better yet, has a bottle of excellent quality sherry and two long stemmed crystal glasses on a marble topped side table in the warm room. She shifts over a bit, catlike with an economy of movements that accentuates her young, lithe figure, and invites her husband to sit by her.

With careful gestures, she offers one of the long-stemmed glasses to her mate.

In a soft voice, that masks her meticulous calculating ambitious mind, she brings forth what has bothered her most of the evening. "That was an excellent gathering, yet I thought you would hint that you would be running for governor as you complete this term as Senator."

Here she pauses for a moment, before she states plainly, "but tonight, when the Vice Presidents of the Anaconda Company and that of the Great Northern Railroad were asking you if you were pursuing that path, this as they prepare to choose the right candidate in the coming Governor's race, you did not respond as you should have."

Senator Bell takes a sip of well-aged sherry and looks quizzically at his wife. She takes this as an invitation to continue, "Are we still somehow being blackmailed by Mr. Woodrow W. Flynt and his Walking Y Ranch or worse yet, are we being bamboozled by that coarse Catholic Irish pugilist who murdered our Hank in cold blood?"

Here she pauses to gauge her husband's mood. She reads his nodding head as an invitation to proceed. That she must, as the events of the past ten days have irritated her. "Blackmail is the only way I can read the fact that we incurred significant pecuniary expenses to replace those cows that Roger righteously shot after our exalted neighbor used our own Ringing Bell cows to get a bank loan. Not only that, but you helped renew that loan and we also paid for those horses that those wild orphans shot while they were riding them, along with all those medical bills. I know we discussed this at the time, but we even paid for the doctor's wife, who tells all in town how she had to nurse that dirty repugnant boy, Frederick Torroni. This, the same boy who shot and wounded our very own manager, Jesse. At this point, it is high time to put a halt to our velvety treatment of Mr. Woodrow W. Flynt's cattle operation."

With color rising to her cheeks, and her posture gaining rigidity, her tone hardens. "How do we make sure that we destroy that confession that Woodrow is holding to blackmail us? He is the sort of obnoxious, miserly, greedy individual who will milk it for everything he can. Look, in the past two weeks we had to back off all the legal actions you had started such as having that Irish scum locked up and that fiend, Eric sent to the reformatory. What does Woody have on us? Do you really suspect that Roger betrayed us?"

Carefully Montana State Senator William Howard Bell the Third takes another sip of the vintage sherry and begins crafting his rebuttal. "My dearest Gabrielle, that setback of not even two weeks ago has been a raw, painful, and humiliating experience. Never have we suffered such a reversal in so few short minutes. Never has a series of witnesses left me standing so momentarily at a loss for a legal maneuver that could save our interest. While I have been transparent with you, there is danger in that turn of events that clashes with our aspirations. We need to tread carefully for a little longer, as the loss of political power now could leave us without the significant income I secured for our interest in the last legislative session and plan to grow in the next."

The Senator stands and walks behind his wife, and touches her soft shoulder, "the problem my dear one is that we are in ignorance as to what Mr. Woodrow W. Flynt may have in his possession that could impact our objectives. Who knows what fabrications he may have about the abduction of those two girls, and how those may be embellished by titillating accounts of a sexual nature by those lassies. All I know is that Woodrow was fully aware of Roger's mission, and somehow he retrieved the girls from that remote cabin from where they should not have been able to escape due to the winter cold. Somehow the Walking Y managed to find and release them. To make it worse, Sherriff Bozeman and his deputy, Tex, could not hold that contemptible Irish Catholic scum in prison where he rightly belongs. So, yes, the Walking Y defeated the men we hired, Roger, Hank, and Dave."

Gabrielle looks back at her husband and raises an eyebrow. "Have you not heard from John Keegan regarding this matter, and has he tracked down Roger or Dave?"

"No, no luck whatsoever with regards to Roger or Dave. Their belongings along with Dave's saddle still grace our bunkhouse. On the other hand, I will soon meet with John in Denver, but so far, I am drawing a blank on Roger and Dave. I even covertly invested a Double Eagle with Randy, the owner of the Silver King Saloon, to be on the lookout and forward any idle chatter, but thus far he has had no luck hearing anything that is of help. What really worries me are the stories Roger may have created and embellished, especially in that so-called confession, which Woody promised I could have after I signed our agreement. Then again, like with everything else, he lied and did not comply."

His wife looks up and takes a very delicate sip of sherry, and comments, "it is a shame that you had Roger on our payroll. You should have fired both Roger and Dave sooner than last week, as their actions, even if fully approved by both of us, may be viewed by some in a fashion to impugn the integrity of our characters."

The Senator nods his head in the affirmative, and states, "from what Woodrow W. Flynt tells me, they implicated us in their disreputable actions including that of kidnapping the girls, leaving them in that cabin naked with only one blanket, with just our employee Dave, and who knows what else. Frustratingly, I have not been able to find any trace of either of our two hoodlums. Thus, I remain without knowledge as to their fate or their location. In fact, I would not be shocked if they were deceased. I do not know if they signed a real confession that falsely implicated us. Worse yet, I remain in ignorance if that was a bit of bluffing by the owner of the Walking Y, may his soul rot in hell."

Gabrielle looks at her husband's tight mouth, and she sits a bit straighter and responds in a quiet voice. "William Howard Bell the Third, you have always said that Woodrow comes at you like a bull on the trail of a cow in heat. Thus, would bluffing not be out of character?"

"Yes, my dear Gabrielle," the Senator replies somewhat at wits end, "that is part of the problem. The Walking Y is behaving erratically and out of character. Woodrow, who was always so predictable, now seems to be listening to those orphans and to that drunken Irish Catholic stump trainer. If anything, I would think that such a label implying bestiality would disqualify him from being his foreman. That ranch has become much harder to predict."

Here he pauses for a bit, looks at his wife to gauge her mood, "I'm trying to gain time while I get information, because there is something that does not register as quite right. For instance, Jesse has seen that team of Belgian draft horses that I purchased for Dave in Lincoln. It was being driven by one of those disreputable orphans, the one called Nick. Why would Dave leave a valuable team behind, and why would Roger, that avaricious man, not have insisted that he get his back pay before I knew that he had signed the confession? I have crafted some rumors in town blaming Roger and Dave for those actions that may be embarrassing, and now state that both are no longer in our employ, but I cannot track either of them down."

His wife stands, and softly steps behind the Senator. Running her hand through his hair, she purrs, "Well, my wonderful Senator, it appears that you must see or contact John. That's where you originally hired Roger for the first-time years ago, and John has never disappointed us until this most recent episode, and of course, he'd better not again. The reality is that we need to kill and bury those kids once and for all. We must dispatch that Irishman Seamus Patrick O'Connor and destroy our illustrious neighbor Mr. Woodrow W. Flynt and his Walking Y once and for all. They are nothing but an irritant and must not be an obstacle to our rightful creation of the largest ranch in the county and one of the largest in the state. Our thus expanded Ringing Bell ranch will be the perfect platform to make you Governor and both of us powerful and rich for the good of all the fine people in this state."

The Senator runs his hand to his head and puts it on top of his wife's velvety fingers. He gives it a gentle squeeze and pontificates, "I am in full concurrence. The good news is that earlier today I received a telegram from John in reply to my letters, and this answer gives me hope. That is why I did not close off the possibility of running for Governor of Montana tonight. Our Butte friend stated from the telegram he sent from his Denver office that he cannot find any trace or scent of Roger nor even of Dave. He thus suspects that they were both killed and were secretly buried, probably by Woodrow and his crew. John affirms that he sought to take advantage of methods that have worked in the past to contact them for employment to no avail. In short, what has always worked in the past to contact them is now a dry well."

Here the Senator pauses for a bit, and in a surge of emotions, turns and looks at his young wife. Finally, he continues, "Better yet, John Keegan postulates that signing a confession is most unlike Roger. John is convinced that Woodrow was bluffing when I signed that agreement. He wants to meet with me later this month, as he promises that he has the ideal couple who will get to the bottom of the mystery."

The Senator now smiles as he continues, "That said, I told John that he must start a concerted campaign against Woodrow W. Flynt. I suggested that he separate Mr. Flynt from that foreman of his, whom the children insist on calling Tony. In short, I informed him to eliminate The Walking Y Ranch and all who work there; however, this time, to wage an operation where we are not directly involved. Where nothing can be traced to the Ringing Bell Ranch."

"I remember John's reply as he nodded his head and said, 'Senator, I can vouch that we are well advanced in the planning stages.'"

The room is quiet for a moment, and Gabrielle and the Senator again sit side by side. Finally, the Senator continues, "Yes, John Keegan wants me to be elected Governor and he wants to know that Montana will get the governor it deserves. John has already secured the support of my candidacy from the Anaconda Mining and Milling Company. He is sure that we can persuade both the Great Northern Railroad and the Burlington Railroad to support my campaign as I have been amicable to the needs of these corporations in the past. Now dear, are you ready to be the first Lady of the State of Montana?"

Gabrielle runs her right hand to her long dark brown hair and sweeps it back from her white visage. Smiling she looks at her husband and nods, "Oh, yes. What I do not understand though, is why don't you tell Woody to get lost, and call his bluff?"

Suddenly looking a bit tired, her husband replies, "First, I want to get that document I was blackmailed into signing, and I want to make sure that there is no confession by Roger and Dave, and more important yet is to make sure that no matter what, they can never talk against us or oppose us even posthumously, in writing. With regards to the Walking Y, if necessary, I fear a fire might ravage his cookhouse with a few bodies inside. John told me he has plans to eliminate Mr. Woodrow W. Flynt along with that Seamus Patrick O'Connor and those five delinquent orphans they absconded with under shady circumstances from the orphanage in Sandpoint, Idaho."

Here the Senator pauses for a moment before resuming, "However, John also insists that he wishes to be a little more subtle and as I already said, he claims he has the ideal couple to solve our problems. He will persuade her to take employment in the heart of the Walking Y, and that way we will kill Woodrow's ranch from the inside. In order to help her in the task, he will also hire him to put external pressure to distract the Walking Y from the true danger. There is too much at stake to do otherwise, and the strong interests I have supported in the past want us in the Governor's mansion in Helena."

Chapter 2

<u>Woody's Hardy</u>

The night westbound train huffs into Hellenville with its whistle blowing, enveloped in a steam cloud, breaking the quiet of a cold snowing evening. The bell sounds muted, as the locomotive brakes hiss and the line of mail cars and coaches behind it clang to a full stop. Among the passengers disgorged on the icy platform is a large black man, who steps off tentatively and stiffly, as the years have taken a toll on his joints. He looks around, his head a bit over that of the other passengers and sees a man he has not seen in decades. Faintly, he smiles, and steps through the crowd.

Wearing a well-worn cowboy hat and a dirt encrusted sheepskin coat, the old stout rancher moves forwards, and extends one of his large, calloused hands. The tall man seizes it with emotion born of warm friendship. Woody looks into the black man's eyes, and a true smile lights his face, momentarily making him look younger and less careworn. The stiff passenger returns the favor and straightens his back. The ranch owner voices a greeting,

"Hardy, so glad to see you, you haven't changed in what, twenty years?"

The tall man, whose build would also be the envy of a brick outhouse, smiles back heartily, "Woody, my God, you look just the same, all the way down to your graying hair. And worn hat. Haven't you ever been able to afford a new hat, or do you buy them worn?"

Both men laugh in camaraderie. Woody affectionately clasps his guest's elbow and Hardy resumes, "Let's see it has been – closer to twenty-one years? You brought a smile to my face with your letter inviting me to join you, even if you're in trouble - again."

Woodrow W. Flynt puts his hand on Hardy's shoulder and steers him towards the secondary exit from the platform. Hardy, or James Thomas Hardyman, carries a large carpet bag in one hand and just enjoys the

"Nick is the next lad; his family was French, and he speaks a bit of that language yet. He is stouter than Eric but would have a way to go to match you. He is a good athlete and loves those big draft horses. That lad has darker reddish-brown hair, and strangely enough green eyes. He was held at knife point and cut up a bit and threatened with being gelded. He feels guilty for telling Roger's man which girls were in the cookhouse. Then there is Fred. He's still gimping from the bullet that nearly killed him. He'll never be strong, but he is the smartest kid I've ever known. He has black hair, and dark brown eyes.

"When Tony, our foreman, is sober – which thankfully he is most of the time – he will tell you how the two girls ran away from the orphanage to join us and the boys. I didn't want them and was livid with that Irish Catholic brawler for bringing them. But they are both worth their weight in gold. They managed to signal us from the cabin where they were held when kidnapped. What I didn't tell you in the letter, is that they were held naked so they could not escape due to the Montana winter. They both made a run for it, and Teri even managed to get away and warn Tony about the ambush Roger and Dave had set up. My, if I had sired girls, I could not have done better. All of that said, they have been through a lot, and I need headquarters to be safe."

Hardy nods his head, encouraging the grizzled owner to talk on.

Woody, twists his short stocky frame around to scan the room, seeing no one, he then continues, "It's just a matter of time before Senator Bell comes back after us. Actually, I am impressed that he has paid us for the cows and horses his men killed, and closed out the legal battles he had created, but I have always said that Senator William Howard Bell the Third is not a man to trifle with, as we have done. I also fear that he has some sort of backup who is powerful and even more ruthless, but I do not know whom. And as you know too well from the first time we met, I don't give a damn about normal conventions and kissing ass. So, let's be honest, I might lose a popularity contest with a skunk if the election for the role was held in this county."

Hardy reflects for a moment and puts on a pair of wire rim spectacles. He leans back in his chair which creaks at holding his strong frame and takes a sip of his beer with large capable hands. "Yeah," he replies slowly in a deep voice, "I see what you mean. Woody, that we get along is only due to the fact that I saved your hide as a young man – which is only fair 'cause you saved mine." Here he smiles a bit as do two comrades at arms. "I'm still amazed that we got out of there. I've heard of foolish things but finding you aways north of Little Big Horn in the late summer prowling for gold with the Indians madder than a hornet was not the smartest thing you or I ever did!"

Hardy smiles and then goes on, "as I told you in my reply letter, my kids, for some obscure reason have all stayed in this part of the world, and I am retired. So, your ranch is a great location between my boy in Missoula, another in Billings, and a daughter in Boise, Idaho. Looking back first from my stint with the Army as a Buffalo soldier and then from my cooking job in Denver, I think we can make this work, and again, I think the pair of us will be underestimated. Just like we were in the summer with those Indians on the prowl."

Both sit quietly for a moment, as one can with those rare friends to whom you would trust your life. Hardy then leans forwards. "Woody, to make this work, you have to treat me like a colored cook. No better, no worse. You can't let people know we go back, nor let people know that I can fight harder than most men half my age. Even at sixty years of age, not many can match me with fists, a handgun, a rifle or even with a knife. I can still hit a quarter with my revolver if you toss it in the air and give you change. These spectacles are a bit of a prop, and I only need them to read. In fact, don't let them know I can read, or any other thing about my past. Limit it to the fact that I asked for a job and cooked for a ranch or two."

He looks around and sees only Mrs. Wilson in the dining hall. "Will she talk?"

Woody looks up, "Fernande," he calls as she comes by the table. "Can you overlook my guest for now?"

"Why yes, of course Woody." Fernande Wilson, the fine figured middle-aged owner of The Prancing Mare stands by the table for a moment as she knows Woody well enough to guess that he has a bit more to state.

"OK Hardy, let's go, and you can trust Fernande in everything. In fact," he adds turning to Fernande, "Hardy here has my full trust. I would trust him with my life. So, if he needs anything, trust him as much as you trust Tony. But please do not tell anybody you saw us here tonight. Hardy will be my colored cook and help me try to keep the orphans safe."

Thereupon both men walk out into the cold dark night after finishing their drinks and closing out their discussions. The ranch buckboard waits for them, and there are very few horses tied at the rail. None wear the Senator's brand, and Woody is content that he managed to have the needed discussion seemingly without arousing any curiosity. Should any have noted them talking, he already plans to tell people that he finished ironing out Hardy's employment terms at the Prancing Mare before bringing him to the ranch.

Surprise is Fred's reaction when he enters the cookhouse the next morning to start breakfast, as he has the unfortunate task on that cold day. The kitchen is already warm, pork chops are already in a cast iron pan, and the table is set. No sooner do these facts click in his brain and a smile of pleasure wraps itself on his face, than a large grey haired black man steps out from the pantry with a loaf of bread. Fred's face drops.

"Who are you?" barks the surprised and normally very polite lad, taken aback by this new person in the kitchen. Seeking to recover, he continues, "strangers are usually not a good thing on this ranch." Realizing that he is just painting himself as totally impolite he stops, and stares with his mouth open.

"The cook," answers the stout man with a genuine smile. "Woody had an ad in the paper, I applied in person last night, and he hired me at the Prancing Mare. Call me Hardy or Cookie."

Teri stumbles down the stairs upon hearing a strange voice and barrels into the kitchen holding a rifle at the ready. Behind her, Michelle whose hair is a mass of confusion thus veiling her face, also holds another single shot twenty-two.

Teri barks, rudely, "What are you doing here," while aggressively holding the rifle as she cocks it. "How did you get in?"

She swivels looking at her friend, "Michelle, I swear, I locked the doors, because Woody said he'd be out late. I thought it was Woody downstairs, not some strange black man."

"Take it easy ladies, and you can put the rifles on the gun rack. Woody hired me last night when I applied, and he told me that none of you would complain at the fact that you have a cook instead of being stuck doing it yourselves."

The girls look at each other uncertainly when at that moment, Tony along with Nick and Eric walk in. The Irishman smiles, extends a hand in greeting and looks at Hardy, "so you must be the new cook, Hardy I believe. This is great. While I'll miss the girls' cooking, I will no longer have to eat my own or Eric's burnt beans or worse yet, Woody's tough steaks. My name is Tony, and you are most welcome here on the Walking Y. Not only that, you're being here also gives me back my full crew."

The Irishman's smile and genuine welcome puts all at ease. This augmented by the smell of a good meal, the bubbling of hot coffee and especially the pot of hot chocolate, and Hardy's grin means that Teri puts her rifle where it belongs, while Michelle does the same and then slips into her chair without hiding too much behind Teri or one of the boys.

Eric on the other hands licks his chops, "Did I hear that you're called Hardy? Boy, am I glad you're here, and now I don't have to cook. Not only that, but I'm also so hungry my stomach is chewing on my backbone."

Woody is the last to arrive in the kitchen, having spent the night in the old cabin his father had built which is just a few steps away from the cookhouse.

He exchanges a stilted polite greeting with Hardy, and the two do not talk much. None note their body language except for Tony, but the Irishman stays mum on the subject. Conversation soon gravitates to the assignments for the day, with the girls tasked with continuing to train their horses, Crowhop and Princess. Woody will work with Nick and Fred on polishing their riding skills and also training their own new mounts. All are ecstatic at finally being rid of kitchen duty, and after an excellent meal, all stand to start the day.

"Those were sure good pork chops," muses Eric while putting his plate full of bones on the counter and reaching for a cinnamon roll to take on his walk to the barn, as he and Tony have some cattle checks ahead of them. Hardy smiles at the lad. Woody smirks.

"Yes, thank you Hardy, breakfast was delicious," adds Teri. She does not turn away from this big sincere man but looks him in the eye. "I didn't mean to sound impolite when I greeted you this morning, but Michelle and I do not feel safe in the cookhouse, so we kind of sleep with our rifles even if Woody only provides us with an inadequate single shot Winchester twenty-two. We should feel safe, but so far it has not worked that way."

"Well Teri and Michelle," answers Hardy with careful words, "I mean to make sure you are safe, and my sixty years have taught me a trick or two if needed. I actually think that's why Mr. Flynt hired me." So saying, he gives a wink and a broad smile. "When you get done with those ponies, I'll have a snack for you, so that you can put your mind at ease."

Chapter 3

<u>John Keegan</u>

The clock strikes two in the large open waiting room of Denver's sumptuous Union Station. The crowd parts as a well-dressed patrician man plows through aiming for the ornate oaken doors on the far side where stands a uniformed doorman guarding the high-class restaurant. The blue-blooded passenger proceeds at a determined pace. Suit, necktie, shining boots are visible as is the expensive coat that covers his frame. His face is stern, well shaven, and sports but a few white hairs. He deigns not to turn his head to the left nor to the right and those around him know that he looks down on them as mere low-class mortals unworthy of notice.

"Sir," greets the doorman seeking some identification from the rapidly advancing well-groomed lean dark-haired man. In reply, he weathers a look that would intimidate any recruit in a military camp when addressed by a master sergeant. The uniformed doorman quietly, bowing his head, opens the door, and bobs in deference as the newest guest passes without a further glance.

Inside, the newfangled electric lights struggle to show the patrician gentleman slowing as he approaches the reservation desk. Without a smile or any greeting whatsoever, he addresses the uniformed clerk. "I am Senator William Howard Bell the Third, and I have a reservation and a meeting with Mr. John Keegan."

"Welcome Senator," replies the young smiling cleanly shaven receptionist from behind his small reservation desk. "Mr. Keegan is waiting at a secluded table. Please follow me."

The Senator shadows the clerk and again neither turns his regard to the right nor left. Yet, his eyes miss nothing, as it is important that he not be accosted in this establishment at this time. In this, he is helped by the inadequate electric illumination and muted afternoon light filtering in the high-ceilinged room from the windows. The pregnant clouds outside scud by to drop snow in a fashion typical of mid-January. Soon the pair turn into a darker corner, bereft of the newfangled bare electric lightbulbs, where a red cloth covers an ornate wooden table that stands apart with a single candle. The corner is guarded by carefully sculpted dark oak paneling on three sides, and a large space on the fourth side.

Only a few chairs surround the remote table, and two chairs are positioned catty-corner to each other so that their occupants can watch the room. One is already occupied. A corpulent balding man, clad in well ironed plaid trousers that are matched by a similar coat, watches and misses nothing. He slowly stands as he fixes a smile on his face that does not reach his eyes and regards the Senator.

"Ah! Senator William Howard Bell, always a pleasure."

"Mr. John Keegan," quietly greets the lawyer. Senator Bell then palms a silver fifty cent piece and drops it into the discreet hand of the clerk, dismissing him without a word. He turns to Mr. John Keegan, and nods a business-like silent greeting, while checking one more time that all adjoining tables are empty, and no ears can overhear the pair.

Mr. Keegan examines the Senator for any changes since the two last met. So doing, he indicates the second chair with his head and waves his hand to the table. "Knowing your punctuality, and our usual need to talk confidentially, I've taken the liberty of ordering a couple appetizers, coffee, and a good bottle of single malt scotch so that we are left alone."

The Senator nods in acknowledgement, removes his long coat and drapes it over an empty chair at their designated stall. He then sits catty-corner from the man he had commanded to be available for this two o'clock meeting. He lets silence reign for a moment and does not move, but studies John Keegan. He knows that this is going to be a delicate meeting and he has not seen the balding man since last hiring him in Butte the prior year. So far, that had not ended well, and any additional failures will not be tolerated.

The politician pulls a cup and saucer closer and reaches for the delicate flowered China coffee pot. Carefully, with studied movements, he fills the cup sitting on a matching flowered saucer. The brown beverage steams and is soon joined by a dash of scotch that is added without a comment.

Keegan takes a small notebook from the breast pocket of his plaid coat and places a small inkwell on the table and produces a silver pen sporting a fine metal tip. Looking at the Senator, he also pours himself a cup of coffee and adds both sugar and cream and then places a small white crustless sandwich on a matching plate. He glances up at the Senator and waits without voicing another word.

"Very well John, I have a parlor car reservation on a six o'clock train to Cheyenne, so we will regrettably have to be brief and to the point as we have much to discuss," he begins in a surprisingly soft voice. "I need to make an announcement soon on my reelection as a Montana State Senator and position myself for a run for governor. But I have encountered a material setback. Roger, whom you recommended a couple times in the past and most recently in Butte last year, has not succeeded in his assignment. That is a disappointing event that I have not experienced previously from any of your agents and has set me back considerably on several fronts. Due to his disappearance, I suspect he has been eliminated by some individual from the Walking Y Ranch, but I cannot ascertain that such is the case. Have you had any communication from him since Christmas?"

Keegan sits up a bit straighter as this verbally matches the last letter he had exchanged with the Senator, and thus far his enquiries as to the fate of Roger and Dave are eliciting no response whatsoever. With sharp eyes digging into the Senator, he replies, "No, he has been quiet for many weeks. His last letter stated that he was eliminating Woody and the Walking Y and had part of the crew at his mercy, a pair of girls named Teri Curtis and Michelle Longmire. Initially, until I heard otherwise from you, I thought you were keeping him quiet and low to the ground, so I had no concerns. I never thought he could not deal with a couple girls. To be sure and between us, I would not have wanted to be one of them."

The Senator now hesitates for a moment before coming to the key part of the setback which obviously enough Mr. Keegan ignores. He plays with his silver teaspoon and adds another generous dash of scotch to his coffee before continuing.

"At the key moment, Roger and that right hand of his, Dave, were defeated. I have not heard from them since. If I did, not only would I not pay the closing fee, but I would also ensure that they were eliminated due to their awful performance. Their incompetence allowed the Walking Y Ranch to present me with a document, allegedly signed by the pair of them, implicating me with unauthorized activities. In more than fifteen years, this is the only time I have been left surprised by Mr. Woodrow Flynt. He and that Irish sidekick, supported by those orphans, secured a document from me that I have to destroy."

Here the politician takes a moment to make sure that he shows no emotions that Mr. Keegan will use against him in a fashion such as raising his fees. He takes a small sandwich and looks out at the room and out the distant window that shows no sign of better weather and then continues.

"Your last advice, namely again securing the services of Roger to ensure that Mr. Flynt's tenure at the Walking Y would come to an end, was incorrect. I will not tolerate disappointment. Do I make myself clear?"

With this question, the Senator bores into the eyes of John Keegan, until the plaid suited man lowers his gaze. The Senator resumes, "I require more efficient individuals to work on my behalf and let me remind you that I do not take such failures lightly. Due to their incompetence, Mr. Woodrow Flynt of the Walking Y Ranch made me sign an agreement that bars me from running for reelection and blackmailed me for funds too; ostensibly to offset the killing of some cows, horses, and to cover the costs for the care of injuries suffered by the orphans allegedly perpetrated by Roger."

Here the Senator pauses to let his concern at the failure of John Keegan's agents sink in. Then, before the plaid coated man can interrupt, he continues. "Not only is your subordinate missing so is his companion in arms, Dave. Indications are that both were somehow eliminated by Mr. Woodrow Flynt, or Seamus Patrick O'Connor, or by one of the orphans. But as the ranch's actions are out of character, I suspect the Irishman or the orphans. If I had to place a bet, I suspect that Michelle Longmire or that Teri Curtis were major players. Mind you, there is also Nicholas Rubattel, but he seems a bit thick, or Eric Smithby but he is a bit of a loose cannon. One or more of those are the culprits. I do not think it was Frederick Torroni as he was recovering from his gunshot wound. Next time, Jesse better shoot a bit more accurately. Much to my disappointment, I had to drop charges against that one, due to Roger's confession."

Here the Senator takes another swallow of his coffee, to wash away the unsavory taste of his tale. Meanwhile, John Keegan begins, "The last discussion I had with Roger was at the beginning of the third week of December. At the time, he had the two meddlesome girls out of action in a remote cabin where he was keeping them so they could not escape. In conjunction with this, Roger stated that Mr. Seamus Patrick O'Connor was incarcerated on a murder charge as he killed our man, Hank. It should have been a guilty verdict and a hangman's noose for that trashy Irish Catholic troublemaker, but again you had to acquiesce to the charge being dropped due to a lack of evidence that it was not self-defense. I also heard that Mr. Woodrow W. Flynt was on his deathbed after his unprovoked attack on your foreman was terminated by one of your riders. In fact, of the entire crew, only one orphan, Nicholas was free. It looked like the Walking Y Ranch had reached its demise. From there, I had no news as to what happened."

    The Senator nods his head. Looking John in the eye, the lawyer fills in more of the tale. "Being a man of my word, I visited the Walking Y to make good on my very generous standing remunerative offer to purchase that spread. I went with a couple of attorneys to conclude the acquisition of the Walking Y Ranch and found that Mr. Woodrow W. Flynt was alive and well. He refused to sell. In addition, all the rest of those individuals including the girls, showed up and they flashed in front of me a document which was a theoretical confession signed by Roger along with Dave. This attested that both those men were working on my orders when they shot Walking Y cows. Furthermore, they said that the document stated that Roger had planned to take advantage of the girls with my implied consent. Regrettably, due to the surprise apparition of the entire crew and this so-called confession, I signed that agreement that had me pay for the loss of Walking Y cattle, horses, and their exaggerated medical costs. In addition, the non-legally binding contract included a clause that I would not run for Governor."

    "I have my copy, but I need Woody's copy and that confession. Somehow, we again have to get someone into the Walking Y. But this time, I want someone a bit smarter than Roger and a bit more insidious. The person needs to gain their confidence and get me those documents while hopefully setting the stage for the sale of that ranch and the acceptance of my very generous standing offer, less fees and numerous expenses of course. In summary, I need a person who can remove Mr. Woodrow W. Flynt and Mr. Seamus Patrick O'Connor along with those pesky orphans. I need you to guide the actions directly, and I cannot have any of your agents in my employ nor on my ranch nor associated with me in any fashion. Do I make myself clear?"

John Keegan takes a small bite of the sandwich and a sip of coffee as his mind races. He looks at the well clad gentleman beside him, scans the room and replies, "That Roger is possibly dead is a shock. He was one of my most ruthless and effective guns. Totally without scruples. Never had he and Dave, when paired up, not delivered. If the Walking Y took them out, and killed them, and no one knows for sure, it means that we will need more than brute force. Tell me more about what is going on with the Walking Y and what the local busybodies discuss regarding that establishment."

"Well, apart from renewing a line of credit from a bank in Great Falls and buying a bunch of new cows at an opportunistic price and a horse or two and most recently hiring a colored cook, they are keeping a low profile. My wife, who was less than pleased when I told her I was considering retiring from politics, has sprung into action. She has taken to frequenting the dining hall at the Prancing Mare Hotel to listen to the gossip, and I have given generous tips to Randy, the owner of the Silver King Saloon, seeking to discern what opportunities there may be to recover from the setback incurred last December."

Here, the Senator looks around discreetly and notes again that no one is idle at any table nearby. He leans into John Keegan, and continues, "From what I can gather, Mr. Woodrow Flynt is looking for a governess to help run the place and keep the girls company. It seems that he would prefer not to have to sleep in the main house, but he must as Michelle and Teri are having nightmares. You know how girls are, flighty and not very brave. Well, it seems as if it is not to Mr. Flynt's taste. The agreeable news is that I read, by incredibly good fortune, an advertisement in the classified of today's *Denver Rocky Mountain Journal*. John, look here under help wanted." Thereupon, the Senator pulls out a page of that morning's newspaper and points to a small advertisement:

> *'Large Montana Ranch seeks a single well-educated lady under the age of forty, to serve as tutor and governess for five orphans. The children have basic schooling but lack deportment having spent too much time outdoors with cattle and horses. Candidate should also be ready to aid and console said children who have been subject to recent hard events. Please contact Mr. Flynt c/o Windsor Hotel with references. Advanced degree a plus.'*

John reads carefully and looks up at the Senator smiling. This is too easy. "It seems like he is going far afield advertising in Denver. I presume that you somehow are footing the bill due to their blackmail. The good news is that this also implies that your exalted neighbor is in Denver for the National Stock Growers Convention."

The Senator leans back and takes a large draught of his scotch infused coffee and reaches for a small pastry. The same thought had crossed his mind, meaning that discretion was more important than ever. He nodded faintly and pocketed the newspaper.

John Keegan rubs his chin and looks the Senator in the eye. He slowly smiles. "I have the perfect answer. She will require a higher fee than Roger, but my Jenny fits the bill, has the needed degree and polish and she will succeed through wiles where brute force has seemingly failed. It will do her some good to get out of Washington, as the Secretary of the Treasury is now in both my client's and my debt thanks to her. It will be her first time out Montana way on an assignment, but my Jenny is good. If you agree to the stipend, I will telegraph her today and she will be on an express in the morning. That should get her to Denver in time."

The Senator leans in, "John, just so that we fully understand each other, I do not think seducing Woody will work as he is immune to any amorous advances unless he is not what I think. He has been a bachelor for decades and is now close to fifty years old. He is impolite, has no social graces, and is generally uncouth. The two years he spent at Yale University were a waste of the family's money and probably a frustrating experience for that establishment. In addition, Mr. Seamus Patrick O'Connor is also a bit crude for any feminine talent with such pedigree. In short, what worked with the Secretary of the Treasury will be wasted on the Walking Y." Here the Senator stops and examines Mr. John Keegan's face.

The plaid clothed man leans towards the Senator and voices his thoughts. "Looking at the situation objectively, my suspicion is that the real weak point will be the children, and a bottle of whiskey will take that Irish scum out of action."

The Senator nods his head in approval, then adds, "I would not focus on the boys, except to make sure that they are blinded to the truth. But they have proven that they have some luck on their side, so it is essential that they are not looked upon as gullible. The most important aspect to consider will be if she can ingratiate herself to the girls or more difficult yet, the owner. If that can be done, she can most probably do the job. However, there are a few other factors to consider."

Both men are quiet for a moment, and both take a swallow of coffee. The Senator straightens his posture a bit and raises his hand slowly to speak, yet remains silent until he has Mr. Keegan's full undivided attention.

"John, I do not think your Jenny can do this alone. We need to pressure the entire structure so that they cannot focus on the internal danger as they confront a series of external threats. Yet these must not be seen as coming from the Ringing Bell Ranch. Unlike last time, where Roger was on my payroll, we must apply constant pressure, and we need a way to communicate without arousing suspicion. There is a bit of a stench left over from the last confrontation and my ability to make a successful run for Governor would be impaired with any setbacks associated with me. I cannot afford any hint of any implication in the travails that are in store for the Walking Y or its crew."

John nods his head knowingly and leans forward. The clouds persist to keep the room gloomy, and snow periodically pelts the window as dusk descends on the land. Both men continue their conversation in hushed tones as they discuss how best to defeat the Walking Y and destroy its crew. This time, they will not use a blunderbuss like Roger, but plan a detailed campaign to throw them off balance while they destroy the crew one way or another, preferably from the inside. In short, they scheme for another hour and a half.

Chapter 4

<u>City Adventure</u>

In a crowded wooden Burlington Railroad coach, a teen-age boy wipes the single pane glass clear trying to see the innumerable lights of the big city of Denver. His companion watches with a smile and ignores the fact that not only are all the seats taken, but many of his fellow passengers are also headed to the National Stock Growers Convention. The hats, coats, worn pants, and burly attire, all shout "Cattlemen".

Finally, the train screeches to a halt, and the boy stops staring about as if the world were a bizarre joke. The older man signals the lad that he should grab his bag with a simple movement of his head and does not waste energy talking in the sea of voices. Most are getting off at Union Station, and soon about halfway down the train, visible in the faint dirty lights of the platform disembark the odd pair, off some ranch or another. Both are clad in blue jeans and sheepskin coats and the teenage boy, with a newer hat, has black circles around his eyes which are visible whenever the light allows. But the stout old rancher, who wears an even more dated attire, shepherds the boy through the chaos. Both carry scruffy smaller suitcases, and both have the rumpled look of passengers who started the trip well before Cheyenne. None pay attention to them at this moment, as the pair look around at the bustle and start towards the main terminal.

"Eric," voices the stout man, "we will check into the Windsor Hotel. I have a reservation for a modest room with two beds. In short, the two-dollar special. Not the Presidential Suite which has even been used by several presidents, but even in our modest room you will be exposed to the best hotel in town. Not only that, but it'll also be warm, and that will be our base for a couple days. The hotel is not too far, but we will get there by shank's mare if you're up to fighting a crowd. It's just up the street from this station and I should still be able to find my way."

The boy looks at the man, and the crowds that jostle about like cattle in a corral, and replies. "Woody, as these pilgrims are smaller than cows, more docile than bulls, and slower than dull eyed horses, I can manage them, as long as there is a good meal in the near future. I'm so hungry that even these sick looking pilgrims might be tasty, and it's not a comfortable feeling. They don't look healthy."

Woody stops momentarily and pulls Eric face to face with a sincere smile. "Well Eric, that is good news, as I've not heard you joke in close to a month. My God, that's progress. Perhaps you are finally getting over the brooding because you might have shot that Dave when he tried to ambush and kill you. In fact, as I told you, getting you away from the ranch is the best thing that I can do for you. None of you kids have fully put that fight with Roger and his scoundrels behind you, so I aim to see what I can do. I've talked to some of my older friends who were in the war between the states, and one bit of advice was to get you on new terrain so that you can sleep a bit better and get rid of the circles around your eyes. They also said that I must keep things boring around us. To that I replied, 'Ha, like that will happen.'"

"Well Woody," answers Eric clearly with a hint of a matching smile, "I'd prefer to be on the Walking Y and working horses with my rump in a saddle and a rifle in my scabbard than fighting my way through this crowd. These people are packed together tighter than shoats in a shed."

On that note, both wander into the large waiting hall, and focus on navigating through the crowds. They quickly exit the building through the main doors. So doing, they do not notice a corpulent balding man in a plaid coat with trousers to match. He watches them intensely.

The stranger's face comes to life as he hears Eric's reply. He turns off the smile and follows the pair at a discreet distance while seeking to stay within earshot of the two ranchers. Mrs. Couchman, the wife of the owner of the General Store in Hellenville, provided accurate information as to their train. Still, he cannot believe his luck, although he had spent quite some time watching these doors as he suspected that the two Walking Ys would be coming through the station on that train from Cheyenne.

Meanwhile, unsuspecting, Eric turns to Woody, "So did you say that our hotel, the Windsor was just up this road?"

Woody looks at the lad, and replies, "Master Smithby, it is and let me tell you that it is the grandest hotel in Denver. In fact, it is such a wonderful place, that it will probably still be the grandest hotel in one hundred years, that is if trains haven't been replaced by birds!"

The ranch owner rubs his unshaven chin, and continues a bit more seriously, "While I have not been there in some time as The Walking Y was being squeezed to death by The Senator's lawsuit, I suspect that the Hotel has not fully recovered from the silver crash, but I am sure that it's still quite grand. I decided to splurge and with the Senator's payment I thought we would travel with some comfort as we look for a prize bull and for ideas on how to improve our cattle. There is nothing like the National Stock Growers Convention to teach us what we need to know or to offer what we need to buy. I aim to do better than the Senator and make the Walking Y hum."

The stranger standing nearby looks lost as he stares in a different direction, his ears attuned to Woody's comment. He drops back content, and once out of sight he turns and heads to a nearby brick building on Larimer Street where he walks into the lobby that includes a plaque listing among the tenants a "J K and Associates." What luck. He now knows for sure that the predictable Woody is on the way to the Windsor Hotel as he guessed. He has already paid the front desk to let him know when they arrive. Now he can taste his fees, and with luck notch another task done for people in power who are willing to pay anything and do anything to have a bit more. It is a profitable business. He already has offices in Butte, Montana focused on the Anaconda Company, along with one in Washington, DC and this one in Denver. Next with a bit of cunning will be Chicago and New York. Never has business been so good. An expanding government breeds naked ambition and powerful individuals need his services.

***

Eric gawks around at the atrium and its opulent furnishings as he enters the hotel. He notes not the fact that the carpet is a bit more used than should be the case, as never has he seen something so grand, and has never dreamt that something manmade could be so enchanting. Woody glances at the lad and smiles faintly as he walks up to the desk. Well at least this part of the plan is working, and the boy is not brooding.

"Reservation for two, under the name Woodrow W. Flynt, of The Walking Y Ranch in Hellenville, Montana."

"Yes sir," replies the clerk arching his eyebrows, "I see your reservation Mr. Flynt, for the two-dollar economy special – each, which includes your meals. Would you care to upgrade Mr. Flynt?"

Woody darts him a withering look, and the clerk looks down at his papers before continuing, "I guess not. I presume the pair of you are here for the National Stock Growers Convention? I have your room, it is on the second floor, and you may take that elevator to get there. Do you wish for a bellhop to take your bags?"

Eric turns around and wonders, what is this bellhop thing? Perhaps one of those young men dressed in a dandy red uniform silently pushing a polished brass cart that looks like a diminutive cargo wagon. He feels surprised at how a carpet covers the floor. His mind races as there is so much to see. He has never been to a city larger than Missoula, and that was some time ago. He had been too young when he moved North from Texas and had probably slept through any stop in Denver.

Woody brings him back to reality. The owner barks, "No, but thanks. We will carry our bags."

Eric guesses he would not find for sure what a bellhop is at this time. On the other hand, he has heard of those elevator things, but has never ridden one. He smiles again. An adventure, but this time hopefully without danger, and for the time being without horses or guns. Well, he misses the horses, but not the nightmares.

Woody cocks a finger, and Eric follows like a bottle raised lamb. They round a corner by a large chandelier with electric lights. Seeing the boy stare open mouthed at the display, Woody informs him that their room will also have electric lights. While gawking about like a country boy, he hears a grating open, and a uniformed man looks at Woody and asks, "Sir, what floor would you like?" Both walk into the iron cage with their suitcases, and Eric looks around.

The grating closes. The uniformed attendant moves a lever that looks like a thick hand on a clock, and – wonders of wonders - the cage moves. Up. He looks out to see the ground dropping below him. What a pleasure. He can hardly wait to get back and tell the tale to the girls. It has been a few hard weeks – since – since the nightmare from hell.

Eric shudders, as he remembers Dave's last rasping breath, words, and then the eyes going blank like the deer he had shot just last fall. His smile fades. The cage lurches to a stop. Eric shakes his head like a dog seeking to dry his pelt and focuses on this adventure to the big city. He must focus on the new sights, as Woody will not want him to cry out in his sleep as he relives that nightmare when Dave died by his gun. Nor does he wish to recall when Roger was blasted but a few feet from him by Tony, who shot him thrice to make sure the bastard was truly dead. His father would not necessarily be proud of him killing a man even if it was in self-defense. But he does not regret his role in saving Michelle and Teri. Good God, riding off into that adventure was not what he anticipated.

It had been hell.

"Eric," repeats Woody, "this is our room. Stop daydreaming. We'll wash up and go and find you a horse to eat, ideally with a tasty rider!"

The lad tosses his head about like a colt to clear the water out of his eyes. Yes, food. That is the ticket. He meekly follows Woody into the room, and lays his suitcase on the second bed, the one away from the window. Woody closes the door and makes a startling announcement. "This place has indoor plumbing. You'll take the first bath, hot water, and I'll get the second later tonight. Then dinner my lad, and tomorrow the National Stock Growers Convention. While you are bathing, I'll step out and make a few inquiries, so we know where to go, and perhaps get a feel for the town. I also must see if we have any applications for a governess to help us get the girls back on an even keel, as I am using a conference room at this hotel for the interviews."

Eric enters the small dark room Woody indicates and pushes in the light switch. "Click" and enjoy light. Electricity. That would be handy on the ranch. He pushes it again, and turns it off, and then again and pushes the switch on. He stares at a white claw footed bathtub. He has never bathed in one before, and this one is rumored to have both running hot and cold water. Should not be too different than the metal hot water tub in the front room of the foreman's house or the main room of the bunkhouse. But he'll have to think carefully so he does not have to ask Woody how to prepare his bath. Thus, he concentrates as he looks at the thing. Why there is even a toilet in that small room. Amazing. He pulls the chain, and it flushes. Well, that's good, as it is probably a very long way to an outhouse in downtown Denver!

***

The large barn is crowded with cattle of all sorts in innumerable stalls. Boys running around washing large bulls adorned with brass nose rings, using cold water in a dank setting while others are grooming their pelts until they shine. This is a new sight; cattle being groomed like horses by the numerous attendants hovering around them. Woody carefully looks at the large bulls, checking their size, their forequarters and their hind quarters. Discreetly Woody also looks under them and between their back legs as he checks their bullhood.

Eric watches the Walking Y owner and smiles, "Woody, why don't you take a sewing tape to see the circumference of their privates and then a small level to make sure they're hanging evenly!"

Woody throws him a nasty look. Eric smirks, "Woody, it's a good thing the girls are not present, this would be embarrassing."

"Eric, this is important. A bull who can't service the cows is worse than useless. We'll have no calves, and you'll go back to that orphanage in Idaho."

The boy self-consciously looks again a bit more critically at the bull and his bullhood.

The male bovines stand patiently with steam clouds issuing from their nostrils. Eric steps carefully, remembering that unlike horses, bulls like cows, cow kick. That back leg will dart out at an angle at lightning speed. With these strong animals, if it makes contact with your human leg, the result is a busted leg.

"Well, Eric," begins the ranch owner, "as the Senator had one of those white Charolais bulls, I think I will go for something different. Most of our cows now are Hereford Texas Longhorn crosses, so I think we need something dissimilar. Come here and look at this red bull. He has nice lines, a masculine face, and is well proportioned. The only thing I don't like on this one is that he has no horns. Don't know how they defend themselves. On the other hand, I hate to see a man gored, and I have seen that more than once. The card here says, 'Polled Red Angus'. Not sure what that word polled means. Come on Eric, we need a bite of food, before we spend more time looking and before I start dickering."

Eric follows Woody, absorbing the sights. Impressive. Last night after his third bath in Denver, and a large steak dinner in the hotel, he had again slept through the night without a nightmare. There is something to say for this travel stuff and looking for the best bulls available in the country, even if this already is the third day of looking.

After a meal, Woody comes back to the bulls and stops as a cleanly dressed gentleman with handlebar mustache approaches him. "Sir, I noted that you have looked at my bull Genesis for the past two days, and judging by your attire and walk, you must be a rancher from out of town. I couldn't help but hearing you state that you did not know what 'polled' means, thus I want you to know that it means that the bull in question has no horns and hence some of his offspring have no horns. Thus, there is no reason to burn off the horns of your calves and there is less damage to your cattle when bulls get to playing push-push and bash each other's heads. It will be the way of the future. Lastly, I would not want Genesis mad, as he can move lightning fast, and the foe that can hurt him does not exist."

Woody stops and considers. He looks at the ribbons hung beside the bull. Maybe, just plain maybe, this is the bull the Walking Y needs. He reaches into his inside coat pocket and pulls out a leather-bound notebook which he opens by releasing the hasp. It reveals a small pencil, and the ranch owner looks up, "How is he on breeding, and how large are his calves?"

"He can cover as many cows as any other bull if not more, and his calves will be about fifty plus pounds. They will grow quickly, and we hope soon that combined with good cows his heifers could be bred back to calve as one-year-olds! You can see for yourself that he is well endowed, and you will not find a better breed anywhere. The packers will pay a premium for his steers. Also, if you have Hereford cows, breeding them to this bull will give you hybrid vigor."

The discussion drones on into the very late afternoon. Eric watches Woody negotiate, and he knows that the old cantankerous owner is making a play for Genesis. Oh, well, that's one of the two reasons they traveled to Denver. From what Woody tells him, the ranch owner will be interviewing candidates tonight at the hotel. He hopes to travel back to the ranch with their new teacher who will also be a female companion to Michelle and Teri. They need that as much as he needs to travel. With any luck, they will stop seeing Roger leering and dying in their dreams.

Woody snaps him out of his daydreams. "Eric, come look at Genesis. He's a red angus, and he's polled – that means that he has no horns, it'll look a bit different than those remaining longhorns and our horned Herefords. I just bought him, and he will be the genesis of the best beef herd in Montana. It'll leave us a bit low on funds, but we need to upgrade."

After a moment of silence as they walk out of the large building, Woody resumes, "We must leave now, as I have some interviews for a governess at the hotel. I hope we can find a good candidate. But, we need to get back to the Windsor now."

Both step out of the main pavilion of the National Stock Growers Convention and flag down a horse drawn coach for hire to go back to the hotel. One hackney that is sitting idle despite the numerous customers in the area pulls up to them as if it was waiting for them.

"Gentlemen," asks the driver in a rasping Irish accented voice while making no eye contact and keeping his face in the shadow of his large hat, "I am at your service. Where may I take you? The Windsor perhaps?" Again, Eric has a nagging feeling, but he suspects that it is due to the events of the prior month.

Woody, his mind still on his expensive red angus bull, nods "yes". Eric does a double take. How does the driver know they are headed to the Windsor Hotel. Is this just a lucky guess or is the driver pursuing a nefarious agenda. The accent is not western, however, there are many newcomers in Denver, and a New York Irish accent like Tony's is probably not an unusual occurrence. They both board as Eric ponders these questions.

Thankfully the coach turns and starts to travel southwest which is correct, although Eric does not recognize the roads. They are a little less traveled than the ones they used on the way to the National Stock Growers Convention from the Hotel. But the aggregate direction is correct, and Eric relaxes. This is still better than walking and taking a tram and fighting the weather. The wind gusts and now grey clouds sire sleet that pelts the window as darkness falls. The coach sways to an easy rhythm, and Eric cannot see much through the snow-covered window. Both he and Woody nod off in an easy slumber accompanied by the motion of the coach and the footfalls of the horse.

They stop, probably an intersection. The door opens. "Gentlemen," says the husky driver cloaked in dark snow-covered clothing, "your coach ride is over."

"Eric, wake up!" barks Woody.

Something in his voice is wrong.

The lad looks out the snow-covered window and then turns and sees Woody's worried look despite the faint light. His gaze moves to the door, and his heart skips a beat. The coachman has drawn a colt and the business end is pointing at Woody's surprised face.

"Gentlemen," says the coachman again, with a nervous twitch of his pistol toting right hand, "I have a strong argument to make, and you better be cooperative. This is a forlorn part of the city, and especially in this weather there is no help to be had. I want your wallets so hand them over and I want your boots, so take them off. Now."

Woody grunts "wallet" as he reaches for it, slowly. It is in the inside pocket of his coat. Gingerly he hands it down while keeping his eyes locked on the driver. The coachman pockets it without looking. Eric watches the ranch owner and seeks to keep his face neutral. Woody has handed him his new leather-bound pocket notebook. Damn, as Tony would say, Woody must be a pure-blooded English bastard.

Hell, that means the game is now up to him. He looks at the ranch owner and says meekly with a touch of resentment.

"Boss, please move slowly to the side so that I have room to take off my boots."

He then looks over to the gunman and adds, "I don't have a wallet, Mr. Flynt here has to pay for everything. He doesn't give me any money, I'm just his indentured servant so to speak."

Eric removes his boots, slowly. The pistol never leaves them unguarded, and the darkly clad man is nervous. Finally, Eric's boots are neatly arrayed under the opposite seat. Woody inquires softly, "now what?"

In a harsh voice, the pistol toting driver glares at Woody and barks, "you take off your boots and like your servant leave them under the seat. Then slowly step out of the coach and give me any loose change you may have."

"Leave my boots, WHAT?" barks the grouchy owner.

"You heard me, you dumb ejit, I'm the one with the gun. Take off your boots and leave them in the coach."

Eric moves first, slowly. Looking at the coachman, he adds, "It's my job to help this half-wit," he says pointing at Woody, "out of his boots and in and out of coaches among other things. He's got a bum leg and is grouchier than a bear coming out of hibernation. He had this thing called a horse fall on him, and he can't negotiate steps without me mollycoddling him."

Thereupon, Woody gingerly, favoring his right side laboriously removes one boot at the time with Eric's clumsy assistance. He then moves to the edge of the step as Eric, already bootless, steps out. The gunman moves back a bit and Woody painstakingly starts to climb out in stocking feet on wobbly legs.

"Damn!" snarls Woody as he clumsily tries to swat at Eric who is seeking to assist him, "give me space. I'm not totally an invalid you dumb idiot."

Eric steps back, moving his dark brown hair out of his eyes, seemingly mortified, and the gunman moves his focus to Woody ignoring the subservient cowed boy.

Woody trips or slips and cries out as he crashes to the wet hard cobblestones. The highway man stares at the ranch owner, as Woody moans in pain. Eric launches a diving tackle. He hits the gunman's knees from the side. The highway man's legs buckle, and there is the faint sound of a bone or knee cartilage snapping. The dark coated brigand pulls the trigger as he falls under the stage. The bullet lodges itself in the upper door frame of the coach.

The horses fidget, whiney and bolt. The stage rumbles off down the road in an erratic path and the locked brake jars into its neutral position. In a clatter of hoofbeats and harness creaks along with the sharp noise of the steel rimmed wheels on the ground and over the brigand, the coach is quickly lost in the wet snow, which mutes the racket of the uncontrolled dash as it disappears in the night. No lights are turned on in the warehouse infested neighborhood which is still some distance from the hotel.

"So, I'm a dumb idiot?" asks Eric still feeling the adrenaline.

"Well, I'm glad as a half-wit to know you're my indentured servant. You're not even a good one."

Both laugh nervously and turn their attention to the inert form on the ground. Woody grumbles and walks over without a limp to the prone figure. He flips the assailant on his back, confirms that there is still a rasping breath and notes that he was simply stunned by the coach as the horses bolted. His hat is now on the ground and a gash in his scalp weeps blood. Meanwhile Eric snags the pistol which is lying on the cobblestones. He checks the loads and moves the cylinder to an empty chamber before handing it to Woody who tucks it out of sight in his belt.

Woody frisk the highwayman. "Not much here," he tells Eric, "Let's see, my notebook, a few gold coins that I'll take as we now need to purchase some new boots, and what's this?" In the darkness he holds a business card he cannot read due to the lack of light. He grumbles on, "I think the only other thing here is this business card. I'll take it and look at it later." He pockets it and gestures to Eric.

"Let's get out of here. It will be a long walk to the Hotel with no boots and I don't want to answer questions with the local constabulary."

"But what about him?" asks the lad seeking to regain his full composure.

"The hell with him. I'm tired of the Walking Y being at the wrong end of a gun. Let's skedaddle now before there is more trouble."

Thereupon, the owner starts to walk at a fast clip. Eric falls beside him, both with only wool socks protecting their feet. Woody, do you think this is an accident or a coincidence?" asks the lad with a nervous voice.

Woody keeps on walking and does not answer for a while. "You know Eric, it most probably is a coincidence, but considering what we went through, and how many people know we were coming to get a bull at the National Stock Growers Convention and how we are also looking to hire a governess, maybe not. We talked to the Doctor and his wife in the general store, and Mrs. Couchman is not our best friend. We also talked about this trip with Fernande at the Prancing Mare. I don't think the Senator is going to roll over dead. He's paid for the cattle, horses and dropped the legal charges, but he has not announced his retirement from politics. Both he and yes, his wife, are very power hungry, and increasingly ruthless."

Chapter 5

Miss Hathaway

John Keegan quietly walks into the Windsor Hotel and marches to the front desk as if he owns the place. He slips a quarter ounce five-dollar gold coin to the manager, and states, "Mr. Woodrow W. Flynt has asked me to do an initial screening of the applicants he has waiting. Hopefully you have already made them feel welcome with tea and hors d'oeuvres?"

The manager nods his head to the affirmative. John then goes on, "Also, can you confirm that they are in the conference room you discussed with him and lastly can you bring me some fresh hot coffee. Mr. Woodrow W. Flynt is being delayed, as he was caught flat footed or maybe that is barefooted so to speak and wishes me to take care of this matter for him."

Pocketing the unexpected generous coin, the manager signals John to follow him. On the ground floor are small rooms for business meetings aligned one after the other, and he leads the plaid jacketed man to one with a brass plaque stating, "Blue Room". At the door, the day manager steps to the side, and signals a busboy to make himself available.

Mr. Keegan walks into the room and surprise registers on his face at the number of candidates waiting. He wastes no time, "Ladies, Mr. Woodrow W. Flynt has asked me to thank you for your interest, and to tell you that regrettably the position has already been filled. He has asked me to give you each a couple silver dollars to defray your expenses of coming here in this inclement weather, and he wishes to thank you for your interest."

Thereupon, he breaks out his purse and gives the half a dozen ladies the stated stipend. Soon the room is empty except for one young, dark brown hair lady, who presents herself in a conservative white blouse and light blue dress. She does not move with the others and stays seated without acknowledging Mr. John Keegan as the other candidates leave. When all others are gone, she looks up.

"Niece, it is so good to see you," he says as he comes up and lightly kisses the thin long-haired English looking woman who remains. "It's been a long time. Delighted you could make it. This time, we are trying to constitute a governor along with our fees, so we need a governess. The assignment is a bit different than your last one in Washington. I'll fill you in quickly before I leave. You'll have to wait a while for Mr. Woodrow Flynt, as he will be late, probably quite late. You will be a key part in an orchestrated attack on his ranch to drive it out of business. Sometimes your situation may be precarious, but triumph means that we will have a future governor of Montana at our beck and call and, as always you will be generously renumerated."

The large brown eyed young lady stands for the cursory kiss on the cheek and returns to her seat. Thereupon the two talk in hushed tones for a while and then, as the hotel shifts are about to change, John Keegan leaves before those who work the late-night rotation can see him. He turns to the lady, and states as he hands her a bundle of books, "Jenny, this is volume one through six of Gibbon's *Decline and Fall of the Roman Empire,* which the Senator noted is a favorite of the owner of that ranch. Remember, he is Woody to his friends, and not much of a fan of his full name which is Woodrow W. Flynt. The right balance might be for you to call him 'Woodrow,' once you are introduced, and I think that he will be vulnerable to your wiles no matter what the Senator says. That is my suggested line of attack into the heart of the ranch."

With these words, he dons his plaid coat, and adds, "Remember Jenny, he should be easy for you to manipulate, as we know he is very lonely. He turned sour after he lost his only love and his first wife to be the day before they were to be wed. For us, it is a good thing that was more than twenty years ago, so he will be receptive to the touch of a beautiful woman. Take advantage of his tremendous years of loneliness and do not mention her. Use his yearning for the touch of a woman to our advantage. The reality is that even I would be easy to manipulate with just a bunch of orphans who are going into puberty and a drunken good for nothing Irish bum who is rumored to have stump trained his mare as companions. Anyway, the Gibbon's books are a good prop and decent history although a bit long, so I'm suggest you start with the second volume, and put the other five in your valise. I bought all lightly used, so they are more convincing. I'm having you start with the second one to imply that you have already read the first."

Jenny looks at Uncle John with no real emotion and tosses her hair back while running her hand through it. She finally replies softly, "Uncle, I could wrap you around my little finger if we weren't related. You trained me well. I had no trouble getting intimate with the Secretary of the Treasury, so some stupid ranch owner will fall easily."

Uncle John Keegan leaves. Jennifer Hathaway sighs, this is a step down from her work in Washington, but she gained too high a notoriety ensnaring the Secretary of the Treasury. Thus, she has to work out of the limelight for a while, and this is what that entails. She looks around the room, where she now sits alone, and she begins to laboriously peruse Volume Two of Gibbon's *Decline and Fall of the Roman Empire*.

***

The clock tolls eleven by the time Woody and Eric hobble up on numb cold, wet, tired and now bare lacerated feet to the front door of the Windsor. The doorman looking down in dismay at the pair, steps into their paths as they seek to enter. With distain, he blocks both of them, "I'm sorry sir, but are you guest here?"

Woody glowers and growls, "Get out of the way!" He hobbles past the uniform doorman without another word. Eric follows in his wake, and he also leaves wet dirty and bloody footprints as mementoes of their passage. Several guests look on in surprise, while the doorman seeks to regain his composure. With a bit more authority in his voice, the doorkeeper barks, "Sir, stop now!"

He signals with his right arm, and suddenly Woody faces a couple large determined looking individuals who step in front of the Walking Y's owner, blocking his access. Woody sneers at the newcomers with no sense of humor.

"NOW WHAT? You damn jackasses. I am a guest in your city, I get held up at gunpoint in your city, I have my boots stolen in your city, I get fired at in your city, I took the gun from the dumb highwayman in your city and now you two think you're going to stop me from getting to my room in your city? Not a chance in hell. Your city stinks. Some highway man had me at the wrong end of a gun, and we lost our boots, but I have his damn gun under this coat. We left that bastard on the ground, so if you think you spook me, let me tell you something, you don't. We just want to get to our room, so, get the hell out of the way."

As he completes his litany, he pushes one of the men to the side. The manager on duty signals the two employees to stand aside. He turns to Woody. "I will keep you company until you are in your room. But we must go by the front desk for your key. I apologize, but like any city there are certain areas of Denver where you should not venture unless you are willing to incur trouble."

Woody glares at the manager. "Damn trouble seems to find me of late." Eric smirks in the background. Woody is an even worse diplomat than he would ever dream of being. The pair gimp up to the front desk with Eric at his side. The stout owner states snippily. "Flynt's the name, our room is 212, and I would like the key – now."

"Ah, Mr. Flynt, have you forgotten you still have the last of several ladies waiting for you in the Blue Room. The others left as you are very late."

Woody does a double take. He had completely forgotten about the interviews for a governess that he had the hotel set up at his request. The incident with the highwayman had obliterated his thoughts of bringing back to Hellenville a governess who would double as a female companion for the girls and be a teacher for all the orphans. He mutters "Damn!" Then replies a bit less brusquely, "Tell her we will be there in a few minutes; we need to tend to our feet."

Thereupon he hobbles to the elevator with both he and Eric leaving wet and somewhat bloody footprints on the clean floor to the consternation of both guests and other employees of the Windsor. Well, they should police their city a bit more. The manager follows in tow, noting that he will have some clean-up duty to assign upon his return.

Ten minutes later, Woody is back on the main floor of the Windsor again with Eric. Both wear matching fluffy hotel room slippers courtesy of the Hotel Manager and clean dry jackets. Still in a foul mood that he has yet to control, Woody barges into the Blue Room and looks at the one remaining lady, the only one he has been told who has had the patience to wait. His face melts into a smile when he sees a cultured woman well into her twenties with good posture, proper attire, seated with dignity reading the second volume of Gibbon's *Decline and Fall of the Roman Empire*.

He beams. Here is the governess he needs for the orphans. Educated, refined, reading a sensible book, not some trash like Jane Austin. He takes in her appearance: conservative, subtle, and discreetly telegraphing politeness which proves that her education is at par with that of any one of the Seven Sisters, if she is not from one of those prestigious northeastern women's schools. She is well worth it. His mind is made up, this is the only candidate he needs. He will hire her now.

Eric stands back and never says a word as he stares with a troubled look at this pretentious woman. It is instant discomfort. His mind races. Is his reaction because he is biased against educated nobs, or is Tony influencing him against the English, or is there a deeper instinct setting the stage? For the moment, watching Woody swoon, he will bide his words and try to discern the root of his discomfort.

time Father Patrick saw her. Both girls look at the kettle with the letter "T" scratched on its side designating the teapot, and both are rubbing their hands over their eyes. They nod their heads at Fred who is at his usual spot by the stove, not noting the foreman in a darker corner.

"Good morning, Teri, Michelle," yaps Tony.

The girls jump and spin around. Teri raises her rifle while Michelle raises her arms. Fear slashes across the two young, frightened faces and the sleepy eyes jump wide open in alarm. Neither had seen the Irishman standing there in the shadows.

"Oh, it's you," croaks Teri.

Slowly the girl relaxes her jaw and lowers the rifle which had instinctively come up to her chest. She looks at her single shot .22 that spent the night beside her bed and sheepishly puts it in the kitchen rifle rack. She affixes a shallow smile on her face and steps to the tea kettle. Michelle stays frozen a bit longer, before unclenching her fists and brushing some of her uncombed long blond hair out of her smudged face. Finally, she looks up at Tony, relaxes a bit, and smiles blandly.

The outside door flies open, and Nick is the last to arrive. He looks at the others sheepishly, and focuses on Tony, "I wanted to check on the palomino team. Gosh darn it, it's cold and the manger was just about empty, so I added some hay. Those two mares have a long day ahead of them, and they're really nice horses. In fact, I don't understand how Dave, who was Roger's sidekick, could have had such a nice team."

Hardy standing by the stove, looks at the red headed lad, and smiles, "Nick, I don't think that this Dave was always all bad. Those two horses have been well tended, carefully trained and gentled. You have to respect such skills." Nick listens, then continues into the kitchen and gets himself a cup of coffee and all slowly gravitate to the table.

Finally, all sit and wait, as Tony begins, "Bless these Thy gifts ……"

Teri hides an impish smile behind her hand thinking how she initially greeted the Irishman, what was the terms she used? Something along the lines of, "I do not like drunken Irish Catholic trash so do not touch me." My times change, even with the memory of that awful cabin and how she slashed Roger with a hoof knife, and – here she shudders a bit – yes, she had mangled him with that hoof knife and can still feel the blade's resistance as it hit the murdering bastard's collar bone. She thinks back to that dull hoof knife saving her and winces. Thank God Tony shot him.

Tony notices her shudder. She looks up sheepishly, "It's the cold. It makes me shiver, just thinking about it."

For the rescue, she would be thankful. Now if she can only put away those awful nightmares that haunt both her and Michelle. They both relive the events at the cabin again and again like some awful endless loop where both of them are cooped up naked, with but that filthy blanket, and that leering Roger wanting to get them.

"Teri and Michelle, eat," commands Tony.

She snaps out of that memory as does Michelle. Looking at the table, she smiles, Hardy knows how the stomach rules. She serves herself an excellent breakfast that tempts her taste buds, as do Michelle, Nick, Tony and Fred.

The Irish foreman looks around, and smiles. "All right lads and lassies, late last night we got a telegram from Woody. In his usual style, you can tell he's counting every penny as it is a bit cryptic. I'll read it fully to you if you are quiet." Not a sound is heard except for the crackling wood in the stove. Tony with exaggerated gestures pulls out a crumpled telegram from his pocket:

BRINGING BULL JAN 28 STOP MEET AFTERNOON TRAIN

"That's today!" booms Nick with a wide smile. "Eric's getting home." Voices rumble before Tony cuts in.

"All right, who's coming with me to the train? I need to pick a couple good riders for the bull, and I need to pick one more to drive the buckboard." He turns to the girls and adds, "I don't know, but I presume your new governess and teacher will be with them."

All look at him with hope. "Ah hell, Woody will scold me, but I think we should all go. But, if and only if all the chores are done, the milk cow milked, and if all the cattle and horses are fed, and if we have plenty of wood by the stoves."

All eat fast and scatter to get the work done with no delays.

It is a joyous Walking Y crew that heads to the station in a warmish early afternoon sun. Nick importantly drives the buckboard, which is pulled by what are rapidly becoming his two palomino Belgian draft horses. The golden horses unlike their previous owners, are well behaved and wonderful calm giants at close to one ton each. Nick enjoys handling the team which he does mostly with verbal commands, and thankfully he is burly enough that their harness is not too heavy for him to handle alone.

Meanwhile Teri along with Michelle and Fred are arrayed around Tony who rides the ornery Sorley. The girls are on their favorite mounts, Crowhop and Princess, while the lad is on Blacky. The short two-mile ride is not stressful, and all are looking forward to seeing the grizzled owner, that rapscallion Eric, and their new teacher who would also be their governess - whatever that means. The sun is shining, and while it is cold, the wind is moderate, and the travails of the prior month fall away as they babble excitedly.

Hellenville's new brick station house gleams in the snow. With clanking, bell ringing, whistling, hissing, and puffing a large black Great Northern locomotive steams into town as if it is the most important stop on the line, and as always it is on time. The normal fanfare of the afternoon mixed train bringing the world to Hellenville, includes all those packages on the eagerly anticipated railroad express service along with the afternoon delivery of US Mail. On this day there are two full express cars that will be partially unloaded to fill numerous carts that will be manhandled into the depot. There is the normal crowd for the afternoon train and the platform is a hive of activity. The Walking Y crew is positioned so that none can escape their notice.

Immediately as the train lurches to a stop, the train crew detaches two freight cars adorning the rear of the train and a small helper locomotive pulls them away as the first passengers disembark from the line of coaches. The two cars shed by the train are nothing unusual, one is a livestock car, the other a box car. The livestock car is immediately shunted off to the corrals and Tony and the girls go that way. Nick waits for the passengers and lounges talking with Fred who keeps him company. Nick is especially impatient for Eric whom he has missed, while Fred is curious as to what the new teacher will be like.

Eric, Woody and Jennifer Hathaway climb down after most of the other passengers. As Nick runs up to greet Eric, he spies the governess wearing an elaborate colorful hat and a light blue coat that looks out of place in Hellenville. Nick comes to a halt abruptly looking open mouthed at the apparition. So much so that Fred who is a little behind him rams into the stout lad. Woody points out the two boys to Miss Hathaway who walks up to them with a smile affixed on her face. Eric lags, as Woody carries Jennifer's heavy valise that contains all six volumes of Gibbon's *Decline and Fall of the Roman Empire*.

The owner beckons the boys, "Nick, Fred come here so I can introduce you to Miss Jennifer Hathaway, or as you will address her, Miss Hathaway." So, saying, the lads remove their hats and walk the last few steps. Nick is perplexed noting Eric's quiet demeanor as his friend holds back.

"Boys, I am pleased to meet you," greets Jennifer with a sweet-sounding voice and an ingratiating smile. "I have heard so much about you. Fred, I've heard you are the scholar in the bunch, and I have some books here that may be of interest. It's the full six volume set of Gibbon's *The Decline and Fall of the Roman Empire*." Fred's face lights up. He had yet to ask Woody's permission to take the owner's treasured copy of the set.

Jennifer Hathaway then turns to Nick, "Nicholas, je parle up peu de Francais. Je suis ravis de te rencontrer (Nick, I speak a little French, pleased to meet you)."

Nick answered confused in rusted French, "avec plaisir". Thereupon he clams up.

He looks again at Eric, who is at the rear of the cortege. The stout lad is perplexed by the quiet demeanor of his normally rambunctious companion. He makes questioning eye contact and mentally notes that there is something that is bothering the hot-tempered lad. He will have to talk to him alone as soon as he can. Something is not right.

Tony joins them, having made arrangements for the baggage, including a large steamer trunk, to be loaded on the buckboard and also to sign papers for the delivery of the new Red Angus bull, Genesis. He steps up to the group and looks at Jennifer and how she stands very close, beside Woody. His steps falter briefly and then he comes up to the ranch owner, with his right hand extended. "Woody, glad to see you."

He then turns to Jennifer, and says quietly, "I am Seamus Patrick O'Connor often called Tony by my friends, I am pleased to meet you."

Jennifer looks at Seamus and smiles. So, this is the ex-boxer and ex-gambler of little skill where her womanly wiles would be wasted. He does not seem dangerous. She is sure she can handle him. After a moment of reflection, she replies. "Mr. O'Connor, it is a pleasure to meet a fellow teacher. I do hope to see more of you in the coming days."

Thereupon, she nods her head and possessively takes Woody's arm and starts to walk forwards. Tony falls back, glances around and discretely sneaks a small snort of medicinal whiskey from his new leather encased metal flask that he keeps, as is his habit, in his breast pocket. Thereafter he follows behind the owner his mind deep in concentration upon the scene before him.

Nick at the back of the cortege, finally gets a chance to talk to Eric. He keeps it light, trying to fathom his friend's subdued demeanor, "Eric, why so quiet. We have a moment as the buckboard is over there. Also, it'll be fun to hear your big city tales."

Eric replies flatly, "Did you bring Moose for me to ride back?"

Nick retorts a bit defensively, "Sorry, no, I didn't bring your gelding. Didn't know I should."

Eric looks sour, and Nick notes the mood. He takes a stab at what is bothering his friend, "Ah, come on Eric. You know you have to do some schooling. At least it'll be on the ranch so you can get out half the day and we can have fun working the cows and training our horses along with raising hell. All of this is much better than that stone cold orphanage in Idaho."

"Yeah," Eric answers unenthusiastically, "guess that's so. The horses, and cows I can handle, and I guess I'll have to do some school. But later tonight I've got to talk to you, you alone. The trip turned sour, or at least some of it leaves me with some foreboding, and I need to think it through."

Shortly all are loaded into the buckboard with baggage. But instead of going directly to the ranch, Woody wants to go to the corrals and talk about Genesis, his prized polled Red Angus bull. The owner carries on, "There is nothing like him in the county and probably not even in the entire state of Montana. Why, he looks much better than that white Charolais bull who makes me think of an overgrown ram the Senator is always prattling on about. I'll take an Angus any day. Come on now. This is exciting. He's our future, and he'll build one doggone hell of a good one."

Jennifer Hathaway gives him the look, and Woody buckles.

A sheepish Woody repeats, "As I meant to say, he'll build us one heck of a good future."

Within minutes, a small crowd gathers by the corrals as Michelle on horseback pushes open a heavy wooden gate giving access to the loading lane. Teri rides in, and at the far end, in a small holding pen, a pawing red bull can be seen through the thick lumber siding of the Great Northern corrals. Both girls work pens like this with ease. While they are still training Crowhop and Princess, there is no missed cue, and the bull snorts looking at them before lowering his head. Michelle has a lariat in her hand, and with a good tap of the knot on his rump she gets the bull moving forward.

Teri leads the procession on her short bay mare with four white socks that is part mustang. The little spirited cow horse, Crowhop, watches the bull behind the pair ready to dance, but the mare likes a challenge. Not bad for a horse that is not much more than fourteen hands tall. In short, the steed's spirit, color and grit matches the girl to perfection.

Between Teri and Michelle, a somewhat confused bull emerges. He snorts and paws the ground with his foreleg and bellows his complaints to an uncaring crew before fully emerging from the corrals after a long train ride. Behind him loops in Tony on his favorite mount, Sorley and Fred on a quiet new horse he has only ridden a few times. She is another black mare to replace the one Jesse had shot and killed under the lad only a little over a month earlier. Like a couple other horses, the Senator footed the bill for this one who regrettably has the unoriginal name of Blacky.

It is quite the pageant that goes by The Prancing Mare Hotel and its shining new front windows. The procession pulls many of the patrons out to watch from the boardwalk in front of the Hotel dining hall. In front are four riders escorting the large Red Angus bull, a breed that most in the county have never seen. Following is a fully loaded buckboard driven by the stout red headed orphan who has the lines carelessly looped over the front of the wagon as he directs the matched team verbally. In the wagon are three other occupants, the grouchy Woody, that troublemaker Eric, and a new face in town who seems out of place. She is a fine-looking lady with long brown hair and matching brown eyes in a fancy hat and a light blue coat. Others join the festivities, and even Eric, wishing he was on Moose, smiles from the back of the buckboard. It is quite the cavalcade.

As they meander along the main street in Hellenville, past the courthouse, town folks come out of the stores to look. Why this creates quite the excitement and having such an unusual bull walk up the middle of Main Street pulls all eyes. He attracts more gawkers than any cattle drive going to the railroad corrals, and in cattle country his size and appearance pull all eyes. The Walking Y enjoys being the center of positive attention, especially as there are smiles for a change. Tony lets the girls ride on the bull's flanks and takes the position as drag rider with Fred to let the girls bask with smiles in the festivities. The Sheriff, Cody Bozeman, waves at the group and does not frown when he sees the Irishman for a change.

"BOOM!"

The silence is shattered by the heavy round of an old buffalo gun.

Chapter 7

Pursuit!

The pedigree high dollar Red Angus bull, the center of all the attention in Hellenville that afternoon, stops and shakes his head lethargically. In the brief moment of silence that follows the bark of the old Buffalo gun, a red liquid flower blossoms in the center of his red-haired forehead. His eyes look uncomprehending about and then glaze over as he slowly crumples to the ground in a dignified sluggish folding of his forelegs.

Around the cortege, some horses panic at the loud shot.

A woman screams.

The crowd disperses in haste, as several men pull guns scanning for the source of the unexpected attack.

Nick talks to hold the team, and with the sudden roiling of the crowd around the horses, he finds that he loses control of the buckboard. The foolishly tied up lines, put thus in a showoff display of how he could verbally direct his heavy horses through the town, handicaps him. Unable to quickly grasp the long leather driving reins, the buckboard rattles forwards at an increasing speed, and tangles beside another wagon that is also spooked by the shot and the commotion of the crowd. Thankfully both are going south. Both veer to the side of the road. Nick scrambles to hold his horses, seeks to regain control before they hit a water trough beside the snow-covered main street. The stout lad brings his team to a stop and breathes a sigh of relief.

In the chaos, Eric leaps free from the Walking Y wagon while pulling the scabbarded rifle that adorns the front of the buckboard. He leaps past Nick who is seeking to calm the draft horses. He slaps a round in the chamber and pivots and looks around madly. Sheriff Bozeman darts into his office and emerges with his rifle. Tex, his deputy, is right behind holding a shotgun. Others look about with guns at the ready seeking the source of the shot that felled Genesis.

Tony on Sorley draws his handgun and notes a dissipating puff of smoke from the roof of the livery stable up the street. He yells and points while urging the willing mare onward. Sorley bolts using her powerful hindquarters and has the Irishman at a flat-out gallop in less than two seconds. The two girls also stay in the saddle and spur their horses behind the Walking Y foreman. Teri pulls her rifle, while Michelle shouts and points. Fred is a bit slower and less graceful. He and his horse careen into the falling bull and add to the chaos.

Woody jumps out from the buckboard and draws the handgun he confiscated from the highway man in Denver. He looks around but misses the puff of smoke and only sees Tony and the girls going hell bent for leather. He is bowled over by Eric, who tosses the rifle he snagged in the owner's lap. The buck toothed boy dashes and purloins Fred's horse. The lad vaults into the saddle paying no attention to the skinny black-haired Fred still lying on the ground shaken. Eric astride Blacky, pulls the rifle Fred had in his saddle scabbard, cusses at the inadequate single shot .22, and joins the chase.

Tony and Sorley have covered about two thirds of the distance to the livery stable with clods of muck and snow flying up behind them. The girls just about twenty yards back also push their horses flat out knackers, while Eric brings up the rear on the slower Blacky when an empty storefront blooms out by the Irishman.

"KWHAMM!"

Main street disappears in a light gray cloud of debris. The vacant storefront explodes and knocks Sorley and Tony over. The blast sends sharp shards of wood, filth, glass and rubble. Fragments fly down on the pair. The cloud rains wreckage on Tony as he and horse crash down in the flowering dust and dirt.

The girls plow skittish horses through chaos, falling bits of building and dust. The detonation slows their mounts but for a moment. Blind, Michelle hugs her mare's neck. Teri screams in rage as she hunches over in the saddle and shields her head with her rifle. Both drive through the bedlam with Eric now but a few yards back. Behind them the momentary quiet gives way to more screams from those who were watching the festivities now turned to mayhem.

Teri on the fastest of the horses, Crowhop, is the first to reach the Livery stable. She jumps clear at the wide street level doors and lunges into the building with her rifle, trusting Crowhop to wait ground tied. She throws herself flat in the dirt just inside the door plowing into the soiled straw in case the gunman is waiting for her. She cocks the rifle and scans the stalls.

Nothing.

There is not a damn thing.

No shot, no gunman, no nothing. Just dirt, cold dirt, and straw and the smell of manure, urine, horse sweat, hay, and leather.

Michelle, just a step back flies around the building to the rear and sneaks a very quick look up at the roof. Nothing there either. She turns around and scans the country behind the livery stable.

Eric joins them, still on horseback. He works the bolt of Fred's rifle and lopes to the other side. The lad sees a figure in the distance on a fast horse hightailing it to the south. Whomever it is has close to a half mile lead on the lad and is going by a short rock ledge that nudges up to the road. Eric knows that those rocks will soon hide the bastard who shot the bull. The lanky lad carefully shoulders the lightweight open sight rifle, guesses as to the needed elevation, and leads the target as he squeezes off a calculated shot seeking to take the wind into account.

"crack"

He sees the rider swerve, look back and then slide to the side of his horse Indian fashion to make himself a smaller target. The bullet must have spooked or even perhaps clipped the rider. Blacky jumps as the green horse is startled by the shot fired by his rider. Eric gives Fred's horse a nudge and channels the fear in a forward dash. The pair takes off in pursuit.

Eric mutters, "God, what I'd give to have Moose under me." Blacky lacks Moose's wild spirit that matches the lad. The girls join the chase down the dirt road that goes south of town and well before the rock ledge, Teri and Michelle are ahead of Blacky and his frustrated rider.

Eric, now lagging, comes by the rock where he threw a round at the bastard who shot Genesis. He sits back and brings Blacky to a sliding stop. A fresh torn envelope flutters in the churned dirt and snow. The glint of new coins catches the lad's avaricious eyes. Gold. He jumps out of the saddle and drops the reins. Blacky thankfully knows how to be ground tied. Eric snags the bounty, noting that half a dozen one-ounce double eagles will help pay for Genesis. He grabs the envelope which he stuffs in his pocket. His ears note that in the distance, the girls are still thundering along in pursuit of the unknown gunman. He looks around quickly, sees nothing else of immediate interest, and jumps back into the saddle and urges Fred's horse onward.

His mind registers that there is no trace of blood nor any other indication as to where his shot landed. Ah, well. At least the scoundrel is a bit poorer. As Fred's horse has no staying power, he holds the mount at a sustainable lope. He will examine the letter later. Ahead, he sees that Teri is in the lead, Michelle trails, and he is good two hundred yards back due to his stop and the quality of Fred's horse. The pursuit continues along the main road south out of Hellenville. Of the livery stable shooter there is just the odd glimpse, as he widens the distance he has on Eric and even to some extent that he has on the two girls.

Soon Teri fades back to the group, as she does not think it wise to outrun both Michelle and Eric, especially as they enter a winding stretch in a canyon with trees perched at all angles along both sides of the road. Soon, they hear bellowing and come around a corner and find a milling mob of cattle blocking their way. The damn things sport a Ringing Bell brand and the Senator's men are moving several hundred cows out of the corrals they recently built beside the throughfare. What rotten luck, of all the days to move them to the pastures and hay mounds closer to Hellenville. Now, this happens, and the bellowing mob allows the shooter to escape. Any tracks are now history. The delay of making it through the cattle gives the culprit a free pass to escape and strike again.

Teri, then Michelle, and finally Eric pull to a stop in frustration. Jesse, the Senator's foreman looks at them mockingly, with the mob of cows milling behind him. The rest of the Senator's crew pointedly ignore the Walking Y riders. Eric rides up to Jesse and impertinently barks, "What the hell are you doing?"

"Moving cows, what does it look like?" counters Jesse, the Senator's manager with a sneer. He then adds with a smirk, "Do you have a problem with our use of the road? and if you do, you should ask yourselves if I care." Thereupon, Jesse spits on Blacky.

Eric's jaw clamps shut. He reaches for his rope to teach the scallywag a well-deserved lesson.

But Michelle rides up and quietly asks, "did you see a rider come on horseback going like the blazes?"

Jesse smirks at the long-haired blonde. "Well little girl, I see no reason to answer you, but I will if you ask politely."

"Can you tell us please if you saw a rider come by with the horse going like the blazes?"

"Well," answers Jesse with a shrug. "Why, yes, he went by just before we opened the gates to get the cows out, or" he adds looking at the frustrated Eric with disdain, "Did we let them out as he rode by to delay you? Take your pick you little bucktooth snot."

"Damn! Of all the rotten luck. That son of a bitch shot our bull," snaps Eric ignoring the Ringing Bell manager's obvious baiting. "How damn many cows do you have coming out of the corrals?"

Jesse turns to his cowboys and barks out, "Well, boys, slow them down. This little snot wants us to count the cows." Thereupon, the Ringing Bell crew, with mocking smiles, slow the cows to a walk, and funnel the front of the mob into a narrow line beside the seething Eric.

The lad sees red. He shouts in frustration, "We'll just plow through the son of a bitching things. Follow me Michelle, Teri." With these words he wades into the bellowing cows. It is slow work, with the front of the mob being held back, and those riding drag pushing up the rear of the herd.

Jesse laughs at Eric's seething frustration, signaling his crew to casually work the cows in the path of the three Walking Y riders. Slowly, the three orphans work through the milling mob, but this leaves three winded Walking Y riders fighting the antics of the Ringing Bell crew instead of chasing their quarry. When they finally break clear, they can hear laughter behind them along with the bellows of cows still clogging the road.

The three youths push on at a mile-eating canter. But soon it is evident that the trail is cold. They debate riding on; however, the road has numerous logging trails and ranches along its length and any of these turnoffs could be a hiding place for the gunman. After covering another mile with no sign of their quarry, the three resign themselves to defeat and start the long trudge back to Hellenville on tired mounts.

Chapter 8

Nick's Girls and Woody's Woes!

Nick drives the buckboard casually and looks around at the townsfolks watching them. He directs the team verbally with the lines draped loosely on the front of the wagon on a cross piece. The shot that kills Genesis ends the festivities and panics his mares. He scrambles to reach the reins. He lunges forwards and elbows the owner. He claws his way to the lines, and simultaneously sings to his beloved large palominos in a surprisingly calm and clear voice,

"Whoa girls! Easy girls! You're safe with me."

He snags the heavy leather driving lines, gently pulls them, to let the horses know that all is well, and that he is watching. Out of the corner of his eyes, he sees the other wagon forge on ahead and notes the girls, then Tony, and finally Eric take off like a rabid hound dogs on the scent of a scared fox. Again, he sings to his magnificent team,

"Easy girls, Whoa!"

They slow and with no harm done, still breathing fast. Nick gets ready to dismount and walk up to their heads and talk to them after the pandemonium sparked by the single Buffalo gun shot, when,

"KWHAMM!"

Suddenly the lad senses a storefront halfway to the livery stable disintegrate in a mushroom cloud of debris. Again, he is off balance as one foot was on the wagon's step. Again, he is in the wrong place to hold and reassure his mares. Horses shriek in panic, humans scream in fear, and his wonderful team bolts. Nick scrambles his way back on the lurching wagon. He lunges for the driving lines. Again. Verbally he cannot hold his mares. He cannot reassure them. The large horses lunge forwards in a powerful panic. They veer to the right.

Nick shouts clearly, "HAW, HAW, HAW."

Somehow the horses hear him and obey, turning to the left just before they crash into the boardwalk. Nick reaches the leather lines and calls out clearly, "Easy girls, easy." The pair begins to slow in the middle of Main Street short of the chaos of falling debris. Nick's relief is brief. Another terrified driverless unmatched team careens towards them.

Nick, hands now clasping the lines, pulls on the right one and yells, "GEE, GEE, GEE!"

Again, the horses hear his clear voice and turn to the right. The other team barrels past them in chaos, cargo flying off the stricken wagon. A wooden crate bounces in front of the buckboard. Nick swears. The front corner of the wagon smashes into the large wooden packing box. The wheels miss the obstacle, but the buckboard lurches over the crate and wood shatters. Nick only hears the doubletree issue a loud "Crack!"

"Whoa, girls Whoa!" stammers the lad, gently pulling back on the lines.

The large horses jump a smaller second box. The buckboard's tongue drives it off course and makes it barrel into a horse water trough. The wagon teeters for a moment. The horses dance to a stop. Nick holds the lines and sees the harness totally askew. The young teamster continues to talk to the horses who now face the blacksmith shop.

His clear voice is heard as he sings, "Easy Girls, Easy."

The Belgians panting, eyes wide, with sweat forming under their disheveled harness, stop. Thankfully, the double tree leaves a loose tongue, but it does not gore them. This time Nick dismounts and walks up to their heads. He firmly holds their bridles while talking to them calmly.

"Good Girls, oh! are you ever such Good Girls. I'm proud of you."

After a minute, seeing nothing else in town except for his beloved horses, he scans their flanks. His eyes miss nothing. Apart from the white of the eyes, and the fear and sweat, the horses look at Nick and lip his outstretched hands. The lead horse tucks her head on his shoulder. He speaks soothingly to the pair and looks back at his team. Artemis and Minerva are safe for now. Only water leaking from the damaged water tank is heard before the next wave of sound registers. The screams of townsfolks caught out by the explosion or hurt in the other runaways.

***

The flying debris, smoke, and deafening noise of the explosion knock both Tony and Sorley to the ground. In the back of his mind, the Irishman sees the girls staying in the saddle and then Eric vaulting on Fred's horse. As to the foreman, head pounding and ears ringing, face lacerated by debris, he notes the last of the shattered wood and glass touch the ground. He sees Eric charge through the dust and smoke with the black horse pounding the frozen road as he pursues the girls.

Tony mouths a short prayer, "Thank you Mary for getting that boy through. They stand a chance."

He then seeks to stand and staggers and falls again. He can neither see the girls who disappear past the smoke nor the hot-tempered boy on Fred's horse. Carefully Tony, dazed, tries to rise again but he crumples to all four. He shakes his head. Coat torn, numerous cuts start to bleed. He hears nothing except for a loud hum. He can't move for a minute, and finally checks Sorley visually. The sorrel mare is now up standing with her head between her forelegs and sweat and lather covering her flank. Thank God she stands.

Her thick winter hair cannot hide the cuts. Blood drips where her hide is ripped open by flying glass shards. Fred comes over, and glances at Sorley. The mare is dazed and spooked. The black-haired lad talks to her and reaches for the reins before he helps Tony to his feet. The Irishman wobbles and holds his wounded horse to help him remain upright. He talks to Sorley gently and then staggers like a drunkard while he checks all four legs. He wants to join the chase. His hand sense and eyes find a deep cut on the right hind quarter. His ears ring. He cannot hear Fred talk nor anything else. He tries to stand straight but cannot and remains hunched like an old man. He wobbles about as he would after a hard blow in the boxing ring like those he collected many times in bouts fought for money in Brooklyn not that long ago. His brain tells him that Sorley needs doctoring, rest and care.

His body tells him that he needs the same. He instinctively reaches to his breast pocket and takes the medicinal whiskey and dabs it on Sorley's cut. For the first time he truly looks at the wreckage strewn around him. He is in the midst of a crowd that gathers around what remains of the storefront. He sees some men grab buckets and fill them at one of the water troughs to extinguish a couple small fires that start in the ruin of the building. Women come back out to see if anyone is hurt. The Irishman looks at the activity and staggers back leading his horse to where he last saw the buckboard.

There another small group assembles and divides its attention between the dead bull lying gracefully on its haunches in the middle of Main Street and the buckboard stopped askew with a broken double tree. The bull's blossoming bullet wound between its eyes somehow looks obscene. Tony's brain registers that someone very familiar slits Genesis' throat before the heart fully stops, and blood flows copiously on the street. He guesses that it's time to try and salvage whatever meat can be salvaged from the pedigree Red Angus bull. The Walking Y's foreman shifts his gaze to the buckboard, perched on the remains of a wooden crate and its contents.

Nick is consoling The Walking Y team while he simultaneously unhitches the harnessed draft horses to move them away from the shattered doubletree. Tony is impressed at how Nick is calm and how his horses pick up on the young man's composure. The horses' eyes lose the fevered panicked look and the lad then hands one of them to Fred who moves up to assist his friend. The studious lad holds the lead horse by gripping the bridle while Nick moves his focus to the second horse.

***

When the bullet rips into Genesis, Woody scans around in haste. No riders down, no horses down, and no one hit in the buckboard. It takes a moment for the bull to collapse to the ground. Woody understands that the bull, his prize bull, the bull who he banks on to rebuild the cattle herd on the Walking Y, is dead. In the middle of his forehead, smack between the eyes, is a weeping bullet wound.

Looking the other way, he sees the last of a dissipating puff of smoke. Hoofbeats make him turn to see Tony taking off on Sorley, and behind him the two girls. Somehow, Fred is on the ground, and Eric vaults in that lad's saddle. Jolted in the buckboard, it registers that Nick is gaining control and he makes a note to thank him. He looks over to Jennifer

Hathaway, and she is holding the seat as if her life depended on it and has a white sheen on her face.

"KWHAMM!"

A blast, a fast-growing cloud reaches out to kiss them.

The livery stable is hidden. The wagon lurches again. A storefront is blown to smithereens. It blocks Main Street about two thirds of the way to the livery stable. Dust and debris fly. Tony, by the store goes down. Three riders low in the saddle gallop into the chaos. Nick scrambles with the team.

Woody shouts uselessly, "Get the bastard!"

Coat torn, looking old, he shouts again, "Damn bastards!"

He seeks to grab Nick to hold him as the buckboard careens out of control. The boy is stepping down and in a terrible position being half in and half out of the buckboard. While Woody pulls, the lad screams "Gee, Gee, Gee!" while guiding his team as he can with the lines. Brave lad. But someone else's team is now out of control.

A crash, horses scream. Wood breaks. Nick tumbles out of the buckboard.

The buckboard comes to a stop.

Woody looks around. Is Jennifer all right? Has he lost any of his crew? He finally sees Tony on all fours, Sorley looks worse for wear, and Nick in what passes for control. He turns his focus back on Jennifer who was thrown from the seat to the floor of the buckboard and has several cuts. All of this probably when the buckboard lurched out of control and broke the doubletree. The blue coat is torn, her arm is smeared with mud and blood. Her hat is missing probably trampled in the snow and mud. The owner notes to his consternation there is a cut on her face that bleeds copiously.

Woody moans overwhelmed, "Oh God, why?"

Among the gawkers that gather around the buckboard, Mrs. Couchman is the first to realize that Miss Jennifer Hathaway is bleeding. She climbs up on the wagon and takes out a clean handkerchief from her large handbag, and begins ministering the well dressed, out of place lady in the buckboard.

"Oh Goodness, Woodrow, what happened?" asks Misses Hathaway in a bit of an English accent.

"How the hell should I know," barks Woody in a fury as he stares again at the crimson flower in the bull's forehead.

He shakes his head and cringes in defeat. All that hard work to gather those carefully nursed dollars come to this. A dead bull, hurt men, bleeding horses, and his Governess nearly killed. He curses again, "That God-awful Senator is back on the warpath. That God Damn Son of a Bitch."

Furious, he leaps off the wagon, pulls his well-honed hunting knife and slits the bull's throat. The blood pulses out, as the heart is still beating its last. "Damn it all to hell."

Woody looks at the blood pooling in the middle of Main Street, and mutters, "Well, sorry Hardy, but we'll be reduced to eating bull for the next few months. There's no choice. It's either that or feed the coyotes and milk the bank account that is already dry." He looks around with pain in his eyes and wipes the blood on his knife with his bandana and sheaves it, tears of frustration and rage and pain flows down his cheeks. All of his toil reduced to this. A dead bull, a downed rider, an endangered governess, and three kids chasing a heartless killer.

He shakes his head to clear the morbid thoughts. Then spares a moment and looks again at the dazed Jennifer and calms down a bit more. He is acting like a cad, again. But Mrs. Couchman comforts her and ministers to her needs. He walks up and ignores the wife of the owner of the General Store as he shunts her aside dismissively and addresses the new governess.

When he speaks, it is in a more normal tone directed at Miss Hathaway, who is new to the west, "Nick lost control of the buckboard when the bull was shot, and then someone blew up a building close to the livery stable. My gut is that was to block any pursuit. I do not know what happened to my hired kids or foreman, but we will try to sort out this mess when I can gather them. We do not have far to go to the ranch, and we have the warm master bedroom waiting for you there. With any luck, there will be no more excitement for today."

Jennifer cries. Her bloody torn coat, missing hat, and look of fear register. He softens his voice and pulls his clean handkerchief from his shirt pocket, and hands it to Miss Hathaway. He gives her a hand, and she sits on the tilting buckboard seat, while letting Nick tend to the horses. "We'll be home soon, Jennifer, and then you can lie down for a bit if you need to.

I have no idea as to what is going on, except that the bull was shot, and that empty storefront was blown to smithereens."

"Where is your foreman Tony, and how did he let this happen?" gently asks Jenny looking Woody in the eye with tears.

Woody is mute for a moment. How is it that Tony is not around where he needs him. The Irishman took off after the girls and Eric and his timing was perfect to end up by that building that blew up. With luck, both horse and rider will be all right, but now, he must help Nick get the buckboard and team underway. He'll need someone to deal with the bull and bring the meat to the cookhouse. Looking at the mess he calculates that first, he'll need a new doubletree to replace the busted one. Just what he wants, another expense. Thank God, it looks like the horses are safe.

On the other hand, he will have to use the milk house to hang Genesis' carcass. Why he can probably salvage a thousand pounds of beef and sell an extra steer. Not much of a return, but it's better than nothing.

That's a blessing.

Woody smiles bitterly for a moment, why the past year has been one blessed thing after another. All right, to work. Untangle the harness and help Nick. Get the Sheriff to do his job for a change. Thinking about it, he must tell the orphans that they should not try and be heroes – again. Trouble is, he did not see this one coming. What else is going to hit the Walking Y and how can he make that damn Senator and his hoodlums back off?

While the Walking Y crew seeks to repair the buckboard which through a strange twist of fate lurched up to the blacksmith shop, Woody spends most of his time with Jennifer Hathaway. He dismisses Mrs. Couchman who remains standing nearby with a frown. He barks a rude "Thanks, we don't need you anymore." Then he waves off Sheriff Cody Bozeman. When Tony comes up to talk limping, he points to the bull, "Can you get some help and gut and quarter and load that. We need to salvage the meat and bring it back to the ranch? We'll hang it in the milk shed, and it looks like we will have award winning pedigree bull on the menu for a while."

Sheriff Bozeman meanders to the storefront. He scans a pile of debris, and as he walks around, he sees a wire that goes from the blown-up storefront towards the livery stable, under the boardwalk of a couple neighboring buildings. Whomever blew up the storefront set off the charge from the livery stable and then in the chaos made good their escape. Or worse yet, walked into the mob of curious townsfolk seeking to help or just to gawk. What a mess.

Of course, the Walking Y would be involved again. Why if that jackass Woody would just sell, life would be a bit more peaceful. Again.

Of course, Mr. Woodrow W. Flynt will abrasively blame the Senator's crew. But he did not see any Ringing Bell riders, nor had he seen any. Nor did he see the Senator, and nor was the politician at the courthouse. In fact, as all hell broke loose, the Sheriff had just reached his office. Theoretically, Tex who was on duty might have seen something, but he was at his desk when the sheriff stuck his head in the office to snag a rifle when the first shot rang out.

Damn. The recent peace was too good to be true. And again, he has no one in custody.

Chapter 9

<u>The Trojan Horse</u>

It is a tired defeated cortege that rides up the tree lined driveway hours later past the white bunkhouse, the white foreman's house, and past the imposing red barn to the large white headquarter Walking Y cookhouse under now cloudy grey skies. There is no prize bull to admire and corral, just four quarters to hang in the milk shed. The matched golden Belgian draft horses look spent. The buckboard shows the raw marks of temporary repairs as the new doubletree has not yet been painted to match the wagon or even the rest of the rig. Sorley, riderless, with the stripped saddle in the back of the wagon, is hobbling, favoring her wounded hind quarter.

Tony is quiet, lost in his thoughts, seated on the tailgate leading his horse. Nick is singularly focused on his two golden draft horses who were endangered by his bravado as when the shot rang, he was not holding the driving lines. Michelle and Teri are in a whispered discussion and look around furtively still clutching rifles in their frozen grips. Fred is in the buckboard with a bandage around his head, and pain coursing through his legs. Eric is alert on Blacky also with a rifle at the ready. Miss Hathaway is quiet, her light blue coat stained by dirt and blood from the small copiously bleeding cut on her forehead and a larger one on her arm. Woody is stone faced, quiet, and angry at the merciless fate that so destroyed his homecoming. Looking from the barn to the cookhouse, they spy an immaculately saddled horse waiting patiently at the cookhouse hitching rail.

Woody curses. "Damn it all to hell. Now what?"

Most go up to the cookhouse wondering what trouble awaits them with their energy momentarily rising. Their hopes for a respite a forlorn wish. The door opens and Senator William Howard Bell the Third steps out of the main door impeccably and perfectly dressed in a new expensive tweed suit and matching coat. Right behind him is a stone-faced Hardy. This is unexpected.

Woody is the first to recover. He spits at the ground by the saddle horse and looks at the politician with loathing. He growls, "What the hell are you doing here Senator?"

"Ah, Mr. Woodrow W. Flynt," states the eloquently dressed lawyer while standing on the top step of the cookhouse looking down at the battered crew, "please inform me what transpired in town to delay your arrival. I have been lingering around here for an extra hour in anticipation of your presence. Your boy here," he goes on, while dismissively pointing back to Hardy, "would not allow me to wait in the comfort of the living room or your office. He insisted that I was not to go beyond the kitchen, and I am unaccustomed to being treated that way by any servant, much less a colored one."

Woody snarls. "He's right. I should have told him to make you stand outside, you pompous ass."

The Senator sneers down at the ranch owner and ignores the comment. "Politeness is obviously not a strong point of yours Mr. Flynt. Come to think of it, it never has been. As to this so-called boy of yours, he was quite forceful in informing me that the hospitality he could offer ended where the kitchen ended. That is unacceptable. I would like you to offer an explanation of such rude behavior along with an accounting of what transpired in town."

Woody spits again from the seat of the wagon. He ignores the Ringing Bell Ranch owner and turns to Jennifer, "Please disembark here. Eric, tell Tony and the rest of the crew to grab a quick coffee and then tend to the horses, rigging, and our expensive beef. It has been a long afternoon, and the animals can wait for a couple minutes. Then have everyone join me at the table. We have a few things to discuss."

Turning back to the door, he feigns surprise at still seeing the Senator. "So, you're still here. What part of 'You're not welcomed here' do you not understand?" Before the pretentious Senator can utter a word, the gruff Woody continues, "Be aware that my 'boy' is following Walking Y policy. I'm surprised he let you in the kitchen. I'll encourage him not to be so polite in the future, but as he is a gentleman, unlike the rest of the people around here including yourself, he will probably ignore my desire to show you the door and he will remain polite."

Woody dismounts from the buckboard and barges up the stairs, past William Howard Bell the Third and goes into the kitchen. The Senator and

Miss Hathaway follow the owner into the house. She turns to Hardy and asks in a tone that expects obedience, "Can you show me to my room, and bring up my baggage. I wish to change out of this bloody coat and these torn garments. It has been a wearisome trip from town, and I need to refresh."

Hardy steps out, snags an armful of her baggage before the buckboard can retreat back to the barn and hefts the lot up the stairs into the large master suite that has been turned over to the governess. Inside, with Jennifer Hathaway in tow, he leads her into the freshly painted and cleaned but dated master bedroom. It is at the far end of the hall from the fire escape and has not been used in some time. It is the largest room in the house with its own privy and fireplace.

Jennifer looks around dismissively at the newly made bed, clean towels and the shining windows and points to an area beside the large armoire and tells Hardy, "Please put all of that there, and you can leave now." Those are the last words that Jennifer directs to the cook as she points to the door. He steps out, she closes the door, and quietly she moves from heating grate to heating grate to better understand how she can eavesdrop from her quarters.

Meanwhile, the Senator, not in the least bit taken aback by Woody's usual and vintage welcome, retorts, "Mr. Woodrow W. Flynt, if we can adjourn to your office, I will not unduly delay you; however, I wish to talk to you of some matters that are of high importance. Privately and now."

Woody grumbles in disgust and throws off his coat in a huff. He ignores the Senator again and walks over to get a cup of coffee. Not the least bit perturbed, the politician gives himself permission to also have a cup of coffee and snags a cinnamon roll Hardy had just pulled from the oven. Both men look at each other, Woody with a look of anger, and Mr. Bell with a bit of a sneer curling his lip. He enjoys taunting the ranch owner in his own house. Finally, Tony walks in for a quick cuppa. He looks at Woody and the Senator and reaches for his breast pocket and takes a little nip of his flask.

"Ah," taunts the intruder, "Mr. Seamus Patrick O'Connor. I see you have a brand-new leather covered metal whiskey flask. That is so very lovely. I wonder what interesting twist of fate met its predecessor?"

Tony, who has played a game of poker or two in his life, looks at the politician and mimics the politician, "Ah, Your Lordship, I see you have polished your arrogant Sassenach bloodlines. That is so very lovely. I wonder what interesting twist of fate allows you to burnish them to an even greater extent?"

At that moment, Michelle and Teri walk in, holding rifles at the ready in a quiet threat directed at their neighbor. Fred hobbles in still limping from his old injury compounded by his fall earlier that same day. He looks at the Senator with hatred, and in a rare display of temper, the scholarly boy lets his tongue get the better of him. He snarls pointing with his chin, "What's it doing here?"

Woody momentarily smiles as he sips his coffee standing at the threshold to the living room. He looks at the three young ones, and tells them, "Fred, Michelle, and Teri once you have all downed a cup, help with the horses and then come in to warm up for dinner. We will call it a day. Hardy will have something for all of us. Tony, after you take off your coat, and get a cup of coffee, join me and our illustrious guest." Fred stands there uncertain, glaring at the Senator as do both Michelle and Teri.

Woody sees this, and growls with a hint of amusement, "Hot coffee or hot tea or hot chocolate, and then take care of the horses, get to it now." They all snag a cup, but Fred takes a rifle off the rack in a rare display of bravado.

The cook comes back down the stairs, and Woody looks at him. "Hardy, it has been a hell of a day, and I will explain as soon as I can. The young ones will warm up for a minute and then put horses and gear away. When they come back let's have dinner and hot beverages and if you have it, a good dessert, they would be most appreciative. Then ask the girls to show Miss Hathaway around headquarters when she comes down after she is done changing."

Tony and Woody each holding a cup head out of the kitchen. The owner, with curt movements, signals their unwelcome guest to follow. The office is no cleaner than the last time the Senator soiled it with his presence, and Woody would still like to slug the son of a bitch; however, for now he will refrain. The owner steps around behind the desk and sits. Tony casually leans against the door jamb, blocking any exit from the room. Innocently, he checks the loads of the pistol he is carrying and drops it back in the holster. The Senator sits in one of the chairs across from the desk, and notes that it is of the correct height. He smiles as he thinks that Woody does not know the most basic rules of power plays. Make the chairs your guests sit in a bit short to put them at a disadvantage. Typical of Woody. He is a blunderbuss.

He is brought back from his observations by Woody's curt tone, "All right Senator, I guess you'll deny it and use your presence here as an alibi, but I think you're the low-down bastard who caused the ruckus in town. So no, I will not fill you in. What do you want?"

Senator Bell sits straight showcasing his full height and looks down his nose at the shorter Woody, "Mr. Woodrow W. Flynt, it is evident that you are reaching conclusions without any evidence, and again feel free to impugn my character, while not even offering me the courtesy of a hot cup of coffee, leaving me to serve myself. That is the case, even if it is only a bit of work for your new cook I have yet to meet as you did not introduce us. There is no reason we cannot be civilized."

The Senator then glares at Woody and Tony and lets the silence speak before he begins again, "My visit is due to the fact that I wish to discuss those items for which I am responsible under our agreement, as I am a public servant who stands by his promises and word."

Tony interrupts, "Well that would be out of character."

Woody, losing his limited patience, glances at his foreman and briefly smirks. But schoolyard antics will not encourage the Senator to get to the point. The lawyer slows, and sneers at the juvenile antics and resumes his verbose dialogue. "Thus, if you do not wish to elaborate as to what delayed you in Hellenville, and wish to levy baseless accusations, I will educate myself when I ride to the courthouse. I am disappointed as to the low level that we have reached in our relationship. That said, Mr. Woodrow W. Flynt, I am here as I must request your assistance in a matter of mutual interest. Per our last discussion in this room on December 20th, 1904, you will note that I have been following through on the agreement that you compelled me to sign under pressure. At the time you did not even allow me the opportunity to see the vile accusations a couple men had directed in my direction. You should be aware that those two men had been fired several days beforehand for insubordination."

Woody looks up startled at this news, and Tony lowers his hand to the colt he has taken to wearing. The Senator, after the appropriate dramatic pause resumes.

"Thus far, I have ensured as a good neighbor and as we agreed that your line of credit with The First Cattleman Bank in Great Falls was renewed, per my efforts. That is despite the fact that you had originally secured the loan through fraudulent means. I have purchased the cows and horses you feloniously implied died due to the activity of my men, to maintain the honor of my word. I have covered the requested compensation without complaint for the ridiculously high nursing fees and other expenses you submitted including initial wages for that colored cook you have dredged up from Lord only knows where. I have done this only as a fellow rancher and out of the goodness of my spirit. However, I have somehow misplaced my original copy of the document. Thus, I am here in order to request an opportunity to review your original so that I can ensure there is no possible point which may be outstanding that I may not remember, as I am a man of my word."

Here the Senator pauses, as Woody remains fixed like a statue, and Tony ensconces himself a little more in the doorway. "Thus, would you be so kind as to allow me to peruse your copy?"

Woody, at the end of his patience, fumes. "Senator, that's a load of bull. You wouldn't 'misplace' something that important, and so no, I will not fetch the document while you watch. You're the kind of low-down rat who'd seek to destroy my copy. So, in short, I will not allow you to know where I keep that document, nor will I allow you to peruse it. In fact, Senator, I can categorically state that you can burn this cookhouse down, and that document and the confession signed by YOUR MEN will be perfectly safe as they are not here."

The Walking Y's owner then glowers at his unwelcome guest before going on, "In addition, I have instructions with my bank, and lawyer, and also with a dear friend as to the document's location. Thus, getting me or my foreman killed will not make those documents disappear. So, I suggest you get that maid of yours to clean your office and find it, or you purchase a pair of spectacles and find it yourself. If you have a specific question, I know the letter you signed by heart, so I can state that you have paid for the cattle, horses, made the bank renew the loan, paid the nursing fees. You and I both know you have a few other tasks ahead of you including stepping aside politically. So do it – NOW!"

The two glare at each other for a moment, and then the Senator carefully puts on his hat, nods his head, and stands to leave the office. Tony, with a barely perceptible signal from Woody, lets the well-manicured lawyer pass. Not another word is spoken, even as he clears the door, walks through the kitchen and steps out to his fine English hunter and his well-polished saddle.

Meanwhile Miss Hathaway in her room on the second floor quickly opens the trunk and takes out a change of clothing. But now, she notes that this house, like many of these large two-story country houses that seek to spread as much of the kitchen heat as possible in the winter, has several grates to the main floor that can be adjusted by the occupants of the bedroom. One of her grates accesses the main sitting room where Woody spent his time injured and this opening to the floor below is beside the small office. Looking around after she makes sure her door is closed, she silently bends down over the grate and brushes her hair back behind her when it slips. She listens as carefully to the Senator leaving as she had to the entire discussion.

She changes into a clean casual dress, and ventures to explore the house starting with the second floor. She locates Michelle's room and also Teri's. She scans the other rooms, the emergency fire escape at the end of the upstairs hallway and even notes the box of cartridges in one of the girl's rooms. After looking around, she ventures downstairs and walks into the kitchen as if she owns the place.

She ambles up to the cook and ignores Tony seated at the table, "I'm Jennifer Hathaway, the new governess. I am pleased to meet you. You are?"

"Miss Hathaway, my friends know me as Hardy, and my full name is James Hardyman."

"I see James, have you worked here for a long time?"

"No ma'am, I started less than two weeks ago. Would you care for some coffee?"

She then considers Tony, and walks up to the foreman extending a hand, as if she wants him to bend over and kiss it. As he stands, she states in lightly accented English, "Now that we do not have guns barking, I would like to make proper introductions. You must be Mr. Seamus Patrick O'Connor. I am pleased to meet you and I have heard so much about you. I am Miss Jennifer Hathaway, the new governess. I will teach the children those subjects you do not, such as proper English, mathematics, and obviously comportment among other things. Where in Ireland are you from originally?"

"County Cork," replies the Irishman flatly.

"Ah, yes, I have been there when I was at the Maryborough estate a few short years ago. Had a lovely time. My hosts were most civilized, and I enjoyed them very much. You must have been from the lower town?"

Without waiting for a reply, Miss Hathaway turns back to the cook and continues a casual conversation for a few minutes, "Yes, James, I like a good English Breakfast tea with milk in the morning. I hope you don't mind my calling you James, I find it so much more refined than Hardy."

Hardy nods his head in the affirmative and resumes his work.

She snags a proper cup of tea with a dainty silver spoon and a saucer, and then ventures into the large sitting room, and looks at the bookcase perusing the titles. She picks up Woody's Volume 1 of Gibbon's *Decline and Fall of the Roman Empire* and opens it with a grimace and while no one watches she shakes it to see if there are any loose documents in the book. When this yields nothing, she goes through the other five volumes the same way while ensuring that she is unobserved. This concluded, she migrates to the ranch office, and looks in. Woody is lost in updating the daily log and going over the bank ledger. He frowns as the loss of that prize bull will hurt, more than he would like to admit, and he needs a few quiet years of successful operations to bring the Walking Y back to life on a sound financial footing. He cannot afford to hire any outside hands, and will have to rely on the orphans, Hardy and Tony.

"Mr. Flynt," begins Jennifer, "I hope I am not disturbing you?"

"No, not at all, how can I help?"

"Can you give me a bit more background on the two girls, and also the three boys. They seem to have taken immediate action when the bull was killed, and I wish to understand what training they have had that makes them so prompt to attack perceived foes, and why they are so quick to snag guns? It is not natural, especially for girls to behave thus."

Woody muses for a second. This is not something they would teach in a city or back east, and Miss Hathaway must see girls with rifles on horses chasing gunmen with no apparent fear as a mystery. "Regrettably," Woody begins, "Montana is not one of the states that has given woman the right to vote as of this time, but it will happen as it already did some years ago next door in Wyoming. Those girls have been through hell, pardon my use of the word, and had they not been resourceful nor willing to act, they would be dead thanks to the men that son of a bitching Senator turned loose on them, if you will excuse my English again. You will teach them more conventional subjects, but I will insist that they also keep that sense of action and maintain that ability to shoot as well as any man. As you saw today, the Walking Y is still a target of some who wish us dead."

"Oh," Miss Jennifer says, batting her eyes in concern, "Mr. Flynt, who would want such a dastardly outcome?"

"As I said, Senator William Howard Bell the Third and his hoodlums. We have had more than one run in with the scummy bastard."

"But the Senator seems to be a gentleman. If you could reach an agreement, I am sure he would honor it. He strikes me as well educated and I hear that he is a lawyer from one of the best schools back east."

Woody does not mince his words. "The Senator is a low-down skunk. I think he hates me because my father left me this ranch that was carved out of the wilderness while he had to buy his and not inherit it. That said, I wouldn't trust that so called Senator as far as I could throw my horse with the wind in my face. He can stoop low enough to undercut a weasel, and I would recommend that you not trust him or his men. He is not a gentleman. Last go around he planted a spy on this ranch and tried to kill the kids using that spy as a hired gun. In fact, Miss Hathaway, I hate to state this, but the Senator's men, had they had the chance, would have had their evil way with the two girls and left them dead. Anyone who hires someone who stoops so low as to kill cows, shoot boys, slaughter horses, kidnap girls, and threaten rape while he holds them naked is just plain evil."

Miss Hathaway seems somewhat stunned by this pronouncement and is quiet for a while. She then hears the outside door and voices. She ventures back to the kitchen to better assess the rest of the crew. As she enters the kitchen, she sees Michelle and Teri whom she briefly met at the train station, along with Seamus and the three boys. She smiles to the girls and stands while James works on preparing dinner. Outside, the wind begins to blow, and despite the looming darkness, snowflakes flit by the window. It's obviously the start of another blizzard.

She walks up to the children before they can sit with a pre-dinner cup of hot chocolate, and addresses all of them. Eric glares, Nick is polite, while Fred smiles excited to have a tutor along with a governess. Teri and Michelle are a bit more restrained as all wait to sit at the table. "I am Miss Hathaway, and I will be your Governess and teacher."

Chapter 10

The Virtuous Senator

The entire crew is eager for dinner after such a foul and disappointing homecoming. The weather now matches their moods, as the wind is biting, and the sky dark grey veering to black earlier than normal for late January. The orphans sit at their habitual places, and Woody walks in and looks around. Trying to sound encouraging he starts;

"Well, that was a long day, and I really appreciate how you all reacted to the shooter, whom I have nicknamed 'The Buffalo Gun.' His rifle sounded like a Sharps, and it is a very deadly weapon. That said, I am also impressed at how well you all reacted to the dynamite." He turns his eyes to the red-haired boy first and goes on, "Nick, excellent work and congratulations at your control of the team, Teri and Michelle well done, and your ability to hold your horses and ride through falling debris. Eric, that was an impressive jump on Blacky, and you probably could have caught the brigand if you had been on Moose. Fred, you recovered well, and you helped Tony stand, and Nick hold the horses. Thanks to all of you."

The wind outside howls as a strong gust makes the house rattle, the damper on the wood cookstove emits a puff of smoke, while cold air chisels its way in. Woody looks around at the flickering kerosene lights and candles and changes tack, "If the feared major cold front comes in, we can split the day tomorrow so that all of you can start your education with Miss Hathaway. Tomorrow morning, Eric and Tony and I will patrol, as we will break into two groups. I do not expect issues if this is a blizzard beyond those of survival. I had hoped we were past the need for those patrols, but the events of the past few hours tell me that we are in someone's bull's eye – pardon the pun."

Woody then sits, and Hardy looks at the crew, "I've got a really good beef stew for dinner, with my homemade bread and for something different, I have a hot plum duff pudding for dessert. Tony, with you in mind, I gave myself the liberty to double the rum ration in the pudding."

The orphans except for Michelle look at the adults in askance. They have never heard of such a dish.

Then the boys chuckle, as Eric winks and tells Fred and Nick "Hardy is going to get us drunk and we'll have to buy a flask like Tony!"

Hardy cuts back in, "Boys, the cooking removes the alcohol."

Jennifer's face lights up for the first time since the shot rang out that afternoon, "Oh Goodness, I have not had plum duff pudding since I was but a girl." She looks over at the foreman, and continues, "But Seamus, growing up poor and Irish, I would expect that the only ingredient you are familiar with, is the rum ration."

Tony takes the barb in stride as he expects nothing better from the English. He pauses for a moment before replying, "As a matter of a fact, all Your Lordships would let us have was the tripe of any bullock. So, yes, we had plum duff pudding, although usually we were a bit short of cinnamon, or the dried fruit. In addition, sometimes we were even short on rum. Even if we were Irish."

Jennifer, seeking perhaps to be funny, tosses another barb at the foreman, "That was probably because your father drank it while helping in the kitchen."

Tony darts a dirty look her way, but keeps quiet and takes another discreet slug of medicinal whiskey. Hardy busies himself placing serving dishes on the table while everyone takes their place. Woody serves himself last and looks around. He passes a platter of beans and then serves himself from the one with the rich stew. Jennifer interrupts. "A proper meal requires a proper grace. Woodrow, would you care to give grace?"

Woody stammers for a moment, and turns with a wicked smile, "Tony, it's your turn."

Tony, out of ingrained habit drummed into his head by monks when a child, bows his head, and recites, "Bless us, O Lord and these Thy gifts, which we are about to receive from Thy bounty, through Christ our Lord. Amen."

Miss Hathaway, with a knowing smile, addresses the orphans. "Thank you, Seamus for that most Catholic grace. I will take the liberty of teaching others to you children so that you may go into high society and know how to make yourselves at home."

Tony glowers at the Lady, and as normal, Eric dives in, and looks up at Hardy, with his mouth half full, and mutters with a now rare smile on his face, "Hardy, this is great. In fact, it's better than Tony's cooking, and I didn't know you didn't have to burn the beans."

Jennifer looks at the lad disapprovingly. Tony smiles and sits back to watch the battle.

Nick seeing this, stuffs his mouth, and in turn looks at Hardy mangling his diction, "Yeah, Hardy, much better than Woody's old socks." As Miss Hathaway's eyes lock in on the lad, he makes it a point of turning to Fred, and continuing after swallowing a bit more at once than polite, "Fred, isn't this better than your own cooking?"

Fred grins, and looks over at the cook, "Hardy, I'll concede your cooking tops anything we were able to muster since we've been here. I think even the girls would say so."

Michelle and Teri, who never liked kitchen duty, both nod their heads in approval. Then in a distinct act of defiance, both turn to Tony and state at the same time as if they had rehearsed the line, "That Tony, finally means that we can ride a bit more, as we are your best cowboys." Thereupon they look at each other and shout, "Ha! Didn't think you had studied your line."

Woody watches the orphans and stays quiet. He does however, put his hand next to Jennifer's to help encourage her to put up with his cantankerous crew. Unnoticed by any in the room, this is the lightest mood the orphans have mustered since the prior December when the girls were kidnapped, and the boys challenged by their injuries or the events around them. In short, the mental jousting moves their minds off the terrible events of the day.

As dessert is being served, a sulky drives up to the cookhouse through the foul weather. Dr. Maxwell and his wife come to the door. "Come in," barks Woody feeling a bit short. He turns to Miss Hathaway with a knowing smile, as the unexpected seems to be the norm at the moment. "It's Doctor Maxwell and his wife." The couple walk in.

The Doctor looks around the table and checks every face. "I thought I would stop by as I was not far away and headed back to town. Did any of you get hurt in today's escapades?"

"No Doctor," answers Tony as Woody is a bit dour, still brooding on his lost bull. "No major physical injuries except I'll ask you, after the meal is completed, to check Miss Hathaway's forehead cut and gouged arm and Fred's leg and hip. He's limping again. But why don't you both join us for dessert. Hardy, our new cook whom you may not have met yet, has made plum duff pudding."

Mrs. Maxwell, who had been frowning upon seeing Woody remove his hand from near Jennifer's, looks up with a sparkle of interest in her eyes. "Plum duff pudding! Oh my, I have not had any in years, and my mother made an excellent one. Yes, we would be delighted, wouldn't we dear?"

Her husband nods his ascent and starts to take off his wife's coat. His eyes lock in on the dish of plum duff pudding and the slightly smaller dish of perfectly whipped cream. As he sits beside his wife with a smile, and he adds "If it's not too much trouble."

Woody growls his consent, and soon all are installed, and the conversation goes to the day's events. Tony looks at Doctor Maxwell and states, "We are glad to see you, it has been a while since we have had a chance to talk. I don't think you've been here since Christmas Eve, when you gave Fred a clean bill of health." He then turns to Mrs. Maxwell, and smiles as he addresses her, "Mrs. Maxwell, I have never had a chance to thank you adequately for the help you gave us in the last month and while Woody was in Denver. If there is anything reasonable that I can do to return the favor, please let me know."

Mrs. Maxwell looks at the Irishman, and in jest replies, "I guess that making you give up your flask would not be classified as 'reasonable'?"

Tony eyes sparkle at the opening and he replies in kind, "Certainly, that is quite a reasonable request, if you would join me in a good Catholic rosery."

Woody sensing a pending debate on the merits of the temperance movement, cuts in, "Mrs. Maxwell, I was just curious if the Senator has been in touch with you?"

"Why yes, he wanted to give me a generous nursing fee as a thank you for my work offsetting the harm his men did without his consent. I asked that he give it to my church instead, which he has."

The Doctor looks at Woody and asks, "would you have any idea as to whom was behind today's attack on your ranch?"

Woody muses here for a moment now in contemplation as to the harsh events of the day. "Yes, I suspect my exalted neighbor. But of course,

I have no proof, but I smell a rat, and William Howard Bell the Third would be the rat."

"Why," answers the Doctor a bit with surprise at Woody's reply, "I am going to tell you what is now being discussed in town. I'll state that because of what I have seen here, I do not agree with the local assessment, but in town it is said that 'the Senator fired that Dave and Roger, because they started an unauthorized vendetta against you.' William Bell has also stated to his crew that 'he apologized to you in person and is compensating you for the unauthorized harm Roger and Dave did to your ranch.' In fact, the Senator has stated that he 'ordered that Roger be fired immediately upon hearing the first hints of his actions against your crew.'"

"What? That's a God Damn lie," counters Teri in astounded surprise. "That bastard couldn't have fired them."

Mrs. Maxwell chokes on her bite of pudding, "Girl," she admonishes as she looks up in shock at the lassie's unacceptable language.

Miss Jennifer Hathaway gasps in surprise at the harsh words voiced by Teri that is more in keeping with that used in a cowboy's bunkhouse.

Meanwhile Eric, Nick and Fred stare open mouthed at the Doctor, holding their bite of pudding halfway to their gullet, awed by the duplicity of the Senator and the ease with which he can fabricate lies.

But the strongest reaction was that of the Walking Y's owner. "Michelle and Teri," interrupts Woody forcefully, "you all know that Roger and Dave left the county after they said that they thought they acted on the Senator's behalf and signed to that effect. While I don't think they will be seen again around here, we will keep our eyes open."

Here Woody turns to the Doctor and his wife along with Jennifer, "That pair was pretty dastardly to the orphans here, and while I am thankful that the Senator is covering the damages his hired guns did to our ranch and people, I still do not trust the son of a bitch."

Mrs. Maxwell gasps again. My, the stories she will have to tell her church friends that will leave them all speechless. In two minutes, she has heard words that she did not want to hear more than once; however, part of her can still picture how hurt each orphan was when she stayed at ranch headquarters doctoring all of them. She still has not finished telling her church group all the details, but has been parsing them out for better effect.

Jennifer not noting the quiet reflective look crossing the Doctor's wife's face pipes in, "Woodrow, I am also thankful that the Senator is a good enough man to recognize that he made a hiring mistake and perhaps you should give him some benefit of the doubt as he is covering the damages. Many men would duck that responsibility."

Now it is Teri's turn to choke on her bite of plum duff, and Tony immediately cuts in giving all the orphans his strictest and most forceful warning gaze, and comments blandly, "I don't know if he will run for Governor, but he told me that he would retire from politics."

The Doctor looks at Tony quizzically, "He has not mentioned anything like that, nor has anyone mentioned that to me. In town, the Senator says whenever he has a chance, and I quote:

'I will not have any hired guns on the Ringing Bell or on my payroll again, and doing so was a grave mistake, but I only did it, as The Walking Y was putting rebranded cows among my Ringing Bell cattle. Mr. Woodrow W. Flynt was seeking to frame me as a cattle rustler, which is not something I would do as an honest public servant. Anyway, the Ringing Bell Ranch can afford to purchase any cows that need to be acquired. But hiring Roger as part of the Ringing Bell crew was one of the worst decisions I ever made, and I have learned a hard lesson.'

Woody looks at the Doctor and ponders for a moment, "I see Doctor. Well, I seem to remember that you were here for Nick's broken arm and concussion before the brand inspector stopped the first cattle shipment. You were also here to see the burned haystack, and shortly after the Sherriff and the brand inspector stopped that railroad consignment due to the fact that there were Walking Y cattle that were not properly sorted." Here he pauses for a moment before continuing, "You also brought Fred back from the edge of death and doctored the girls upon their return from the kidnapping and heard of their treatment in captivity."

The Doctor replies seriously, "Woody, I am telling you what I overheard, or what is being said in town. This is what the Senator stated when talking with the town council at the Prancing Mare Hotel the last time I was eating in the restaurant there. He loudly told all who would listen that maybe it was Roger who rebranded those cows, and that is why he paid you for the loss or any other claim you may have had. He is turning the events in such a fashion that he looks virtuous. And Woody, often your antics and that of your crew makes this easy."

On this bit of news, Eric, who is slurping his hot chocolate, chokes and gasp for air. With tears in his eyes, he tells Mrs. Maxwell, "I think it went down the wrong pipe. I'm sorry."

Miss Hathaway looks around the table, "Could it not be possible that the Senator, who still strikes me as a gentleman, made a mistake and is now trying to rectify it?"

Woody looks around, and with a glance at Jennifer replies, "As you are not from here, and were not around last fall, I can see how you would ask such a question. However, the Senator and his crew are evil. The Doctor and his wife witnessed just how truly evil and depraved the entire campaign was against my ranch and crew."

Thereupon, the conversation drifted to safer subjects and Miss Jennifer Hathaway's new role at the ranch. The Doctor's wife looks at Jennifer, and states with great conviction, "I am so glad you are here, and" turning to the Walking Y's owner, "you, Woody thought it sufficiently important to have a governess. This ranch is a bit of a rough place to raise two young ladies like Teri and Michelle," then glancing at Tony she adds, "and the boys are picking up some bad habits."

After dinner, the doctor retires to one of the bedrooms upstairs and checks on Miss Hathaway's injuries which he declares should heal with no scarring on her beautiful forehead; however, she will have a small scar on her arm which he rebandages with care. Fred gets a clean bill of health despite a couple ugly new bruises. He is admonished to rest his leg for a couple days which includes the order of 'no riding'.

Chapter 11

<u>The Card</u>

A few days later, after dinner, five angry youths and Tony meet in the common room of the foreman's house. The door is secured and closed, and Tony walks around before he steps back in to talk with the five youngsters. "We need to keep our voices low, and be quiet, as I fear some of the ears around here. You heard the Doctor and Mrs. Maxwell some days ago, and you all understand how the Senator is trying to turn our victory to his advantage. He is not to be trusted, and we MUST not let the world know that the demon Roger is dead as is his sidekick and how both are buried on this ranch."

Before he can get much further, the wiry brown-haired Eric spits out, "Why that low down lying snake, if the truth was light, he would be in the darkest hole hiding from it."

"Come on," voices his stout red headed friend, Nick, "that's unfair to snakes. Why the Devil himself must be proud of his student."

Michelle cuts in with a shudder, "Oh, come on, that is also unfair, and understates the Senator's skills. Why that so called Senator could give the Devil a lesson or two."

Teri just sits there barking, "I just hate him. I hate him. I really hate that son of a bitch," for lack of a better term of damnation.

Fred stammers, and unusually for him, chokes with raw emotion, "That bastard is a thorough paced scoundrel."

Tony cuts in and purposely lowers his voice to a near whisper looking around carefully, "We all know he is a scoundrel, a ruffian, and many other terms. But the key is that we are warned, and more than ever, we must watch our tongues. No one is to know that Roger and Dave are dead and will be pushing daisies this spring. Watch what you say. The

Senator is smart, devious, and devoid of any morals. Worse yet, we wounded him, and he is a very, very dangerous animal. This time, it will not be a blundering fool like Roger coming in the open, this time, we will fight shadows while that bastard works on setting us at each other's throats."

Eric mutters what Tony is thinking since his meeting with Woody that first night in the office, "Jennifer!"

The lad then gasps in dismay, "My, Tony, I forgot."

He runs to his room and fishes in the bottom of a drawer and returns sheepishly to Tony. "In the excitement of the last few days, I forgot to show you these." He lays out the six double eagles and then digs around for what he remembers as a torn document. "I found a torn envelope with the gold, but I can't find it now. I seem to have mislaid it."

Tony takes the gold, and pockets it. "I'll set these aside for the ranch, ideally, we'll hold it to try to get a replacement for Genesis. It's not enough, but every bit helps. I know Woody's broken hearted about the bull."

Eric nods his head. With a smile he then begins, "He spent three days looking at that bull. It was kind of funny, and I thought he was going to get a level as he even looked really carefully at, eh" - here Eric pauses while all look at him. His face turns red as he avoids eye contact with both Teri and Michelle, before ending lamely, "you know, what makes him a bull."

Teri laughs at the lad's embarrassment, while both she and Michelle have no intention of letting him off the hook. Teri looks quizzically with a smirk, "Just what do you mean, Eric?"

The lad's cheeks turn red, and suddenly the room feels hot.

So much so, Tony runs to his rescue, "For a bull you check the reproductive track, and if it looks wrong or is too small, you do not purchase him. If they're deficient in that area, it might mean that you have no calf crop, and for most ranches and definitively this one, it means that you go under. Questions?"

***

Later yet, after the girls are back upstairs in the cookhouse and hopefully sleeping and while Jennifer Hathaway is ensconced in her room putting a horrifying first few days behind her, Woody burns the late oil working in his office. While the ranch is alive, the recent events have left the grouchy owner fretful of the future. He sits looking at the ledger, and there is enough money in the bank to pay Jennifer for a few months, and the normal minimal ranch expenses, but he cannot afford to replace the bull. He will have to make do with what he has. Meanwhile, Tony will have to survive on half pay or less – again, until next fall when the ranch can sell some weanlings steers. Regrettably, Hardy will be in the same boat, and the kids will simply get IOUs instead of the pittance he had negotiated when he hired Hardy and Jennifer.

Good thing he has been honest with all his own crew, and maybe he will incorporate to give them all a fraction of the ranch. But the Senator is up to no good. Thinking back to his trip with Eric to the National Stock Growers Convention, Woody muses, and his mind flashes back to the brigand who left them barefooted. He gets up, and rifles through his overnight bag which sits in a corner where it had been tossed days earlier due to the chaos. He pulls the still damp clothing and the now ripe torn and bloody socks out of the bag and digs for the pants he had worn that night. In them, he pulls what might be the key to this set of very well-planned attacks on the Walking Y. The card he pocketed, when attacked by that louse in Denver, who left them afoot without boots. The now damp business card he threw into his trouser pocket might be the key to survival. He stares at it carefully:

J. K. & Associates
Detectives, Investigators, and Fixers
Larimer Street, Denver

Woody muses, and idly turns the card over in his hand, thinking. Startled he looks again. That is most unusual, there is printing on the back of the card that mimics the front.

J. K. & Associates
Detectives, Investigators, and Fixers
Anaconda Company Office, Butte, Montana

Surprise lines his face. It was too much of a coincidence. An office in Butte, Montana. Did that mean that the attack he and Eric foiled in Denver was related to the campaign against The Walking Y. If so, then the bastards had time to set up and plan how to kill the bull. Genesis' death was perhaps a warning, or perhaps a diversion, or perhaps even the start of a vicious campaign. He'd have to talk to Hardy when it was quiet. He'd also have to talk with Teri, Michelle, and Eric to see if they had any more information as to the bull's shooter.

The buffalo hunting days are in the past, so that bastard could be an old timer. It was what, a six hundred yard shot from the livery stable roof to where the bull was downed. But the way the shooter escaped meant that it most probably is a younger man who learned from the best, and who knows explosives. And the son of a gun is for hire. And, dammit, he is a good shot. Better than Eric, or even Hardy or himself. And he is still on the prowl, an unknown threat. That is darn dangerous.

Too many coincidences. Denver. The bull. The explosion. The Senator's visit. In addition, there are new people; James Hardyman, and Miss Jennifer Hathaway. Somehow all are linked. The answer lies in those links. Woody paces and does not react to the occasional creak coming from the ceiling.

Jennifer pulls the upper part of the heating grate and makes fast changes. The quick removal of the baffles allows her to look in the office, still out of sight protected by the stamped metal ceiling mesh. But now she can get her head down to that cover, and she can see and hear undetected. For better security she can hide her handywork under her empty trunk when she is not using her spy hole as she is now. She must find the documents. She must inform John as to what Woody and Tony are thinking, planning and how they are holding up to the pressure. One advantage was meeting Mrs. Couchman on that first day. She is the hired link back to her uncle. As to the children and the colored cook, they are of no importance.

The key is Woody, and any and all means to bring him down are fair. She will enchant and ensnare him, spy on him, and seduce as needed, and turn him into clay to mold as she sees fit. After all, he should be easier than a Secretary of the Treasury. He is lonely, and for twenty years he has not confided in a woman. She watches Woody work, and she freezes. Her heart stops and a cold clammy sensation fills her gut. The familiar looking card. How did Woody get that card?

As Woody dims the light, Jennifer pulls away and carefully puts the trunk over the grate. She checks herself in the vanity and passes a brush through her hair. In a revealing red nightgown, she slinks down the stairs, arriving at the landing at the same time as the owner is walking to the kitchen from closing the office door.

"Oh, Woody, I am surprised to see that you are still up. I'm having trouble resting after all the events since arriving here, and I was coming down for a cup of warm milk that I hope will help me sleep. Woody, I am scared of nightmares. Visions of someone breaking into this large house send shivers down my spine. I'm alone in this house with just that colored cook and two infantile girls. I was not brought up in such a rough environment."

Woody pauses, his eyes linger on her gown, and he ignores his first answer that the two "infantile girls" have already proven themselves resourceful tigresses whom he would not want to confront even if paid all the tea in China. Jennifer's fears seem real, her presence close, and her genteel upbringing and college degree from one of the 'Seven Sisters' would not provide training for such a rough world.

Grasping for air forces his mind to work, "Miss Hathaway, I have never known rough men in this part of the world to attack women. Well, except for Roger and his ilk, and they preferred to go after young girls. Generally, if you threaten women in the west, you'll find yourself pushing daisies. So, you should be quite safe. That colored cook is competent, or so he seems to me, and my suspicion is that I would prefer to wrestle with a hungry bear than have him on my bad side. So, all in all, you are safer here than in one of those fancy eastern cities like New York or Washington. Come to think of it, Tony is from New York, and he's one tough fighter and he learned most of those skills there, in that so called genteel city."

Jennifer sheds a tear, and clutches the ranch owner's arm, "It's not my world. I never dreamed people could be so perfidious. Woody, I'm scared, and this house is where I hear the girls were kidnapped. Roger ripped Michelle's dress off in a room upstairs. They got in. Twice. I don't want to stay here. Specially alone."

"Tell you what I'll do," replies the owner handing her a clean bandana for her tears, "I'll sleep in my office as there is space for a cot as

Hardy has my old room. That way, not only will Hardy be here, but so will I."

Miss Hathaway hoists a wan smile to her lips, and nods her head, "That will help. Thank you. I'll try to do better, but I have never been anything else but a student or a teacher. I have not been around rough people, and sometimes the way Tony struts leaves me uncomfortable. That might help me sleep tonight, but what about tomorrow night or the subsequent night?"

"I'll make the office my home for a while, so you have nothing to worry about."

They talk and talk. Miss Hathaway and Woody share a few drams of whiskey and she clutches his arm. Soon she sits a little closer. Woodrow W. Flynt does not move away, and smiles as the lines on his face are muted for the first time in years.

Finally, Miss Hathaway goes back to her room.

Woody dons his coat and gathers a few things from his father's old cabin, comes back and makes himself comfortable in his office. Propping his rifle in the corner by his desk, he pulls off his boots and hides his old revolver under his pillow. Clad in old, faded long underwear, the owner lowers himself on the makeshift bed and in cat-like movements pulls himself under the heavy blankets thinking this is not all bad, as that cabin is cold and lonely.

Chapter 12

<u>Routine</u>

While there is a bit of a glow to the southeast, the pale sun has yet to peek through the low hanging clouds at a frigid landscape as the crew gathers for breakfast. Woody stares at his empty cup as he muses with his nose in his notebook looking at the hay inventory and the calendar, oblivious to those around him. Jennifer sits with a hot cup of coffee beside Teri and Michelle. Tony grumbles as he removes his coat and brushes the frost off his whiskers upon coming through the door. Behind him, rambunctious come the three boys.

Eric brays as he enters the kitchen, "Damn it Hardy, its colder than a witch's tit out there."

Miss Hathaway's jaw drops, "Young man, that is not appropriate."

"Well," he counters with a wicked smile, "It is colder than a witches' tit. Obviously, you haven't stuck your nose out there yet!"

"Eric, you'll stay in this morning instead of going out as punishment. You will write two hundred times: I shall mind my manners and my language."

Eric looks up stunned. Jennifer is serious. But Nick comes to his rescue and makes him smile, "Ma'am, Eric's wrong. It's colder than a witch's ass! Now do I get to stay in and do lines?"

Teri looks up defiantly, "Nick, you don't know these things. It is colder than a witch's tit. Not her ass. Good, now I get to stay warm and write lines?" Here she looks at the Irishman and chuckles, "Tony shut up as you get to work alone, as the debate is not finished!"

Woody cuts in. "All right you little tyrants. No one is getting out of work for having a smart mouth, because nothing would ever get done around here. You all are on feed runs this morning, and you WILL have classes with Miss Hathaway this afternoon and you WILL show her respect. Are there any questions?"

Tony smiles, "Woody, as I am not a little tyrant, do I have the morning off? After all I have a sore hangnail when it's cold?"

The orphans laugh as Woody darts a severe look at the Irishman. Hardy starts to lay platters on the table, and Miss Hathaway cuts herself back into the conversation. "I'll say grace, and I want you all to learn one that is appropriate in the proper circles of society."

Breakfast is devoured, and Woody and the crew all bundle up as the sun now struggles to break through low clouds to light up the frigid landscape. Wisps of snow curl off the roof, as the cold sky announces that the animals will be very hungry on this subzero morning. As the last boots are jammed onto wool stockinged feet, Tony announces the tasks. "We'll run two teams this morning with Nick driving his mares with Michelle and Eric, and I'll take the other with Fred and Teri. Woody is taking Jake for a short ride to patrol, check water holes and break ice. Everything must be done before lunch which will be late. This afternoon, Jennifer gets to tell all of you how you will state the temperature in a civilized fashion and how to calculate exactly how cold it is."

Grumbles meet this pronouncement.

Before they head out as the sun begins its climb, Mrs. Couchman shows up in a sulky. Woody glares at this intrusion, and points to the door. "All right, we're running late. Get to work all of you." He then turns to Mrs. Couchman, and asks, "What can I do for you?"

"Ah, Woody, I am here to see Miss Hathaway. On this rough place where you are all a bit crude, she needs a lady friend."

With those words, she walks in, and goes into the main living room. Where she expects Jennifer to join her, and Hardy to bring her a proper cup of tea. The workdays follow this pattern, including the unwelcomed visits by Mrs. Couchman who has taken an unusual interest in Miss Hathaway, and the two see each other often in town at the store or when the shopkeeper drives her sulky out to the ranch.

The afternoons are a different kind of challenge for the governess.

"Eric, if you want to be a rancher, you must calculate how much hay you will need for the winter. So, if you have 120 cows, and they eat 30 pounds of hay each a day, and winter feeding goes on for four and a half months, how many loads of hay must be in the hay mound if each load weighs two tons."

"Miss Hathaway, it seems like a total stupid waste if you need one hundred and twenty-one and a half loads assuming your months have thirty days. You should either sneak on a bit more hay on each load or remember to feed your draft horses and include them in your calculation, because only a real greenhorn or city slicker would go for half a load or forget to feed the horses."

'Fred, when did the Roman Empire finally fall?"

"Miss Hathaway, the book you're using says 476 A.D., but my research would support a case for using the date 529 A.D. when they had the last horse race at the forum. In my mind, that is the true end of the empire because that is when the culture of the empire officially ended."

"Teri, if the American Indians were forced off their land from the beginning of American History in 1776 and only recently has Geronimo been brought to heel, does this make this war the longest in history or was the hundred-year war a bit longer?"

"No Miss Hathaway. I'd say the longest war ever is still going on. It is between those who are sedentary like us farmers and ranchers, and those who are nomadic. That war, as you should know started on the bank of the Tigris and Euphrates Rivers in about 4000 BC. So that makes it a war that has been going on for close to 6,000 years or a bit longer than you have been alive."

It is a tired Miss Hathaway come dinner, but the children learn and some of their trials fade in the past. Yet, her day drags on.

"Eric, don't use your left hand to shovel food in your mouth with a fork, use your right hand and take smaller bites and keep your napkin on your lap."

"But, Miss Hathaway, Hardy made this steak so rare that I'm afraid it'll run off my plate and kick me, and I keep my napkin handy to blindfold it so if I have to shoot, it won't take my gun from me."

"Eric," Tony cuts in, "That's why you should cut it in two. They don't move as much then, and Hardy tells me that he never had one that was cut in two attack him with a skillet."

Nick counters, "But Mr. O'Connor, I heard Hardy talk about how he had one attack him with a skillet when he was a cook on a cattle drive. The darn thing took the skillet and even attacked the trail boss! Thus, Eric, you're being smart, 'cause according to Hardy, the trail boss had to shoot it. Twice!"

"Boys!" cuts in Woody looking at a stone-faced Miss Hathaway, "no need to be smart asses."

Michelle smiles and looks at the owner, "Teri, you and I are off the hook then, and we can continue to be smart asses, despite Miss Hathaway who is always saying, 'You are young ladies, and you should act like young ladies.'"

After dinner, the young ones study at the kitchen table, coming and going from the living room and the surprisingly good library Woody and his father had assembled over the years. All five work quietly as Miss Hathaway reads in the living room seated on the couch by the office drinking a cup of tea.

Woody and Tony meanwhile are in the office, planning and looking at the ranch books. Both are looking at the ledgers and the herd record book with consternation. Tony digs into his pockets, and smiles.

"Woody, I have some good news for you that I have been forgetting to tell you. Eric found these where he took a shot at The Buffalo Gun." Thereupon he drops three double eagles on the owners cluttered desk. Woody stares at the coins as if they were gold from heaven. As they are gold from heaven so to speak, Tony continues, "Now, do we have enough money to buy some oats? The bin is just about empty."

The owner counters, "Let me look at the ledger, because I would like to save most of this for a new bull in the future. Now where is the damn ledger. You'd think that after twenty years I'd have this office organized so I could find the bank ledger, but no. It's still a dusty mess in here. So, I'll say we and the horses, and the cows will have to do with this." He pushes one coin back to Tony. "Get what you can, and we also need salt for the animals. Anything else, we will have to live without."

Tony smiles and pockets the double eagle. It should be enough. Woody looks around at the clutter throughout the office and shrugs. "Look Tony, we'll have to move the replacement heifers we bought closer to the creek, as the water holes are freezing in that pasture to the west of the barn."

"Woody, we can get that done, if you will allow me to put Michelle, Teri and Eric on it right after lunch. That will also give me Nick and Fred to get more firewood, as we are burning a lot. We'll have to take a sled up to the 12,000-acre pasture woods."

The grizzled owner frowns, "but Jennifer wants more time with them, especially the girls. She wants to start comportment without Eric being in the class to disrupt it."

"Well, then pick. It's your ranch. You get two of three, either move cows, or get wood, or have the girls learn to curtsy. Your choice."

"Well, it is my ranch. All three need to be done. Could you just have Eric and Fred move them while you and Nick get the wood?"

"Woody, it's bloody cold out there. Those heifers are hiding in the trees and will make a run for the bulls. Not only that, when it's twenty below, Nick and I will not get many trees felled before our hands are numb. We had to break ice off the horses' snouts so they could breathe this morning. I don't want to do that."

"It's my ranch and my pay, so do it my way."

"Woody, you old grouch, you told me I'm the foreman, or manager and your pay is just a bunch of IOUs. I need three on each task. It's colder than an Englishman's heart out there. Also, I don't need to remind you that your pay is so generous that I can't afford to refill my flask or go to the Silver King of late. So, throw me a bone, and let me have three people on each task."

When the old clock in the living room chimes nine, all call it a day. Tony, Eric, Fred, and Nick troop over to the foreman's house, while the girls head up to their rooms. Woody works on a bit and later in the evening finds himself nestled on the couch with Jennifer where they talk in each other's warm company. Woody relaxes and enjoys the younger woman's company. It has been a long and lonely twenty years since his wife-to-be died.

Chapter 13

<u>JK's card</u>

Tony and the boys remain awake and are stirring in the Foreman's house later than normal, as it is Saturday. That means that the following morning's feed run will be an hour later. So, Tony and the boys stay up, playing poker for points, as after all, as Eric states, "we're all too poor to pay attention."

"Tonight, I've got to teach you how to play with the Senator."

"What Tony, I wouldn't play with him, as he's crooked as a dog's hind leg."

"Eric, you've got to know how to play with card-cheats who are on a first name basis with the bottom of the deck."

So, they play, and Tony teaches. While the bedrooms face the cookhouse, the main living and dining room with the wood stove face the barn and cannot be seen from the cookhouse. Which is just fine with the four of them. After a while, Tony holds the cards.

"Get some hot chocolate boys, because I want to ask Eric here a few questions. We need to talk and think." He turns to the wild lad, and resumes, "We never did grill you on your trip to Denver, and exactly what happened after the bull was shot, because the Senator, may his soul rest in hell, was at the house. We should have done this a couple weeks ago, but we needed the right time. The right time is now.

Tony, Eric, Fred and Nick drink hot chocolate with Tony's being fortified with a little medicinal whiskey.

"All right my boy, tell me again everything you saw and did. But this time start from when you left the ranch and went to Denver with Woody."

"Tony, apart from looking at bulls, hiring Miss Hathaway there wasn't much to the trip. The Windsor Hotel is fancy and full of prissy dudes. Let's see, how would Mrs. Maxwell phrase it? She would state with a smile that it's 'Grand'. Yup, that's the word she would use. That's where we hired Jennifer. We were late, because we were attacked by the coach driver."

"Ah, Eric, you leave out little details that could be important. Now tell me, how did you get attacked and why were you late. Who else interviewed for the position?"

"Tony, I told you, we looked at the bulls, and telling you how Woody looked at his privates still makes me blush. He just about took a ruler and a level to his balls. Anyway, he bought him, and then we headed to the hotel. We left the National Stock Growers Convention, and this bloke in a plaid coat signaled for a coach, and one came from beside the line and picked us up. It was dark, and the driver had a low hat and high turned up collar because it was cold. He took us in the correct direction but on secondary roads. He wanted our boots and our money. We got him, but the horse panicked and bolted with the coach. We frisked the son of a gun, and – wait – I forgot to tell you, Woody got a business card from the bastard. Anyway, we had to walk a couple miles in sleet with no boots. So, we were late to interview the candidates. There was only one left, Jennifer. She was reading one of Woody's history books. You know the one he always is going on about."

"You mean *The Decline and Fall of the Roman Empire*?"

"Yeah, that's it. Anyway, she got the job."

"What about when we met you at the train boy? What did you see after Sorley, and I were blasted off our feet?"

Fred pipes in, "You mean after Eric took my Blacky?"

"Sorry, that was rude, he was your horse. Well, I wanted to catch the girls, and even more so, catch the shooter. That bull didn't deserve to be shot. Anyway, I told you, I, eh Tony I forgot. This could be important." Here, Eric stops and jumps up in excitement and runs to his room. Coming back in with his lighter raincoat, he resumes excited. "I told you that I tried a long-range half a mile shot to get him. I missed, but I must have come close. I checked the ground, and saw no blood, and he did not seem hurt as he rode on. But I forgot. While I gave you the six double eagles, I finally found that envelope, strangely enough today as I was looking for something else in my room."

With impatient gestures, he rifles through the inside pockets and tosses anything he finds on the floor as the other three watch. In surprise, Eric shouts, "I got it. This is it, and I didn't have time to look. He pulls out the mangled envelope. It is only the upper left-hand corner that has anything left to read, and the return address is partially legible.

> J. K. & Assoc
> Larimer S
> Den

Eric opens the envelope and pulls out a single sheet of paper. "Look at this Tony!" All stare at the sheet that Eric lays out on top of the scattered cards.

> *January 26, 1905*
> *Dear GUN,*
> *Shoot only the polled red angus bull in Hellenville, not our agent whom you know well. They come in on the afternoon train Jan 28. Partial pay enclosed.*
> *Other orders follow. Make sure you plan your escape.*
> *JK*

All look. "That's something," says the Irishman. "We can fill in a bit. With regards to the address, that word is probably associates, and Den is probably Denver, so that would be Larimer Street. I'll check with Woody tomorrow to see if he has someone who can look them up in Denver."

Fred pipes up, "Tony, whose 'our agent'?"

All look at the lad, he has just pointed out the fact that there is a Judas in the area, perhaps even on the ranch.

Tony speaks up, "Well, if the agent is on the ranch, there are only two possible candidates, Hardy and Jennifer. But as Jennifer was hired in Denver, and as you were delayed and only Jennifer was there to apply when you were late, I would say she is our primary suspect."

"Tony," counters Fred, "we need to expose her."

"Yes, my lad, but that won't be easy. Woody knows my suspicions and has his own and he even told me about a small incident that first night, but he is lonely, believes in redemption and is close to her."

"I have it," Fred replies quietly thinking hard. "Woody loves Gibbons. If she's a fraud, she has not studied or enjoyed *The Decline and Fall of the Roman Empire*. Why don't we trip her up?"

Tony nods. "I hate to say it, as Gibbons is an Englishman, and was an indolent member of that parliament. So, I never admit it, but he did write a good history, even if there are parts of his work that strike me as wrong footed."

"Like what Tony?"

"He states as fact that The Catholic Church helped bring an end to the Roman Empire. I do not think it would have lasted any longer even if the Catholic Church had not been around to replace the pagan idolatry that existed. What killed it was the loss of virtues such as the Roman farmer who was also a fierce soldier. Indolence replaced self-reliance."

"I see Tony, so you studied Chapters fifteen and sixteen carefully."

"Yes Fred, I have."

The other kids stay quiet as Fred and Tony converse about details in Gibbons. They discuss how to entrap Jennifer the next morning at breakfast to see if they can put Woody a little more on his guard.

After the Gibbons discussion, Tony adds, "I'll bring this envelope with me to present to Woody when he seems like he will be receptive. Perhaps at breakfast, before we all go out for the morning's work."

Eric pipes in, "don't forget to ask to see the card we found in the highway man's pocket when he tried to rob us in Denver. Thinking about that, I still don't know why he wanted our boots. That's a bit bizarre.

Tony muses for a moment. "If you want to know what I think, your attacker set out to make you late. He took your boots to delay and hurt, but not to kill you. That Jennifer is a fraud or a plant or both."

"Ah," voices Nick, "you don't like her because she's English."

"But he likes Woody," replies Fred.

"Yes, but that's the exception that proves the rule," counters Nick. "Have you ever heard Tony say anything good about the English?"

"Now boys," voices Tony with a smile, "there is nothing good about the English. Look at Woody. Half the time I want to slug the hardheaded mule. He's good, but only for an Englishman!" With these words, Tony reaches in his breast pocket and tries to take a small nip. He puts it back with a frown, as it is empty. "Ok, Eric, let's go over this again, what did you see?"

Chapter 14

Gibbons' Decline

"Good morning, Hardy," voices Tony amicably as he walks into the cookhouse. "Looks like another nice Montana winter day, just a bit grey, not too cold – our thermometer reads about twenty below, with not too much wind maybe thirty to forty miles per hour. We just have a little blowing snow, and a bunch of hungry livestock. So do you want to join the boys and me, because it must break your heart to have to stay in the warm cookhouse every day?"

Hardy looks around, smiles at the Irishman. "Good morning, Mick, how's my favorite Paddy today? With regards to your offer if I remember how you burn food, and how much you all eat, I'll join you the second the crew votes to have you as cook. In the meantime, I think I'll suffer here in this kitchen."

"Yup, just keep on cooking away Hardy, and I see you have some chocolate cakes underway, so I'll take it easy with the cows and feed them."

Both laugh, and the crew sits at the table noisily, joining Teri and Michelle who are already in front of a cup of hot chocolate in a whispered conversation. The girls look up furtively and stop talking while blushing faintly. That said, the game is given away, as their lingering eyes focus on the empty chairs of the two that are still missing. Woody and Jennifer are very present in their absence, and all others note the empty seats.

"So, where's the boss?" barks Tony with his usual subtilty.

Hardy stays mum. After a short silence, Teri whispers while blushing a bit, "They're still upstairs."

Michelle adds in a whisper giggling, "In her room."

Thereupon the boys all chuckle, and also blush a bit. Tony arches his eyebrows. He looks around and makes eye contact with each orphan and then in a low voice begins a serious lesson.

"Children, listen carefully, because it's important that you understand that Woody is a good man. He's still a bachelor, not because he wanted to be, but one night when we were talking, he sent me in the office to get his Special Reserve. I stumbled on something that explains a lot. He was clearing out some papers trying to neaten up, and I stumbled on a wedding announcement. Woody's! Turns out that the day before the wedding, his wife-to-be was killed in a runaway coach. That was a couple years before the lawsuit. He's been very lonely for a very long time. I'd even say it has made him a bit bitter. Now, the problem here is that Jennifer is English. I don't trust the English and, especially, I don't trust her at all. That said, be kind to Woody. He's been lonely for years, and I'm hoping I'm not right about Jennifer, because if I am, she'll break his heart. Again."

Hardy stops laying out the food on the table, and looks at all of them, letting his eyes linger on Tony, before he voices his thoughts. "Woody is a private person, and that tragedy is a closely guarded secret. He did not like how people in town talked, and how loose tongues took pity on him. I know you have not noticed because of how cuddly he is, but the owner of the Walking Y is not one who likes pity. It drives him nuts. So, please keep this to yourselves. The only reason I know, is the last time I saw Woody, I was to be his best, eh, well, I just know from when our paths crossed in the past."

"In short," Tony adds with the young faces turning to him intently, "do not give him a hard time for spending nights with Jennifer. We all can be an eejit at times." Here he looks at Eric who is smirking, "Even you Eric have been known to be an eejit, or to put it in terms you understand well, and idiot."

Eric reaches over and cuffs the Irishman. "But," Tony adds without rising to Eric's bait, and with a serious tone he continues, "as she is English, from a long line of English, do not take her too much in your trust." Looking up at Hardy, he adds, "Even you Hardy."

Fred cuts in, "So, you're saying do not put Woody between a rock and a hard place."

Tony nods his head, yes.

There is a moment of silence while the cook is placing a large platter of beans – strategically in front of Eric. Quietly he hovers near the table where he can hear everything while tending to the platters holding scrambled eggs, sausages, toast, and lastly a large serving dish which holds enough pancakes to feed a small army along with corn syrup. Eric starts to spoon beans on his plate with a smile when he is brought up short by the Irishman.

"Good, so as the foreman, let's lay out the day's activities while we eat. But first Grace. Eric, as you are starving, you can lead us in Grace."

"What? Are you out of your mind?" retorts the lad snorting.

"Nope, you should be able to do that at all times. You'd be amazed at how often I have been called on, as you noted the first night Jennifer was here."

Eric looks around with a mischievous grin, "I know, I heard this one from my father." Here he adopts a mock serious face and bows his head, "God bless the meat, God bless the fat, God damn the bones, you can't eat that."

Nick and Fred chortle as they dig in, while Tony looks disapprovingly at the lad for a moment before smiling. "Well, boy, that might not get you a job with the English or in the Church, but you could get one with a bunch of hungry cowboys! Shame they aren't the ones doing the hiring on any ranch."

Eric defers the attention from the mild reprimand by slurring his words with a full mouthful and looking up at the cook, "Again, you did it Hardy, these are sure good beans."

Nick nods his head, "For a change this time he's right. Sorry Tony, but yours were generally burned."

Looking around the table in a conspiratorial fashion, Tony resumes clearly as he hears Woody coming down the steps, "I have nothing solid, so I will have to think this through. All of you, do not raise the issue of 'J. K.' at this time as we planned at breakfast – especially if she is around. We have to be smart about this. But Fred, we'll proceed with Gibbons."

Woody, who walks in sheepishly and grabs a cup of coffee and sits at his usual place, leans over and snags some hotcakes and a few links without saying a word. As he takes his first mouthful, Jennifer comes downstairs dressed for a day on a ranch and for a change has mimicked the girls and wears a clean pair of blue jeans. She feigns embarrassment at the attire, and Teri cannot resist, "Miss Hathaway, I see you are wearing something practical for a ranch. Bravo."

Fred looked up in feigned surprise at Teri. "Ah, come on. Miss Hathaway is quite practical. Not only that, anyone who reads Gibbons' *The*

Decline and Fall of the Roman Empire has a practical mind, as by studying the fall of that Empire, you can discern what mistakes you do not want to make as a society to avoid going back into the Dark Ages."

Eric snorts, "That's a useless set of books. It does not tell you how to avoid being gored by a mad bull, or how to note that a cow who's furious at you for branding her calf, and wants to stomp you, or even nowadays how to avoid having your prize bull killed beside you by the despicable son of a bitch who should be in hell for trying to kill you with a buffalo gun."

Jennifer looks startled at the change in topic, and Woody remembering how distraught Jennifer was in town at the display of raw violence, changes the discussion back to safe territory. "Miss Hathaway is a Gibbons scholar Fred. She was reading volume two when I first saw her, and that is the reason I decided to hire her on the spot."

Jennifer, blushing lightly cuts in, "Regrettably, I would not call myself a scholar of the great man's work. I have just read bits and pieces, as he does write well, and it gives me some cues as to the cycle of history."

Tony sits back and drains his coffee and nods his head to Hardy who is making a round with a fresh pot. Once the cup is full, he turns back, "Even though he's English, and served in Parliament, and never considered us Catholic Irish to be worthy of his time, I will confess to having perused his works."

Woody looks up startled, "What, you studied Gibbons?"

Tony laughs. "Woody, reading and education means that you must study people you don't like. Remember, I was a teacher in New York. Mind you, I now prefer to be outside and on horseback. So now I limit myself to teaching all I learn about life to these young ones."

Nick cuts in, "Yeah, like poker. I like that game, and I already have some IOUs from Eric."

Eric, quick as a whip rebuts, "well, I'll give you some IOUs I have from Woody here to pay off my debt. And no, Nick, you may not have Moose because he would ditch you and he's my best friend. I love that horse."

The owner shakes his head. Jennifer looks horrified. The kids are laughing. Michelle cuts in, "I think Fred and I have the biggest set of IOUs from both you and Eric. You can pay them off by doing chores…"

"Like bringing in the wood for the stoves," cuts in Teri.

All laugh. Tony goes around again. "Ok you young rascals, this is important. Like, Jennifer, let's teach a bit. What do you say about Gibbons stating that the Roman Empire lasted an extra couple hundred years due to the Catholic church's influence in restoring morality and the finer attributes of Roman civilization?"

Jennifer looks startled. Lamely she replies, "I actually agree, although I am not a fan of that church."

Woody shakes his head. So do Fred, Eric, and the two girls.

Fred cuts in on cue. "Tony and Miss Hathaway, you're both wrong. In Chapters fifteen and sixteen, Gibbons states clearly that the Catholic Church was a corrosive influence on the old Roman Empire, as it was the final force that destroyed the old virtues and supporting religious beliefs. I personally think that Gibbons was influenced by the Church of England, and the anti-Catholic influence pervasive in late eighteenth century in England. Remember, the Papist were persecuted in England since before Cromwell. And that leader was not a good friend of the Catholic Irish. Right Tony?"

Tony looks at Jennifer and Woody. "Woody, isn't Fred, right?"

Woody looks at Jennifer, and around the table which is suddenly quite serious. He puts his hand on Miss Hathaway's hand and pauses for a moment. "Well Fred is correct, and lad, I would hate to debate you on the subject of Gibbon's work. I have read him several times and Tony; I suspect you knew you were full of blarney when you said that about the Catholic Church enhancing the life of the Empire."

Here the owner's tone hardens, "You, Tony, are not a better poker player than I was once, or Hardy is to this day. You set out to see if Jennifer here knew her Gibbons. Nicely done. I'm not impressed. She already stated that she's learning, and Miss Hathaway here has my full trust and confidence. I have nothing but respect for the lady and how she has put up with all of you thus far. She has a miserable job trying to civilize all of you, actually all of us, and I would like it if you all gave her full cooperation."

Silence follows this monologue.

Woody cuts in again, "Are there any questions about what I just said?"

A chorus of muttered replies stating, "No Woody," makes a round from all at the table.

Jennifer Hathway looks at the owner, carefully. "It's all right Woody. I need to study him a bit more closely if I'm going to claim knowing his work. And it's a good thing that all of these kids seem to know a bit of Gibbons. It means that we are making progress on educating these orphans."

Woody replies with passion, "Well said. But all of you need to respect Miss Hathaway. She is here to improve your minds and your behavior. She is new to us, to the West. She knows very little of what happened to The Walking Y. She would never condone it." Here the owner turns to Miss Hathaway, "You have already stated and shown that you do not like violence."

Tony, Fred, and Eric shake their heads as would a bull when clubbed by a strong thick branch. But the topic gravitates back to a discussion of chores, what hay remains where, and how the animals look.

Less than half an hour later, all are wrapping up their breakfast. Tony looks around handing out assignments, "All right, Nick you drive the team. Fred, you join him in feeding. Girls, you saddle up, and do a loop through the cattle. We need to make sure none of the new ones are sick, as we will soon merge all the cows that are due to calve. Lastly, because of how the bull was shot, we continue to ride with rifles, and in pairs. I'm going to check the bulls, and Eric you get stuck with me this morning."

Here in turn, he faces the unsmiling Woody and stern Jennifer, "We'll have your young ones in class this afternoon with Miss Hathaway."

Everyone stands, and heads for the door, as Hardy begins to clear the table. Jennifer goes to the stove to pour herself a fresh cup of tea, her cheeks sporting a pink cast and her hand a slight shake. Tony looks up, and turns to Eric, "Can you saddle my horse, so that I can talk with Woody for a moment?" The young ones troop out to the porch and start to put on warm boots and clothing.

The Irishman does not snag another cup of coffee, but sits beside Woody whose jaw is still clamped closed. Miss Hathaway sits on Woody's other side, and daintily takes a single piece of buttered toast, and reaches for the jar of jam while possessively putting a hand on Woody's lap. Tony lets the owner take a bit more coffee and clean his plate before he starts, "Woody, I need to talk to you and check on today's instructions. Can you meet me in the barn, we have to clear the air a bit?"

"BOOM!" echoes in the distance.

Woody barks, "DAMMIT!"
Tony cries out, "Not again!"
Eric howls, "That's The Buffalo Gun."
Jennifer whispers, "Oh no, not now."
Woody and Tony stand. Jennifer shrinks in her chair.
The orphans still on the porch jump as if a rat is crawling up their legs.

"That damn son of a bitch," shouts Eric as he jams on the last boot, grabs his rifle and opens the door with his coat still flapping, while snagging his gloves.

"BOOM!" reverberates again in the distance.

Chapter 15

A Friend's Death

Tony leaps up and grabs his loaded rifle from the rack and his coat off its hook. He is out of the door scrambling to the barn. The orphans run pell-mell. Woody slow witted, as his mind was elsewhere, is a little way back.

"That bastard is after the bulls, all of you get your horses with guns now!" barks Tony.

"BOOM!" That awful sound resonates again.

Frantic, all scramble into the barn, and Eric leaps on Moose, bareback with a rifle in his hand not even bothering to use a headstall. That pair, dashes out as a mad centaur, clears the front door already at a full charge. Others scramble to saddle, ensure that guns are loaded, and join the pursuit marked by the sound of Eric's mad race.

The lad does not open the gate to the back field but sails over it gracefully with full cooperation from his like spirited equine friend, Moose. Woody, who's well back, reaches the barn as Michelle and Teri, also bareback, but with headstalls on Crowhop and Princess, gallop out of the barn nearly bowling over the grizzled owner. Each girl is also clutching their own single shot twenty-two. Their horses follow Moose who is a good forty yards ahead moving fast.

The girls also sail over the impeding gate without opening it, and dash after Eric with snow flying behind them thrown by their horses' hooves.

Tony is the next one out. The first with a saddled horse, he jumps into the saddle and he lopes to the gate and opens it from horseback and leaves it that way. He rushes after the bareback riders. Nick is the next to leave, and he joins the chase at a gallop. Fred and Woody are still saddling their mounts and then are the last pair to take off in a mad scramble.

Eric, bent low around Moose's neck, flies through field and cottonwoods on the banks of the creek that meanders through these pastures. While doing so, he glances back to see Teri and just a few horse lengths behind her, Michelle riding like mad in his wake. He knows that the rest are probably also getting underway. He'd prefer to be in a saddle, but time is of the essence. Looking ahead, he tries to discern where that damn bastard and his damn buffalo gun are hiding. The son of a bitch has already proven he is an excellent shot at up to half a mile, so the trick is to make sure he cannot get a clean shot.

Eric veers into the cottonwoods.

"BOOM!"

"You God Damn Son of a Bitch!" shouts Eric in fury as he watches a spray of wood shards break open just a couple feet from his head.

Teri sees Eric's maneuver and hears his cry. She also swerves into the cottonwoods and continues a mad dash with Michelle just a short way back as they both assess the origination of the shots, while changing their riding to be more erratic.

"BOOM!"

Ducking through the trees, Eric hears the shot fly by his head, and sees a fleeting puff of smoke on the far side of the field. He kisses Moose's neck and angles through the barren cottonwoods towards the source. He turns and crosses an open stretch hoping to cover the ground while the bastard rechambers. Moose senses a small embankment and lunges up in a mighty arc powered by strong hindquarters.

BOOM!"

Moose staggers and rolls ass over his slumping head and forequarters. Eric vaults off as the buckskin spins in the air. The lad rolls in the snow still clutching his rifle screaming a silent lament.

Teri shouts back to Michelle, "Help Eric!"

She passes yards from the prone cowboy and his mangled horse and now leads the pursuit. She angles through rougher terrain and guides her short mare with her legs while attempting to point her single shot rifle at the black powder puff. She has to spoil his aim. Michelle and Eric are sitting ducks. She spies some movement in the next tree line, by the dissipating smoke, and fires by instinct.

"crack"

Amazingly the single shot twenty-two seems to have had an effect. The movement in that tree line changes. She sees a dark form on a large dark horse heading towards town on old cattle trails. Teri changes course to try and cut off the bastard with his heavy buffalo gun when,

"KWHAMM!"

A large tree explodes a hundred feet away. Teri's Crowhop swerves, slips, and the girl loses her balance and lands in the snow rolling several times with her head tucked into her chest before coming to a stop. Crowhop, freed from her rider, spooked by the dynamite, with the white of her eyes showing, wants to panic. She looks towards safety, preferably her barn, but feels her reins on the ground and heeds the girls long hours of training, and stays ground tied.

***

At the cookhouse Hardy dashes to the door and steps out on the stoop to watch the frenzied departure of the Walking Y riders. He shakes his head in dismay as he sees, first Eric, and then the girls ride off towards the bull pasture, bareback. Tony is taking too long, but he finally emerges with Nick, and both have saddled horses with rifle scabbards, and he can spy that the Irishman has taken a moment to don a revolver.

That's a bit better.

"Boom!"

Is Eric the target? The barn blocks his vision.

Hardy ducks back into his kitchen and grabs his coat, gloves, boots and his own heavy rifle that he keeps out of sight behind the wood box. He steps outside as he then sees Woody and Fred on fully saddled horses, each sporting a rifle, join the pursuit. That's much better. What next? Hardy runs towards the barn, thinking that the team and sled might be needed, and if not, that will be good news.

Shots and hoofbeats are still reverberating when he hears the tree explode. That damn bastard likes dynamite and hides behind it to escape. Hardy enters the barn and aims for the team, unharnessed, still tied in their stalls. He hefts the first harness, off a hook by the lead horse, and drapes it over her rump, and rolls it forwards. In no time, he has both in place, along with the collars and hames.

Jennifer watches Hardy run off and looks around hastily. She backs out of the kitchen and ducks into the large living room. The office door is open, and she glances out the window and spies Hardy now entering the barn. He's probably getting a team, and that will keep him busy for a couple minutes. She slinks into the office, and with an economy of moves that would put most thieves to shame, she scans the room and heads to the desk.

Quickly she pulls the first drawer, locked. "Damn." She reaches for the next drawer, "damn." It is also locked. She mutters, "I'll get them later." Methodologically she canvases those drawers she can access, the top of the desk, and the bookshelves and other flat surfaces. All this before a single minute passes.

A crumpled form and type font jumps out of the disorderly paperwork. She picks up a tattered familiar business card and stares at it, astonished. Thank God, she heard them. This is what she feared. Unless she makes this disappear, Woody and his crew might connect the dots. The card is toxic. She will have to give her Uncle John a piece of her mind about his habit of trying to impress scum by handing out his business card. This is a more serious game than intimidating some Wobbly or 'Taking care of' some union recruiter in Butte, or having her seduce some foolish politician.

If John is not careful, someone might climb back up the chain by following how he earns his fees and how he takes care of his customers by showing no remorse for his foes. Come to think of it, she is also deeply implicated as she has – more than once – used her womanly wiles to ensnare some stupid male. Thinking she looks again at the card, as all those thoughts took no more than a breath or two of time.

J.K. & Associates
Detectives, Investigators, and Fixers
Larimer Street, Denver, Colorado

Jennifer Hathaway stands there like a statue for but a moment. Open mouthed, she stammers, "How did Flynt get this card? This is awful. He should not have this card; he should not know about John Keegan." Here she pauses, listens carefully to make sure that Hardy has not doubled back. Her mind races, do I have anything that ties me to John? I'd better check when I get a chance. She flips it over, and yes, the back is printed.

J.K. & Associates
Serving the Anaconda Mining Corporation
Detectives, Investigators, and Fixers
Butte Office, Montana

Miss Hathaway mutters in dismay, "Good God, I'd better get out, so I have an alibi."

With a shaking hand, she puts the card inside the upper part of her dress and steps furtively out of the office. Looking around like a trapped bird, she quietly dashes to her room and snags a heavy sweater and winter outerwear. Scrambling to put these on, she staggers down the stairs and shambles through the door, and into the yard. There she stops for a moment and steadies her breath, and ventures towards the barn.

As she gets to the wide-open doors, Hardy is already leading the two palomino Belgian draft horses out to the hay sled, and without a word he hitches the obliging team. Without an invitation, Jennifer steps on the low-slung sled, and Hardy looks in askance. He then drops his rifle in the affixed scabbard and clucks to the team.

The horses sail through the gate with room to spare on both sides, and Hardy brings them to an easy lope. His efficiency and the fashion in which he handles the rifle and drops it in the scabbard takes Jennifer aback. She is quiet for a moment, and then as the silence drags on, she begins to chatter, "I wanted to join you in the pursuit. I do not want to stay in the house alone, as there is too much going on. It's where Michelle and Teri were attacked and taken. Can I go with you, please?"

Hardy nods his head in askance, but keeps quiet for a moment before he replies, "There's been some shooting and there might be some more." The team follows the tracks made by the riders who are now out of sight. Hardy ties the lines, and simply talks to the horses. He uses his hands to snag his rifle and chamber a round. The sled is surprisingly smooth compared to a wagon and Jennifer quickly notes that it will make an excellent platform from which to take an acceptable shot.

He clucks twice in quick succession, and then continues, "Come on now girls," in an even tone. The pair of large heads turn his way, and large brown eyes consider his request for a moment and then in a dignified manner, the pair dash with the sled following quietly, with just the creaking of the harness attesting to the movement. The rig is ghostly, as Hardy had taken the time to remove the bells. The cook scans the landscape and within a few minutes spies Eric, his prone horse, and Michele holding the reins to her horse in one hand and her rifle at the ready in the other. Of Tony, Woody, Nick, Fred and Teri, there is no sign.

    He brings the team to a stop beside Eric who looks up with tears pouring down his face. The sobbing boy is convulsed in complete agony. Michelle stands speechless beside him staring at Moose and the bloody flower marring his intelligent forehead. There is no need to ask any questions, as the lad's grief-stricken face tells Hardy what has happened. The boy's best friend since his first ride on the Walking Y is no more.

Chapter 16

<u>Defeat</u>

"Follow me, Nick!" barks Tony as they drive after Teri who is now in front, but the gap has narrowed to not more than fifty yards. The girl, while riding hard, is now ducking through the trees for safety as are Tony and Nick.

"KWHAMM!"

A tree mushrooms out in a loud bloom. Teri and Crowhop disappear in the flying debris and blossoming smoke.

"Bastard!" Howls Tony urging Sorley onward. Nick, a few yards behind the foreman, hunches in the saddle. Fear drives his mount. the pair dive into the pelting falling shards of the exploded tree. They emerge to see Crowhop standing with sweat on his flanks. Teri struggling to her feet urging them on. They resume the frantic chase for The Buffalo Gun.

The two veer into the cottonwoods, and charge on a well-trod cow path that cuts towards town. Tony catches fleeting glimpses in the distance of a dark horse and rider, and knows that Teri is probably behind him bareback also in pursuit. Branches reach out and lacerate the Irishman as he focuses on getting the best possible speed out of Sorley. Nick does his best to follow, but the gap widens, and Teri passes him while the boy can sense Woody gaining on him astride Jake.

A train whistles in the distance.

The renegade angles to the sound. The pursuers turn towards the tracks.

The lumbering freight train screams, again.

The fleeting shadow lunges to and ahead of the smoke belching locomotive and jumps across the tracks. Tony reaches the rails in a desperate bid to outrace the train and fails. He turns and stops, defeated. Sorley, flanks heaving, hide covered in lather, sways. Teri and then Woody join him. Jake and Crowhop blow thick clouds of steam from their nostrils.

A minute later as the train still clatters interminably on the tracks, Nick finally catches the group as all now fight for breath.

"That damn son of a bitch English bastard likes dynamite," utters the Irishman staring at the moving boxcar wall.

Woody nods in agreement, "We'd better walk our horses back and check on the others. Michelle is with Eric, and Fred is probably with them. Come on Nick, Teri."

Frustration burning in his soul, Tony gently turns Sorley and the others follow as the caboose sways past them mockingly. No one is visible on the far side of the line. Shoulders slumped, they shamble back towards the ranch, and their downed companions.

Back on Walking Y land, the riders find a cluster around Eric and Moose. Teri now assumes the guard position with her single shot rifle. Fred holds Blacky. Hardy and Michelle help the broken-hearted Eric, who is still clutching his rifle as tears streak down his face onto the sled. Jennifer's eyes drift from the broken-hearted sobbing boy to fixate on the mangled horsehead that is all that remains of Moose's intelligent forehead. Miss Hathaway's heart cries and real tears fall from her eyes.

Hardy frees Eric's saddle and gear from the inert buckskin, and tosses all of it on the wooden deck of the sled. He then climbs on the platform set to begin the long trek back to headquarters. Woody halts him with a hand gesture and looks around with a stony face. "Tony and Hardy, lead them back and keep an eye on Eric, and I hate to ask this Nick, but can you assemble whomever you can and start feeding the cows. Teri, I know you're bareback, but can you join me to check the bulls? I want to see how many were shot and slit the throat of any that are lying there badly wounded. No animal of mine deserves to be eaten alive by either coyote or cougar, just like no animal should be killed in cold blood for no reason at all except to enhance the power of some crooked, stone hearted, power-hungry individual."

With these words, two riders fork away from the sled and head toward the bull pasture on what is again a still morning except for the cows clamoring for feed. On the sled, Hardy drives stone faced focusing on the horses stating, "Eric, Moose saved your life with his jump up that embankment. That Buffalo Gun and his employer have no scruples. Children are fair targets."

Jennifer finds herself shedding a tear as she comforts the sobbing vulnerable lad who has lost his first and very best friend on the Walking Y after he escaped that stone cold orphanage in Sandpoint, Idaho. Worse yet, Miss Hathaway knows that this tragedy is partially due to her perfidy.

***

All work hard upon their return to the barn with Hardy heading back to the cookhouse with the governess after he hands the team to a willing Nick. Michelle and Fred volunteer to help the lad get the first team out on a feeding run after their saddle horses are brushed down and turned back out for the day. Tony drafts Eric to prepare the second team and sled for work, as he plans to keep the lethargic Eric working hard. He knows of no better medicine for his broken heart than to put him to work. Thus, the Walking Y tries to salvage the workday.

By the time all come in for lunch, a bit late and despite the robust fare Hardy has prepared for all augmented by a surprise chocolate cake waiting on the table for dessert, it is the quiet meal of a defeated crew which is eaten in the early afternoon. Woody sees their fatigue and breaks the silence with news that he spent the morning creating in his mind as he checked the slaughter in the bull pasture.

"Well Eric, Teri, and Michelle, I want to thank the three of you for keeping the carnage in the bull pen to a minimum. Teri and I found only four dead bulls, so that leaves us with eighteen for the coming years. If we can limit future damage, we should have enough bulls to fully cover a little over four hundred females. Now, looking at those dead bulls, I'm just about sure they were shot with a Sharps .50-90, which was made to kill buffalo. That is a hell of a gun, and we're outclassed. Because the charges against Tony for the so-called murder of Hank were dropped last year, I still have some of the $216 back in the ranches' secret stash. So," turning to Jennifer he adds, "I'm also going to pull the girls from a few afternoon classes and give them and Fred a better rifle than a single shot 22."

The girls look up exited, Fred looks up startled. The owner goes on, "I've been stupid, and more than once the girls have been exposed to grave danger or charged into trouble with an inadequate gun. I'm eying lever action Winchester 25-20s for each one of you girls and you too Fred. I want you all to be good with it. It has more power than a .22, and the kick should be de minimis. Using the same ammo for all of you will be an advantage. A single shot Winchester 22 is no match for a son of a bitch who has a damn good eye with a black powder Sharps buffalo gun and an affinity for sticks of dynamite."

Jennifer looks disapprovingly at the owner of the ranch as his language is not suitable for such young ladies. The girls smile and Woody is oblivious to the governess's discomfort as he goes on. "I fear that gangster is but the tip of the spear. The Senator has a go-between orchestrating this attack. That cowardly scum wants to keep his hands clean, and we are in worse danger than from Roger. At least we knew who the gunman was last time, and now we have yet to get a look at the son of a bitch who has us in his rifle sights. We need to find him and also find the Senator's go-between. Questions?"

All around the table stay quiet waiting for Woody to go on. Hardy, at the stove working on that night's dinner, is quietly paying full attention to the ranch owner who goes on to the next subject. "I might buy a couple new horses as we are short. I'm going to use that Buffalo Gun's money, as unless we defeat him, we will never need a pedigree bull. Michelle you and Teri have a good string, but I would like it if you used your seconds more often."

Eric's shoulders sag a bit more. Yet the owner is not done. "But I want to resume patrols from before dawn to after dark. To do so, we all need good horses, so I want to rotate horses around a bit. Nick, you get the golden team you like so much, so you are now head teamster. But I'll take your second saddle horse for myself. Eric, I want you to take Jake. You need a good lead horse, and he is one of the best I have ever had. He needs a younger rider who is fearless and can jump on him bareback. I was too timid to do so today, and thus I was too late to be of any use at any time. I have Red as my second horse, and he's a good one. As I'll be one short, I'm taking your second horse Nick."

Eric, whose head looked up at the owner at the mention of Jake stirs. "Woody, I don't need you to feel sorry for me, and Jake will not replace Moose. So, I don't want him."

Woody eyes the lad, and carefully replies, "Eric, I'm not being charitable. I should have been beside you, and you should not have been alone at the point of the attack. Moose should not have been the first target in the chase. I'm getting older, and ten years ago, I could have done what you did, namely take off on a horse with just a rifle and no saddle and no headstall. I can't anymore. Jake is a darn good young horse. But I can't push him to save our necks like you can if you work with him. Our lives, our animals' lives, and this ranch depend on catching that crazy dangerous dynamite loving sharpshooter. We need you on a damn fast horse, where you can be riding hell bent for leather without taking time to dilly dally getting a horse ready. Jake is the only animal on the place that will do that and match your spirit except, perhaps, for one of the girls', and it would be unfair to take one of the girl's horses."

"But Woody, I don't want Jake. He can't replace my poor Moose."

Woody ignores the lad. Turning to Nick and Fred, he adds, "Sorry Nick, but your riding is not up to the task, although you are probably our best teamster. Fred, you know as well as anybody that you are not skilled enough to do that kind of riding. So, we will leave you with Blacky. That said, you were right there today, and next time, I want you to be just as brave and daring."

Eric cuts in, "Woody, listen to me, I don't want Jake."

Jennifer pipes in, "I agree with Eric. Tony, as foreman, you should be able to ride Jake into danger bareback and Woody, shouldn't you keep the boys and the girls safe?"

Eric sits up steaming. "Are you out of your mind Lady. I don't need to be kept safe. I'm a damn sight better at riding bareback than Tony." Then glaring at Miss Hathaway defiantly, Eric declares with certitude, "Woody, I'll take him."

None except for Tony note Jennifer look up startled and shake her head as does a dog that has just been unexpectantly cuffed. Or Woody who seems to expect the boy's reaction. All others look at Eric's show of energy, and how he dares to defy Miss Hathaway.

Chapter 17

The Missing Card

To Jennifer's disgust, after a dinner a couple days later, where she again made scant progress on impressing on them the need for proper etiquette, the orphans decide to stay in the kitchen. Hardy clears the table and places mugs of steaming hot chocolate for all. Nick and Fred smile as they exclaim how they will teach the girls poker, and all those games and terms they have learned from Tony. Eric sits still and quiet while Fred gives instructions while shuffling an old deck.

"Michelle, this is a real neat game, and it's called seven-card stud."

"You mean like a stallion?"

"Yup, but there's no horse, just these cards. What you want to do is keep an inscrutable face."

"A what?"

"Yeah, Tony taught me that fancy word, 'inscrutable', which means you don't let your face tell others what you have or if you are happy or mad at your cards. So, just the opposite of Woody who always looks like a grouch."

"Or Jennifer," adds Nick not realizing that she is still within earshot, "Who looks at us boys like we're something the dog dragged in."

Michelle looks at the lad disgusted, "You mean like a dead rat?"

"Nah, I was thinking what you have after the dog eats the rat. Anyway, back to poker, you want to get a pair, or better yet, two pairs or three of a kind or a full hose."

"Nick," cuts in Fred, "that's a full house, not a full hose."

"Oh…"

Tony looks in and notes that Eric stares halfheartedly around the table, quiet. The foreman catches the boy's eye and cocks his finger calling him. The Irishman then looks at the cook, "Hardy, you've probably played a game or two in your time, so why don't you join them and teach? I need Eric for a bit."

While the kids are bickering drinking hot chocolate and Hardy joins them sipping on steaming coffee, Tony drifts to the office with Eric behind him. Jennifer, frowning at the uncomplimentary smart comments emanating from the table puts her dime novel on the couch by the office, and quietly goes upstairs to her room. Both Walking Y riders enter Woody's office and Tony closes the door tightly leaving the intruding young voices playing cards on the outside.

Tony eyes Woody, who is again behind the desk, and voices his concern. "Woody, that Senator is after us again. Eric's horse was not an accident. And we're in trouble because we don't know who, or what is going to hit us. Eric's loss is the proof that whoever is shooting that buffalo gun has a deadly aim and combine that with his dynamite, he'll kill one of us sooner or later unless we act. I've been asking around in town, and the Senator does not have any such executioner working on the Ringing Bell Ranch, so we don't know how to strike back."

Woody leans back in his worn chair, "Tony, we have a whole bunch of worries. We are going under. If he kills any more bulls, we might not have enough to breed all the cows. I already can't pay you or the kids. I've moved Hardy to a bunch of IOUs. I don't want dead orphans. Look at the pattern, first the bull in town, now this. He aims well and will not hesitate to kill. I'd prefer Roger who thought he was a good shot. This shooter is a good shot, from a long way off. He can hit the sweet spot between the eyes from half a mile away. And he plans his escapes and makes pursuit dangerous. I don't know about you, but I'm not sure I want us to chase him again."

Tony points to Eric, "Both of us think the first attack in this wave was in Denver." Woody looks up startled and the ex-New Yorker continues, "Please listen. You both were left barefooted. We think it was to make you late, so that she would be the only one available, thus the governess would be Jennifer."

"Damn it, Tony," barks the owner as if he is acting, "Since she arrived, you have had a problem with her because she's English. At this time, I will not put up with that kind of bull. She is a fine lady, and she is not part of the Senator's crew. If you can't leave her be, I want you to leave right away."

"Woody," Eric cuts in quietly changing the subject and diffusing the looming fight between the two adults, "can we see the business card you picked up in Denver after we took that highway man out?"

The owner glares for a moment and turns to reach for the card. It is not where he thought he left it. Quickly he begins to scan the flat surfaces, and then more carefully he looks around with no luck. He walks around the office and then checks under the desk. It is not to be found. After a bit, he looks at Tony and gestures that he has no idea where the card might be laying. "Eric, what the hell do you want to see it for?"

Eric answers, "Woody, can you remember what name or address was on the card?"

Woody pauses and is quiet for a moment. "Something like J T and Associates on both sides and the Anaconda Company in Butte and some address on Larimer Street in Denver. Why?"

Eric digs in his pocket and pulls out a crumpled torn envelope. "Take a look at this and tell me if this is the same as the business card."

J K & Associates
Larimer S
Den

Woody stares for a long time and then looks at Eric carefully. "Where did you get this?"

"Woody, I asked you if it is the same as the business card?"

"Yes. Now where did you get it?"

Eric inhales slowly and nods his head. "Woody, right after the bull was shot in town, I took off after the two girls on Blacky. That horse is too slow for me, so I saw the shooter going into the rocks to the south of town, and I took a ranging shot at over 800 yards with Nick's rifle. I got close to him, or I might have creased him. He ducked behind his horse, and we have not been cursed with his presence for some time now until earlier this week. Well, I found that torn envelope on the ground where he was when I took my shot. I found that and a few gold coins that I pocketed, which you should have by now. No one would leave one-ounce gold coins on the road, so they had to come from him. He's linked to the highway man who picked us up at the National Stock Growers Convention. Remember, our so-called taxi came from a different line. I think it was specifically waiting for us and called for us."

Woody stays quiet for only a moment and begins as if he is repeating the lines he has already stated, "Eric, as I told Tony, I will not put up with you saying that this J K planted Jennifer on this ranch. This J K must be a coincidence. As to Miss Hathaway, she is a real fine lady. There is no way she is part of the Senator's crew. In the wagon in town when we arrived and the bull was shot, I could tell that she is not used to violence, and you saw that just a couple days ago at how she blanched when we reached your dead horse. If you can't understand that we'll end this conversation right away."

Eric sinks in his chair looking a bit defeated. Upstairs, Jennifer looks at what she can see of Woody, and hears how he believes in her. She smiles fondly. Meanwhile, Tony looks unperturbed.

He pipes in. "Woody, we'll drop that, even if we do not agree. Let's move on. I wanted to thank you for handing Jake over to Eric. That was generous, but more important yet, it was smart. Real smart. We can't have the girls alone in the vanguard attacking some shooter with a buffalo gun, worse yet a Sharps .50-90. Don't know if you recall, but some time ago, Billy Dixon is rumored to have killed a man at over 1,500 yards with one. Jake is the only horse on the place that can outrun Crowhop. Teri and Michelle might be having nightmares because of Roger; however, the Senator's threats have not taken the fight out of those two girls."

Both men now eye Eric. The lad looks defiantly at the ranch owner and his foreman. "All right, I said I'd take Jake. No need to rub it in. He isn't as good as Moose, and that fiend who shot him needs to pay. I need a good horse to catch the brute. So I'll take him, and work with him, and make him my partner, but I can't guarantee I can protect the girls. I failed last time, but I can state that I'll not let them get into trouble without my company. So there, are you satisfied?"

Woody looks around, and snags three dirty shot glasses and opens a locked drawer and pulls out a fifth of bourbon and fills them. Tony arches his eyebrow thinking of his empty flask. "Well boss, I see you've been holding out on me. I'll keep that in mind next time you want a dram."

The ranch owner smiles at Tony. "All right, we have a deal. Those girls are hellions, as are Nick and Fred. So, let's toast to the fact that Eric here along with you Tony and I will keep them all safe."

With these words, Tony and Woody each down the shot glass in one easy swallow. Eric chokes a bit, and with tears in his eyes finally downs the light brown fire water. The two older men chuckle, watching Eric's face gain a pink tint.

Woody starts in the next part of his agenda, looking at the lad, "All right now we need to determine how we patrol the cows, bulls, and cover normal ranch chores. First check goes out in the next hour. I'd prefer two on each patrol, and with Hardy and Jennifer here we don't need to leave anyone else to cover the cookhouse. So, one of Eric, Tony or myself must be on each patrol. OK, who is more of a morning person, and who likes to work late…" With those words he breaks out a sheet of paper and dips a quill into the inkwell. They then sit and walk through the activities for the next few weeks and the patrols to try and protect both the ranch and the livestock.

Tony must pull Teri from the poker game which has graduated to five-card draw. All the others call it a night, as Eric accompanied by Michelle have the first patrol before dawn. They will only come in after the first feeding crew consisting of Nick driving the team with Fred to help him and Woody nearby on horseback are at work. In the afternoon, Eric must start training with Jake so that the pair can work together at his high standards while the others get to practice with their shooting. The girls and Fred need to discover and learn their upgraded rifles, brand new gleaming lever action Winchester 25-20s.

The following morning, with two already out working, breakfast is a quiet affair, and no whispered conversation or comments takes place as Woody comes down from the second floor daring anyone to utter any wisecracks. Tony innocently, smiles. The owner gives him a murderous look that fades as Tony cuts in. "Woody, I was chuckling as I wonder if Eric had trouble getting up this morning after his little snort of whiskey, or if Michelle had to dump a bucket of water on him?"

The stout man replies with a sudden smile, "Yup, I probably shouldn't have given him that shot. But he is just about a man now, and he does a man's work around here like everybody else." Here Woody's smile fades and he goes on, "That said, he loved that horse, and I have rarely seen such pain in a lad's eye. So, if he fights a bit of a hangover, it'll help him focus on Jake and the danger from The Buffalo Gun. Michelle is a morning person, so it should go well."

Chapter 18

Butte

Thus, a couple weeks go by when a full-fledged blizzard gives Tony a chance to huddle in the barn with the five orphans shortly before lunch. As the six sit in the tack room on a couple benches that allow the crew to don spurs or change their boots. Tony looks around right after the feeding run and after Woody has drifted back to the cookhouse.

"OK, what we need to make sure is that we are focused on The Buffalo Gun. Woody thinks it's a Sharps .50-90, which was made with buffalo in mind. So, executing some bulls is not that different, mind you you'd have to load your own, which you girls will learn how to do for that Winchester .25-20. Knowing that and seeing the way it's brought down Moose and five bulls, we need to be careful. Eric and all of you, keep in mind that both Woody and I think that the shooter is not staying in the area, but is drifting here from a neighboring town. As you chased him south, he's probably staying in one of those towns going towards Garrison. Woody has asked the Widow Wilson to keep her eyes open, and Fernande tells him that no stranger with that kind of gear has set foot in her hotel or been seen."

Here Tony pauses, before going on, "Woody even talked to Mrs. Maxwell and had her check at the General Store if a stranger has been buying black powder or even lead to make their own rounds. She even asked about any purchases of dynamite, fuse, or blasters. Mrs. Couchman said that there is nothing to report."

"You mean he asked the Doctor's wife to nose around town for him? I thought he called her," here Teri hesitates and then mimics Woody's gruff voice, "'a dried-up old ditty who sticks her nose in everybody else's business.'"

All laugh at Teri's role playing. Eric cuts in, "Woody's really scrambling. I know she assisted us, but that must of cost him to ask her for help."

"Eric, I can tell you in confidence that I don't like the English or people of English descent..."

"Nah! Never would have guessed," cuts in Nick smiling, "I don't think you have said anything like that in the past."

"Yeah, no more than one or two thousand times," adds Teri.

"A day," cuts in Michelle. All are really laughing now.

Tony reaches for his flask, brings it up to his mouth and still finds it empty. His startled and disgusted look draws even more laughter. He puts it back in its allocated breast pocket and looks around sternly bringing their laughter to a close, "Kids, I hate to remind you, but Eric and I think that Miss Hathaway may not be totally honest. So, we can't discuss these things around her, or worse yet, Woody. He seems infatuated with her which means we have to walk on eggshells, or at least I have to."

All instinctively know that Tony is right, and none challenge him. Tony then goes on, "Quick reminders, do not mention that Roger and Dave are buried on this place, and do not discuss this mysterious J.K. and Associates. I think that is the key, but Woody won't hear that whomever this J.K. is might be responsible for planting her here."

Now as he has their full attention, he goes on, "As Woody is intransigent, I'm going to leave for a couple days starting tomorrow. I'm going to Butte by train to get information on this J.K. I'm telling Woody that I have a 'Fenians' meeting for the old country in Missoula, so that's the story."

Here Tony stops talking. His face turns white. As if he sees a ghost. A long-lost apparition. A stunned quiet moment passes.

"What is it, Tony?" asks Eric.

"I just realized where I've seen that kind of work with dynamite before." Pensively he hesitates before resuming, "I hope I'm wrong. But I was just a wee lad. Understand, I was a lowly snot nosed boy, but I was proud to be a runner for the Fenians. The Irish fighters used us boys to move guns and dynamite around to blow things up in England. Mom found out what I was doing, and next I knew we're on a boat to New York. She thought I'd get killed. I wonder. Well, no matter."

The Irishman stays quiet for a moment and shakes his head. "Where was I, yes, while I'm gone, Woody will lead the night patrol with Michelle. Eric you'll have the morning one with Teri. Woody will cover the feeding run also, so he'll be working like a dog. I need you all to behave. Eric, as I discussed with you, every day you need to check for my daily telegram at the train station. Do so early afternoon."

He looks at the others and adds, "Eric's paying for the trip with the three double eagles I held back from Woody." He looks at the lad who is perplexed, "That Eric would be the same gold you found when you clipped that Sharps toting renegade."

Eric looks at Tony and smiles, "Why Tony, you must be a pure-blooded English Bastard, holding back on the boss in case you saw the need to do something he wouldn't approve of."

Tony darts him a furious look. All the others laugh.

After a moment, sheepishly Tony goes on, "All right you win that one. Now, I'll send you the agreed upon one-word telegram each day. If I go quiet or say the wrong word, it means that I need your help, Eric. I don't know what we are facing, but we can't just sit here like steers waiting for slaughter. So, I will leave you with two of the double eagles, I'll take the other, and I have a few coins saved for an emergency."

The orphans look at Tony concerned.

Teri glares at Eric. "We'll go to Butte to help."

Eric swivels his head startled, "We?"

"Yes Eric, you can't go and rescue Tony alone. Either one or two of us go along, or I'm telling Woody."

With fire in his eyes, Eric retorts, "Teri, didn't you ever hear, 'we don't like tattle tales'?"

"Tony," cuts in Michelle diplomatically, "Eric alone won't work. If you get into trouble, you'll be needing at least two of us. Won't you?"

Tony looks around. "I won't let some English bastards get the better of me. So, no, I won't get into trouble. But I see wisdom in a couple of you going to town to get the telegraph because of that Sharps toting killer. So, Eric, keep an open mind, and young man you have enough cash to buy more than one train ticket all the way to Butte and back if you need to."

***

Butte in the early evening is a roiling mass of humanity. Sidewalks are crowded with men in dirty clothing coming from the mines and mills, spewing workers in and out of bars. Children dart about in dirty clothes. Women seek to stretch their meager food budgets and bring home groceries before the stores close. In the background, coal driven boilers spew black smoke in the air, mine whistles merge with those of shunting trains as copper ore is moved for concentration and smelting. Other trains load up these valuable cargoes and shunt them to the nearby town of Anaconda for smelting and thence to Great Falls for refining.

Horses compete for space on the roads with a few new horseless carriages, wooden poles carry an obscene number of copper wires that move those two modern wonders, electricity and telephone. Telegraph lines flank the main rail lines in a never-ending row of post with copper wire, much of it from Butte, to shrink the world. The country is alive with change. Over it all, lords a few hard rich men who sire these wonders ruling the plebes with an iron fist.

Toiling men, hard muscled men, men in filthy dirt encrusted overalls or worn jeans seek food, drink, and companionship. Women toil to bring civilization that makes a still raw land tamer with painted houses, churches, and schools. Red brick buildings line both sides of every major street. Seamus inhales the acrid smell going back in his mind to Brooklyn, or as a wee lad, to Cork. Like many others, the breath he exhales reeks the pungent odor of cheap whiskey. He wants information. In his head, he looks at another bar, near the corner of Main on Granite. He walks in, and watches as when the bartender steps back when he asks, "where can I find J. K. and Associates?"

After a stiff examination, the barkeep looks at him carefully. "Can you fight?"

"A bit, did some rounds in Brooklyn for money not that long ago."

"And its J.K. you want? Why?"

"I was told he paid well, and needed men like me."

"What about if you need to bash Irish scum?"

"For money, it's not my concern who I bash."

The bartender examines Tony's face. "Those labor agitators, Wobblies, are nothing but trouble. So, you'll probably have to pound some union agitators. Well, it's your call. OK, go to Broadway, just west of Main on the North side. Third or fourth door, there's a little plaque that reads J.

K. & Associates. Go there. But, let me warn you, they don't like to be double crossed."

Tony walks out, and he soon finds the sought for brass plaque. There is a small non-descript dry goods store on the ground floor, and offices above reached by a narrow staircase. Seamus knocks, and there is no reply. Not a big surprise, as the building is dark, but the street is alive. Our Irishman walks to the back of the building in a dingy lane, and steps into a dark corner. Even here, there are people and eyes watching.

For cover, he pretends he is a bit drunk and pisses in the dirty snow like an alcoholic while his senses note every little activity around him. There is a small back door that hangs a bit askew in a shadow that might be a way into the building housing J. K. and Associates. There are probably back stairs, and the shadows mean that Tony won't be seen if he times springing the lock well.

A burly man notes him relieving himself and barks in a familiar Irish brogue. "Hey, Paddy, move on. That's not a latrine."

Tony hitches up his trousers and then teeters away, pretending to be drunk.

So, there is a watchman. Irish by the sounds of him. But he did not see the face. No matter, from a corner leaning as a drunkard against a cold raw brick wall, he watches the burly man make his rounds. Tony reaches in his breast pocket and touches the cap to his lips. He is stone cold sober but wants his breath to stink. Soon he notes that the guard does two rounds an hour. Predictable. It should give him close to thirty minutes. He has a candle stub, and if quiet, he should have a quarter of an hour to browse. Time enough to search through J.K.'s office for some clues as to what is going on and for proof that the Senator is paying for the Walking Y's troubles.

After the next round, Tony staggers across the back lane, and in the shadows furtively peeks about. He sees no one. He pulls a thin metal blade and clicks the lock. Still, no one about. He enters sealing the door locked behind him. He waits for a moment and moves up the back stairs as close to the wall as he dares. All is dark. Carefully he lights his stub of a candle and shields the light with his hand. On ghost like feet, he walks the long straight hallway the length of the second floor and scans the painted frosted glass panels on each door. No luck. He goes up to the third and he hits the mother lode as painted on the frosted window he reads. "J. Keegan and

Associates". He glances around, and quickly jimmies that lock. He enters. Carefully he locks the door behind himself.

The window shades are drawn, so he can keep the candle burning, as long as he is careful. He goes straight to the largest desk in the room ignoring a couple small used roller topped workstations that are obviously for underlings. He begins to scan papers. File after file shows nothing that means anything for the Walking Y. He reaches for the top drawer of the oaken file cabinet beside the desk, and it is locked. Tony takes a moment to trick the lock, again using his thin blade.

The folders are alphabetical. He checks "Bell", nothing. He checks "Ringing Bell" which also draws a blank. Same with "Walking Y", "Hellenville", "Roger". Frustrated he checks "Senator" again nothing. He thinks intently and as a lark he looks up "Ding Dong". Eureka. A thick folder. He smiles. Yup, that would be the Honorable Senator William Howard Bell the Third. He pulls it. Lays it on the desk and rifles it. A forgotten name from his early childhood jumps out and leaves him breathless.

Chapter 19

Festus O'Leary

The Irishman stares at the paper in the folder tagged with the ridiculous moniker, "Ding Dong." My God, it couldn't be. Fate wasn't so cruel. What a nightmare. Hands shake, heart beats madly. Tony rubs his eyes again, looks at the name written in a neat handwriting on off white paper.

"Festus O'Leary".

"Impossible." What are the chances. Why, of the millions of Irish in America, this cannot be. Fate couldn't be so cruel. But, Festus O'Leary, using old hard killing skills in a city that will richly pay for them to keep hard workers in line. That should not be surprising. His skills are rare, and now he works for new masters for a comfortable income. Tony's face turns white even in the feeble candlelight. His memory floats back in time to a nightmare in his childhood:

A rainy day in Cork. In a dank stone hovel on the edge of town, little Seamus Patrick O'Connor stands in a gloomy corner staring with large green eyes at a tableau he would never forget. A cold dark eyed young man stares with contempt at a trembling shopkeeper clad in wet clothing.

'You sold us out. If Seamus hadn't told us the Poms were in your warehouse, we would have been caught with the goods. You know what happens to traitors.'

With a look of terror, the shopkeeper answers, 'By Mary, Joseph and Jesus, Festus, I didn't know that the Brits were in the warehouse. I've been home and I've been loyal. They raided all those warehouses along the dock road. You should know that.'

'Not good enough. You know the punishment.' The merchant blanches and cries in terror, 'No, for God's sakes, no! Festus, have pity.'

Fast as a flash, a black gun is in his hero's hand, and it barks. The shopkeeper falls to the ground clutching his mangled leg. Kneecapped. The shopkeeper's knee is a mass of mangled flesh, blood and bone.

God, little Seamus doesn't know what to do. Festus turns to him, 'Remember, that's what happens to traitors."

Little Seamus retches with tears in his eyes. He just wants to help Ireland, not kill.

Tony's entrapped mind does not register the slight sound behind him until it's too late. He turns. A click bathes the room in light. An electric bulb on the ceiling. The foreman's mind races. Too sluggishly.

"Don't move Seamus. Unless you'd like a .45 and a kneecapping."

Tony stares, comprehending the danger, but too slowly. He lamely voices, "Festus. I should have recognized you."

"Seamus, you always were a bit of a Melter. I should have kneecapped you when you was a wee filthy lad in Cork. Ah well, we meet again. Now tell me, did you piss yourself when that bobby chased you and you dropped the bundle? That was my dynamite. Is that why you were on a boat with your old biddy?"

"Leave my mother out of this Festus. Anyway, I heard you died in the old country."

"Ah yes. The old country. Piss on it. You're not so lucky. Because you dropped that bundle, I had to run. Got here just in time to shoot the last of the buffalo. Handy skill if I can say so. Did you enjoy my work? Pretty good, that bull in town. In fact, the only shot I missed of late was that boy. Stupid horse threw his head up, and puff. That was the end of that. Now I'd like to end you, and I'll even get paid to end you and that annoying Walking Y."

Fetus' tone hardens, as he waves another man into the room. "You're going to comply. As you showed the guts of a coward as a sordid wee thing when you dropped the bundle. YOU should have killed that bobby by pulling the striker. You could have killed him and taken a bunch of Bodachs with you. I trained you to blow yourself to heaven. Coward."

Color drains from Tony's face, as he staggers back as if he had been slapped.

Festus moves up a bit, grinning at Seamus, a Colt .45 steady in his hand, "We have you covered. I think John would like to talk to you. Shame he's out of town because I would love to kneecap you right here."

Festus turns a bit, and he barks to his companion, "Mack, pat him down for knives or a gun."

Mack first pulls a thin blade from its sheath on Tony's belt and tosses it to the floor. Then with relish, he pats him down, hard. He takes extra time to sneak in a nasty punch in his manhood. Tony grunts doubled over in pain and sweat beads on the foreman's forehead.

"Nothing else boss, no gun."

"Well Seamus, no gun. You always were yellow. GET ON THE FLOOR, NOW! On your stomach. Good God, how I'd love to kneecap you, and I think you weren't so young that you don't remember how I do that. So, you'd better be an angel, or I'll make you one."

Festus then turns back to Mack, and orders, "Tie his hands behind him, hard."

Mack looks at Festus quizzically, "I need rope."

Turning his head, Festus barks, "Get a rope from that armoire." While they are thus distracted, Tony on the floor reaches up and moves his flask to one of his back pants pockets.

As Mack completes the job, Festus turns with a smile and mocks Seamus with his handgun and dry shoots him in the knee. "Click." With a vicious grin he adds, "You and I are going to take a bit of a walk. John will want you, regrettably alive. At least for now. Oh, and Mack is coming along too. So, behave, or not. I don't really care."

They step out the back door and lock it behind them. Three to four hours before dawn, and Butte is dark. Even most of the bars are closed, and Tony feels exposed as he walks a short way ahead of Festus. Running is not an option, anyway it's hard to do with your hands tied behind your back, and Festus would love an excuse to kill him. They angle up Main Street one block to Granite Street, hook east past the now last of the closing bars where the dirt is being swept out of the door. Seamus notes that it's the very bar where he was given the direction to the offices of J.K. & Associates. His eyes lock in on the tired barkeep, and he is pushed from behind. They continue till the Irishman sees only a small shack ahead of him with a large hoist frame in the background.

"See that," laughs Festus pointing to the solid shack, "you'll call it home for a while. It's nice and remote. Even if you cry for help, which I would not recommend, no one can hear you. Mind you, Mack might decide that such a cry will be your last."

A train whistle blows, not far away, as a short ore train comes creaking down the uneven track. Tony slips and falls, hard, in the icy mud with his shoulder striking a horse trough with a loud smack. Festus snarls, "Up you bastard." Tony turns, and his pale knee shows through a gash in his pants, and his hands are still tied behind his back. He gets up, gingerly rolls over, struggles up, and gimps with his face creased in pain.

"Damn, that hurts," mutters the Walking Y foreman while drawing his captor's attention.

Festus and Mack both snarl, "Get moving damn it!"

Tony moves slowly, in obvious pain. He hobbles and he favors his right knee and the bloody gash there. Unseen in the theatrics, Tony leaves his treasured flask behind, against the horse trough in the muck out of the traffic. The only thing ahead of him now is that dark cold forlorn cabin.

As they walk in, Festus shoves the gimping Tony to the floor. He turns to Mack, "Untie the wee thing."

Laughing he mocks the foreman, "Coat, boots, belt and socks off. Now. I'll be taking them and be thankful that I'm not taking everything as Mr. Keegan wants us to strip any captive naked. He says it's harder for them to cause trouble that way." With a momentary pause he goes on, "Offsetting Mr. Keegan's orders is the fact I don't want to see that much of you."

While Festus and Mack chuckle, Tony complies. When The Buffalo Gun, that dynamite toting gangster snags Tony's items, he signals with his .45 that Tony should move "in here." Tony finds himself in a very stoutly built small room that once held powder for one of the mines. He is alone, with no shoes, no socks, no belt, and no coat and one putrid mouse infested blanket. Tony surveys the lone roughhewn wooden bed stinking of neglect and rodents. No window. He turns and sees that a little candlelight and air come in a very small grate above the door. So, it is dark. For now, he limits himself to trying to figure out how to signal Eric for help or how to signal his location.

***

His captors leave. The cabin is frigid. The bastards did not even stoke the woodstove that was added when the building was no longer used for explosive storage. Tony finds himself shivering and sneezing in the putrid blanket staring at nothing. With no candle in the other room, with no moon, and a dawn that never comes, he can see little. A couple times he walks around inside his cell, and a couple times he tries to claw his way up to see out the grating, but he is a bit short for that task.

In the dark, he lowers himself on the floor and feels it carefully. There is no exit that he can discern that way, but he feels the wooden stump of his rough-hewn bed. They could make stilts, and that might allow him to look. He could put them back where at a quick glance no one would notice that he savaged his bunk. He puts his feet against the far wall and heaves with all his power. The first leg does not budge. He rests for a moment and tries again. And again. And again.

It budges. He gives himself a moment rest. The exercise has warmed him, and the project gives him purpose. He heaves with all his muscles straining. Years of boxing in Brooklyn, years of training, and then half a year as a cowboy mean that the large nails slowly release their hold. Soon the first leg is off. One more leg to go, and then the bed will only be fastened to the wall. But he'll have a club or two. Awkward as only a four by four can be, but clubs none the less. Now one more to go and then try and see out the grate, and to see if it's as solid as Festus assumes it is.

Tony rants in anger, alone, "Call me a coward you bastard. You just like to shoot from a distance, and have kids blow things up. I notice now that you always kept your ass out of trouble." Mimicking Festus' rough brogue, he begins "Little Seamus, YOU showed the guts of a coward as a sordid wee thing when you dropped the bundle. YOU should have killed that bobby by pulling the striker. You could have killed him and taken a bunch of Bodachs with you. I trained you to blow yourself to heaven. Coward."

Fumbling in the dark to place his body to push the second leg free, Tony goes on, "Festus, you bastard. How many little boys did you train to blow themselves to heaven. Jesus, Mary, Joseph, I can't believe I believed in you. Darn good thing Mama took me to New York. You are as bad as the English."

With those words, he heaves and pries off the second leg to his cot. He stands them, and carefully climbs and looks out the grating. He sees little that is of help. The opening is not more than about one foot wide, and no more than three inches high. The edges are rough cut two by sixes. Not something bare hands can destroy. The wooden legs will not fit in, so he cannot use them to try and break his way out. The Walking Y manager slides back down in his cell to think. Perhaps he can bash in the door next.

No sooner does he slide down; he hears the outside door open. A match strikes and a kerosene lantern sputters to life. A little blessed light filters into the cell.

"Hey Paddy," snaps a strange voice. "Just letting you know that I'm Brogan, and I'm on guard duty. Festus, Mack and Cormac have some hunting to do up your way, and Mr. John Keegan is not due back for a while, so you'll just have to stew. I'm opening the door and give me the slightest excuse and I'll blow you away, as it would make my life easier. So, get to the far end of your pen. Festus says that for old times sakes and due to the fact we don't want this place to stink, I should give you an empty coffee can to piss in."

In a mocking tone he adds, "So don't piss on the floor or do anything else on the floor because you'll be living in it."

With these warm words, the door opens inward a few inches, and the unknown guard tosses an old tin coffee can into the cell. The door slams shut. Tony, shivering, puts his makeshift latrine in the far corner. So much for the hope of getting out to go to an outhouse and having that opportunity to escape. Then quietly, he places the legs back on the bed, sufficiently so that they will hold it up while he rests, but he knows he can grab one in a hurry to use as a club. Time dawdles on. Tony sighs. He has a good day to figure out how to signal Eric. If he gets to Butte, and with any luck the lad will be on the train that afternoon, when he fails to send a telegram. He also has a good day to plan his escape.

Musing, Tony mutters, "I wonder what hunting Festus and Mack have up Hellenville way?"

Chapter 20

Cold Comfort

    Eric bounds up the snow-covered entrance of the depot two steps at the time and hurries into the red brick building. He sprints for the black iron grated ticket window leaving snow on the polished stone floor. He looks through the grate and sees a uniformed railroad employee lounging with his feet up on a worn desk reading a cheap book.
    With bated breath, the lad shouts out his question, "Do you have a telegraph for me?"
    The spectacled older thin man beside the telegraph key looks up from his book in askance at this insolent youth and slowly puts down his dime western. He cannot resist teaching a bit of a lesson to the impudent lad, so he moves sluggishly and comes all the way to the window and answers in a mocking tone.
    "'A telegram for ME?' now Sir, would that be for Master Eric Smithby, or would 'ME' be The Walking Y Cattle Company, or would 'ME' be Mr. Woodrow W. Flynt, or perhaps 'ME' is Mr. Seamus Patrick O'Connor, or in your case, 'ME' might even be Miss Jennifer Hathaway or someone else who lives at that ranch you work on?"
    "Any of those, Ben," retorts the fuming Eric.
    "Let me check, Sir." Leisurely the telegraph operator walks to an alphabetized set of cubicles that is glaringly empty, he looks about carefully for a bit, and then shuffles to the window to face the impatient lad. "No Sir, there is nothing for any of your 'MEs'. Do you want me to check for anything else, Sir?"
    Eric swivels and leaves in a huff. As to the telegraph operator, with a smirk, he goes back to his desk, picks up his dime store novel and ignores the annoying youth's irritating departure, as Eric slams the door, bounds down the steps, and looks at the girls on horseback. He leaps into the saddle. Jake shakes his head at the rider's mood. Eric frowns and growls,

"Nothing. Not a darn thing. I've got to go to Butte. Quick. Let's get back, I need to gather a few things so that I can make the afternoon train."

Faster than Eric's ears can grasp, Teri counters, "Not alone you don't. We're going with you. Tony said we could."

All three turn their horses and start back at a mile eating lope. Eric looks at the girls and barks, "Did not."

Teri smiles, and counters, "Did so, or we'll tell Woody."

They ride on, bickering at a canter to get a few items and some of that Buffalo Gun's gold. As they close in on the ranch, Teri says, "We only have about an hour before the train pulls through, and we'll need someone to bring our horses home. Fred, Nick and Woody are on a feed run."

Eric counters, "That would be you and Michelle."

Teri fires back, "No, we'll get Hardy to do it. On Blacky. Fred's on the sled feeding."

"Teri, Michelle, did you forget that Miss Hathaway needs you for schooling. So, you both stay here."

"No. It'll take all three of us. If you argue, we'll tell Woody and delay you, and you'll endanger Tony."

Eric rides up to the barn steaming.

He turns to the girls and spits. "Darn it, all right. Just move. Grab some dark non-descript clothing and steal Woody's large carpet bag. I want your rifles wrapped up with plenty of shells inside your clothing. Get Hardy to give us food for the trip, as we don't have any excess money for the dining car. Also, as it was your idea, get Hardy to ride Blacky to lead the horses back. If he says 'NO!' then I go alone. You have ten minutes. I'll get my stuff and a pistol."

The cook spies the girls running towards the cookhouse. Now what? Before a moment passes, they barge in without removing their boots. Jennifer is at the table, planning her day's schooling. Dinner, a large pot roast with potatoes and carrots is at the back of the wood burning cookstove simmering.

Hardy turns to prepare some hot chocolate as the girls scamper into the kitchen. Teri ignores him and the hot chocolate. She runs to the office, leaving wet and muddy tracks.

Michelle, in her wake like Teri does not even bother to remove her coat nor her scarf, looks at Hardy and ignores Jennifer. Panting she begins, "Hardy, we need your help. Can you ride Blacky into town with us and bring our horses back? Now? And can we have some sandwiches and food to take with us, now? We're leaving in five minutes. Got to catch the afternoon train."

Miss Hathaway looks up startled, "But you have classes in half an hour."

Michelle ignores the governess and turns and bounds into the living room and up the stairs leaving tracks the whole way. Teri comes barreling into the kitchen with Woody's carpet bag. She snags both new Winchesters from the gun rack and pulls a box of cartridges from the shelf below them. These she lays on the table beside the well-worn carpet bag. Meanwhile Hardy efficiently cuts bread and slabs of cold corn beef.

Jennifer looks over at the commotion and the rifles being packed. Incensed she demands, "Just what do you think you're doing young lady?"

"Leaving. Going to rescue Tony. Now. Don't get in the way Miss Hathaway, as we don't have time to debate. Hardy, we have to leave. Now."

Michelle tears into the kitchen with old dark clothing, and both wrap the rifles in the bleak attire Eric suggested. Hardy forks over a satchel of food that is swept into the large canvas carpetbag.

Jennifer, stands and stares astounded. She turns to the cook. "Boy, I order you to stop them. They're just little girls. Stop them now."

Hardy looks at her and hooks his old coat that is behind the door along with a large, well-worn sheathed knife that he drops in the bag as Teri closes it. "Sorry ma'am, I don't work for you, or anyone else that calls me 'boy' in that tone." With those words, all three run out to the barn meeting Eric who is coming at a jog from the Foreman's house, with a set of bulging saddle bags that include Tony's old revolver.

***

The excitement of travel by rail was missing despite the novelty. While all three had little experience on trains, they were lost in whispering to each other as the passenger car swayed and clicked along the rails. Eric was looking at the schedule, 'Teri, Michelle, we arrive in Butte at night, and we need a place to stay."

Michelle stays quiet and Teri states one problem. "But Eric, Miss Hathaway is always telling us that girls galivanting on their own are not welcomed in any real hotel because they might be girls of ill repute."

"Yeah, I've heard her. Sometimes when she's talking with Woody she says," here he dons a grimace and seeks to imitate Miss Jennifer Hathaway's voice, "those girls are as modest as tarts and are headed for trouble.'"

All three laugh at Eric's imitation of the maligned teacher.

After a moment, Eric considers the girls, "Teri, you and Michelle will hide your hair. In fact, before we get there put Michelle's hair up in a bun then hide it in those winter stocking caps. You'll also put on more clothing so that you both look like boys. Smear some dirt on your faces so that your skin looks rough. I'll rent the room for the three of us at a cheap place where they might not ask questions if I slip the clerk an extra dollar. We'll pretend we are brothers, and that our father will meet us there after his work as a consulting engineer at the Anaconda Mine."

Miles clatter by while they iron out those details, and then Eric comes to the crux of the matter, "I still don't know how we'll find Tony. He should have taken his gun, that's the one I snagged."

"Eric," counters Teri, "you told me that in his first fight with Roger in the Silver King, he wasn't wearing one. He prefers to fight with his fists."

"That's right Teri. Nice thing is that I have the revolver, but I still don't know how we'll find him."

The short haired brown eyed girl looks excited for a moment, "We'll pretend were his kids looking for him as Mom wants him home, and we'll go and ask around for him in the bars. One more thing. I think that the first thing we should do in Butte is get a room. Then we'll go looking for Tony."

All gesture their heads in concurrence. After a moment of quiet, while the few other passengers are not paying too much attention, Teri nods to her friend and says, "Now Michelle, let's go to the powder room and change into boys." Both giggle.

Discreetly Teri and Michelle leave Eric behind watching their seats, and venture to change into the dingy dark non-descript clothing they snagged in the cookhouse. Once the task is complete, none of the other passengers note them coming out in shabby well-worn dark clothing, and with dirty faces. Michelle's hair is out of sight under an ugly hat and winter coats hide their other feminine features. Eric even does a double take before smiling. He will be the older brother.

As to Butte it is a rich mining town, but as that wealth is fully controlled by corporate interest, poor clothing on immigrant miners or their kids will not arouse any curiosity. Thus, the disguise is perfect.

***

Eric pushes the battered front door of a cheap hotel in the heart of town and walks on a threadbare carpet. The grand foyer of the hotel chosen by the orphans as the most probable one to get a place to sleep is not very clean, nor is it in one of the newer buildings. Yet it holds the promise of rooms that might have more than one bed with its brick clad exterior and three floors. At the counter, in the still dark and dank lobby, Eric's voice sounds out of sorts as he walks to the front desk. Michelle and Teri hang back, as the shy younger brothers.

"Can we have a room with two beds please?"

The disheveled clerk behind the short, battered counter at the rundown Hotel Harris in Butte stares at the kid who wants a room. The little brat is in dirty ranching clothing and doesn't really have to shave yet. And his two brothers standing back shyly are definitively sissies with their limp hands and smooth yet dirty skin. Well, the standing order is to send any whores packing, but they don't cover this scenario. He frowns at this trio.

"You isn't old enough. So, get lost." That should send them packing.

"Dad will be here shortly, he had to go to the mine, and he told us to get a room here and wait for him."

The clerk glares at the lad. "What are you, dense or persistent? Anyway, I don't buy your story, I need cash. Real money, now. Not when your father decides to come here from whatever tart he's with."

"I can pay now for the first night. Cash, and Dad told me to give you an extra dollar." Here Eric tosses a silver dollar in the air and catches it deftly.

Avarice glints in the clerk's eyes, he perks up a bit. "Let me see it."

Eric opens his palm, and flashes two silver dollars. The man behind the counter reaches for them. Eric closes his hand and pulls it back. The clerk shoots him a greedy calculating look. "I want another dollar to give you a room with two beds."

Smiling, Eric counters, "I'll give you an extra four bits."

Eric digs in his pocket and takes out a fifty-cent piece. The pale faced man nods approval and reaches with scrawny hands and grabs all three coins. He sneaks two of the coins into a pocket of his dirty trousers and pats them in place. Only one silver dollar goes into the shallow drawer. He grabs a short pencil and stabs his finger into a dirty ledger. "Room 31, sign here."

Eric signs "Frank Jameson and additional guest sons Derrick, Terry, and Mitch."

The clerk does not look twice. The girls see the names and nod. It is as they discussed on the train. Close enough to their real names that if one makes a mistake, it should be easier to cover the faux pas. Finally, the three troop up the creaking wooden stairs to the third floor of the cheaply built hotel to claim their rundown lodging. The door is thin, and the room reveals beds that are sagging, a grimy window with a scenic view of a neighboring rooftop chimney belching smoke, all complimenting the brick wall of a taller building. In short, the room is cold and dirty, and not worth one dollar a night. But it will have to do, and it gives them a base from which to search for Tony.

Eric looks at the disappointed girls and voices the next step of their plan. "OK, we'll hide the rifles under the mattress, and dump everything else on top of the bed. I'll bring Tony's gun, tucked away so it's not visible and we'll get a bit of food in a cheap restaurant. Then we'll start checking all the bars."

Teri looks up from her bag, hiding her disenchantment at the first hotel room to ever greet her, "There's a lot of them. Must be an easy hundred saloons and bars and that's not counting the ones connected to brothels in the red-light district."

Eric is startled but does not bite, "Yeah, I noticed. We won't need to check those. Tony is here to get information. I wonder if we could safely split up?"

"I propose Michelle and I do one side of the street, while you, Eric do the other. I can pass as a boy, and Michelle can be my younger brother, and she can watch my back."

Eric hesitates and thinks out loud, "I don't like it. It's a rough town. You'll see and hear stuff you shouldn't."

Teri smirks, "Eric, since when did you become Miss 'nice little girls shouldn't know this stuff' Hathaway?"

Eric lowers his head in guilt and grumbles to hide his embarrassment. He changes back to the important subject, "You win, after dinner we'll split up but check with each other before moving on to the next block. But now, let's eat. I am famished."

Teri teases him, "Eric, you're hungry. Why I never would have guessed. I don't think I've ever seen you worry about a meal before."

A quick dinner, that includes preparing the questions they plan to use in the bars is on the menu. So armed, the trio walks south on Main Street rehearsing and work their way North. Eric recaps the game plan as they prepare to enter the first saloon looking for the Irishman. "We look for Tony, by describing him, and we assume that he was last asking questions yesterday evening sometimes. If the bartender is chatty, or we find someone who is talkative and seems somewhat trustworthy, we mention that he was looking for J. K. as he wanted to discuss business with him."

Teri adds, "Tony's our father, and mom is sick, so we need him at home."

Then begins a long night. Getting anyone to answer or even finding someone with the time to listen to a question or two is difficult. Eric and the two girls meet at the end of every block, and sometimes one or the other must wait. The moon has set, and all three are tired and stinking of cheap booze, cigarette and pipe tobacco. Worse yet are the cigars, and the unwashed bodies retching of cheap booze. A couple times, individually, one of them have their tail pinched, and they glare at the guilty before retreating out of the bar, leaving the obnoxious patron behind. However, overall, the working men taking a moment for a drink and to socialize, are polite and want to help the children.

At the corner of Main and Broadway, Eric looks at the fatigue in Teri's face, and the dismay in Michelle's. "Let's both do one more block, and at the next intersection we will call it a night and try our luck in the morning."

"Eric," counters Teri, "We need to cover at least two more. Why don't we run another hour and finish whatever block we are on."

Michelle stays quiet but nods her head in agreement with Teri. Eric sees this, and answers, "OK, we'll run to eleven, and then finish whatever block we are on."

Later, the boy looks at a clock in the bank and sees that it is only quarter to eleven. The girls have just gone into a saloon on Main at the intersection with Granite. So, Eric goes east on Granite to try one more bar and forces his back straight as he walks into another establishment. The bartender watches the lad, and is about to boot him out, when Eric interrupts his words, "I'm looking for my father, he's Irish and quite stout. He was wearing ranching clothing and was trying to track down J. K. for a job. Mom's sick, and I need to bring him home."

The bartender stops and looks at the lad. Not much family resemblance. Possibly a tall tale, but that name. Again. He looks around him, and notes that none are paying him any attention and the background noise coupled with the self-playing piano will drown out his words.

"I wouldn't mess around with Keegan. He plays for keep." Here the barkeep looks around, and grabs Eric's shoulder and points him to the door. As he is unobserved, he continues in a quiet voice, "I think I saw him, as I was closing and it was dark. He was going east on Granite and he had his hands behind him and a couple burly men 'escorting' him. I'd be careful if I were you. Now get out, while you can," so saying, the bartender grabs Eric's arm and tosses him out the door. As the boy looks back, the bartender points East. "That way." Then Eric finds himself alone on the boardwalk, looking at the closed door. He debates his next action and recalls that he is off track, and the girls must be waiting. And its late.

He spies the girls shivering waiting for him on the corner, outside in the dim yellow light cast by a streetlight and away from their last bar that was a futile stop. Eric comes running up.

"I've got to talk to you, but let's find a warm spot where we can get some coffee and maybe a slice of pie." So, saying, he points to a small eatery across the street. The trio walks into the establishment.

"Three coffees and three slices of apple pie please,"

"Bit young to be out at night, and a bit young for coffee, aren't we," and then after a momentary hesitation, the waitress adds the word, "boys?"

'Dad's working late," answers Eric blushing a bit. "And we're hungry, why I could eat a horse."

The waitress smiles, "I know, and chase the rider. Three pies it is, with a bit of cream and three hot chocolates instead of coffee?"

As she steps away, the three-huddle close together and whisper. Eric starts in, "He was seen, and J. K. or this man called Keegan is said to play for keeps. So, we have to think. He was being marched east on Granite, 'escorted' by a couple burly men. Town peters out fast in that direction, as you get into mining operations. We'll look carefully. But I think we should go back to the hotel first."

With wide eyes, Teri guesses, "You mean to get the rifles?"

"Yes, but also, I want to get a couple chocolate bars so we'll get everything, and Michelle, we may want you as a girl."

"Now?" asks the bewildered long-haired blonde.

"No, but have everything ready. We don't know where Tony is, but we may have to check some buildings. We can sneak around and maybe get shot, or you can go as a girl with a made-up story like someone from J. K.'s office asked you to bring them some chocolate bars as it is cold and they're working hard."

They snarf the last of their snack, Michelle being a bit slower to finish than the other two. Eric bounds into the hotel with Michelle, while Teri watches out of sight by the front door. Within a minute they bound down the creaky steps, and the same clerk yells at them.

"Where are you going with that bag at this hour?"

Eric barks back as he leaps out the door with Michelle, "Dad asked for some clean clothing. He got stuck and soaked in a wet dirty shaft in the mine and wants to change."

Keeping to the shadows, the three youths bound up the street and turn east on Granite. Here they slow, and Teri brings them to a stop as she has an inspiration. "It's a long shot, but we should spread out and look for signs of Tony. He may somehow have left a trail or sign or something. Move along, but look closely."

With these words, the three spread out, footsteps now drowned out by the noises of the Anaconda mine nearby. Teri holds the large carpet bag with the loaded rifles, and Eric clutches Tony's revolver under his coat. The last bars are left behind them, and only a faded moon casts a feeble glow on the mud, ice- and snow-covered road. Eric and Teri are impatient, while Michelle tarries a bit behind, shivering a bit despite her coat. Paying little attention, she nearly stumbles into a half-frozen horse watering trough near the last old storefront that gives way to open churned terrain. She slips, and falls.

In an urgent low sound, she exclaims, "Eric, Teri, come here."

She points, and all three see a familiar leather pocket flask.

Eric looks around foolishly and pulls out Tony's revolver.

Teri recovers first, "Eric, hide that."

Michelle reaches for the prized flask. Reverently she lifts it into the cold moonlight. All three stare at it. The flask is a newer one, and just about empty. Scratched in the leather is an upside-down Y. Eric reverently states the obvious. "That's got to be Tony's."

Their eyes scan the area. Not much left beyond the building by the water trough. It is a rundown store that has seen better days, but there is a lantern burning in the back room. Michelle stares at it and in a scared voice says, "I guess it's my turn." She takes off her hat, drops her hair, braids it real fast and ties a couple large bows. "Well, do I look like Michelle?"

The other two nod yes.

With those words she walks up and knocks. Teri and Eric dash out of sight, but with the boy again pulling the revolver. Quietly, Teri pulls her new rifle and feeds a round into the chamber.

There is no answer. Michelle knocks again, and the lantern inside moves. The door creaks open, and an old woman bundled in a heavy coat looks down at Michelle, "Yes?"

Michelle stammers, "I was sent by J.K. to bring you a snack."

Mystified the old lady looks at the long-haired girl. "We stay away from J.K., I don't think he'd give us anything." She turns to the back, and calls, "Harold, come here."

More steps, and a geriatric man limps into the doorway. These could not be guards. Why they are hard pressed to walk. There is no way that they can be holding a prisoner. Michelle flashes her most innocent smile and says, "I'm sorry to have disturbed you, but I think I have the wrong address."

Looking over his spectacles, Harold replies, "Well little lady, you should be getting home and to bed." With these words, he closes the door, and Michelle slowly drifts around to the side of the building away from any windows. One moment later, the three-huddle shivering in the cold. Again.

Eric points, "Well, the only thing away from town this way is that building over there." All three look at a strongly built weathered tar paper covered structure beside a slapped in rail spur. There is a feeble light in the one window. Eric looks back to the girls, and hastily plans. "Michelle, can you do it again? This time let's position ourselves. The back of that building is dark and has no windows. Let's go there, plan, and then Teri and I will be ready to help if needed."

The girls nod their heads, and all three carefully go around to the back of the structure, staying away from the lone window. The muted sounds of the round the clock mining activities, and the rumble of a nearby mill cover any noise they make. For a couple minutes, they huddle at a whisper. With their dark clothing, they blend in with the wet tar papered and weathered wood of the old mine building.

"Michelle, you knock. Teri will cover the window with the rifle, and I'll be close to the door with the revolver." As he says these words, Eric reaches into the bag, and pulls Hardy's knife. He looks at the blonde girl, reaches under her coat, and places it in the inside pocket. "Have this handy so at least you'll have something. If that's where Tony is being held, his guard won't be there because he's a nice guy."

Chapter 21

Melee

Tony shivers in his dank cold cell. The coffee can, now well used, stinks as does his prison. He was told to pour it out himself. Brogan laughed as he said, "There's a mouse hole in the corner, pour out your piss carefully so you keep your cell clean. If you want to, you can try pissing directly in the hole, but that's hard to do considering where it's located and how we have you in the dark."

To the best of Tony's judgement, it's been close to twenty-four hours since he was locked up. No food, one jug of water. So, his stomach growls and it's obviously late night, again. He lies quietly on his bed when a large something prowls on the outside wall. Listening carefully as he snoozes, he can very faintly hear Eric coming to his rescue in his dreams. "Michelle, ... I'll be close to the door ... revolver."

Startled he sits up. They're out there. My God, how did they find him? What great kids. Damn. He needs to do something to help. Now. Before Brogan can hurt them.

What?

He rolls off his bed and in a swift move reaches for the bedposts. Any noise is lost to the background racket of a mining town that never sleeps. He goes to the cell door and hears a knock on the front door.

Brogan moves. "Who's there?"

A girl's voice answers, "J.K.'s office sent me to bring you something."

Using one of the bedposts, Tony climbs to the grate and looks out just in time to see the door open. Michelle is there alone. Scared. What the hell? What kind of a rescue is this?

Brogan stares at the girl as if she were a ghost. The very white-faced lassie addresses the gruff warder in a soft innocent voice, "Hi, I was asked to bring you these chocolate bars by someone from J.K.'s office."

Brogan continues to stare open mouthed and does not close the door behind her. From a small satchel she pulls out a couple newfangled Hershey milk chocolate bars. He sees them and shakes his head like a mad bull who has just been struck in the forehead by a little heifer with a dandelion. Even as dense as he is, Brogan is astonished.

He says to both himself, and the shy trembling girl, "This doesn't feel right. John doesn't send chocolate bars out in the middle of the night. Who the hell are you?"

Quick as a snake, his arm whips out and his large right hand grabs the girl's neck. He pulls the frail girl towards him. He snarls, "What the hell are you?" Michelle smells his unwashed body and his alcohol tainted breath. Brogan feels her frail windpipe in the claw like grip of his right hand. He holds her. The little harlot is much lighter than expected, and he gropes her with his left. "You're a little tart, why you can't be older than thirteen or fourteen. Who sent you? Are you with that scum in there?" So, saying he points to the cell door, and his eyes open wide.

Eric jumps into the doorway pointing Tony's pistol. Brogan senses him, and whirls back around dropping Michelle. She reaches in her coat and pulls Hardy's knife unseen by Brogan. Eric hesitates, scared to fire and endanger Michelle.

The beefy man looks at his sudden foe, gropes for his own gun, and pulls it. He is kicked from behind by the long-haired blonde girl as he takes a fast shot at Eric. He misses. The bullet lodges itself above the lad's head in the door jamb. Eric throws himself through the doorway.

Tony's voice echoes into the front room, "I'm coming."

A loud crack reverberates throughout the building as Tony batters the door with the bedpost using all his might. It does not open.

Eric, now on the floor, seeks to aim.

Michelle's kick and Eric's intrusion and Tony's pounding confuse Brogan. His fist lashes out at the girl. He misses as she bounds back into the wall. He turns and again aims for the armed rescuer on the floor. The girl is not the primary threat. Michelle lunges forwards and slashes out with the sharp knife. It cuts deep through Brogan's jacket. The blade sinks into his broad muscled right shoulder. Brogan howls in pain and drops the gun. With his left, he delivers a hard slap that knocks the feisty bitch flat across the room.

Eric finally pulls the trigger, and his first shot misses.

Another large crash on the inside of the cell door. Again, Tony shouts like a demented berserker, "I'm coming."

Brogan turns, confused by the multitude of attackers. He snags his gun off the floor with his uninjured left. He seeks to aim it at one of the assailants. He chooses Tony and the cell door, assessing that the Irishman is a greater threat than the multitude of brats pestering him.

Tony screaming "I'm coming" smashes a bedpost with all his might seeking to bash his way out of his cell, again.

The sound of the post hitting the cell door reverberates like a drum. Brogan's first shot hits true, but Tony is to the side readying another blow. The second bullet cleaves through the door's latch.

Already, the jailor hears a new danger. Breaking glass and a rifle pokes into the room from the lone window. Brogan turns and fires his third shot with his awkward left hand, while his right arm flounders in pain.

That rifle shoots.

The bullet hits Brogan's right shoulder.

Eric, on the floor, fires point blank. A puff in the dirty jacket on the torso is his reward.

Tony smashes through the door, foaming at the mouth. It splinters.

The rifle barks, again. The shot is true. Another hit to the torso. Brogan swivels, staggers, falls and faces the two kids from the floor. He sees Eric, lifts his left hand, and fans off a wild shot.

Tony claws his way into the room like a demented bear swinging the bedpost as a club. On the wooden floor, Brogan's arm lifts the revolver. The frenzied Tony, spittle flying from his snarling mouth, smashes his makeshift club onto his jailor's head with a thud. The crazed Irishman lifts his club again, and swings to the left side, and the violent blow crushes Brogan's left arm just below the shoulder.

Eric lowers his handgun. Michelle lowers the knife. White faced Teri dashes in, frantically working the lever action on her rifle for a possible third shot.

All is quiet.

Brogan lies there unseeing in his thick winter clothing, with multiple wounds. The jailor is dead. On a cold floor in a dimly lit room at the edge of town, with the noise of the battle having merged with the sounds of the Anaconda Mine whose hard-working headframe is but a few hundred feet away. The four Walking Ys look at each other, amazed at being alive. The multi-pronged attack worked. Then reality sinks in.

Eric, shaking, speaks first. "God, that's awful." He replaces the revolver in its holster under his coat, and reels to the door, greedily gulping air.

Teri staggers and lowers her rifle listlessly, all color draining from her face. She teeters to the corner and leans against the wall and bends over retching, her body convulsing. "Oh God," she moans. "Oh God, help me."

Michelle gawps in horror at the accusatory blood on her hand. She wipes it in revulsion on the dark coat she snagged in the cookhouse. Tears form and streak her color drained face. She hands the knife and sheath Hardy gave her, that now repulsive pair, to Teri who secures it out of habit, and squirrels it out of sight, deep in her jacket.

Tony recovers first. He looks around at the chaos and walks over to Brogan. He quickly searches the gangster and snags whatever he can find. With a bit of wonder, he finds himself looking at a handful of twenty-dollar double eagles. He also pulls a business card that reads J. K. & Associates. He pockets Brogan's gun, and then looks around at the poorly kept room and spies his boots, socks, belt and coat. Shivering he tosses them on and then rapidly scavenges a couple broken pieces of wood from the door he battered and wedges them across the window.

He lowers the flame in the lantern and turns to the orphans who have remained mired in their turmoil. He looks from one to the other, and states firmly, "I'll have to pray, as I killed the poor sod with that club. I shouldn't have hit him twice, that was morbid. The gunshot wounds hurt him, but were not fatal, being as they went into the shoulder and arm."

He hopes his words sink in a bit, and then he barks, "We've got to get out of here. Now."

With this command, he points to the door, and urges the youths' forwards. Teri and the others, in a trance of pained emotions, ignore him and remain in the center of the room. They stare down at the still warm cadaver, drowning in an emotional tsunami. Tony glances at each one of the young white faces, seeking to penetrate their consciousness. He tries again, talking clearly and slowly, "As I said, I hit him bloody hard. I heard his head snap. Sorry to tell you this, I am the one who killed him. It was that, or see you die trying to rescue me. Now we have to leave. The police here work for the mines, and this is John Keegan's town where he pushes for the mining companies' interest against the workers. We don't want to be caught."

The others continue to stare mesmerized.

Tony points to the door again and orders. "Out now. Go behind the building. Get whatever stuff you have outside and stash your weapons. We've got to catch a train out of here now. John Keegan has more than one man working for him, and in this town, he also probably has the law on his side." He very gently pushes the inert young ones towards the door.

"Move. Now! Those shots could have been heard."

His order penetrates the orphans' minds. All shamble out into the darkness, and gravitate behind the building, instinctively away from any accusatory eyes. Tony, the last one out, checks Brogan's body again and makes it a point to leave the jailor's wallet and silver in the man's pockets. Perhaps fewer questions that way. Carefully, he kills the lantern, and closes and locks the door and tosses the key in the snow and mud, some distance away. He walks a few feet and looks back. All looks normal despite the violence, and nothing seems amiss on this dark night in the loud mining town of Butte.

Once he joins the orphans, he leads them away from the abandoned mining structure, following rails for a while and then turns them all downhill looking for churned tracks or bare ground. After a few minutes, he steers them back into town, and slows to talk. "We'll go to the depot. Is there anything essential you forgot in town? Anything that will identify who you are?"

"I don't think so," Eric replies looking at the girls. "We brought everything from the hotel when we found your flask."

"Brave lad and lassies, you found it. I was hoping you would."

While Tony says these words, Eric stops. The others do the same, and Eric digs into his pocket and produces the prized flask. For the first time since freeing Tony, Eric sports a wan smile. Tony tries for a swig and finds very little in the way of solace.

"I'm going to make Woody fill it. He owes us. Now let's get back to the Walking Y."

With these words, the four of them begin the long walk to the south side of town and the large depot awaiting them there. There are still several hours left in what is a long sleepless night. That dirty hotel room will stay empty with the beds made and nothing much to show for their passage or silver. Sometimes past three in the morning, a bedraggled exhausted crew staggers up to the railroad station, only to find it closed and locked. A faded sign, barely legible in the glow of a dimmed lantern states that it will only open at five, and the first train is half an hour later. Thus, they must sit on a wooden bench outside, shivering, snoozing, and reliving the melee in that mining shed.

The minutes pass slowly. Their minds still seeking to comprehend the clash that left Brogan's body on the floor. Now fear joins the guilt. Has the cadaver been found? Will it be found before the train arrives? All fight fatigue and the need to sleep. Slowly the children doze off, crowded together on the bench for warmth on a freezing dank night.

Tony sits up sharply and looks around in a panic. The others wake. He looks at Eric white faced and frantically inquires, "Good God, I forgot to ask you, what name did you use at the hotel?"

Eric, sharper than one would expect considering the gunfight and the lack of sleep pauses for a while before answering. "Why Tony, we signed Woodrow W. Flynt, Seamus Patrick O'Connor and William Bell the Third."

Tony's entire body sags.

Eric chuckles. The strange sound is amplified by a light laughter from the two girls. Tony audibly gasps, the girls laugh harder as the Irishman croaks out, "That's not funny. They'll check the hotel registers when they find Brogan and track us down."

"Seriously," replies Eric smiling despite the stress of the last few hours. "Teri and Michelle and I discussed this on the train, coming here to get you. We used names that could be confused for our first names, and as we mentally had you as our father, we used yours." The lad watches Tony's face seeking to comprehend. The foreman's face sags. The lad continues, "but we called you Frank Jameson to make you look like an Irish protestant. Frank!"

Tony smiles wanly. "I should have known you brats would pull my leg a bit. I deserve it. My turn now, I have both good news and bad news. Which do you want first?"

"The good." Michelle says instinctively while yawning and shivering wondering if the accusatory blood was still visible on her hands.

"I know who is behind that buffalo gun. That would be an Irish scallywag by the name of Festus O'Leary. Regrettably, he and I go back a long way. The good news is that he thinks I am a coward, so he might underestimate what we can do."

"And the bad?" counters Teri.

"He and his sidekick Mack are on their way to Hellenville now. They have a head start on us. I expect they will strike later this morning. So, we have to sleep on the train and be ready for trouble as we arrive home.

With those words, the exhausted group hear the depot stir to life. Shivering, they enter the warming main waiting room, and snag benches right beside the glowing potbellied stove. Tony uses Brogan's gold to purchase tickets to a rail junction, where he will purchase another set. Painfully, he watches the minutes tick by as he awaits their departure. The orphans snooze exhausted anticipating escape on the first train of the day.

Chapter 22

<u>Woody's temper</u>

Woody stands imperiously in the kitchen by the large oaken dining room table on another cold Montana evening. He glares around the room while a cowed Fred and a cautious Nick munch on their dinner not even tasting another excellent meal that tonight regrettably comes with a side of guile. Strenuously, they avoid making eye contact with the irritated owner, and they close off their ears to the rising voices that threaten their world - even more so than the disappearance of Eric, Teri, and Michelle. Woody leans forwards on his feet and glowers at the cook.

In a nasty voice that brokers no good will, he continues in a bellicose tone, "What did you say James? Jennifer tells me that you helped Eric, and the girls leave on the afternoon train. What in tarnation makes sense about helping them go to Butte to rescue Tony, who's nothing but a lying drunken low-down double-crossing Irishman. That lout told me he was going to Missoula for a couple days for a meeting with The Irish Brethren. He did not tell me he was going to Butte to track down that murdering low down skunk, John Keegan."

James Hardiman does not flinch under Woody's onslaught, nor does he seem particularly perturbed. "Woody," he answers forcefully without yelling, "you told me when I agreed to come here that I was to use my head. I did, and I have no regrets. When you sit down and eat your dinner like a good boy and rein in your temper, I will explain my logic."

Woody puffs out a bit, as even Jennifer lowers her head to make herself small. "My Miss Jennifer Hathaway told me that you ignored her efforts to stop the three of them, and that you were impolite when she made the mistake of calling you 'boy'. She also tells me that you ignored the logic of her position. What the hell has gotten into you 'boy'?"

Hardy momentarily looks furious but controls his emotions within less than a second. Turning his head slightly, he replies in a dangerous tone, "You call me that again in that tone Woody, and I'll knock you down a peg or two. You might not remember, but I have done it in the past when you needed it, and I can do it again. In fact, that's why you're alive. Now, if it weren't for the fact that you and your crew need me here more than ever, I would walk out. But I know your temper. So, before you say another stupid word, I suggest you think for once, or go to your room and get past that tantrum of yours. You know as well as I do that it's gotten you into deep trouble more than once, and if you keep it up, I won't be around to beat sense in your thick skull."

Jennifer looks stunned. There is obviously more to this relationship than meets the eye.

Woody sways as he stands at his place. In a low voice he mutters, "I don't have to take this from you or from anybody."

With those words he steps away from the table and stomps out the main door. He slams it shut, and one pane falls to the floor and shatters. The owner does not hear it, and heads to the cold cabin his father built just to the North of the cookhouse, and where he has occasionally slept since the orphans arrived and turned his world upside down. It seems to be his safe refuge.

Hardy watches him go and smiles lightly. "Now, that wasn't so bad. A moment alone will cool that bull like sulk of his, and he'll be better off. Nick, Fred, you'd better both eat well, because with the others away, you're going to have to work twice as hard. Woody will get past this, and I'll help feed."

In the kitchen Jennifer stands, scared as her protector stomps out like a small boy in a temper tantrum. She looks around the table and faces eyes accusing her of stoking a dangerous fire, namely Woody's temper. Sheepishly she mutters to no one in particular, "Oh, how I hate violence and fighting."

Hardy looks up sharply. "Well, if you hate violence, you sure have a tendency to stir up plenty of strife and you have since you've been here. Perhaps you should look in a mirror." Nick and Fred nod their heads in agreement.

Jennifer stares from one face to the next. None offer comfort. She hunches down in her chair, hurt by the truth and the role for which she is amply paid. She mulls eating the excellent pot roast that lies steaming in her bowl. She breathes in deeply, and the smell of Hardy's home-made buttermilk biscuits tickle her nostrils. She hesitantly takes a bite while seeking to regain composure. With this act, the two boys dig in a bit more. They have not finished their work that day, as they still need to ride a possibly dangerous patrol after dinner, and the next day promises both a morning feed run and another in the afternoon along with more patrols. And that is if everything goes well. Which it usually doesn't.

In that quiet lull after she finishes her portion of pot roast and biscuits, Jennifer puts her fork down, and looks around the table confused. To no one in particular, she begins, "This is hard and unfamiliar for me. It confuses me. Please excuse me if I take some time by myself. " With those words, Miss Hathaway leaves the table and walks to the living room and up the stairs.

The two boys look at each other, feeling their appetite shrivel. The large table now seems empty, and the wind outside blows snow around, and flakes and cold roll where there is now a missing pane. Nick shivers and looks at the only other person seated at the table, "Well Fred, if it weren't for the fact that we have a couple patrols, I think I would prefer to be studying history. It's cold out there."

Fred looks up. "I love history. I've asked Jennifer if she knows Latin because I'd like to learn it. Think, I could read Julius Caesar in exactly the language he wrote in, and ..."

His soliloquy is interrupted by a flying roll. Nick's aim is accurate. "Hurry up and eat. We have a patrol next, not an oration. I wonder if Woody will help?"

Hardy stops and looks at the lads. "Look, this is a tempest in a teapot. Sometimes one is needed to clear the air. I'll talk to Woody after he has had a few minutes, and I'll put something over that window. He's a good man, and I would follow him to hell. And I have. But as you might have noticed, he does have a temper, and he is a grouch."

With those words, Hardy places more food in front of the boys, shuffles around in the pantry and comes out with a bit of wood pried off a packing crate, a hammer and small nails. He patches the hole left by the missing pane. He then sweeps the floor and then snags his coat, winks at the boys, and walks out of the cookhouse.

In Woodrow's father's old cabin, the original building on the Walking Y, the owner lights a fire in the frigid old potbellied stove, as he has been staying upstairs in the cookhouse. The stout man paces while the room warms a bit, and then sits in thought. Minutes later, the door opens and Hardy steps in without bothering to knock. Woody looks around and does not say anything to the strong grey haired black man.

"Woodrow," begins Hardy, "If you'll listen now, I've got to explain why I didn't stop them. Eric was hot under the collar. In a way, he has your temper. I could have said 'NO' as much as I wanted to, and he would have gone off anyway. This way, he left with backup, bags properly packed, and food. He also left with a couple girls who like to think and aren't as hot headed as him, and that might just save his life. As for Tony, he wants to solve that J. K. mystery. He figured that we could wait here and get shot from half a mile away by someone with a heavy buffalo gun, or he could try to get information and take the fight to them."

Woody spins around, "Don't you think I don't know all of that. Damn it Hardy, I have you here to keep them safe, and Eric has his favorite horse, his companion, shot out under him. I couldn't stand it if I had to bury that lad. And those girls, do they think this is a lark? Whomever is behind that buffalo gun is a killer. Whomever ordered and paid for him is a killer, whatever lost soul he has as a sidekick is also a killer. Just last month, Roger wanted to rape and mutilate those two girls."

Here Woody brings his heavy flannel shirt sleeve to his eyes and clears them as he stares at Hardy. "They're just little girls. I should never have taken them in. All I have done is use them as gun fodder to try and selfishly save this ranch. My father worked like a dog building it with blood and sweat, and he gave it to me, and we are going under anyway. I am so God awfully mad, I could scream in frustration. Any time someone comes to the house, I'm thinking 'Now What'."

Hardy looks at the twisted face. "Woody, those kids wouldn't change a thing. They hated that orphanage, and here they're alive. You can't lock them up. Anyway, didn't you tell me that, and I quote:

> *'You can't keep a boy away from horses with a bit of spirit any more than you can keep him away from girls. Yes, they're both dangerous, but you can't keep a boy away from either and expect him to grow up.'"*

Here Hardy pauses to let the words sink in, "I'll add, it's the same thing for girls. Raising them is also giving them the room to grow, and hopefully not make too many bad mistakes. But you have to respect their judgement. That is essential. Look, when we were young, you and your father fought like demented tigers. He was a strong man, and often he didn't give you room to grow. So, you ran. You're worried about the girls. Well, I am also, so I gave Teri and Michelle my knife. You know, the one I had when we were young. The one that saved us more than once when we were both runaways. Now come on, everyone here needs you to have a strong back."

Here he looks at Woody and adds with a twinkle in his eyes, "Even Jennifer."

Woody looking sad replies softly, "You don't need me to have a strong back."

"Well Woody, I do, but not in the same way. Being here is making me young again. So much so, that I'll help with the patrols and cattle feeding runs till we have a full crew. I'll take one patrol with you tonight for old times sakes, and we can let those two boys sleep. That said, I think we should have them in the cookhouse tonight."

Hesitantly Woody puts on his coat and goes back to the cookhouse. Hardy goes upstairs and gently knocks at Jennifer's door. She listens to him from behind her door, "If you would join us for dessert, it will bring us together for a bit. Woody and I have had a chance to clear the air, and he understands why I couldn't listen to you. If you come down, I will calmly explain everything to you, as you have the right to know. Also, by joining us you will help the old man."

Jennifer steps into the hallway with puffy eyes, and hesitantly walks down the stairs behind Hardy to join the group at the table. Once seated, with Hardy calmly manning the stove, Woody looks around at the quiet group, and says, "You know, I've already told this to Fred and Nick and the other orphans. 'Old grouches are grouchy, and if I act that way, you are to give me a cup of coffee without the cup, as that will cure me.' Any questions?"

All remain quiet. He darts a knowing glance to Jennifer and adds with a smile, "That does not apply to you, because you would."

Jennifer laughs a bit and the cloud of discord lifts. With gusto, the dessert is devoured, tales are told over tea and coffee. The work schedule and the menu are revised so that Fred and Nick can also have some lessons with Miss Hathaway, while Hardy can leave the confines of the cookhouse for patrols with Woody. Miss Hathaway on the other hand inherits the dishes and the preparation of a couple of meals.

***

Tony looks at the wan faces on the train with him, when Michelle voices the universal concern. "Good God, I can't wait to be home. I hope all is well there."

The Irishman stares about and again notes that their chosen seat, against the polished oaken end of the car with a coal burning stove on the other side of the aisle means that as long as the seat ahead of them stays empty, none should be able to overhear them. Looking at the schedule in his hand, he grumbles, "I hate to say this, but this rail line was built by English idiots who handed off the scheduling to their pampered brats. Not only do we have to change trains in Helena, but we are also on a milk run so we won't get there until next year."

"What's a milk run?" inquires Teri while fighting fatigue and the nightmare of that rifle bucking in her hand and watching that Brogan swirl in surprise as the slug hit him. Eric is also looking at Tony perplexed.

"Yes, that means that this train stops at every single solitary siding between here and Helena to get milk. It'll be the slowest train of the day. In fact, it's slower than a covered wagon. There are a couple cars up front with empty metal milk jugs, and they pick up full ones with milk from the farmers along the route and drop off the empties. The only good thing is that no self-respecting scoundrel running from the law would be foolish enough to take such a slow train. So, we should be safe."

As the sun rises, and the train moseys along, Eric looks up from under his hat where he had buried his face to sleep and catches the Irishman's attention. "Hey Tony, does that schedule tell us when we might eat?"

"We have an hour in Helena. I propose we wash up in the bathrooms, and then get a good meal before the next leg thankfully on a faster train."

Eric nods ascent, and none of the others have the mental or physical energy to reply. The train stops again, and a farm buckboard is on the side of the tracks with two draft horses looking bored and a burly farmwife getting ready to heft milk jugs. "Look at that, can you imagine raising milk cows. You'd never have a moment of rest."

Teri looks up and tiredly counters, "You mean just like us and the daily feeding runs, chores, getting firewood, and patrols. That is if you do not count Miss 'that's not acceptable behavior for a young lady' Hathaway?" The train resumes its forward speed and must reach a good twenty miles per hour before the next stop.

Daylight is coming to a close by the time they reach Hellenville and stagger off a late afternoon train. The exhausted Walking Y crew looks at the platform with disappointment. No one is waiting for them.

"That's funny," muses Tony as they stand around somewhat stumped, "I sent a telegram from Helena. Woody or Hardy should be here."

Chapter 23

<u>J. K.'s Fling</u>

All except for Miss Hathaway on the Walking Y are getting ready after lunch to go back out for chores and work as Tony, Eric, Michelle, and Teri mosey on the milk run out of Butte. Woody and Hardy are bundling up for their next patrol. The preparation for a long afternoon is interrupted by a knock at the door. A shadow is visible, but the ice crystals mean that as Hardy gets ready to opens the door, it flies open. Mrs. Couchman greets the surprised cook with her vintage pasted-on smile. Undetected and in the background, Jennifer's shoulders sag a bit. The governess forces a grin to her lips that does not take away from the troubled look in her eyes.

The General Store co-owner dismissively looks at the colored cook. In a tone that will broker no questions, she discharges him; "James, I have here some feminine items that would be foreign to you and are not of your concern. However, Miss Hathaway mentioned her needs the last time we met, and the order just came in on the late morning train. Being concerned about her welfare as the only true female in the house, I thought I would bring them."

With those words, Mrs. Couchman walks into the kitchen as Woody glowers as he would if a bad nickel landed in his hand. He grunts a curt, "Hello Mrs. Couchman," and walks out of the door with that "James" behind him who is now putting on his coat. Nick and Fred follow. Mrs. Couchman gives herself a cup of steaming coffee and sits herself importantly at the table while the boys now make their exit. Jennifer hesitantly joins her, leaving two chairs empty between them.

Mrs. Couchman looks around, and whispers. "I have John's telegram for you telling you this is the day, and I intercepted one for Woody. Looks like that drunken bum of a foreman is on his way back with Eric and all. I've already told John about that one. They're both in the bag with your feminine products. I can tell you that the comedy is coming to an end, and you soon will leave THIS place."

Jennifer's face sags a bit, and she looks around the room, sad.

Mrs. Couchman reaches over and pats Miss Hathaway's hand, "No need to worry my dear. It must have been brutal having to put up with that indecorous Mr. Woodrow W. Flynt. I don't know how you lasted this long or could stand getting close to that ill-mannered oaf. No one in town can stand him, and whatever happens it will serve both him and that drunken stump training Irish foreman of his, right. The kids, if they're not stupid, can go back to that orphanage in Idaho or get real work."

Mrs. Couchman takes a moment to sip her coffee and let Miss Hathaway regain her composure on what has been a miserable assignment. She finally resumes, "Mr. John Keegan has sent you special instructions as he plans to rid the county of Mr. Woodrow W. Flynt. He wanted me to tell you that your ongoing information and that my being your courier has been very helpful, and that he will give us both a special bonus when he brings this comedy to an end. I can see why you work with your uncle, who is quite the gentleman. He thinks of everything and is a generous soul."

A moment of silence passes, where Jennifer looks sad. "Yes, my uncle thinks of everything. He has kept me employed since I was a young girl not much older than Michelle or Teri. I have developed skills entrapping men to provide me with shelter and much money. Woodrow is a bit different than what I expected. Most men are rather shallow and focus on their immediate pleasures. Mr. Flynt is a bit more difficult, while he is a grouch, he has been more difficult."

Mrs. Couchman taps Jennifer's hand again. "Yes, he is difficult. I did not think anyone could get through that prickly personality of his, but you succeeded, and your uncle is proud of you. He has another engagement lined up in Albany in New York. That one is with someone close to the Governor there. You should be able to leave in the next day or two."

Jennifer greets the news with a sigh. Mrs. Couchman hears her, and cuts in, "I asked Mr. Keegan to give you a few days off in a spa, and I think that is just the ticket. You've done good work keeping John updated even if some of your dispatches were a bit boring, like having to teach those coarse ungrateful children, or putting up with that crude Irishman, and an ungrateful colored cook." Here Mrs. Couchman pries a bit, "But worse of all was having to get intimate with that awful Woodrow. That alone would drain anyone, and maybe even leave them feeling dirty. In fact, that's why I think a spa would be good to clean off the stench of this place. So, if you ask your Uncle John, I think he will give you a few days off along with your bonus. It'll be just the ticket to recover from these dreadful bores."

Miss Hathaway listens without a word. After a bit, she gets up and takes a cup of tea with a shaking hand, and asks in a quavering voice, "Can we please discuss the telegram and the last part of my role here?"

Mrs. Couchman beams and pulls out the crumpled paper and expands upon it, as she spent a luxurious hour with that gentleman, Mr. John Keegan. She talks on for a good half hour before taking her leave. Miss Hathaway watches the sulky take the storekeeper away, and sighs. The next hours might be the most difficult of her life, or at least the most difficult one since her parents were shot, and she fell into Uncle John's rapacious care.

***

It is a long ride to the far end of their sweep. Woody and Hardy look at the bulls from the fence line of the pasture. All is quiet, and Hardy takes out a small pouch of chewing tobacco enjoying the feel of the saddle and the clean winter air. He looks at his friend and comments.

"Well Woody, not much here. I wonder how the boys are doing with the feeding?"

Woody holds out his hand for quiet. Hardy can read the trouble in Woody's eyes and puts the pouch back into its pocket without taking any. He then slowly pulls the rifle out of his scabbard, and chambers a round. Woody does the same, and suddenly signals his horse to a forward leap into some cottonwoods. Hardy mimics his friend. In the shelter of the trees, Woody turns to Hardy and whispers. "A flock of birds flew up over half a mile away, to the North. There's something out there that shouldn't be there."

The cook, checking his rifle softly states, "Probably The Buffalo Gun."

"I agree, Hardy I don't know if he saw us. Let's split up and check. You take the right, I'll go left, and let's come in together over by the far fence in those woods, straight north."

Carefully, using the terrain to mask their approach, they each meander stealthfully to the designated spot. Within fifteen minutes they meet, and stare at unknown tracks that stopped about thirty yards from where they met. The horse prints then turned around and whomever it was is already headed back from whence they came. Dismounting, both men study the trail, and follow it for another thirty yards. The unknown rider dismounted and cleared the snow off a branch where he rested something. A rifle perhaps. Looking from the perch, Woody can see both the bull field, and the far end of their sweep. But no one fired. Woody spies a bit of wool snagged to the branch. Orange.

Woody looks stumped. "That's strange. No one trying to go unnoticed wears orange."

Hardy is quiet for a moment. Then carefully he looks at Woody, very serious. "It's as if he wanted us to see him, and this unknown rider wanted us to meander further from the cookhouse."

The owner barks, "Ride."

Both jump in the saddle, and ride as if the demons of hell were after them. To the cookhouse.

***

Nick and Fred feed fast. Nick's ability to talk the golden draft horses through the day's work means that both lads can focus on feeding in the straight line that minimizes wasted hay. Having two pitchforks constantly moving hay accelerates the process. While Fred is getting stronger, Nick's ability to focus on the pitchfork reduces Fred's workload. The two head back by midafternoon and aim for the large red barn and its eighty stalls which regrettably stand mostly empty.

Fred jokes, "Nick, that's the best time we've ever made on that feeding run. We must have shaved half an hour off the task." Both laugh. They turn to ranch headquarters along the tree lined drive as an unknown wagon leaves the cookhouse going the other way out towards the county road.

Nick chuckles lightly. "I bet you that's a food delivery and that Hardy knows that Eric 'I could eat a horse and chase the rider' is on his way back."

Fred voices a concern, "But Nick, you nearly eat as much as Eric. In fact, sometimes you eat more. But Hardy's out on patrol with Woody."

Nick looks serious, "Darn, I forgot. That's bizarre." Both boys reach for the rifles in the scabbards at the front of the sled. "You know, just in case."

Fred nods his head in agreement. Something about that wagon doesn't feel right. Momentarily, they are out of sight of the cookhouse. Thus, shielded from view, they stop the team and work the bolt of their rifles, making sure that each has a round in the chamber. Both lads have been practicing at Woody's insistence, and all the orphans now know how to use both bolt action as well as lever action rifles. Ready, they watch carefully and bring the team to the barn and in sight of the cookhouse. They keep the rifles out of sight, until they are behind that building, and the boys unharness the horses and release them without grooming them.

Then both walk back through the barn and exit behind the corral fencing. To keep a lower profile, they also use the milking shed and the blacksmith shop for cover. From that last building, they lunge across to the cookhouse, and barge into the kitchen with rifles at the ready, Nick in the lead as he is the better shot.

The tableau that greets them is anything but what they expect. Miss Jennifer Hathaway stands in the kitchen white faced. An unknown dark clad burly man with a bandage on his scalp holds an old navy Colt to her head. He smiles seeing their shock.

"All right kids, drop the guns, or she gets it."

Nick and Fred, open mouthed seeing Miss Hathaway being held captive, put their rifles on the table. "Don't hurt Miss Hathaway." Pleads the black-haired lad as he looks at her with concern. Nick eyes the burly man defiantly waiting for the next instructions.

He smirks, "Good boys, so you like your teacher. You'd better listen. Now lie down on the floor on your stomach. Spread eagle." The boys comply.

The burly man looks over and calls to another probable thug in the living room, "Mack, it worked. We'll tie them up."

Nick and Fred blanch as if punched in the gut when they both hear the brigand's next statement. "Jenny, nice acting. You really looked scared. Those little brats thought we'd shoot you." The second man walks into the room, and the bandit reholstering his colt turns to Mack and hears him stating, "Good thinking Cormac."

The boys lift their faces to see Jennifer Hathaway step away unharmed and obviously in cahoots with the brigands. She will not make eye contact with either of them. Fred grimaces in sorrow with tears soiling his young face. He looks her way, hoping for a miracle and cries out, "But Miss Hathaway, I believed in you. How could you?"

Mack hears the pain riven sorrow in the youngster's voice. He smiles and cannot resist mocking Fred. He looks at Cormac and rubs salt in the boy's mental wound. "Oh, little master Fred had his feelings hurt. Did you hear that Jenny," and creating a high pitch wine of a pre-pubescent boy mimics, "'But Miss Hathaway, I believed in you. How could you?'"

Both men laugh and Mack spits in the crying Fred's face. Nick tries to get up to defend his friend and gets kicked back down for his efforts. Mack barks, "When I tell you to behave, I mean it." Then he turns to the tightlipped Miss Hathaway, and mockingly baits her, "OK, Jenny, I know you can't stand the rough stuff, so I won't slice him open. At least not now. But hand me that rope on the chair."

With a pained expression on her face, Miss Jennifer Hathaway reaches for the rope and hands it to Mack. She then leaves the kitchen to avoid the accusatory eyes of the two lads. She hears Mack counting out the score. "Well, that's two down, and it leaves us two more who should come in about now if Festus did his part, which is a given. Then we have a few hours off before we get the other four."

Cormac is the quiet one. He just nods his head in approval. Mack sums up the task ahead, "Easy money. It's real nice to know their routine. It takes a lot of guess work out of this assignment, thank you Jenny for setting this up from the inside. Nothing like having our target work his way into our spy. You know, that's real nice. Now we can kill them without risking our neck. Stupid trusting suckers!"

He turns and yells into the living room, "Jenny, your Uncle John said you did a good job reporting everything that was going on. He's pleased with you, and I hear that he has another job lined up for you, back east somewhere. There's another dolt who needs to be ensnared."

Both men laugh. They harshly tie up the boys' hands behind their back and gag them tightly with their own bandanas that had been adorned around their necks. Mack looks over to his companion and barks "Cormac, we'll leave them tied up on their beds. They should rest for a while there, like a long while."

Chuckling, the two brigands proceed and order the boys upstairs. While Cormac moves favoring his right side with a limp, Fred's footsteps betray the fact that his hands are tied behind his back. Three times he stumbles, and Mack or Cormac take delight in administrating a swat for moving too cautiously. Once upstairs, kicks are added for good measure. Each is thrown face down on unmade beds, and their legs are tied together. Then, each is tightly bound to the metal bed frames.

Jennifer watches the boys being hauled upstairs and makes no comments. She simply sits in Woody's favorite chair looking deflated and exhausted and winces each time one of the lads gets a good smack. John Keegan's cohorts come downstairs laughing at the ease with which they disarmed the lads.

Cormac smiles and proposes how to deal with Woody and Hardy. "Why don't we hold Jenny at gun point when Mr. Woodrow W. Flynt and that James Hardyman walk in."

Mack nods his head, and adds, "We'll gag her for good measure, just in case she weakens like all females. It worked last time and should this next time. It looks like they all liked their little strumpet. We'll just tell them to drop their guns, or we shoot her. Those idiots will. And what I really like about it, is the reaction when they realize that Jenny is on our side. Think of Woody mimicking Fred, 'Oh, but Miss Hathaway, I believed in you. How could you?'"

Mack then smiles and sarcastically, he commands, "Hey Miss Jennifer Hathaway, come here. We need you one more time so that there is no shooting in this house, 'cause you don't like rough play. We'll try it again, but this time we'll gag you. Woody won't endanger you and Hardy, well he's just a colored cook, so not much danger there." So, saying, they begin to replicate the prior set up.

Meanwhile, Woody and Hardy make good time at a mile eating lope back. Instead of taking their horses to the barn, as they close in on headquarters, Woody proposes, "Hardy, why don't you take the horses, and

I'll go in the cookhouse. If I don't call you in, you know that they control the cookhouse."

Hardy mulls it over. "Well, that is the opposite of any military doctrine, which is not to fritter away your forces, but I see no option. We don't know what's going on at headquarters, and we can't see inside the cookhouse. The only option I see is that we reverse the order. I go in, and you get the horses."

Woody mulls his answer. "No, the way I look at it, they will underestimate you. Leaving you behind won't sound like a plan but will look more like I am treating you as an underling. So, you go to the barn. Your best approach to the cookhouse is out the back of the barn…"

"Woody, I know. I'll try to sneak in. But it's not a given I can make it. I'll obviously come carefully. That is if you don't give me the all-clear."

With these words, both ride up to the cookhouse, and Woody jumps off his horse. Hardy then leads both animals to the barn, looking like a pure picture of servitude. Woody, delays going in for a minute while Hardy covers the ground to the barn and walks in. The owner then opens the door into the cookhouse and enters the kitchen.

There, he finds Jennifer Hathaway tied, gagged, and bound to a chair, and a smiling Mack barely visible behind the wall partition going to the living room. Woody throws himself to the floor and rolls behind the table while snagging his pistol in his right hand. He fires a quick round into the doorjamb before Mack has a chance to say a word. He then crawls into the pantry and fires another round at the doorway.

"All right, you son of a bitch," growls Mack, "If you don't surrender now, I'll kill the bound biddy you like so much."

Woody fires two shots in quick succession while bounding back into the kitchen, and he bashes Jennifer's chair to the ground. As he does so, he fires one more time towards the doorway, and pulls his knife. In a flash, he slashes the rope that ties Jennifer to the chair and tosses her into the pantry and safety. He fires another shot to make as much of the door jamb possible splinter to induce caution in his foe.

Jennifer staggers to her feet, and Woody unceremoniously shoves her deeper into the pantry. Gruffly he orders. "Get down behind the dry goods and stay low. You're safe now, I've got you covered." Mack peeks around the corner, and Woody fans a shot in that direction. At this point he takes a moment to reload, fishing for new shells from his belt.

Hardy has just finished haltering the horses at the mangers when he hears the first shot. The cook snags the rifle from his saddle holster, checks his hip for his old Army Colt, and bounds out the front door of the barn at a dash as another shot rings in the cookhouse. He recognizes the distinct sound of Woody's revolver. As all are busy with that firefight, Hardy sprints to the house, keeping in line with the trees that run beside the driveway.

At the corner of the building, he looks about quickly, and dashes for the fire escape. He vaults up the steps two rungs at the time and does not slow when he reaches the top. Instead of fighting what he knows is a locked door, he punches through the window, tearing both his gloves and his coat, and releases the lock from the inside. He barrels into the hallway.

A shadow flits from one of the rooms, and he throws himself on the floor. "Boom!" All the panes behind him shatter, as do the pictures on the wall. That bastard uses a shotgun. Hardy fans off a shot and tosses his hat into the hallway.

"Boom!" His hat is shredded.

"Ha," he shouts as he flies across the hallway into a room occupied by a trussed-up Nick. "What the hell?" He looks back and falls to the floor. A quick peek, and a shot rings out. This one a Colt. Chips fly from the doorjamb where his head should have been. Hardy jumps back and throws the bed over. Nick, bed and all crash to the floor. Hardy barks out, "Nick don't move." He then smiles. Trussed up like a sausage, that was a useless command.

Suddenly Fred cries out in agony.

A gruff Irish voice sings out, "Hey, Darky, want to see how this kid bleeds red?"

Hardy mutters, "Darn. Now what?"

He peeks into the hallway, and Fred is standing there, face bloodied, still tied up and with just a gloved hand holding a knife near the lad's throat. Cormac laughs, using the boy as a shield.

"Go ahead, try for my hand. He dies with me. Go ahead darky. Let's see if you have the guts to kill this little shrimp to get me. What are you darky, gutless?"

Hardy ducks back into Nick's room at a loss. He hears Cormac yelling down the stairs. "Woody, I've got that little black-haired kid. You heard him. Unless you and your Darky friend toss down your guns, I'll kill this useless boy. Your call. I'll give you thirty seconds."

A moment of silence passes, and Mack yells up the stairs. "Well done, Cormac. We've got them now."

All hear a horse ride up. Mack shouts in relief. "It's John. Cormac, we've got them. Kill the boy if you hear a single shot. You hear me, kill the boy if you hear a single shot."

Woody yells up to Hardy, "I'm tossing out my guns, and Hardy, I want you to do the same. Don't let them hurt Fred." The cook then hears the sound of the gun hitting the floor in the kitchen as Woody shouts clearly, "I'm coming out with my hands up."

Hardy hears the door open, and John Keegan exclaims. "Excellent work, Mack. I see you have this one under control. Are there any others of his ilk around?"

"Yes, Cormac. Kill the kid if that cook doesn't do the same. Now."

Hardy calls out, "I'm coming out with my hands up." He tosses his handgun in the hallway, hoping that perhaps they will not see the rifle in the room across the hall, and walks out with his hands raised and where Fred stands shivering with a bloody face in soiled clothing.

Looking at the lad, he softly says, "I'm sorry lad. They had the jump on us." Cormac comes out grinning like a Cheshire cat. He walks out and points his gun at Hardy, still keeping a safe distance, and elbows the battered boy in the stomach. Hardy gasps in horror as Fred crumples to the floor.

Smirking, Cormac looks at Hardy. "Do something boy, I dare you. If it weren't for the fact that J.K. has other plans, I'd kill you myself here and now. I don't like uppity cooks."

So saying, he gestures Hardy to go down the stairs ahead of him. As Hardy is part way down, Cormac kicks him in the back and sends him tumbling into the living room. As the bandit reaches the landing, he looks down at John Keegan and Mack and Woody who is covered by a couple guns. He says with a vicious grin, "That's the last of this lot. I guess we can tie him up."

At that moment, Jennifer staggers in, and looks at Woody and Hardy with tears in her eyes. John looks at her, and points to a chair. "Why don't you sit down Jenny, we have this under control. Well done, as these two are a bit tougher than we thought."

Woody looks up sad. John notices, and laughs. "Woodrow W. Flynt, I guess I can tell you now that Miss Jennifer Hathaway is my niece and works for me. So, kind of you to fall for her. You're not the first man she has ensnared, nor will you be her last. She's good at it as I trained her. I pay her well because of it."

Woody's face sags in utter defeat. Hardy looks over at what should be a mocking Miss Hathaway and sees only misery written on her face. He looks back at his lifelong friend and wishes he could save him from this pain. A bullet to the heart would have been more merciful.

Cormac turns and barks out, "Jenny, go upstairs and make sure Fred is back on the bed, and well tied. So, help me, if he is not, as I'll check. Get the other one out from under the mattress, but you can leave him on the floor. I'll check his knots also." Miss Hathaway obediently goes up the stairs. Cormac laughs behind her. 'That'll keep her busy."

Chapter 24

Tony's Tumble

Tony and his three rescuers quietly scan for Woody or Hardy or Nick as the train whistle sounds forlorn with the increasing distance as it moves on, uncaring as to the lack of any welcome for the Walking Y riders. Michelle, still reeling from the sensation in her arm as Hardy's knife cut into Brogan's flesh, feels sick. Teri is wordless staring at nothing, while Eric relives the sickening pit in his stomach like when he possibly shot Dave the prior month. Tony looks at the group and digs in his heart for the energy to take charge and try and relieve their pain.

He spies a familiar, but unfriendly face. That said, Mrs. Couchman who owns the general store with her husband, has never turned down a possible sale nor a possible coin. In short, he'll make her greed work for him. He walks up to her, and she deigns to cast a glance his way. Before she can dismiss him and move on, he smiles and makes a proposal that takes her aback, "Mrs. Couchman, I have a five-dollar gold coin with your name on it if you would take the four of us back to the ranch. It's only a bit more than a couple miles, and the girls are exhausted."

Mrs. Couchman stops as if a treasure chest landed at her feet. She casts Tony an inscrutable look and looks back at her buckboard. Then she looks back at Tony. "Pay now and load up."

Not believing their good fortune, all four load up, bringing the carpet bag and the satchel that holds their weapons. Mrs. Couchman, who has let it be known throughout town that she does not like drunken Catholic Irish trash tells the girls, "You sit beside me on the bench." Then looking back, she adds dismissively, "You Seamus, can make yourself at home with that boy in the bottom of the wagon in back."

She slaps the lines on the rumps of her two Morgan horses, and they begin the return journey to the Walking Y. In no time at all, they arrive at the cookhouse. Here, Mrs. Couchman stays in her seat and shouts, "Hardy, your crew is back. Tony and Eric and the two girls look hungry. Better get ready to welcome them."

Tony thinks nothing of this behavior, but is focused on helping his young charges out of the deep merchandise box and off the bench. Moving sluggishly, he passes the carpet bag and the satchel to Teri who is looking up at him. Michelle stands beside her, and all are focused on Tony who is the last to disembark.

Mrs. Couchman looks back, smirking, "Hope they have a warm welcome for you in the kitchen, you all look cold. I'll be leaving now." With those words, she swings her horses around, and takes off at an easy jog with her team.

Teri looks in surprise, "What's wrong with her?"

Tony smiles, "Well first she's English, and secondly, she does not like either The Walking Y nor drunken Catholic Irish. So, it was a close fight between her covetousness and her abhorrence at helping us, and she definitively does not want us to thank her."

Eric smirks and states, "You mean greed won!"

Smiling, all turn around and start to climb the wooden steps to the kitchen. Jennifer opens the door, and as the crew enters, she helpfully takes the carpet bag and the satchel. There is a pot of coffee on the stove, and all think of a hot beverage. Teri takes off her heavy jacket and hangs it on one of the chairs around the kitchen. The others aim for hot beverages. Surprisingly, the governess steps into the pantry and closes the door.

"What in hell's name?" barks Eric.

Three men come into the kitchen, two with pistols and one with a shotgun. None are smiling. "Well, you must be the famous Seamus Patrick O'Connor," states the well-dressed one clad in plaid in the middle of the trio. "And these must be Michelle and Teri. Eric, you don't know me, as I did not introduce myself when I saw you a couple times in Denver. Most recently when you needed a hackney."

Eric stares hard for a moment, "I remember you now. So, you're John Keegan."

"Precisely young man. Glad to see you can still think. Good, now we can have a bit of a conversation in comfort, would you please step up one at the time so that Mack here can frisk you for any weapons, like guns and knives." With those words, he calls over to the pantry. "Jenny, you can come out now. No violence, which is how you prefer your victims to fall."

The pantry opens, and a white-faced Jennifer Hathaway steps out uncertainly, and puts the bags on the table, where she dumps the contents, and all see the two rifles, and Tony's revolver. She steps over behind her "uncle" who is laughing at the loot. The look on Michelle's face is one of shock. Teri scorches the Governess with her foulest glare. Eric wrinkles his nose as if he just smelled something unpleasant. Tony shakes his head in disappointment. As to Jennifer, she goes into the living room and slumps white faced into Woody's favorite chair.

John signals to Michelle to step forwards to be frisked. She hesitates, and Tony nudges her forwards. Mack takes his time groping, enough so to make her very uncomfortable before he finally clears her. Cormac motions her into the living room, where she sees Woody gagged with a black eye, and blood drying on his chin and face. Hardy is also gagged and has a puffy eye. Apart from that, the cook is seemingly untouched, and both are tied up on straight backed chairs. She gently sits on the couch near them, trying to force her mind into action.

She looks back and sees Mack now subjecting Teri to the same filthy hands under the guise of a check for any weapons. Michelle realizes that maybe, just plain maybe, she shouldn't feel guilty for slashing that Brogan. Thinking about it, she'd do it again, but this time it would be that monster frisking her friend. Finally, Teri can sit, ashen faced beside Michelle. Both girls then look at the gagged Woody and turn to see Tony given the same weapon check. This time with brutality. Once cleared the Irishman is ordered into a chair. John now turns to cover him with his handgun and Mack ties up Tony's arms harshly behind him so he cannot move. His feet are also lashed to the chair. The girls ponder as to how, fortunately they do not see them as possibly dangerous.

When Eric steps forwards and is frisked by cruel hands.

"Get in the living room boy, now" orders John who faces him.

The boy steps forwards, and Cormac slugs the lad in the stomach as he steps over the threshold. The buck toothed youngster doubles over retching the little in the way of sustenance remaining in his stomach while sucking for air that will not come. The bandit then shoves him forwards with his foot, and Eric crashes to the floor in pain. "That will teach you, you filthy little bastard, not to mess with me again. Once you stop bawling like a baby, you'll see I also gave your boss a bit of a correction. We also met in Denver, punk, in a hackney." Looking down at the lad, the scoundrel spits in the boy's face.

Mr. Keegan looks up at Mack, who checks the knots on the Walking Y foreman who is now trussed up in his own chairs. John stares at the assembly and looks around, victorious as he warns, "Mack here also would like an excuse to administer a correction or two. I have told them that their first targets will be the kids upstairs, so he will bring down the last of our little group. I need all of you here, for our discussion to make sense. Mack, Cormac get Nick and Fred. Preferably alive. Please."

The two muscle clad men move up the stairs, Mack bounds up two at the time, while Cormac is a bit slower taking them one miserable step at the time and using the railing to balance himself. Shortly, Fred, whose bloody face has coagulated is escorted down with a harsh hand clamped on his shoulder. Then Nick comes down the stairs gingerly as both have their hands still tied behind their backs. Soon, the pair is seated on the couch and the tableau is complete. Fred seeks out Miss Hathaway's face, but she avoids all eye contact and sits like a white-faced statue, unmoving and says nothing.

Chapter 25

<u>The Interrogation</u>

Mr. John Keegan walks around the room and stares at his prisoners one at the time. "Well, looks like we're all here except for one, who will join us. We are finally arrayed in a fashion we can have a short conversation. First a few introductions. That there with a limp he acquired in Denver is Cormac. He feels he is owed a bit of a revenge, as he will have that limp to his dying day. My other companion is Mack, and he's good with both a knife and a gun. So, I suggest you respect that fact. He'll have no trouble killing you, if need be, and I think his preference is to make you suffer a bit. He's better than Brogan who could not be here to give you a personal greeting. But we'll get to that later, especially if you do not cooperate."

Miss Hathaway remains slumped in Woody's chair. She says nothing and makes no sound. Her face reflects misery and confusion as she watches the tableau unfold. Meanwhile all attention is on her uncle who takes a moment to glare at Tony along with Eric and the girls. Then he goes on, "Second, we have a few business items to take care of, so I'll have Mack remove the gags on Mr. Woodrow W. Flynt and Mr. James Hardyman so they can help. I am guessing, but you must be Teri", and with those words he points to the short brown haired and brown eyed girl who glowers at the suited man. He remains unphased, as he continues "And you would be Michelle. Cormac, you've earned your turn."

The dark clad man smiles mischievously and moves into the center of the room with a limp. "Mr. Keegan here told me I could get some satisfaction for the fact two of you left me hurt without my hackney on a cold wet snowy night in Denver. I'd like an excuse to punish more of you if you don't cooperate."

Mr. Keegan signals Cormac back to a chair on the side of the room, and resumes, "I forgot to mention that Cormac is good with a gun. In fact, he is better with a gun and a knife than he demonstrated in Denver when he made the mistake of underestimating that young punk there who is still gasping for air. So, I suggest you not try his patience. I did, as a consolation prize, allow him to give a short correction to a couple of you. For starts, he would love to kneecap your boss and the buck tooth snot."

Here the plaid suited man pauses for dramatic effect before continuing, "Not here yet, as he is bringing a wagon, and I told him to do it only after you all arrived is Festus O'Leary. According to the dispatches I regularly received as to activities here, you call him 'The Buffalo Gun'. As you have noticed more than once, he's also good with dynamite and other pyrotechnics. He used to be a prized member of the Fenians, and he knows you well, Mr. Seamus Patrick O'Connor. In fact, he still rightfully calls you 'a bloody coward.'"

Another pause, while the orator looks at the impassive Tony. Like a clock that has just been wound up, he resumes, "The last member of our little crew assigned to this case, you've already met, and that would be Miss Jennifer Hathaway. She's my niece and has a great skill at making good money by ensnaring any male I ask her to entrap. Jennifer is a lady and does not like foul language or violence. So, I am going to ask you all to use proper English and if I must administer a correction, I will ask her to leave the room on some task or another if I have time."

Painfully, he pauses again, before resuming, "Lastly, I'm Mr. John Keegan of John Keegan and Associates with offices in Butte, Denver and Washington, DC. We have one opening in New York and another in Chicago as business is good. With the expansion of government, there is money to be made by those who are willing to serve themselves. At J. K. and Associates, we pride ourselves in doing dirty work for men in power and doing such work with full discretion. You may not have heard of us before, as we usually keep a very low profile and keep the number of live witnesses of our activities to a minimum. Do you understand Mr. Woodrow W. Flynt?"

So saying, John turns to Woody and demands a reply. The owner of the Walking Y keeps his mouth shut, despite the fury in his eyes.

"No, that will not do," adds Keegan.

He walks over to the couch, and slaps Michelle in the face, hard. The girl yelps and brings her hands up in a defensive posture as blood drips from her nose. Woody growls and tries to stand. The plaid clad man looks over innocently at the ranch owner, and adds with steel in his voice, "Mr.

Woodrow W. Flynt, when I ask a question, I expect a polite reply. If you are not polite, and do not answer to my satisfaction, someone will pay. Do I make myself perfectly clear?"

Woody replies through gritted teeth, "Yeah. You do."

"No, that is not good enough. Teri, which cheek would you like to present, because if Woodrow cannot say, "'Yes, Mr. Keegan, I understand' or 'Yes Sir, I fully understand,' in the next five seconds it will be your turn to taste a needed correction."

Through tears of rage, Woody croaks out, "Yes, Mr. Keegan, I fully understand."

"That's better. For proper deportment, manners are needed. I can now see how much of an impossible task I gave my Jenny. Now where to begin." He then turns.

"Mr. Seamus Patrick O'Connor, do you understand the required etiquette?"

"Yes, Mr. John Keegan, I do understand."

"Very good. Now tell me, who killed Brogan?"

"Yes, Mr. Keegan, I will tell you. I did, and quite savagely at that. I fear I went berserk."

John Keegan stands again, and this time grabs a riding crop that was by his chair. He looks at it and adds, "For your edification, I presume you all know how to use one of these with uncooperative animals. I bring my own, made of good English leather and I keep it oiled to perfection. It helps maintain an open dialogue."

Mr. Keegan then walks over to Tony and puts the end of the crop under the Irishman's chin and lifts it a bit. "Now, Mr. O'Connor, how did you escape to kill him?"

"Mr. Keegan, I will tell you. I pried the legs off the bed quietly, and then used it to bash through the door. Brogan fired at the door, trying to gun me down, but I was behind the stout wall, so he missed. After a few shots, and I was counting them, he did not realize he was on empty, so I crashed in and bashed his head in. The kids arrived with one holding a rifle and another a handgun. I was a bit berserker, and I took both weapons and then shot him repeatedly. Somewhere in there, in my fury I also think I slashed him."

"I see Mr. O'Connor. So, you did this alone. None of those impudent brats helped?"

"Oh, they inadvertently helped Mr. Keegan. I couldn't have shot Brogan so well if they had not showed up. Right after I thought I killed that bastard with the bedpost, he moved. As I said, they had tracked me down. When I was being marched to my cell, I left my whiskey flask where they would find it. It gave them a clue as to where I was."

Mr. John Keegan glares at the foreman and walks towards Teri. Tony cuts back in, "So Mr. Keegan, sir, they thus found me. And when they walked in, I grabbed the guns I needed to make sure he was dead. It was self-defense and I am not proud of the fact that I went insane and made damn sure he was dead. Mr. Keegan, they inadvertently helped. Then they had to calm me down and told me we had to run for a train. All in all, those kids are not that hard. They are uncomfortable holding those guns against men and scared to use them. They think they're tough, but not for work like that. I learned from the best, I learned from Festus."

The plaid clad man continues his walk around the room calmly, and then back over to Tony and contemplates his reaction. He slashes the foreman as hard as he can in the face using his right arm and the switch. Blood welts up across the Irishman's visage. Tony spits a bloody mouthful at Mr. Keegan and it lands true, on his fancy plaid jacket. Mr. Keegan slashes again and again with all of his strength. He hits Tony's torso, and then his legs. In a rage, the beating continues as Jennifer closes her eyes and lowers her head and sobs huddled up in a fetal position in Woody's chair.

After a moment, John, sits and looks at the five orphans. He holds his gaze on Teri, Michelle and Eric. "It's a good thing that Irish trash killed my man; otherwise, I'd have to whip you three as well." With those words, he walks around again seeking to control his breath. Then he sits.

Silence follows the outburst, where the only sound is Jennifer crying in her chair. John looks up at her and barks, "For God sakes Jenny, get us some coffee in the kitchen instead of sniveling." Miss Hathaway walks out in a daze.

The wood in the wood stove crackles in the oppressive quiet as Mr. John Keegan regains his composure. Finally, he resumes, "you see Mr. Woodrow W. Flynt, I'm in total control here. I hope you understand that the current circumstances dictate such a state?"

With a grimace of anger, controlling his irascible temper at great cost to his blood pressure, Woody answers politely, "Yes, Mr. Keegan, I understand that you are in full control."

"Very well, when I have some coffee, we will continue what I hope will be a constructive discussion."

At that moment, in a contrast to her usual primness and with a rare tremor in her hands, Miss Jennifer Hathaway walks in stiffly with tears on her face. She looks disheveled now clad in Teri's coat and delivers three cups of coffee silently. The first to Uncle John and the other two to Mack and Cormac. Reading her uncle's inquisitive glance, she adds, "I was cold Uncle John, so I took this coat, as it was on the chair."

The plaid suited man nods his head in understanding and takes a sip of the coffee. "Excellent my dear Jenny. Nice of you to get it right in terms of sugar and milk. Thank you."

Thereupon he turns to Woody, and in a deceptively calm voice begins, "Mr. Woodrow W. Flynt, I need a couple documents from you. The first is that so called confession you have from Roger and Dave and the second is your copy of the agreement you signed with The Honorable Senator William Howard Bell the Third. Please tell me where they are in this house. Now."

Woody nods his head and smiles innocently. "Mr. Keegan, I have already informed Senator William Howard Bell the Third that neither document is in this house. I sought a secure location out of reach to stow the aforementioned documents. I have also left instructions with my lawyer as to how to access these papers in the event of my death, but not before then."

Mr. Keegan stands up slowly and takes another sip of coffee. Moving with deliberation, he picks up the riding crop he used on Tony and walks slowly towards the ranch owner.

"Mr. Flynt, this is not some sort of a game. Tell me where you have stashed these documents?"

"Mr. Keegan, through the Senator, you know that I have a loan with a bank in Great Falls, The First Cattleman's Bank. I have a safe deposit box there and I stashed the documents out of sight in a such a safe place. Viewing I was wrong about Miss Jennifer Hathaway, she probably can tell you she could not find them in either my office or in this house." Jennifer winces at these words. Uncle John ignores her. She had already told him she could not find them.

J.K. slashes Woody in a swift arc with the riding crop.

Slowly a painful red welt crosses the owner's face, and blood oozes down his cheek. "Mr. Flynt, do I need to ask you again? Next time, someone else will pay for your insubordination." So, saying he drifts over to Eric's chair.

Woody looks up in pain and fear. He needs to think how to stop this. Eric sees Woody's hesitation and remembers the gruesome fight against the Senator's men the month before. He cries out, "Woody, KEEP YOUR MOUTH SHUT. I can take it."

These are the wrong words.

Keegan lunges over to Eric and viciously slashes the lad several times on the torso and legs with all of his power.

Eric yowls in agony, slumps in his chair, and sobs in pain.

John Keegan looks at his handywork with a smirk, turns and calmly states, "Mr. Woodrow W. Flynt. I want answers now. I have four more adolescents I can work over along with your manager and your cook. I want answers, now." So saying, he drifts over towards Michelle. The girl winces back away from the fiend.

At that moment, a wagon leading a saddled horse is spied coming up the driveway in the early evening moonlight through the living room windows. For one brief moment, hope flutters in the heart of the Walking Y. It fades as a smile appears on all three villains. Mr. Keegan calmly looks at his hostages and pontificates with delight, "Ah, you will get to meet the so-called Buffalo Gun, Mr. Festus O'Leary. Seamus, it is my understanding that you worked for him in Ireland until your mother ran with you after you turned yellow. He will join us and has a little work to do here before I leave."

With those words, he walks into the kitchen and opens the door for Festus. Tony cringes as he hears the familiar Irish brogue spewed by a man with no heart. "Ah, Mr. Keegan. The false trail seems to have worked. Have you had a chance to give little Seamus Patrick O'Connor a lesson yet, or can I get in on the act?"

Thus, discussing lessons, the pair walk into the living room, and the newcomer's eyes lock in on Tony, "Well Seamus, you look better with that welt. Shame I wasn't the one whipping you. You are lucky, Mr. Keegan told me that I'm not allowed to kneecap you, but as you killed Brogan, he might allow me to give you the next correction that will come as it seems that Mr. Flynt is uncooperative."

Tony eyes the newcomer and smiles despite his beating, "Ah, Festus O'Leary, I regret to say that as a wee lad, I looked up to you. I told my mum that you were my hero. As I got older, I learned better. I now understand what courage is. Regrettably, you have none and I am sure that will be in your style to hit a man who is tied down."

John Keegan hands the riding crop to Festus, who steps up and whips Tony in the face again and again, "you will address me as Mr. O'Leary, coward."

He then hands the crop back to Keegan who turns to Woody. "Let's see what next. Where are Roger and Dave buried?"

Woody looks in innocence, "I did not know they were dead, Mr. Keegan."

John turns to Jennifer, "I suggest you get out of here, niece, regrettably, I'm now going to have to get rough." Jennifer leaves, cowed.

He then turns back to Woody, "WHERE ARE THEY BURIED?" Before Woody has a chance to answer, J.K. slashes Hardy in the stomach. So much so, the cook's chair topples over. Furious, Keegan yells again, "WHERE?"

Woody gambles. "Mr. Keegan, please let the others go, and I will tell you everything, and even sign the ranch over to the Senator."

"Ha! You postulate that I'll turn you free? Sorry to disappoint you Woody. I'll not play that game." He steps back and randomly lashes Nick with the quirt. The lad yelps in pain, it is Nick's turn to watch blood ooze, this time through his blue jeans.

"Stop please Mr. Keegan, you win. I'll tell you everything." Shouts the white-faced owner of the Walking Y, His cry is so loud that even Jennifer walks back to the doorway to see him. Woody goes on with rage and passion, "Let them live. Please, Mr. Keegan. I don't care about me, but please let those kids live."

J. K. looks over at the white-faced owner, toys with the quirt, and walks over to him. He lifts Woody's face with the horse crop, and steps closer. "Very well Mr. Woodrow W. Flynt. Are you ready to be levelheaded. Let me ask you again, is Roger's confession that implicated Senator Bell real, or were you bluffing?"

"Please let the others go Mr. Keegan, and I will answer everything."

"Woodrow, this does not work that way. You tell me everything now, and I'll consider your request." So, saying, J.K. walks lazily past each of his captives. He lifts Fred's tear-stricken face with the end of the horse crop, and says softly, "It would be a pity to mar such a young face, but Mr. Flynt, you are giving me no choice." He turns to Woody, "Now, is the confession real, or were you bluffing?"

Woody, looking defeated, answers clearly, "Mr. Keegan, I was bluffing, sir."

"You were bluffing, Mr. Flynt. You treated my client, the Honorable Senator William Howard Bell the Third as if he were no more than a mark in a poker game. How can I let the others go if you lied to get that agreement with Senator Bell. You do realize that you have just admitted that the agreement you signed with the Senator is invalid. And now you expect me to let these others free despite the fact that they helped you in such treachery?"

Woody remains silent, praying for a miracle. To have come so far, and to have Tony and Hardy and these orphans killed because he cannot find a way to free them leaves him searching for the key to their safety. J. K. moves over to Hardy, with the whip in his right hand.

"Mack, put him up again, so that I can teach this bastard a lesson if Woody remains stubborn." Mack hefts the cook, still tied to his chair, up. John Keegan comes back to the owner of the Walking Y.

"All right, Mr. Flynt, please tell me where you buried Roger and Dave?"

Woody hesitates for a moment. J.K. steps back and slashes Hardy across the torso. "Next time, pretty boy gets it in the face. I said tell me Mr. Flynt, now."

"Mr. Keegan, they are buried in the bull field, by the cottonwoods. The place is under snow now, but there's a small sign that reads, 'Rogue Bull.' Please let my crew go. I will sign over everything I own. But please let them live."

"Very well Mr. Flynt. You or your men murdered Roger and Dave. You buried them on this ranch, and never told any authorities. You let their families worry when you killed my men in cold blood. Perhaps if I do not get a clean answer to my next question, I will whip one of your orphans to death. It would serve you and them right. A bit of an eye for an eye, and my inclination is that Eric here should be terminated. Do I make myself clear. Let's try again Mr. Flynt. Where is your copy of the agreement?"

"Mr. Keegan, the agreement is under the cab…"

Nick yells in passion, "NO WOODY, SHUT UP. DON'T TELL THAT BASTARD, HE'LL KILL US ANY…."

Festus leaps across the room and punches the squirming shouting lad. Nick crashes to the floor, and the wild punch leaves his arm and shoulder pulsating in agony. Keegan comes over and looks at the kid on the floor and kicks him as the lad assumes a fetal position. He then lashes him a couple times with his riding crop. As Nick sobs, John Keegan collects himself, and walks back over to Woody and addresses him in a dangerously even voice. "You'd better resume telling me, or that little, long haired blonde gets it next. I'm done being nice."

Woody sobs in frustration, and replies, "Yes Mr. Keegan, as I was saying, my copy of the agreement is under the cabin my father built next door. Go into the cabin, pull the middle nail of the third board from my big bookcase. You will find a small compartment, and the agreement is there."

"Get it," barks Uncle John to Jenny.

Miss Hathaway meekly steps out of the room which is now quiet except for Nicks' whimpering. A few minutes pass slowly, and then Jennifer Hathaway steps back into the living room shivering despite Teri's jacket and hands the agreement over to her Uncle John. He looks at it and smiles.

"All right. Where were we?"

Woody repeats, "Mr. Keegan, please let the others go, we have told you everything and I will sign over the ranch now to your employer, Senator William Howard Bell the Third. Please Sir."

"Well, while this is most informative, Mr. Woodrow W. Flynt, it is too late for that Woodrow. It was just a question of how much pain you would suffer before you all die. Just so you understand, I surmised that you killed Roger and Dave, and that they were buried on this ranch. I also suspected that the confession was a bluff. So, if Mr. O'Leary will prepare another pyrotechnic display for your benefit, we can end this comedy. Anyway, we have a train to catch, first to Thermopolis and the Grand Hotel there where I will leave my Jenny to rest and clean up after dealing with you. I expect that a few days will be sufficient, and then she has another profitable assignment. Meanwhile I must immediately travel to Albany,

New York, to set up her next engagement and ensure proper payment. Meanwhile, you are all going to die in your sleep tonight when this cookhouse accidentally burns down."

J. K. then looks at Woody, and adds with a sneer, "I already talked to the Senator about this, and he is not perturbed by my torching this large cookhouse. He sees it as a crude structure that he would have to take down anyway when he acquires The Walking Y properly from the bank with an ironclad title. A future Governor of the State of Montana needs a place with a bit more class than this. Your barn passes the test, but this cookhouse does not."

Mr. Keegan then turns to Mack and Cormac and calmly orders, "Take them upstairs and tie them to their beds. Make sure you pull their boots off, as no one sleeps with them on. Put Woody in Jenny's bed, as he knows how soft it is. It will serve him right to have deluded himself that she is in any fashion attracted to him or any other scum on this ranch. Slap the cook in the room down here, and to make it simple, toss that drunken stump trainer on the couch there. Make sure they are well tied, but not gagged." He then turns to Festus, and goes on, "get the fire setup we discussed ready. It should give us about one hour to catch the train after we leave, so that we have alibis. You know the rest of your role."

Festus goes to the kitchen and carries a box into the pantry. Jennifer stands in the office doorway, captivated by the unfolding scheme, as Mr. Keegan ransacks Woody's office, and the two grunts carry the children upstairs. John Keegan looks at her, and orders. "Niece, go upstairs and get your personal items packed. You will tell them at the train station that you were fired. Mack can carry your trunk down."

Jenny obediently goes to her room.

Chapter 26

<u>Miss Hathaway's Play</u>

The wagon Mr. O'Leary rented from the livery stable is fully loaded, and Festus has taken off on his horse. All are ready bundled for the cold evening, and Miss Hathaway is still in Teri's jacket while her trunk and valises are loaded at the back of the wagon. John Keegan clucks to the team and starts them towards the train station when Jennifer yelps, "Uncle, please stop. My mother's wedding ring. I forgot it in the living room on the table by the easy chair I was using. Please uncle, she was your sister."

John Keegan shouts, "Whoa" to the team and barks. "Get it quickly you fool, Mack, keep her company."

Both jump off the wagon, Mack takes a moment to unlock the door, and both barrel into the house. They rush into the living room where just a couple lanterns still provide a dim light, and Tony is trussed up on the couch with a bloody face. Miss Hathaway dashes to the table by Woody's chair.

"Oh no, it must be upstairs on my vanity. Can you get it Mack. I couldn't bear to see the orphans tied on their beds. Please. I'll give you a nice favor in the future. Please Mack, I need that ring. It's all I have left from my mother."

Mack looks uncertainly at Jenny. She goes to the bottom step and signals him onward with a smile and a hand gesture, he wavers and sprints up the stairs.

Miss Hathaway watches him go, and dashes into Hardy's room. She pulls the sharp blade from inside Teri's coat. She signals Hardy to shush. She slices the ropes binding his hands, and whispers, "Tell Woody I love him. Also, Festus is with his buffalo gun about half a mile away ready to kill if you go out or if the fire set to go off in the pantry does not burn the place down."

Then she races out and postures with a bored look at the bottom of the staircase. No sooner does she position herself at the lowest step, does

Mack come down grinning. "I have the ring, but it was in the middle of the dressing table. I took an extra second to spit in Woodrow's face. The stupid sucker looks desperate. Damn bastard. It'll serve him right to burn to a crisp. Now get on the wagon."

With those words, Jenny starts for the exit, while Mack checks Tony's knots and the fuse in the pantry. They step out the door, and Mack locks it behind them. The governess climbs with the brigand's assistance to sit beside J. K. and the hired muscle jumps in the back of the wagon and perches himself with a rifle at the ready on Miss Hathaway's trunk.

Mr. Keegan turns to asks Jenny who seems tense, "Do you have the ring?"

The ex-governess holds the gold and diamond ring in her open palm. It glistens. She looks and coyly answers, "Thank you, uncle. It means so much to me."

He turns away and clucks at the team. Jenny looks back at the cookhouse which was so different from what she expected. They leave the Walking Y's headquarters behind and cover the short two miles to Hellenville and thence all four go into the railroad station and join other passengers. There is still a good three quarters of an hour before the night train pulls through town. J.K. has booked all of them in the club car at the back of the train, where he hopes to see the glow from the fire on the Walking Y.

Instead, a couple minutes before the train pulls into Hellenville, the sound of an explosion reverberates through the air, coming somewhere from that Walking Y land closest to town. Most who hear the explosion are not perturbed, but John Keegan knows that this is not per plan. He paces the platform, and feels some comfort that Festus was left behind as an insurance policy. Perhaps, somehow, unexpected guests released the Walking Ys, or perhaps the knots were not as tight as they should have been. Thinking, he sees that he has no choice but to leave as planned, as he and the rest need the several alibis established by their presence at the station. No matter, the firebomb is out of sight, and probably not disabled. The good thing is that Festus hid it in the far end of that pantry behind boxes of tinned goods, so it would not be easy to find. And the so called Buffalo Gun is there with his Sharps, ready to kill if need be.

That club car is not crowded on this cold mid-week February night, and John Keegan hands the conductor a generous tip to ensure he is remembered, and the group has privacy all the way at the back, where the fire should be visible. Mr. Keegan watches for the glow of the burning cookhouse on the Walking Y, but as it is lacking, he also judiciously watches Mack and Jenny. Should there be no glow, he will interrogate them. The train leaves Hellenville and rolls through mountains. There is no glow.

Uncle John Keegan reviews everything in his mind, what comes to concern him, is that perhaps her assignment watching, seducing, and ensnaring Mr. Woodrow W. Flynt had been too long. Perhaps she had formed an attachment to the irascible rapscallion or to those wild orphans. But her letters did not seem to indicate any issues. Before questioning her, he would look at a few of them again. They are in his bag, clipped in order. He should be able to do so without her or anyone else noticing.

As the rail ride rattles on, with all headed to Denver, John reviews the "spying" letters that Jenny wrote about activities on the Walking Y. These letters were frequent and detailed, and he congratulated himself on having Mrs. Couchman as a contact. She had been excellent, and it was a shame the lady was not located in an area with more demand for his services.

January 30, 1905:
"Woodrow W. Flynt has called all the crew together to try and improve their manners at my behest. It is easy to cause friction, as Mr. Seamus O'Connor is a crude drunkard, and the orphans are little terrors with no class whatsoever. I cased Mr. Flynt's office and did not find either the confession or the so-called agreement he signed with Senator William Howard Bell the Third. I have also figured out how to listen to his 'confidential' conversations with his foreman.

February 9, 1905
"Woody corrected Eric again for his language and seems to be taking my efforts to heart. He has also scolded Tony for teaching the boys how to play poker. When the boys then taught the girls, he was upset; however, he said that Rome was not built in one day. Talking of Rome, I am still left surprised that he believed me when Tony and Fred caught me being wrong about Gibbons. I told him that I had not finished reading The Decline and Fall of The Roman Empire *and was learning it. Thus, I had*

not reached Chapters 15 and 16. That idiot who owns the place actually believed me.

I did sneak into Mr. Flynt's office and removed your business card that he had taken from Cormac back in Denver. He will not suspect it, as I timed it such that I was outside with James Hardyman when he went to retrieve Eric after the lad's horse was shot. The boy cried for hours, and no one could console him. Thus, the card was forgotten.

There was a subtle pattern of name changes and perspective changes that could indicate that loyalties were shifting. John then spent an hour thinking with a single malt whiskey while the rest of the crew slept in their spacious club chairs. On this most recent excursion to the ranch, when the entire crew was subjugated, she was constantly with one or more other members of his crew. As knots were checked, any betrayal had to be late in the process, after he had deemed that the best way to deal with the Walking Y was to kill all of them as per the plan, in a fashion that would not arouse suspicion.

Hence, he brought Festus in the house to set up a time delayed fire to incinerate them, including Woody, his foreman Seamus, Eric, the two other boys and the two nettlesome girls, along with the no account colored cook. Festus chose the pantry, as it was close to the kitchen, on the lower floor, and any fire starting in the area of the kitchen would arouse less suspicions. But at all times she was watched. But she did come into the living room with that girl's jacket and was still wearing it. It was baggy and could have hidden a derringer or a knife. But how would it have been delivered if his Jenny betrayed him?

Damn it.

When she went in for the ring. She betrayed him when she went in for the ring. Something about her behavior flagged in his mind. He should have stopped when she showed him the ring. He should have questioned her then. She is just a typical weak female even weaker than in his prior estimation.

He was sure of it. He would check innocently, but he would find out. Such a possibility was hard to believe, especially after all he did for her. He raised her when the parents were shot. He was the one who found her and trained her, and he was the one who gave her employment that was ideal for such a good-looking wench. And she was the one who was good at entrapping and betraying men. She had now carried on working for him and later at his behest with Festus by entrapping men since she was a young girl. And had now, as a thank you for giving her these skills, she had perhaps betrayed him – and Festus.

John Keegan's hands shake with barely controlled anger. He breathes deeply and takes another whiskey. First, he must wake Mack. She has somehow entrapped or ensnared or fooled Mack. Did the little wench ensnare Mack by promising some favor in the future?

If so, Mack will pay.

So will Jenny.

The train rolls on with the mournful whistle through to the plains of Montana. The clickety clickety clack of the wheels on the stick rails seems to sing of betrayal, and John Keegan contemplates his next actions for some time. He rises from his chair, and nudges Mack. The hoodlum looks up, and nods like a dog eager to please his master. John's mind wonders. He signals the man to join him, and they go up to the bar at the other end of the parlor car. John orders Mack a whiskey. The man takes a sip with a smile. "What can I do for you, boss?"

"Mack, when you went back into the cookhouse on the Walking Y with Jenny to get her mother's ring, did you stay with her at all times?"

Like a puppy dog, eager to please his owner, the hoodlum answers ingratiatingly, "Yes boss. I went in with her and came out with her. That's what I thought you wanted me to do."

"And where did she get the ring, on the table in the living room?"

Mack looks inquiringly at John Keegan.

"Where was the ring?" demands John.

Mack tilts his head, thinking. Sounding a bit dense, he answers, "Upstairs on her dressing table. She told me it was on the vanity, so it took me a minute to get it."

J. K. stops for a second. His face turning red, he retorts, "She told you?"

Mack, not seeing the issue replies compliantly, "Why, yes boss. She stayed by the stairs in the living room, because she didn't want to see the kids trussed up ready to cook. So, I got it, and I took advantage of the fact I was up there to spit in Woody's face. I hate that arrogant son of a bitch."

Leaning forwards, Mr. John Keegan continues eagerly, "So, she was alone? In the house, downstairs?"

"Just for a minute, boss. But she stood waiting by the stairs."

"Could she have gone anywhere in that time?"

"Nah, she's not that smart. Anyway, she wouldn't have had time, because she didn't know I would walk in and take a moment to spit in Woody's face. Not only that, I checked that Irish swine's knots and the fire fuse in the pantry."

In a dangerously calm voice, the plaid suited man continues, "But it took you time to find the ring?"

Eagerly Mack answers, "Not too long. She thought it was on the vanity as I told you and it wasn't. It took me a minute of looking to find it in the middle of the dressing table. The room was not well lit."

J. K. stands there for a minute controlling his emotions. He takes a small sip of his whiskey and looks at his dimwitted hired hand. Finally, he answers in as even a voice as he can muster, "Very well Mack. Why don't you go back to sleep. But do me a favor, send Jenny here."

Moments later, Jenny walks up rubbing her sleepy red eyes clad in a well cut very dark blue dress, a heavy black sweater, but still wearing Teri's heavy winter jacket. On her feet she still has the same boots that she wore that morning on the Walking Y. Practical warm black boots with good tread for winter use. On her right arm, she holds her thin deer hide leather handbag. Yawning, she looks at J. K., "Uncle, you called for me?"

John stares at her for a moment, wondering if she has betrayed him. "Jenny, you know how I taught you everything you know, and you know how I took you in when your parents died?"

"Yes, Uncle John" she answers not thinking clearly and a bit defensive. "You usually start in on how you saved me when you prepared me as a young girl to work with you and for you. I'm grateful, we've both earned good money, and will continue to do so. Thankfully now, I am no longer a little helpless girl, so I can do the New York assignment. You gave me the skills I need and that have kept us alive and well cared for. We have worked for each other's mutual benefit. So, thank you." With some bitterness apparent, she then goes on, "Are you worried about the New York job, and if I have what it takes so that you can get those New York government contracts and bribes?"

John Keegan looks around for a moment and turns to her with a severe face. "You're feeling sure of yourself, aren't you girl. Well, let me remind you that you are nothing without me. You will do as I say, and you will show me the proper respect. Is that clear?"

Looking contrite, Jenny looks to the ground, and whispers, "Yes Uncle John. I apologize and I was out of line. I guess you caught me still a bit sleepy."

The conductor sticks his head in the car, and yells out, "Moccasin, next stop Moccasin. Three minutes stop in Moccasin."

John's hand reaches out, and he snags Jenny's chin forcefully and lifts her face up so he can see her eye to eye. "I expect complete obedience. Look me in the eye girl and tell me that you didn't give Woody a knife or some means to escape. Did you betray me?"

"Uncle John," she replies as she raises her left hand to his hand on her chin, "Oww! That hurts. I can tell you I didn't give Woody anything. You had Mack with me."

"Listen little girl. You owe me everything. Did you betray me?"

"Uncle, I did not see Woody alone at any time before we left. You were there, and when I went back in Mack was there. He even took time to spit in Woody's face."

J. K. is quiet for a moment. His hand does not release Jenny. "Mack tells me that he left you downstairs when he got the ring. What did you do?"

Jennifer Hathaway lowers her head despite his hand and looks at the ground and mutters. "I waited for him at the stairs."

John sees the body language.

He hauls her head up, "You little wench! You are lying. Who did you help downstairs? Tony, nah, Mack would have noticed when he checked. Who else was down there. Damn. You helped that boy in the back room on the main floor, that no account colored cook. You're a damn lying little slut!"

John slaps her hard in the face.

She slaps him back with more than eighteen years of fury at how Uncle John used her since she was but a little girl.

He lifts his arm to strike her again when it is stilled by an unknown calloused hand.

"Sir, that is not acceptable. You hit her again and I will deck you." John turns and looks at the strong cattleman who is not smiling. He also notes that this rancher has an even stouter companion who is also getting off in Moccasin. The pair would be hard adversaries. While he contemplates his next step, Jennifer Hathaway ducks across to the ladies' powder room and locks the door.

J. K. notes her departure, but he already knows that there is no other exit from the lady's powder room. He breathes deeply. "Thank you, sir, I let my temper get the better of me. You have my word that it will not happen again."

"OK partner. Remember, we don't cotton up to hitting women 'round here. The next time you might find yourself with a fat lip. So don't let it happen again. Do you understand?"

"Yes sir. I will apologize to the lady."

The cattleman and his sidekick seem appeased by his words.

The train slows and pulls up to an empty platform in Moccasin, Montana. Due to the late hour, there is no one waiting except for the agent who is wheeling a cart to the U S Mail Express car at the front of the train. The unknown cattleman and his friend climb down giving John Keegan a hard look. Jennifer stays in the locked powder room. No one else boards the Parlor Car. J. K. signals for another whiskey and downs it with a shaking hand in one gulp.

He politely knocks on the powder room door. "Jenny, come out now."

A soft scared voice answers, "In a moment Uncle."

The conductor shouts to the empty platform, "All Aboard, Laurel, Thermopolis, and Denver along with all points between. This train is now leaving." The railroad employee then ducks in the parlor car and shouts to all, "Next rest stop Mossmain in ninety minutes."

In the Powder room, Jennifer looks about frantically, and opens the window during the commotion between the cattleman and her uncle. She assesses her ability to fit through the small opening and waits. Once the conductor is back closing the doors and slamming the metal plate over the car's steps, and the train has not yet begun to move, she forces herself into the window. She tosses her handbag on the dark trampled snow of the poorly lit platform and strips off Teri's coat and drops it. As the train starts to roll, she levers herself into the opening and dangles out of the car holding on to the cold wooden frame. The train picks up speed. Jennifer says softly "God Help Me!" She pushes herself off the side of the car and rolls helter-skelter in the snow unnoticed as the train chugs out of sight.

John Keegan downs yet another drink and sits where he can watch the powder room door. The little bitch can stay for as long as she wants, and then he will administer a well needed correction when she steps out. Time passes, and his head rolls in fatigue. The whore is still moping. Oh well, he'll hear her open the door to exit. Thus watching, swaying to the rhythm of the stick rails under the car, he falls asleep. When he wakes in Wyoming, he assumes that his little strumpet has done the same, as the door still shows the red mark that says that she is still locked in. The pattern continues. It is not until Denver that he suspects that somehow the little wench has gotten away…

Chapter 27

__Gunfight__

Earlier that evening, as Hardy struggles to free himself from the tight bonds that lash his hands together, he ponders if he is dreaming when Jennifer cuts his hands free and leaves the knife beside his wide-open eyes. At first, he immediately hides the knife under him, and keeps his hands in place as if still tied. He takes a moment to listen to the team leave and ponders her words. A slight smile plays on his lips, and he murmurs, "There might be hope for the lady yet."

Finally, he rubs his wrist, and looks at the shades in his room. They are drawn. Inside light at night with naked windows means that Festus, who is still lurking somewhere, might see any movement. He'll have to be careful. He cuts the ropes binding his feet, and slowly rolls off the bed. Bare footed, he sneaks to the living room. In a whisper, he calls, "Tony, no noise. I'm going to cut you free, but move slowly. Festus is somewhere outside with that buffalo gun, and he is watching. Can you take my knife and free the others upstairs and tell them that Festus is watching. Get them all down to the kitchen and tell them to sit under the table. I'll be there or join you there. Can you do that Tony?"

With a smile, the foreman answers, "Oh, Mary mother of God, my prayers have been answered, even if you're not as good looking as the Archangel. Yes Hardy, I can do that."

Freed from his own ropes, moving despite the pain from the whipping he suffered, Tony creeps up the stairs to free, first Woody and Eric and then the other four orphans. All stay quiet and grab their boots which were by each bed. All move cat-like down the stairs, while staying away from unshaded windows. Soon they are gathered under the kitchen table, where thankfully it is still quite warm.

Hardy joins them from the pantry. "I found it," he whispers, "and I put out the candle that would have triggered the fire. The Buffalo Gun's kerosene bomb is now in the washing tank with water, but it's still quite dangerous, as kerosene floats. But at least there is no trigger. I'd guess we have about thirty minutes before Festus starts to suspect anything."

Woody asks with urgency, "How did you get free?"

"Miss Hathaway. She snuck in the room, cut my hands free and gave me back my knife. She had it hidden in your coat, Teri, so you lost your coat to a good cause."

Woody asks with urgency, "Did she say anything?"

Hardy trying to stop his old friend, "Yes, Woody. She warned about Festus being with a gun and watching."

"What exactly did she say?"

"Woody this is not the time to tell you word for word."

"Tell me, damn it. Now."

"Well, you asked. Remember you asked me, so don't get mad. She said, word for word, I quote, 'Tell Woody I love him. Also, Festus is with his buffalo gun about half a mile away ready to kill if you go out, or if the fire set to go off in the pantry does not burn the place down.'"

The first smiles in hours suddenly adorn the orphans' faces, and all chuckle openly. Eric and Nick even chant very softly "Woody's in L - O – V – E." Tony chokes a bit, and reaches for his flask, which amazingly enough, he still has. He takes it, and says, "I think there's enough for all to have a little medicinal whiskey. He sips a very small swallow and passes it to Eric who does the same and hands it to Michelle who does the same and passes it on. As the ever-present leather covered metal flask makes the round in less than a minute. Woody, like the rest of the crew is still crouched under the table. Even in the dim light, he blushes a bit staring at nothing like a fool. He also takes a small sip of whiskey, which seems to bring him back to reality.

The owner turns solemn. "All right, what horses are in the barn, and where are the rifles?"

Hardy replies seriously, "I looked. All rifles are where they belong, in the gun rack except for the one upstairs. It's still in one of the bedrooms. Someone moved it behind the door, probably Miss Hathaway maybe so we would have at least one, but we have them all."

Fred speaks up for the first time, "I have an idea. If he's watching, why don't I parade a mannequin in front of the windows and perhaps on the porch to see if I can draw fire. While I'm setting that up, the rest of you take ten minutes to get your horses ready in the barn and be on the lookout as to where any shot is fired from."

In a couple minutes the plan is agreed to. However, Woody decides, "Hardy will stay in the cookhouse well-armed to both provide cover, and to give instructions if need be to those in the barn as to where any shot originates."

Quickly, all except Fred and Hardy duck soundlessly out from under the table and don winter coats, scarves, boots and hats. When ready, they slip into the night holding to the shadows and reach the barn with no shots. They plan to only ride those horses that are already in the building, thankfully their first string. They use only one small lantern in a corner of the tack room with the inside door closed, chosen because the light must not be cast onto a window and betray them.

Meanwhile, Fred and Hardy clothe a couple sticks hastily assembled to mimic a silhouette. After ten minutes, they turn on a couple more kerosene lanterns and parade their decoy in various windows, starting to the South of the house. When there is no reaction, they move to the West and then the North windows on the second floor. They begin to suspect that perhaps Festus is not taking the bait, or they were misled as they move to the East windows upstairs.

Fred is just about to stand when, the window shatters in conjunction with the dreaded distant,

"BOOM!".

Simultaneously, the broom handle decoy is ripped out of the lad's hand. Hardy, who is beside the window kills the lantern and allows himself a glance out the shattered frame. He does not shoot, but tries to pin the general direction from whence the incoming round originated.

This is the signal for the riders in the barn. As they were watching, and saw the decoy obliterated in an East window, they head out the safe west facing front door of the barn. At a mad gallop they loop into the nearby cottonwoods holding rifles at the ready. The noise alerts The Buffalo Gun, and a couple shots are directed their way. Apart from shards of bark raining down on Eric, none are the worse. The element of surprise worked. The few seconds where they are exposed during their unexpected appearance has provided safety. The hunt is on.

Woody splits his posse into three groups: himself and Michelle, Tony and Teri, and lastly Eric with Nick. As they are to drive as hard as they can eastwards, keeping to the trees and staying in sight with each other Woody barks out the last-minute instructions. "We'll split up to make that bastard with his buffalo gun work hard at tracking all six of us. But, be under no illusions, as not only has The Buffalo Gun proven to be an excellent shot, but he probably has set up explosives to try and kill us. Eric, I want you and Nick to swing very wide and come in from the south."

The three pairs split.

***

Festus positions himself as an insurance policy. Like all such tasks, he chooses his spot to watch the cookhouse very carefully after scanning the ground on numerous occasions. One area in particular has caught his eye. Any attack will come through the cottonwoods so that any pursuers are concealed by the trees. Thus, the trees while providing cover also hide a danger to any that come after him. In several instances riders will be channeled into a narrow path, and on two of these he ties bundles of dynamite with carefully cut fuses. One is for ten minutes. This one is near a gully. The other is timed for thirty minutes and is closer to his current spot of concealment. If the house burns as expected, he will pull his bundles for future use. But if anything goes wrong, both are where he can light them quickly and where they will give him cover as he retreats towards his horse while trying to shoot anyone still alive.

But he sees his bundles as insurance. He fully expects that he will see the house burn, and Mr. Woodrow W. Flynt and his crew roasting. Good riddance. Good money. Another easy job for John Keegan, and his Jenny's next assignment promises him even more profit.

Otherwise, if he sees anything suspicious at the house, he has the traps set to go. This done, he takes out an old gold watch, and notes that soon the house should erupt in flames. As a lookout, he waits while sluggishly the time inches by.

Time crawls by and - Nothing.

The fire should be starting. He fumes and his eyes focus on the Walking Y's cookhouse and in one window he sees movement. This is not good. Oh, well he has this covered. Unhurried, he takes careful aim, and squeezes off a round. The silhouette falls. The shot strikes true. One down.

He sprints back to his horse, and lopes to the shorter timed ambuscade to light the fuse. He can make out the pursuit. He fires a couple quick rounds to make them worried. He covers the rest of his dash to the second fuse and in less than a few minutes he regains his chosen perch and leaves his horse waiting out of sight.

Listening carefully, he still can hear hoofbeats in the distance. They are after him. He does not need to move yet, and he smiles as he thinks about the two safety snares he has waiting in the trees. Each should be good for one rider. He carefully watches the terrain, and he faintly can make out two or so pairs of riders coming his way. Well, time to scare them and slow them. Despite the trees and the poor light, he waits and then squeezes off one more round. That shot will channel a couple riders into his short, fused booby trap at the perfect moment.

A scream and loud explosion shatter the evening. Both happen at just the perfect moment. Good. Probably one or two more down.

That should slow the others. He can hold his spot a bit longer. Scanning the field, he is surprised to see a pair of riders forgo the protective embrace of the cottonwoods along the creek. He takes aim and squeezes off a round. One disappears. Now probably three down. Perhaps two left at the cookhouse, so no more than three still after him. They do not have him located. It's not time to move, yet. He's chosen a good vantage.

"Crack!" sounds faintly.

An incoming round. Festus smiles. It's well wide. They do not have him pinned yet.

There, in the trees by a gully. He squeezes off another round. The rider disappears. Probably a miss, and they will be a bit more cautious. Still not time to move. He checks his watch and listens carefully. There is but one rider there, maybe two. Festus reloads and is ready. His attention is on the incoming horsemen. Suddenly three closely spaced shots break the quiet. From the house. A heavy gun. All three rounds crash right around him, a bit too close. He aims for the familiar window and squeezes off a round.

"BOOM!"

That should take care of that bastard in the cookhouse. He was a clever one, back calculating the source of the shot that killed the first one to venture by that upstairs window. He has probably taken four or five of them down. Two or three riders who ventured in his sights, and perhaps two at the house. He can hold this ground for now, as he has a few minutes before the next explosion. Now he must force one or two of them into that trap.

***

The middle pair are Teri on Crowhop and Tony on Sorley. They dash among the trees rifle in hand, beside an iced over creek in the cottonwoods. The stream soon falls below level ground in a gully, and a cluster of bushes forces the two to momentarily ride side by side. Teri is near the drop off. She looks back at Tony in the shadowy darkness of the moonlight, and,

"TONY, THERE!" she screams in panic pointing to a sparkle in the trees beside them.

Tony swivels, sees the sparkle, and smashes Sorley into Crowhop. Both horses and their riders tumble down the edge of the six-foot-deep gully.

Teri howls and the world reverberates with a loud, "KaBOOM!".

Horses scream as they land pell-mell in an unfriendly tangle of wild plum thickets. Riders focus on being clear of their mounts, and smash hard into the unfriendly snow and ice-covered branches. Shards of wood and debris land on top of all, and ears ring and pop from the percussion.

Crowhop is the first to recover. She stands unsteady and shakes her head. The saddle is askew, and the bridle is partially off her head. The reins are missing, and even in the moonlight, gashes and dark spreading stains are visible. Her rider, Teri looks around from under the thicket, and sees little beyond chaos, and ice. Amazingly enough, she still holds her rifle, but this has yet to register. She tries to stand, and finds her coat ripped and tangled in the greedy fingers of the thicket.

Sorley is furious.

Useless Tony did not protect her. In anger, the mare stands, fear, pain, and fury course through her veins. Shaking her head, she notes that Crowhop is already up. She goes to the mare and bites her on the rump.

"Move!" orders Sorley. "We're going back to the barn. That's plenty of bedlam for one night."

Tony stands to see two dark equine rumps rapidly leaving their riders behind. The message is clear. "Walk, you two legged things. We've had enough."

The foreman shakes his head and were it not for the fact that there is so much at stake, he would bow to equine wisdom. Instead, as he is in a dark gully, and cannot see Teri. He reaches in a pocket and pulls out a small box of matches. He strikes one into a bright flame which he cups with his hand.

Softly he calls, "Teri, are you here?"

"Coming."

"Good. Do you have your rifle?"

"Yes, Tony, I held on to it."

"Good girl."

Flatfooted, he starts to look around for his own. "Hallelujah," it's but a few feet away. Sheepishly he retrieves it. The match goes out. "Join me. We'll check and clean the bores to make our rifles safe. If we can, I'd like to go after the bastard afoot."

Teri limps up to the Irishman, uttering a few words Miss Hathaway would not have expected her to know. Tony smiles, as he had used even worst ones as they tumbled down the embankment and the pyrotechnics left for their benefit by The Buffalo Gun. The foreman thinks for a second and pulls the stub of a candle out of another pocket, and lights it.

"Quick, gun check, and ammunition check." As Teri begins to do this, he reaches in his breast pocket for a little snort of medicinal whiskey.

"Damn it Tony, do what you ordered me to do," barks out the girl with no mercy.

Somewhere, a distant heavy rifle fires three shots.

The buffalo gun booms in reply.

Tony puts the flask back without taking any and begins to check his rifle's bore.

Another shot, this time one of the hunting rifles barks in reply.

He then glances at the handgun in the holster under his torn winter jacket. Fully loaded and ready to go. Good. Within a very little time, both feel that their rifles and Tony's handgun are functional.

"This gully angles east. We'll stay down here for a couple hundred yards, and then we'll peek up. That shot was still a few hundred yards away. Stay back about forty feet and try to be quiet."

"Yes Tony, same as hunting deer. I plan to get one with this new rifle of mine, even if it is an 1894 model. First let's get rid of that two-legged coyote."

***

Woody and Michelle are dodging branches making more noise than either would like. The owner is a bit surprised by their unchallenged progress when a muffled cry immediately followed by a loud explosion shatters the night. A hundred yards or so to the right, the bastard has just blown up some trees where Tony and Teri should be riding. They both stop, and watch. Nothing. Faintly they hear a couple horses, headed back. The riderless horses crest the gulley and are framed by snow in a field, empty saddles mean that both Teri and Tony are now walking or worse.

Michelle watches Crowhop and Sorley and gasp, "Teri?"

The owner hesitates, "Come on Michelle, we don't have a choice. We can't leave Eric and Nick alone against Festus. The son of a bitch is a killer. That Buffalo Gun is damn accurate." With his hands he signals onward. Hiding more than before, they resume their advance, seeking to gain more shelter in the cottonwoods. Not even a hundred yards are covered, when three distant shots ring out and The Buffalo Gun's reply echoes through the night.

Woody growls, "He's after Eric and Nick." He plows ahead with Michelle following.

A moment later, a hunting rifle replies. Michelle quietly retorts with relief, "That's Eric's!"

***

From the moment the riders split up, the impulsive lanky young man cannot hold himself. Eric and Nick charge south eastwards in a wide loop towards the suspected position. The hot-tempered lad wants to cover ground at a gallop, and he angles away from the cottonwoods on undulating terrain. Both he and Nick cover ground with the hoofbeats muted by the snow. Due to the wide loop, they hear the distant sound of an explosion and exchanged shots. Both have their rifles at the ready and are well wide of the other riders. Eric's eye catches a movement.

"TURN!" and with this word, the lad jags Jake back to the shadow of the cottonwoods. Nick follows instinctively. The ground falls but a couple feet. Enough to save a life.

"BOOM!" barks the damn buffalo gun.

"Son of a bitch." Eric instinctively brings his rifle up and "Crack", he flings a round where a fleeting movement saved his life. "Follow," he orders. So doing, he twists down into the gulley amongst the cottonwoods. They ride for minutes and he turns to finds Nick holding his reins in his mouth, behind him seeking to fire a shot.

"Don't! We'll pop out and get the bastard in a bit."

Riding like a mad centaur, Eric leads Nick, who begins to lag. The young cowboy sees a small cross draw and turns. The trees swallow him. Nick follows, and his horse slips and falls. His steed gets up, and ground tied, does not leave. The large lad tries to stand, but his left leg will not hold his weight. "Damn, that hurts."

"Boom!" the buffalo gun barks again.

Eric barely hears that second shot. Shards of bark lacerate his face, and he plunges into the woods at a full gallop. Momentarily he is but a background noise.

Nick cusses, "Damn!"

He staggers to one foot and catches the horn of his saddle. He leans over and pulls his spare ammunition. Carefully he hobbles up the embankment, watching to keep the bore clear of the snow. He positions himself behind a beaver downed tree, hopefully facing The Buffalo Gun and waits. Watching intently. His horse, despite being ground tied, slowly moves back a few feet at the time, towards the barn.

**

Hardy, as the riders dash from the barn, rushes out keeping to the shadows. He darts into each building to check for any "presents" left behind by the dynamite loving Buffalo Gun and finds none. The barn he peruses a bit longer, and then he runs back towards the house when an explosion rents the night air. Using the cover of the chaos created, Hardy darts back into the house and snags his heavy hunting rifle from behind the wood box in the kitchen. Fred turns to follow him cradling his own new rifle, but the large man orders, "Stay put!"

Hardy lopes up the stairs taking two at the time and goes into the east room where the cold wind sweeps in through the shattered window, and the mannequin lies in a tangled mess on the floor. He picks up the base, places it where it was when shot, and looks at the far wall. The shot ripped a hole that continues through several rooms. He studies the angle and lifts the rear sight to eight hundred yards on his own Winchester Model 1886 45-70. The rifle is a common one on the frontier, and in capable hands such as his, it can take down a grizzly bear. Positioning himself carefully, he levers off three rounds, and falls to the floor. An incoming round slams into the wall behind him and continues reverberating through several rooms.

Hardy snakes out on his stomach, and dashes down the stairs with his rifle, where Fred is holding his own rifle at the ready fully alert to the danger. Hardy, while tossing on his winter gear including no nonsense walking boots looks at the frail white-faced but determined black-haired lad.

"Fred, lock the doors, and shoot Festus if he shows up. You have a rifle just like the girls, and that Winchester .25-20 will knock him down. I don't think he will get around all of us, but that Buffalo Gun is a cunning one. Better yet, bundle up like mad and hunker down in the blacksmith shop with plenty of ammo. Just stay alert. I know his kind, and I know how Woody operates, so I know how I can help the boss and the rest of them. They need me. Now." With these words, Hardy takes off at a run, angling east cross country, keeping to the low ground.

Frederick Torroni, while a frail lad, is determined to do his part. He bundles up in his winter clothing, takes a pot of tea and some cookies along with his rifle and ammunition, a sharp knife and trudges to the blacksmith shop; however, he makes sure that his tracks are obliterated. He locks himself in the small building and scans the one room including the forge and the brick fire pit. As to the only door in, he not only uses the latch but secures the double swinging door with a heavy wooden bar that he locks in place using the framework of the building. From the modest front window of the stout building, he can see the cookhouse. From the only side window, he can see to the milking shed and part of the barn. He props both open to hear, and to shoot safely. Then he settles down on a tall stool in a dark corner, from where he can see out both windows to some extent. Reviewing the layout in his mind looking at it as a chessboard, he knows that his illustrious ancestors could not do better with the time allowed.

***

Festus listens carefully. He can hear a lone rider crashing through the brush to his left. But that is but one rider. Somewhere ahead of him, he can sense two riders. Yet something makes him uneasy. Perhaps he has a foe coming at him afoot. The instinct has been correct too many times before to be ignored. Carefully, he leaves his chosen vantage, and crouched low doubles back towards his horse. He has to dash across a short open clearing, but it is not more than thirty feet. He looks up at the sky and waits for a cloud. The partial moon is shaded, and he dashes.

"Crack! Crack!" Tony and Teri each aim a round at the fleeting shadow.

A slug rips at his shoulder, the second is wide. Festus turns and fires a hasty round where he saw movement as he rejoins the shadows.

Tony yells, "Festus, toss your gun out. We'll kill you otherwise."

Seamus Patrick O'Connor. That yellow bellied bastard knows where he is, and he has someone with him. Festus falls to his stomach and turns away from his horse. The spot was too logical, and Tony remembers how he operates. How he'd love to get the yellow-bellied bastard who dropped that bundle where the Bodachs could collect it. Too yellow to blow himself and those damn Brits with him for the cause. Seamus could have had glory for Ireland, and he chickened out. He deserves to die.

Woody and Michelle riding up a draw about one hundred yards to The Buffalo Gun's right also hear Tony. The owner holds his hand up signaling Michelle to stop. They freeze. And listen. Were it not for the horses' breath, and their own heartbeats, they would hear their foe who is now angling towards ranch headquarters. Woody dismounts, and has Michelle do the same.

Eric stops his mount, as he hears the two shots. Then he hears Tony. Well, that was both smart and stupid of Tony to shout like that. He resumes his advance, but now angles further away from ranch headquarters. If The Buffalo Gun has a horse, which he must, it will be hidden behind him. He will wait astride for him there.

Hardy hears the two rounds and changes his path just a bit to angle into the trees. Those were lighter Winchesters. From the shout, he presumes that it was Tony, although the words were indistinct. He decides to hold until he can hear or see something that tells him which way The Buffalo Gun is moving.

Nick is startled by the shots, but notes that the rifles that barked were lighter than the Sharps carried by The Buffalo Gun. Shivering, he advances gimping. He carefully angles towards Tony and what he presumes is Teri. The big danger now is being shot by his friends. He toys with shouting his name but defers. It will also alert the wily bastard who is out to kill them. Turning around he spots a sparkle in a tree just above him.

"OH SHIT!"

He springs up, ignores the sharp pain in his foot, and dashes for a hollow a few yards ahead. He plunges headfirst.

"KaBOOM!"

His world erupts in flames, as he flies through the air. Welcoming darkness wraps its arms around him.

Festus smiles. Sounds like he got one of the little bastards.

As the explosion reverberates through the night, Festus dashes for a few seconds, and gets past where Tony is watching, and slows to a crawl. To himself he whispers, "I love dynamite. It always takes the bastards by surprise, wish I had more." He now decides that he will steal a horse from the corrals at ranch headquarters after he kills off any guards there. Then he will make tracks and come back to hunt these kids. Why this is much more challenging than just killing Brits with dynamite. Thankfully his shoulder wound is not too bad, just a welt that will hurt like the blazes in a couple hours.

Tony turns in fear for the lad while Michelle gasp, "Nick?" It was the boy's cry. A curse of pure panic, just before the explosion.

Never would Nick utter such a word unless, unless he sensed death. Distracted, they stare in the wrong direction seeking to understand what happened to the lad as his voice cried out in terror just before the explosion. Inadvertently they let The Buffalo Gun sneak by their position when the moon is obscured by clouds.

Woody on Red, now his first-string horse, finds himself fighting to retain control and his seat. The equine panic transmits itself to Princess who wants to run back to the barn. Both riders calm their horses who sense danger. Precious seconds are wasted in a skittish dance. By the time the pair get their steeds back under control and in the dark night and with the echoes of the explosion ringing in their ears, any noise Festus makes while he moves on shank mares is undetected. Shortly thereafter, Woody hears a meadowlark and pauses with a smile before resuming the hunt.

Hardy moves forwards and hears Nick's shout and the immediate explosion. He mutters, "That bastard and his damn dynamite." The cook stands, and dashes forwards with all of his speed, caution be damned. Doing so, he makes noise in the brush. His first priority now is the lad caught by the explosion. The expletive means that Nick probably saw the fuse and had but a second to take action. No more than a second, and he may be out there injured. He'll have Woody carry on the hunt, and he'll bring the boy back, dead or alive. He mimics a meadowlark and knows that Woody will hear him.

Festus hears nothing from where Seamus called him. So those two are not moving. He senses two horses in a gully or a ravine a little way over. Thus, he has four of them located. And one more taken out by his present. That's five. All behind him. Good. He runs forwards at a crouch and hears a meadowlark. He's heard that before, he's not a tenderfoot. He stares in the correct direction and spies a form coming from the cookhouse afoot. That would be the no account colored cook, so not much of a threat. He'll let that one pass, and perhaps they'll shoot each other. Smiling to himself, he crouches forwards. Soon he sees the house, with lanterns still lit inside, looming ahead. He slows and advances cautiously into the shadow of the large barn. He peeks in, and senses that there are still a couple horses in their stalls. Good.

Now for the cookhouse. Any kid left at headquarters would be in the main house, backlit by the apparent safety of lights and flimsy locks. Well, he has killed kids before. Not that hard, just a smaller target. So now he can add an American or two in his tally that includes a couple little Irish cowards like Seamus, and a few British nits who happened to get ensnared in his bombs.

Angling out of the barn, he goes behind it. As he crosses the open ground to the shadow of the milkshed, Fred sees his movement. The lad quietly chambers a round and checks the windows. Good thing he propped them open. He can shoot out and hear movement if it comes to that. He moves off his chair and pictures the area like he would a chess board. He envisions himself as a knight, but behind a pawn, somewhat out of sight. The problem is, he does not know if he can kill someone without seeking surrender first. How does that commandment, "Thou Shall Not Kill" apply in this situation?

The Buffalo Gun goes behind the milking shed and looks at the blacksmith shop. It is dark, in need of paint with missing windows and quiet. He logs its location, and its door in his mind, and steps to the cookhouse. Cautiously, he shoulders his hunting rifle and pulls out a revolver. He sneaks up the wooden steps, holding himself to the side where someone watching the door from the inside could not see him. He reaches for the handle,

"Freeze Mister!"

In one lightning motion, The Buffalo Gun spins, jumps, and shoots. "Crack!"

Return fire, "Crack!" The deer rifle slug misses, sounding like an angry hornet dashing by Festus' ears.

It came from the blacksmith shop. Stupid little bastard. Should have shot first. The Buffalo Gun smiles crouched behind the steps and looks at the dark rectangular shape of the open blacksmith shop window. He spies movement. He wings off two shots from his revolver, and sprints around the cookhouse. With luck, he will have killed the little runt. If not, that kid will lose any waiting game. He'll go around the house, around that old cabin, and come up to the blacksmith shop on its blind side.

A couple minutes pass slowly, as Festus makes his circle.

Fred, untouched by The Buffalo Gun's revolver shots, knows that he also missed. Picturing his chess board, he knows that Festus will next try the door. He takes an old branding iron and puts his hat on it. This he drapes in the shadow by the front window. That provide some protection from the front, a decoy pawn so to speak. The lad then hides with his rifle at the ready, and a fresh round in the chamber behind the forge. The knight hiding behind his rook with a decoy sacrificial pawn. That rook, or brick forge, should stop any slug that can cleave its sway through the wooden siding of the building. He waits in the dark, his hands shaking.

Festus skulks beside the building on feet that instinctively know how to be quiet. Handgun at the ready, he looks at the front of the building, and sees the outline of his foes hat looking out the window to the cookhouse. He fires a round, and the hat falls. But it didn't fall right. Nasty little squirt. It was a decoy.

He looks at the door, and throws himself at it, at a low crouch, so that any shot goes over him. "Thump!" The door cracks, but he bounces off. The little weasel has braced it. Smart little snot.

"Crack!"

A bullet smashes outward through the door, and wings Festus in the arm. The same side that already had a welt. The little runt shot low. Of course, the snot's crouching. Festus fires four shots in quick succession into the building reeling from the pain in his arm. That's the second injury on this dark night. If he had a stick of dynamite, he would just light the fuse, and toss it in to kill the little bastard.

He reloads his revolver and thinks by the corner of the building. Out of sight. A sound penetrates his consciousness. Hoofbeats. He'd better run to fight again. Festus, at a crouch, heads for the barn making sure that he is not visible from the blacksmith shop. The detour and staying in the shadows take time. He finally ducks into the dark horse barn and grabs one of two horses that are munching in an open stall. Both are saddled. He looks at the pair in the dim light coming from the open tack room door, and takes the taller one. He hops in the saddle still in the alleyway and notes that the stirrups are a bit off, so be it. He turns the unknown horse through the door and slaps its' rump hard with the nice long bull hide reins.

Sorley has had it.

It's not her rider, and enough is enough.

She arches her back and bucks aiming to land this unknown brute on the moon. Festus was not born in the saddle like Eric, has not learned as fast as Tony, nor has he been thrown as often as Woody. All of them would find such antics a lark. Festus on the other hand, lacking the help of stirrups, flies out of the saddle, and Sorley thunders on furious.

In the recesses of his mind, Festus hears hoofbeats. Staggering to his feet, he senses danger. He reaches for his handgun while turning. A horse and rider smash into him and send him sprawling. Disoriented, he looks up when another familiar horse stomps him into the ground. Badly hurt, he rolls and gets up instinctively still holding his handgun in his left hand. He turns, bleeding profusely, looking for danger, crouched. Ready to shoot, he is struck down by one or more bullets as a series of shots echoes through the night.

Chapter 28

Pieces

When Nick flies through the air, the reverberations of the explosion lead to a rash of activities. Eric urges Jake to an all-out gallop that covers the hundred yards or so to where he would have stashed a getaway horse. All those hours in the saddle exploring and working the land between the Walking Y and town pay off in spades. In the shadow of a couple of tall ponderosas, tied to a tree, Eric spies a horse waiting patiently. He goes up to the mount and offers the steed a chance to smell his hand. He then takes the lead rope, mounts Jake and tries leading the horse at a walk. It is willing. He moves up to a jog, and it follows with no hesitation. Eric tempts fate and urges Jake to a fast lope. The unknown horse does not fight, but matches Jake, stride for stride. Eric turns to the back road by the fairgrounds. He will go back to the cookhouse on the county road.

Hardy turns and heads to the explosion. He arrives to contemplate the destruction of numerous cottonwood trees and is at a loss for a moment. Listening carefully, he hears a rasping sound. Probably labored breathing. He plunges into a thicket of downed branches and staggers into a hollow. His hand strikes a human form, and he senses blood. Looking around furtively, he takes a chance. He lights a match in a cupped hand and sees Nick's prone form. The lad is breathing, and the large branch on his back should not be a problem. Straining, he lifts it and hefts it over. Nick groans incoherent.

"All right lad, I'll check for broken bones, and then take you home."

He very gently feels the lad, and finds that both arms, both legs, and his torso and pelvic area feel intact. The blood is from a gash on his scalp by his back, and another is more serious, in his upper thigh rump area where the jagged edge of a branch tore through his coat, pants, and long underwear ripping his skin, into the muscle. Looking around, he hears a horse taking off towards the fairgrounds, and figures that is the escaping Buffalo Gun.

Good riddance.

He stands up and mimics a meadowlark.

A meadow lark replies.

He shouts, "Woody, come here."

Woody and Michelle come into view on horseback.

The cook looks up, "Woody, he's hurt bad and bleeding like a stuck pig. We have to get him back. Now."

The owner looks at the unconscious lad, and states, "Let's put Nick on my horse with me, can you load him in front of me? I can hold him. Michelle, you can lead and be the guard as I think Festus just ran for it. Bastard. We won't catch him this time."

Hardy nods his head, and with concern looking at Nick's bleeding replies, "Give me a minute to try and create a bandage. Michelle, I need your scarf."

The girl hands over the scarf she is wearing. Hardy shakes it out, and carefully runs it between Nick's legs and then back around his waist as tight as he can make it. It stems the blood flow, and will hopefully hold until they can get him back to the cookhouse.

Hardy looks at the girl, and points, "Lead Woody and Nick back by the county roads through the fairgrounds. I'll hoof it back, it's not too far, and I'm a bit heavy for your horse." With those words, Hardy takes off at an easy jog cross country towards the cookhouse. Woody, Michelle, and Nick ride off to the county road treating Nick with as little jarring as possible.

Tony and Teri, afoot, hear what they think is the Buffalo Gun escaping after the explosion and stop. Tony looks at the girl and indicates the way back, "Let's go to the barn, as I suspect that Crowhop and Sorley are waiting for us. If I know them, they will be in the open mangers eating. Anyway, I think our quarry has escaped again."

Michelle nods her tired head in ascent, and they track back from whence they came. They have no more than about six hundred yards to cover, and like all are still aided by the moon. None are back to the barn when all hear the muted shout and a couple shots. All fired by lighter guns.

"My God, that's Fred," notes Michelle, as she suddenly quickens her pace. Tony and the girl begin a shuffling run taking care to hold their rifles clear of the snow and ice.

***

Eric vaguely hears only the shots from the county road, but he can do nothing to accelerate his pace. Already he has Jake at a lope, and The Buffalo Gun's getaway horse is trailing on a lead rope. Once close to headquarters, he will cut through some trees and come out by the barn. That is the best he can do.

On the other hand, Hardy breaks into a run. The wily son of a bitch doubled back, and Fred is in danger. The cook slugs through the snow, sweats profusely, and dashes with all his energy. But he lugs a heavy rifle and feels his age as it holds him to a seeming crawl. His heart beats frantically. Fred needs him. Now. His mind races at how that cunning Buffalo Gun worked his way around all of them.

Granted he found and tended to Nick, who might not have made it had he not staunched the bleeding from the deep rip in his backside. But he, Hardy, is not where he was hired to be, at the cookhouse, protecting those there. Yet, even out of place, afoot, he is probably the closest of the lot to Fred's position. He aims for the blacksmith shop, and Fred, where the thin lad is fighting for his life.

Woody, Michelle and Nick hear the whisper of a couple shots and look at each other. With Nick unconscious, they must hold to a steady pace, as the lad is injured. Michelle breaks out her rifle and holds it at the ready antsy to take off at a lope, when Woody growls, "Girl, take a position about thirty yards ahead of me, because I can't both hold Nick and defend us. You're our only shield if that thug comes back this way with a purloined horse."

All are making good time when a fusillade breaks out at headquarters. Hardy, Eric, Teri and Tony can each make out the crack of Fred's rifle and the pop of a revolver. The boy is alive and fighting The Buffalo Gun. Alone. A frail lad known as a terrible shot. Every one of them has joked that he would be hard pressed to hit the broad side of a barn from the inside. Had Tony not been wheezing so hard for breath, he would have been praying.

When Eric surges out by the barn, he sees Sorley dash out of the front door, a strange rider lashing her with Tony's heavy bull-hide reins. It crosses the boy's mind that one should not treat Sorley thus. The lad urges his horse to greater speed and struggles to undo the dally. His cold hands, and the gloves make him clumsy, and when he looks up, he sees The Buffalo Gun fly through the air. The boy gives up on releasing the horse he is leading and aims Jake to trample the downed rider.

As the brigand seeks to get up, Eric mows him over with Jake. The lad has one hand on the reins to direct Jake through his target, and one hand is still fighting the lead rope. While speeding, he feels the sickening impact of horse buffeting a man trying to stand. He rides through Festus. A moment later, the horse he is leading tramples The Buffalo Gun for a second time in as many seconds.

Eric and horses, still at a gallop, careen into the darkness on the side of the barn.

Shots ring out.

One a heavy round from an old-style rifle, aimed by a large dark man with sweat on his brow. Another two shots ring out in close succession, the first being Tony's rifle, and the second of these the distinctive lighter crack from Teri's new deer rifle.

Silence.

Fred's voice comes from the blacksmith shop. "Did you get him?"

Tony replies tired, "Yes. You're safe now."

The boy pushes open the door that he had successfully barred. Hardy rushes back to the lad who is running towards them and wraps him in a warm embrace. "God, I have never been so happy to see anyone." They both drift back to the solemn group around Festus.

Tony walks up to The Buffalo Gun and gently rolls him on his back. Unseeing eyes stare at the sky. The Irishman makes the sign of the cross and utters, "May your soul rest in greater peace than you deserve." He then walks to Teri who is wobbling, sickly white, and hugs her. "He won't hurt any of us again."

Eric brings his horses back at a walk, looks around while moving both horses to cool them. Jake and The Buffalo Gun's horse slowly turn in a nervous circle. Eric sheaths his rifle.

Festus lies on the ground. Mangled. Battered. With multiple gunshot wounds, and grotesquely dead. The question of whom among the crew was the one that killed him can never be answered. For all anyone knows, the guilty may have been Jake or even his own horse. But at no point did The Buffalo Gun ask for nor expect any leniency. He had grown up and lived in hard times that showed no compassion. In return he did the same to himself and those around him.

Teri looks frazzled as Michelle, Woody, and Nick ride up. She asks the owner, "Do we need to call for the Sheriff?"

Woody takes charge, "Teri, the Sheriff has his position thanks to the Senator. Hardy, please tend to Nick. Tony, please check out The Buffalo Gun for anything that will help us, including money, as we don't have any extra. Take any gold for the ranch and leave the silver so it's not obvious we did that. Eric, make sure all the horses are cooled down and groomed. Put that bastard's horse in the back of the barn. He's ours now. Teri and Michelle, help Hardy with Nick. I'll leave and get Doctor Maxwell."

Woody starts to ride to town when he stops and looks back at his foreman. "Tony, can you also wrap Festus in an old blanket and put him on the sled by the barn for the Sheriff to look at, as I guess if I have time, I'll have to get that so called lawman."

Chapter 29

<u>Uncle John's Web</u>

The typical weak female, fresh from jumping out of a small train window on a dark night where clouds obscure the moon, in Moccasin, Montana, looks around at the deserted platform. The few people who greeted the train or disembarked have moved on. The dark lonely gloom suits her mood, as she needs to plan a bit further ahead. That said, she is glad none noted her unconventional exit out of the Great Northern parlor car. She is also thankful that it is ninety minutes before the train stops again. For now, she is safe with many fears coursing through her soul.

She gathers her belongings and thanks the lucky stars that she somehow stole Teri's jacket. The short grass prairie wind is biting, and gusts drive dancing snowflakes around her feet. The town is sleeping. Alone she walks up Central Avenue in the small settlement looking for a room for the night. She looks at the dark doors and windows shivering and finally spots a small sign over a house porch dimly lit by a low flame in a lantern. "Rooms for Rent." She turns up the walkway shaking from both the cold and the stress of the last few hours. Jennifer looks through her tears and sees a small plaque reading Mrs. Statley. She knocks.

The door creaks open a bit and noting that the person outside is a chilled lady holding her purse, Mrs. Statley opens wide and beams a hearty welcome. "My," voices the matronly middle-aged woman with a sincere smile and greying hair as she opens the door wide, "you must be cold. Guess you jumped off the night train? Why, do come in."

Soon Jennifer finds herself in the warm front room, which is dressed in well-worn furniture, amply covered in hand made doilies. She is Mrs. Statley's guest as they share a steaming teapot with matching flowered China teacups and saucers. Jennifer admires the small, mismatched silver spoons. The matronly lady brings out a couple dainty plates each with a few cookies to compliment the sugar bowl and the delicate milk pitcher, and finally sits and looks at the disheveled young woman disgorged by the train with no bags. Polite discourse does not last long before Mary Statley dives to the obvious issue.

"My dear young lady, it is none of my business, but I fear you have had a hard time. You obviously were on the train that just pulled through town, and you find yourself in Moccasin. Looks like you have no relatives or friends to greet you. So, you are alone in a town with no real hotel, yet. You have no bags and a coat that does not fit you properly. You have a fresh welt across your face. If you ask me, granted I should not stick my nose in your business, someone on that train slapped you hard, and you jumped out unnoticed here."

The matronly lady pauses and watches Jennifer's reaction before continuing, "Well, I can tell you from what I have learned in life and from The Good Book, that is the bravest thing you could do. So now, relax and let me pamper you, and if you want, I can be a good ear. Sometimes talking things out is the best way to make a decision, and it is obvious you have not had a friendly female to help you in some time. For now, just call me Mary, that is my name."

Both ladies sip tea as the wind whistles forlornly through the deserted streets and a dusting of snow swirls outside the front window. The mentally exhausted and ever apparently so proper Miss Jennifer Hathaway finds herself fighting back a tear or two. She leans forwards with eyes locking in on Mary. She has nothing to lose and talks more than she has in a long time.

"Mary, I have not always been a good girl. But what happened today was terrible, just terrible."

Mary Statley nods in encouragement and tells the ex-governess in a soothing voice, "I can swear that you can talk in full confidence. I have needed a shoulder in my life and per the Good Book, I want to return the favor."

"Oh, Mary, I betrayed Uncle today. He slapped me, because I was disloyal, and my actions may bring down his empire. But I had no choice. He left those kids and that fine grouchy Woody along with his foreman, Tony and the nice colored cook, Hardy tied up in their beds with a device that was going to burn the house down around them. They would have all died, and it would have looked like an accident. I don't like violence, and to have me sit there or stand in the kitchen while Uncle John whipped those kids and that Hardy, made me listen to my long-forgotten conscience. I couldn't let Uncle kill them. So, I snuck in and cut Hardy free and told him that Festus was in the woods with a rifle ready to kill if they escaped the house."

Here, Jennifer stops to catch her breath, before going on sobbing, "Mary, I don't know what happened after that, but that grouchy Woody, who I entrapped, actually believed in me when I was caught lying about how I studied *The Decline and Fall of the Roman Empire*. Mary, that man actually believed in me, not because he sought advantage, but he somehow saw that I could be good. I had long since forgotten that I could be. I could no longer see any path to anything good, I was evil. And that Woodrow is not a soft man. Let's be honest about it, he's a grouch. But he saw good in me. He did not just see me as a loose woman, but he saw me as a child of God."

The ex-governess takes a small sip of tea, and carries on with tears, "But Festus won't back down as he likes to kill and he is paid to murder Woody and the others. He also really loathes Seamus. I greatly fear there's been a terrible gun fight at that ranch, and someone will be killed because I freed Hardy. I left Hellenville on the early evening train with Uncle John. Oh, Mary, those poor ornery orphans likewise will not shy away from trouble, especially that Eric and that Teri. And where those two go, Michelle along with Nick and Fred also go. None of them will let Woodrow and Tony fight alone. But Uncle John managed to read the perfidy in my face, and he slugged me."

Here Jennifer sobs, "Mary, worse yet, is that I have been unfaithful to my husband, and in my shame, I may have set him up to be killed." Here Jennifer wipes her tear-stricken face. Mary leans over and pats her shoulders and hands her a clean white handkerchief.

"My dear, why don't you start at the beginning and take your time."

"Oh, Mary. My luck went bad when I was a young girl, and when I was nine, both my parents were shot and killed. I can remember being a little lost girl crying in our forlorn home when Uncle John showed up. He was impeccably dressed in plaid, and he took me to his well adorned house and told me that now I was his beautiful little girl. At first all was well, but I would catch the servant girls looking at me with pity and sorrow and the stable boys leering and laughing. He had me schooled in high society and trained me to be comfortable around men. Then within a few short years, Uncle John talked me into helping him. He was going after a government official and wanted me to entrap him. Oh, I agreed, as Uncle John had rescued me. But afterwards, how I felt dirty, yet Uncle was so pleased with me. He pampered me and bought me nice clothes, my own poney and candy. From there, the pattern never ended as candy morphed into jewelry."

Jennifer takes a sip of her tea, and shudders a bit before continuing, "Then some years ago, he told me that I was getting married, and introduced me to Mr. O'Leary. Part of me was relieved, as I would be out of the vicious trap Uncle spun for me. But, no, everything just went darker. Uncle John wanted Festus to partner with him, doing nasty jobs and taking care of individuals who were problematic. The marriage gave Keegan and Associates another tool that was not honorable. The ability to eliminate problematic people for money. Uncle John and Festus simply split the money they made using me, and I was only a wife between jobs. I am evil, and I was working hard at destroying people while I devastated my soul."

A moment of quiet passes while both allow their minds to catch up to the spoken word. Finally, Miss Jennifer Hathaway closes her story. "Mary, if Woody ever found out I am married to Festus O'Leary, he would disown me. And one or both of them may have killed each other as we left Hellenville."

Mary Statley stands carefully and opens a cupboard and pulls out her well-thumbed bible and goes to the kitchen to fetch a freshly baked pecan pie. She puts the bible on the table, along with a couple small plates each adorned with a sliver of rich pecan pie. She also brings another pot of tea, and she refills the teacups, and tops the cups with a touch of sugar and a dash of warm milk.

"Jennifer," Mary begins softly, "you are the bravest of the brave to jump off that train after your Uncle John slugged you, and the hand of providence is with you. Tonight, we will sleep and say a short prayer. In the morning I will suggest that you contact this Mr. Woodrow W. Flynt at The Walking Y in the coming days, and I will encourage you to take the train back to Hellenville. You will stay on the train unless they meet you. If they meet you, you will go with this Mr. Flynt and his crew back to the ranch. You will find out what happened, and you will be totally honest with Mr. Flynt. He may not react well at first, but give him a chance to think things through. If he is an honorable man, The Lord will give him the wisdom to forgive you and thank you for saving his loved ones."

Mary brings her cup to her lips, looks at Jennifer, and adds, "As to those evil ones, the Lord will help you."

The clock is heard chiming out the middle of the night. Mrs. Statley opens the Good Book and gravitates to Joshua. "Here it is, the story of Rahab, and how she protected the spies against the depraved Canaanites. Take a moment and read it. Your Canaanites are your Uncle John and evil men such as Festus, who did not protect you as a husband and family should. Your actions in saving those orphans and all of Woody's crew are a sign of your virtue. In the Lord's eyes you are not evil. You turned away from the devil, and the Lord will help you."

Jennifer reads in the quiet room, and afterwards the pair talk on. Soon the first light of dawn shimmers to the southeast. Both women agree that Jennifer should rest for a couple days, and then on Tuesday morning, they walk to the train station to send Woody a telegram and purchase a ticket for Jennifer to return through Hellenville and continue on her journey if Woody does not greet her.

Chapter 30

<u>Woodrow's Dilemma</u>

Mrs. Maxwell is again in the cookhouse specifically an upstairs bedroom, once more tending to a wounded Walking Y orphan. She turns to her husband as he sows in the final stitch on the gouge in Nick's upper thigh and rump while the lad rests gritting his teeth. The boy looks pale, and vulnerable exposed to the doctor's ministrations. His head is bandaged, and numerous small cuts and lacerations are visible. Each is washed and as before, Michelle and Teri are nearby, and Nick was stripped of his filthy torn clothing, washed, and encased in clean linens. The Doctor finally folds the fresh white sheet and a blanket over his patient and looks up at his concerned audience.

"Well, regrettably you know the routine. Keep him warm, with plenty of fluids and keep everything around him clean. The lad is strong, and he should recover. The gouge is deep but should heal. I can tell he also had a terrible concussion from the explosion, but I am surprised it was not worse. From what I can see from his injuries, it is apparent that he was already jumping away, so it's not as bad as could have been the case."

The cavalcade then moves downstairs to the large table in the kitchen. Hardy has both a pot of coffee and another of hot tea ready for the group, and breaks out some crackers, cheese and home canned preserves along with some cookies. The doctor's wife looks around the table, and asks,

"What happened to that lovely young lady who was your governess?"

The crew as one man, looks at Woody. The owner is flat footed. Finally, he mumbles, "She had to leave in a hurry."

Such an obvious obfuscation leaves so much unsaid, that Mrs. Maxwell looks around now prying, "Why I've heard better explanations from a lump of snow. Do tell me?"

Woody stammers.

Hardy jumps to his rescue. "Mrs. Maxwell, do you believe in redemption, in this case Jennifer Hathaway's redemption?"

The Walking Y crew looks at Hardy intensely. The doctor looks up startled. Mrs. Maxwell looks up stunned. "Why I certainly do. It's all very clear in The Good Book. For women there is Mary Magdalene in the New Testament and in the Old Testament the story of the harlot, Rahab, who was spared with her family in the fall of Jericho. There are others, but these two are the key to understanding redemption for us women. Why do you ask?"

Hardy calmly states, "Miss Jennifer Hathaway was working with those who did that to the boy upstairs. She was put here to spy on us and destroy us. But, Mrs. Maxwell, the Lord can move in mysterious ways, and were it not for her actions, we would all be dead. Everyone on this ranch owes their life to her redemption. She saved us. Alone, and to her own grave danger. We hope to see her again to thank her and welcome her back into our extended family."

Tony nods his head, and instinctively reaches in his breast pocket for a small nip of medicinal whiskey. The doctor's wife is so stunned by the words, that she does not notice the Irishman, but instead looks at Woody who is lost in his own world. Finally, as heads around the table nod in agreement to Hardy's words, she says, "I do hope so Hardy. I always thought of her as a grand lady with troubles somewhere in her past. Remember, the good Lord forgave Mary Magdalene. We should all focus on the good and praise it."

Her husband nods his head in acquiescence and takes a sip of his coffee.

As all relax, they note a stranger's horse going up to the barn. Woody silently steps out.

"Oh, my it's Sheriff Bozeman," notes Mrs. Maxwell. Tony dons his coat and joins the owner and the Sheriff by the barn. The trio remains outside for several minutes before coming back to the cookhouse as the Doctor and Mrs. Maxwell are getting ready to leave.

"Doctor," barks the Sheriff, "I want you to examine the body before you leave. It's obvious he was battered, theoretically by a horse or two, and was shot several times, by different guns. I want to know about every single wound and the cause of death." He then turns and glares at the crew, "I fear that Mr. Woodrow W. Flynt and Mr. Seamus Patrick O'Connor have spun another web of lies."

The Doctor nods his head and walks out with his black bag to comply with the law's request. Once he is gone, Cody resumes and points to the orphans with his index finger locking in on Eric, "Look you little ones, ever since you, Eric, arrived in Hellenville, there has been nothing but trouble on this ranch. And every time it's the same story, namely that somehow it is Senator Bell's fault. I need to ask you all some questions, privately and one at the time."

He pauses and looks around a bit, and snaps out, "Where's that third boy, the one who likes to drive Dave's old team?"

Mrs. Maxwell cuts in, "He's upstairs injured by that Buffalo Gun when that so called 'body' set up a booby trap of dynamite like he did in town. You should be happy that this crew finally got the real culprit, as the law has not been making headway."

Sheriff Bozeman shakes his head like a dog who was just hit by a bone. Mrs. Maxwell and her gossiping abilities are not something to be ignored. Caution dictates that he temper his haughty demeanor. He looks at Teri, and says in an even voice, "Can I talk to you first? Perhaps in the living room please, alone."

Teri nods her concurrence. The Doctor's wife remains seated offering moral support to the children who are called one by one. The Doctor walks back in at about the same time as the Sheriff finishes his interrogations. Both men meet in the kitchen with Hardy handing each one a steaming hot cup of coffee.

The Doctor looks around at the group, and begins, "Well, Cody, the cause of death is hard to determine. He was alive when the two horses ran him over, but he was probably dead by the time the last of half a dozen or so bullets struck him. So, I cannot tell you exactly what killed him, and will state so in my report."

The Sheriff looks subdued. He replies a bit more humbly, "All of the testimony here matches what you just said and what I saw, and I will state so in my report. I will vouch for self-defense and I think that the body is the primary suspect regarding that explosion in town. No matter how some might twist the facts. I examined his buffalo gun, a Sharps, and heard consistent testimony about the explosions. The lad upstairs was injured in an explosion and it is my judgment that you have finally caught the fiend who hurt so many on Main Street. Thus, I must thank you." He looks at each orphan in turn and nods his head stiffly. "Is there anything else Doctor?"

"Well Sheriff, I know you would have gotten around to it, but I took the liberty of checking his saddle bags. They held half a dozen sticks of dynamite, and a letter with a time to be at The Walking Y early today. It was signed by a J. K., and in it, the unknown man talks about his niece as Festus's wife."

A wall of silence so thick, you can hear the wood crackle in the stove greets this announcement. Woody sits impassive and utters not a word.

***

Early the following week, Hardy rushes into the cookhouse at lunchtime from his run to town for supplies. As the crew comes in, and with Nick who joins them for the first time since his injury, seated in a comfortable chair with his leg propped up, Hardy places the hearty stew on the table. As all sit, and Woody mumbles through grace lost in his lonely thoughts as he has since he heard the Doctor. Yet today, Hardy stands by the stove as if the floor was made of red-hot coals.

"Damn it Hardy, stop jumping around as if you had a snake in your shirt," shouts an exasperated ranch owner.

"Woody, we have a telegram."

"Now what! Darn it, my back is still sore from digging that Buffalo Gun's grave in the frozen ground. So, now what?"

"Woody, I don't know why, but you've been more of a grouch than usual since The Buffalo Gun was killed. Well let's see if we can cheer you up. We can't work this afternoon. We all have to go to the train."

"What the hell are you talking about Hardy. We need to check the cows, I want to move that sign by the cottonwoods that indicates where Roger and Dave are buried, and Tony and Fred need to finish patching up all those holes in the blacksmith shop. So, talk, damn it."

Smiling, unphased by the grumbling owner, Hardy digs into his pocket. "Wait, I'll read the telegram. Let's see, where did I put it?" Hardy, as steady a man as God ever put on this earth, enjoys a moment of drama teasing his cranky boss, by rifling through one pocket after the other.

With a flourish, he takes out his reading spectacles, which all had long since noticed were not essential in order to read short documents. Taking his time to adjust them on his nose, he then reaches around for the telegram, and states the obvious. "Ah yes, here it is. If you'll pay attention, I'll read it."

The Walking Y's owner, in obvious turmoil since Jennifer's departure and talking with the Sheriff growls, "Read it damn you, instead of standing there like a calf trying to suckle a steer. Come on. Read. Now!"

Tony, looking nervous, forces a laugh, as the young ones all chuckle. Woody's face begins to gain a red tint, as he is on the verge of an apoplectic fit.

"All right, here I go:
WALKING Y - STOP - WILL BE ON AFTERNOON TRAIN TUESDAY - STOP - IF I SEE YOU – STOP - I WILL GET OFF – STOP - HATHAWAY

A loud cheer reverberates through the cookhouse. Even Eric sports the famous grin of the cat who ate the canary. Tony frowns in concentration as he watches the owner carefully out of the corner of his eyes, while forcing a smile on his face.

Woody sits like a foolish very confused and conflicted statue. Lost in thought. The Sheriff's words from a few days before rattling in his head, and he had yet to trust anyone, including Hardy with any discussions of the lawmaker's announcement. Yet, logically, Tony should have read the letter when he checked The Buffalo Gun's pockets and belongings. After all, Tony had brought the two hundred and forty gold dollars that were on the man to the ranch owner for the communal till. He also left the dynamite in the saddle bags for the Sheriff to find, although the Doctor found those.

Woody looks at Tony and reads the truth. With venom dripping from his lips, he turns to the Irishman, "You damn bastard, why didn't you tell me instead of letting me learn from the doctor in front of everybody? You saw it, you read it, didn't you?" With those words, Woody storms outside and goes to his father's old cabin, slamming the door.

All smiles around the table die. Hardy freezes on the spot as he looks at the departing owner, and the shrinking Tony. Before the foreman can reach in his breast pocket, Hardy walks towards him, and demands, "All right, what is going on here?"

Tony sinks in his chair with a sigh. "It was not up to me to tell Woody that Jennifer was married to The Buffalo Gun. It was not up to me to open the discussion. That Jennifer, she's English, and was duplicitous. That was a letter from JK to Festus in the saddle bags, which the Doctor found and discussed with Woody and the Sheriff. It was very clear and talks about Festus' wife, Jennifer, and how she spied on us to eliminate us."

The wind blows cold outside, and the room freezes with those words, as Hardy says softly, "But she saved us, and we all knew she was a spy well before the letter."

Tony replies in anguish, "Hardy, Woody and all of us didn't know she was married, and to The Buffalo Gun at that."

***

Jennifer stares out the window thankfully alone on the hard seat as Montana rumbles by. The snow-covered short grass prairie gives way to snow covered hills and trees interspersed with large, blanketed meadows. Finally, Hellenville comes in sight. She is on the platform side towards the front of the train, so she will have time to scan and see if any of the Walking Y is waiting for her. Her heart beats fast, and she can feel her anxiety all the way through her bones.

What will she do if Woody and the Walking Y are not waiting? For hours this question has played in her head. The only options are teaching or being a governess, but her ability to secure a good position in these professions will be limited as she has no references. She smiles at how a cover letter stating the truth would be read, but would definitively not secure her respectable employment. In her mind she sees the document:

...can ensnare any man or perhaps any boy – Yes, mothers would love that line both with concerns as to their husband's fidelity and their son's chastity.

...gifted at blackmail of politicians and prior successful targets have included a Secretary of the Treasury – Yes, unethical business mores may be lucrative, but do not hire her as a teacher or as a Governess.

...ethically challenged from a young age, and wants to share that virtue – Yes, school administrators would love that - Excellent recommendation. But not for a teacher.

...gifted with expensive habits, now trying to live modestly; however, if that is not to Jennifer's taste, she has skills such as picking locks or wallets that will allow her to live more extravagantly - Yes, the local law would love that line.

The train slows. Miss Jennifer Hathaway anxiously glues her face to the window. The final curve going into Hellenville from the southeast. She scans the platform, she sees no one from the Walking Y. She stares at the depot doors, she sees no one from the Walking Y. She opens her window and looks with a sinking feeling and spies no one from the Walking Y. She pulls her head in and watches the road to the depot from the Walking Y for any buckboard or rider going like mad, late for the train. She sees no one from the Walking Y.

She sags in her seat. Tears pool in her eyes. Her heart pounds slowly and she fears it will break. She will use her ticket to Missoula, and then, confront the cold cruel world. Her hands shake, and a tear lands in her lap as the Great Northern train begins to chug out of Hellenville, going west. It picks up speed, and Jennifer sits crying softly, in self-pity. She wants to be alone in her misery.

In the background, she hears the normal sounds on the coach, the conductor asking for tickets from those who got on. The doors between the cars are opened by some passenger or another, and Jennifer tries to sit a bit smaller.

"I'm sorry, is this seat taken?"

Jennifer feels she must be dreaming. She knows that voice.

"I'm sorry, can I sit here?"

Hesitantly she answers, "Why, yes of course."

The stout rancher sits, his bones tired. It has been a hard year. "I wanted to thank you for freeing Hardy and saving those kids. They mean a lot to me."

"That Woody, I had to do. If I had not, I could never have lived with myself, and I would have given up on any moral compass."

A moment of silence follows, "Do you have regrets? You know The Walking Y is hard work, those kids are a bunch of hellions, and the ranch is basically broke."

Jennifer smiles lightly, "I know Woody, I went through your books. Uncle John asked me to see what you had left."

Woody now smiles. "Yes, J. K. planted you on the ranch to destroy us. At this point, what do you want from The Walking Y?"

"My old job, but now with The Walking Y as my only boss."

"Before you ask for that, you should know that your husband, Festus O'Leary, was killed on the ranch. He was caught in a crossfire after being run over by a couple horses, so any of us might have been the one who killed him. And you two were married."

"Woody, I discussed that with Mary Statley in Moccasin. I need to finish what should have been my real job on the ranch, being a good governess. I'll explain everything that I've done in the past if you want me to. It's not a nice picture, and I am not proud of what I have done for Uncle John. But I would like to redeem myself and the first step would be for me to be a good Governess and complete the task you gave me a few short weeks ago at the Windsor in Denver. You can pay me with IOUs like you pay Tony, Hardy, and the kids."

"Jennifer," answers Woody seriously, "we would love to have you back; however, you must be ready to be slandered. Not by any of us, as all of us will fight for you, but by your uncle and also by the Senator. It will not be direct, but will be public through rumors that will be printed, all impugning your character, your morality and your sanity. It will be ugly and vulgar. They need to destroy your credibility so that you cannot use your knowledge to attack them, nor use it to defend the Walking Y."

Jennifer is taken aback by this statement. While Mary Statley had touched upon this possibility while discussing Mary Magdelene, she never considered the possible impact to both herself and those around her. She mulls Woody's statement, when the conductor comes through the swaying car shouting,

"Next stop, Drummond in two minutes, Drummond."

Woody looks at Jennifer and stands up. "This is my stop; Nick is waiting with the buckboard, and it'll take a few hours to get back to the ranch. If you want to be the Governess you were hired to be, you can get off in Drummond." Here he is quiet for a moment and steps away towards the exit. Then he turns back to her with a smile, "Mind you, I'll have to pay you with some IOUs."

Woody walks forward to the door, Jennifer hesitates but for a moment. She snags Teri's jacket and rushes to join him. They step off the train and see Nick waiting patiently with Artemis and Minerva whose noses are buried in their own feedbags. Nick helps Miss Hathaway onto the buckboard's seat, and Woody takes the outside. On the drive to Hellenville and the Walking Y, there will be plenty of time to talk, and if Nick hears the horrible truth, that is part of coming to grip with the world.

Chapter 31

<u>Gabrielle's Iron</u>

On a cloudy snowy day, in a walk up building on Larimer Street in Denver two men are meeting. Both are seated in the corner office of a modestly furnished suite, where no ears can overhear them. Senator William Howard Bell the Third takes a sip of his coffee infused with Scotch whiskey and looks at Mr. John Keegan who is seated behind his desk. Choosing his words carefully, the Senator goes on:

"As I see it, Mr. Keegan, you have half a loaf for me. On the positive side, you inform me that the so-called confession was a deception, and that Roger and Dave are deceased. You also enlightened me that both of those men are buried on the Walking Y, by a sign that Mr. Woodrow W. Flynt will probably have moved by now. Thus, you apprise me that my aspiration of a gubernatorial office is safely open."

"However, on the negative side, you are telling me that your so-called niece has betrayed you, and has moved back to the Walking Y. In another development, you state that your best operative, the executioner Festus O'Leary is dead, and Mrs. Couchman has informed you that a horse wearing his brand has been seen in Hellenville, ridden by the afore mentioned Mr. Woodrow W. Flynt."

"With such mixed results, I feel that I can only pay you half of your fee. There was no ambiguity in my agreement that I wanted the Walking Y eliminated once and for all, and that I wanted to purchase the afore mentioned ranch and graft it onto my Ringing Bell. Furthermore, such an outcome would have given me the largest ranch in the county and one of the largest in the state as a basis for my personal story in my run for Governor. I did give you permission to eliminate their cookhouse as I would have to build a large house more to my style and that expected of a great Governor."

"In short, I am disappointed. What will you do to redress the unfortunate shortcomings of your mission thus far?"

John Keegan takes a sip of his coffee which is infused with very little scotch, weaker than that the Senator holds in his hand, "Senator Bell, we have done better than Roger's work last year. First, you will note that no rumors in town associate you in any way to Mr. Woodrow W. Flynt's travails. Second, you now have confirmation that the so-called confession was a fabrication designed to malign you. Third, we have begun the process of destroying Miss Jennifer Hathaway's credibility. Lastly, you are now in an excellent position to make a run for Governor. While I agree that the task is not complete, it would be fair to state that we have done three quarters of the needed work, and the rest is but a minor setback that I am already planning to remediate."

"However," continues Mr. Keegan with a sense of victory, "I do have Woody's copy of the agreement you signed back in December."

William Howard Bell cannot help but to look relieved and smile. "If that is the case, that is good news and would increase my willingness to cover more of your charges. Let's say 60%, after you hand me the document."

Mr. John Keegan smiles. The Senator is not as hard as his reputation, and he ignores the rumors regarding the Senator's wife, Gabrielle, being the iron behind the politician. He reaches into a desk drawer and pulls the one-page document. He unfolds it carefully, and hands it over to the Senator who seizes it greedily. While so doing, he adds, "due to the minor setbacks why don't we settle at two thirds of the agreed upon charge. As you can see, the route is clear for you to run for Governor."

The back and forth continues for a few minutes, and finally, the Senator brings this to a close, "Very well, Mr. Keegan, we will settle on two thirds. But what are your plans?"

JK leans forwards, and begins, "As we have a long relationship, which I hope to continue when you are Governor, that is an acceptable offer. Now the important issue is how we will complete the task. The weak point in Woody's armor is the same one that was my weak point. Miss Jennifer Hathaway is but an easily swayed female. I will use that, and the specter left behind by The Buffalo Gun. Let me explain…"

The Senator leans in and listens carefully as Mr. John Keegan lays out his new approach. The Senator agrees halfheartedly; however, he turns to J. K. and states, "Before we start that phase, I would like to review the plan in Butte, as that is where I would also like to review all of our past activities. I want to make sure there is no pattern that can incriminate me. Can we meet in Butte in – say next week?"

John Keegan pulls his calendar and looks. "Yes, I have to be in Butte then, so that should work. But I can tell you with certainty that there is no pattern. I am one of the best in the country for this type of work and put myself on par with operations as far afield as Chicago. So, Senator, you are perfectly safe, and even with our temporary setback of Festus being eliminated and Benedict Jennifer Arnold, we will prevail. I also, as I told you, have plans to deal with my wayward niece. She is not a danger. She will be destroyed and if need be eliminated. If not, it will be that I died working on such an outcome. I am that committed and sure of myself.

Here Mr. John Keegan pauses, before adding, "While her perfidy has been a setback, I was already grooming a replacement as she could not have worked for me once she was over thirty years of age. No one courts a scandal with an old maid on their arm. So, I have the needs of my organization covered, and these skills will be available to you as Governor."

Thereupon the two shake hands and agree to meet in Butte.

***

Gabrielle dims the lights in the warm glass enclosed sitting room, part of the large master bedroom. She looks around and makes sure that the ceramic coffee pot is on a warming candle, and that the whiskey decanter is three quarters full. She looks at the sterling, and notes not a single smudge, while the crystal dish with the Senator's favorite mixed nuts is properly arrayed. Satisfied that the stage is set for William Howard Bell the Third's return from Denver, she scans the room one last time. As nothing is amiss, and her husband should arrive within less than a quarter of an hour, she walks back into the bedroom and sits at her vanity.

There she focuses on her face and hands. Already her hair has been groomed to perfection by the little Mexican lady who has served as her servant for the past decade. She scans the first age lines around her eyes and mouth but finds nothing amiss. For her age, she looks very young, and she works hard at holding the clock at bay. She applies one last touch of lipstick, a relatively neutral color that enhances her cheeks, and as her husband likes refined understatement, it is the perfect choice. She dabs her eyes with a bit of neutral powder that will highlight her blue eyes. Checking one last time, she stands. She walks to the full-length mirror and rotates slowly. All is perfect.

Now to complete the scene. She pulls Grant's biography off the shelf and slowly reads an enclosed note that she wrote while he was in Denver. She needs to be the backbone, as poor William is too kind. Tonight, Mr. John Keegan must fall. After perusing the one white sheet of paper with its blue ink curves in her handwriting, she stands and walks to the fireplace. Carefully, she places the open paper in its yellow embrace, and the document curls from the edges as she reads it one last time.

Danger: Mr. John Keegan knows too much about Senator Bells' efforts to position himself for a gubernatorial run, including:
- *The death of some blackmailing trollop in Butte some years ago,*
- *The campaigns against the Walking Y (Roger & Dave and the current one),*
- *Using JK to hire Festus O'Leary, now dead,*
- *Sherriff found an incriminating document on Festus from JK, including a notation on how Festus and Jennifer H. are/were husband and wife,*
- *J H has seemingly escaped J K's control with the death of Festus,*
- *And, now Mr. John Keegan fails us, and this creates a danger.*

Thus Mr. John Keegan must be taken care of in a fashion that will not arouse interest, as must his files.

The paper turns to ashes as Gabrielle watches. When she can no longer read a single word, she walks away. Gracefully she seats herself on the divan, and no sooner assumes the desired pose with President Grant's memoirs than she hears her husband coming up the steps to the door. Innocently, she smiles as he walks in.

"Ah, Gabrielle, I've had a most interesting trip to Denver. Do you want the key details?"

"My dear husband, I always want to hear the details, and what is behind them."

"Well, to the positive, Mr. John Keegan has secured Woodrow's copy of our agreement, so that is a major victory. On the more neutral side, he has a new plan to solve our vexing problem with Miss Jennifer Hathaway and The Walking Y. But his plan feels stale, and I fear that it is no match for the expanding crew that Woodrow W. Flynt is assembling. Let me get a coffee and let's discuss the chances of success. We must also discuss if we permit him to try again, or if we consider that he has failed us for the last time. I do think Woodrow W. Flynt will sue for a truce, and that is something we accept no matter what we plan. We will demand their silence during our campaign."

Gabrielle nods her head in concurrence, and opens the backup discussion with her husband, "My dear Senator, we need to discuss how we remove the danger that a weak Mr. Keegan presents. As you said, John's plan is stale, and Mr. Flynt has already defeated better ones. This means that J. K. has documents that could prove embarrassing, and it is time to eliminate any threat from that direction."

"What do you mean?"

"Well, I picture you elected and in the Governor's mansion, and if John fails again, he will be exposed, as will both the men who were involved in the recent attempt against Mr. Flynt. All three are a danger, and John Keegan knows how you operate, and he knows what we have asked him to do for the good of Montana over the years. Both JK and his files could be misconstrued and used against us. We need to plan for that contingency."

"My dear Gabrielle, I am meeting with John next week in Butte to see if there is a pattern. Which is per your suggestion. As you suggested, I asked him to bring all of the files related to our account with him for a full review. That should be adequate I would think."

The grandfather clock in the entryway on the first floor strikes one before Mr. & Mrs. Bell call it a day.

***

Senator William Howard Bell the Third tires of being on the train for days. First, he boards in Hellenville with a ticket for Billings. In that town, with cash and using the unoriginal moniker of Bill Howard, he purchases a Pullman ticket to Chicago on the Burlington Railroad. For this leg, he changes his appearance by wearing reading glasses and cheaper pre-made clothing. He avoids the dining car, and has the porter bring him meals. For the long haul to Chicago, he cultivates the look of an itinerant salesman, and even has some boring brochures extoling a rising line of farm and ranch equipment that was merged into a massive company, International Harvester, courtesy of J. P. Morgan.

That trip is over one and a half days each way, and few people want to hear another itinerant salesman. Thankfully, with a Pullman sleeper, he has the benefit of some comfort. He also has a stack of paperwork, but nothing particularly proprietary. Upon arrival in Chicago, he has an introductory letter from John Keegan that makes him smirk. He would find the skill he needs. Gabrielle is correct. Mr. Keegan has failed, and in his failure endangers everything that William Howard Bell the Third has schemed to accomplish for the past many years. That failure must be punished permanently, but discreetly.

After a fruitful meeting in Chicago, William Howard Bell the Third retraces his steps back to Hellenville. By the time he steps out of the Pullman car, he has shed his glasses, donned impeccably tailored clothing, and deployed his politician's smile and demeanor. Next target is the Governor's mansion and ensuring that all traces of prior contact with John Keegan are obliterated.

Chapter 32

The Senator Runs

Hardy looks out the window, hoping that the immaculately dressed man on a manicured hunter is not whom he thinks it is. He shakes his head. Not now, not with everything else that has hit the Walking Y since he started not that long ago. Mind you it does feel like he is growing old in the cookhouse on a Sunday afternoon. Why occasionally a day goes according to script, but he cannot remember when that last happened.

He steps away from the stove, and sticks his head into the living room, where Woody and Tony are in a quiet discussion. Teri, Michelle, Fred and Eric are lounging, doing homework, or in this case reading under the watchful eye of Miss Jennifer Hathaway. For the first time since his injury, Nick is also in the common room, reading.

"Well Eric," voices the cook knowing that the lad would by far prefer to be mucking out a barn than sitting in a warm room furthering his education. "I know you'd rather not be reading Kipling, so I thought I would toss in a distraction." Eric looks up, as the others pause.

Hardy then locks his eyes on Woody, "The Senator is on his way to our door, now."

Woody sits up like he had just been prodded with a red-hot branding iron, "That God Awful Son of a Bitch is coming here? Of all the gall. Tell the bastard he's not welcome."

Hardy, knowing his old companion in arms well, replies "Woody, you know I can't do that."

Jennifer stands up sharply and spills the last bit of coffee in her cup. All eyes lock in on her, while she looks around like a caged animal. She looks at Hardy and exclaims, "I'm headed upstairs. I don't want to listen to him."

Eric chuckles, "Miss Hearalot, can I speak?"

Jennifer stops and looks at the lad who is laughing along with the others in the room. "That was impolite. What do you want?"

"Just to let you know you can stay down here to listen; you don't have to go to your room and listen by the heating vent. Right Woody?"

Jennifer looks around and sees them all chuckling. She huffs and controls herself despite her reddening face. "Eric, you are a, a, eh, a …"

The lad smiles, and fills in, "Nuisance?"

"Yes." She looks around, and all are looking at her. "You all knew, since when?"

Woody answers, "well that first day when you listened, both Tony and I saw a bit of your hair dangling from the heating vent. Just for a moment mind you. But I thought to myself, 'she's much too nice a lady to be totally besotted with those ogres.' And I was right. Some of the others had to wait a while before we told them."

"So, you all knew?"

All heads nod. Jennifer collapses in her chair. Why, the Walking Y Ranch has been one surprise after the other.

"But you all still like me?"

They all nod their heads yes, as a knock disrupts Miss Hathaway's discomfort.

Hardy steps away and goes to the kitchen and opens the door. Woody stands and follows the cook hoping to head off the unwelcome politician. All the others sit and listen, and Hardy is heard in the other room greeting the lawyer, "Why, Senator Bell, what a surprise, please come in."

"Thank you very much Mr. James Hardyman, if I remember properly. Your hospitality is esteemed. If I could have a cup of hot coffee with a dash of milk and sugar it would be appreciated. After that cold ride to see your employer, I would enjoy a warm beverage."

Here the cany lawyer looks at Woody and makes a superfluous statement. "I do presume that you, Mr. Woodrow W. Flynt, are available. If you are, I have matters of some importance that I would prefer all of you hear directly from me. I presume on this Sunday afternoon, the crew is in? In short, all are invited and welcome to hear important good news that will impact all the fine citizens of this state."

Hardy leads the lawyer past the doorway into the living room, where all are gathered. The Senator looks around and smiles blandly. "Ah, I see that we have a full crew, including possible voters like Mr. Woodrow Flynt, and Mr. James Hardyman. Should I be successful, we also have future voters including Miss Jennifer Hathaway, Miss Teri Curtis, Miss

Michelle Longmire, Masters Nicholas Rubatel, Frederick Torroni, and Eric Smithby. As I have good news that I wish to share with you, shall we all sit, and make ourselves comfortable?"

As Woody is still standing looking at his neighbor with some repugnance, the Senator sits himself in Woody's chair leaving the ranch owner chairless. Woody looks so miffed, that both Teri and Eric chuckle at the owner's discomfort. As to the Senator, he pompously looks around, and teasingly looks at Woody.

"Why Woodrow, why don't you fetch a chair from the kitchen, and make yourself comfortable. After all you and your cook are the only ones here who may be entitled to vote, as I doubt the Irishman is naturalized." Here the Senator turns to Tony and adds with a dismissive smirk, "and anyway, there is a law against stump trainers voting in Montana."

Before Tony can react, Hardy nudges him with a whiskey decanter, and the foreman snags it from the smiling cook's hands. He downs an unusually large slug of medicinal whiskey while the Senator watches him with mirth.

"Gentlemen, and Ladies of course, I came to let you know that after serious reflection, and upon learning that you fabricated slanderous documentation as to an alleged confession from a couple ex-cowboys of mine, that I no longer feel bound by the patently unenforceable agreement you, Woodrow, asked me to sign a few weeks ago."

"I have asked the Sherriff to look into the possibility that my ex-employees were murdered on the Walking Y or elsewhere in the county, and he will reluctantly be doing so. In the interim, dear neighbor, as the agreement was secured under false pretenses, I have excellent news for you. I will run for reelection as your Montana State Senator. Unless of course," here the Ringing Bell's owner pauses for dramatic effect and he then repeats himself, "unless of course, I can secure the nomination from my party to be your candidate for Governor of the Great State of Montana." All look at Senator William Howard Bell with distain. Yet, he goes on, "Should that happen, I will focus my efforts on being your Governor."

Here the Senator turns to the owner and looks him in the eye, "Mr. Flynt, as such a campaign requires some financial backing, I am hoping that you can be a contributor?" Woody looks up startled as if he had just swallowed a wasp. Dramatically the politician goes on, "Perhaps by providing me with some of those gold coins you probably took from Miss

Jennifer Hathaway's husband, when he was trampled by a pair of horses and then gunned down in cold blood on this ranch."

Woody's face is livid.

Tony reaches for the decanter, but as Hardy fears it will be thrown thus wasting precious bourbon, he has already pulled it out of range. Instead, the cook reaches over, and picks up the Senator's cup, and politely gestures to the door. "Mr. William Howard Bell the Third, I suggest that you leave now, as you are not welcome here, nor are your words and effrontery."

The Senator stands and throws a mock salute to his audience and calmy walks out humming. All of the Walking Y crew stands as he leaves each wondering if they should toss him out on his backside. As he is about to clear the door, Jennifer talks clearly for all, "Senator, I did not think it possible, but you are a lower life form than my deceased husband. I make a promise to all that I will somehow secure Uncle John's papers and see if I can land you in jail where you rightly belong."

Senator Bell stops. He reaches into his coat pocket and tosses out a copy of the *Butte Daily Bugle* on the kitchen table. "Miss Jennifer Hathaway, you are a bit late. I suggest you read the most unfortunate news, about another death in your family. I feel great regret at your loss so soon after that of your deceased husband. Mind you Festus was killed by your current paramour, so what does that make you? But then again, that is the way of such Jezebels' as yourself."

With those words, he walks out, leaving many perplexed looks behind him. While Senator William Howard Bell the Third rides away sitting tall in the saddle, all scramble to look at the cover page of *The Butte Daily Bugle* on the dining room table where two articles scream for attention side by side:

John Keegan Kills Himself: *Mr. John Keegan, aged 49, was found dead last night in his local apartment. Police ruled that Mr. Keegan's death a suicide. Apparently, he died of a self-inflicted shotgun wound in the back and was thus killed while hanging himself. The gun was found twenty feet away from the victim, thrown there by the kickback of the double barreled twelve gauge...*

Fred gasps, "Woody look there," he shouts as he points to the second of the articles on the front page of the newspaper.

Deadly Fire at the corner of Granite and Mountain: *A potentially serious blaze was extinguished at the corner of Granite and Mountain in a three-story brick building. The fire was brought under control thanks to the new fire engine given to the city by the benevolent Anaconda Company and started in the offices of John Keegan & Associates. While Mr. Keegan was not in the offices, two of his employees were not so fortunate. Mack Murphy and Cormac O'Toole were found dead with smoke inhalation. Both had been seen a few hours earlier drinking heavily at local saloons. It is presumed that they were holding an improvised wake for Mr. Keegan, who was suffering from acute depression and killed himself a few hours earlier. Mr. Keegan was aggrieved by serious misfortune when a couple weeks ago his beloved son in law, Festus O'Leary, was gunned down on the Walking Y Ranch in Hellenville. This was aggravated by the infidelity of his niece, Miss Jennifer Hathaway (see story on page 7 and lead story on page 1). She is rumored to have taken up residence with her husband's murderer (see pictures on page 5). The fire...*

"That's utter and absolute bull," shouts a red-faced Miss Hathaway, using language that she would never use under any other circumstances.

Teri's jaw drops open at hearing the term from the prissy governess. Jennifer does not see the girl and continues. "That's an absolute and a downright lie. Uncle John was never depressed, not for one single solitary moment. He used people and earned great pleasure in doing so. For instance, Festus O'Leary was in his employ for several years before that job about eleven years ago when that so called Buffalo Gun murdered more than fifty-seven people dynamiting and burning down that hall in Butte. My dear Uncle John was always scheming on how to get more power and money. I lived with him for too long, so I know. Oh, goodness how I know."

Jennifer stops for a moment for a lungful of air and then resumes her tirade. "He sold me as a Jezebel when I wasn't old enough to know better. Uncle had no soul, and feelings were something to be exploited.

There was not a remorseful toenail in Mr. John Keegan. That's what he taught me all the time I lived with him. That article is all wrong."

Here she looks at Woody, and tilts her head as if she is struck by another note in the article, "Anyway, how do you shoot yourself with a shotgun in the back and then hang yourself?"

Fred begins, "Well, you'd have to rig up a string and secure the shotgun so that you could pull the string as you hang yourself. It's not that difficult." Incredulous eyes stare at him from all directions. "But the article did not mention the needed string…"

Woody puts his hand on the governess' shoulder. "Jennifer, we're dealing with the Senator here, ever expanding government, and also monied corporate interests. You know that article is bull, we all know that article is bull, the Senator is laughing because he knows that the article is bull, but we cannot prove it."

Hardy clears the newspaper to the side, and hands out empty cups. "There is nothing like a good hot beverage to dispel stupidity. So, here is some fresh coffee and shortly fresh hot chocolate. And Woody, we need to make sure that no one here is suicidal, as young master Fred will tell them how to do it so that it looks impossible."

All laugh but Woody who remains serious.

"Hardy, thank you for the snack and beverage. We need to talk. All of us. We are in danger, because now he intends to be our governor, and big money intends to make him our governor. The article shows how the police force in Butte is working for the Anaconda Company, and that company wants Senator Bell to be governor. It would help them with the Wobblies, and the union agitators. They have great power, and now we are in greater danger than ever."

Tony pipes in, "Yup, how convenient, the bastard must be pure blooded English." Seeing Jennifer and Woody's reaction, he hastens to add, 'meaning no offence to the current company, of course."

Thereupon, Hardy banishes the serious gloomy talk from his kitchen. "Out, all of you with your Senatorial clouds, and with your newspapers crowing about suicide. We all know that Butte is corrupt, and that power corrupts, and absolute power corrupts absolutely. So, I will exercise my absolute power in this kitchen and banish all of you 'till dinner once you finish your hot drinks."

The crew dissipates to afternoon chores. Hardy demands that the young ones bring him more dry firewood and take extra care milking the ornery cow. "Yesterday, I had straw in the cheese. If that happens again, Mr. Eric Smithby, I will personally make sure that you get it in your serving of whipped cream and may add a bit more."

Dinner that night starts off rambunctious. Teri initiates it by making Woody choke when she says, "we could geld the Senator. If he talked like a girl, he'd lose."

Jennifer barges in, "Teri, enough of that. Some decorum is needed."

Eric adds, "Decorum, yeah, we'll decorum his, well never mind."

Tony replies, "Well, I've never seen that done, but we have a few months to figure that one out."

But, Fred cuts in serious, "With all that money behind him, he'll have a lot of power. So far, we've been lucky. We'll need to outsmart them."

"Lucky Fred. Let's see how lucky," cuts in Michelle counting dramatically on her fingers, "We've been shot, clubbed, kidnapped, jailed, and blown to smithereens. Let's see, you had a horse killed under you and were shot, so did Nick whose arm was broken and then his ass was ripped open by a large branch in an explosion. Eric also had Moose killed under him, and Teri and I were kidnapped, Woody was clubbed, Hardy was whipped, and Tony had to break out of jail and out of Butte. It's lucky he's only had a couple ideas on how to attack us, because I'd hate to be unlucky."

Eric goes back to the black-haired boy, "All right Fred, how do we outsmart them?"

Fred reaches over, looking scared. He grabs the newspaper and opens it and suddenly blanches, "I haven't figured out how to outsmart them yet, but more important, Woody, we have a problem. The only other loose end is Miss Jennifer."

"What do you mean?" queries a surprised Woody.

"Well, think. Everybody who was working for the Senator on eliminating us has been killed: Roger, Dave, Hank, Cormac, Mack, Brogan, Festus and John Keegan. All are dead except our Jennifer, who must be on their list."

Tony looks at the Governess in mock seriousness, "We'd better keep you away from the shotguns. Are you depressed or mildly suicidal?"

Incensed, she replies, "But I'm not feeling suicidal."

Woody cuts in, "You just told us that Uncle John was not either."

A heavy quiet greets this announcement. All look at Jennifer. Woody rubs his chin, "Jennifer, I'm putting you on the next train to Mary's. So, it's back to Moccasin for you as you are in greater danger than is the Walking Y."

Jennifer shakes her head no. "I'm staying here if you are all willing to let me. They will track me down. I will be safer here than anywhere and The Walking Y is my home and is also my fight. Additionally, now that I know some of Hardy's past, and this last round, please let me stay. I'm at home here, and you trust me. You've proven it time and time again."

Woody slowly nods in agreement. "Upon reflection, actually, I agree. We will do a couple things to allow us to rest and enjoy Hardy's excellent food. First, I do think I should get a dog or two and secondly, Tony and I will see the Senator and work out a truce through the election. That is what he wants the most, and will give us what we need the most, quiet time to work a ranch to build up our cattle numbers and our bank account and have you young ones do some schooling."

Tony looks over, "Woody, he's a pure-blooded bodach bastard. How can you trust him?"

"Tony, in December last year, we reached an agreement. He replaced horses and cattle that his crew killed and abided by it for a few short weeks. I'll take anything we can get, because Jennifer will be on his short list, and he can probably find Jennifer in Moccasin. We need to have a quiet stretch to focus on calving, I'd like to purchase a couple common line bulls, and that money we found on Festus will allow us to do that, and I'd like to see what we can do to make ourselves stronger. Remember, this ranch can hold four thousand head of cattle and we only have a bit more than four hundred. We need to focus on ranching for five minutes and maybe do such things as boarding other people's cattle. Questions?"

Chapter 33

Truce

Woody and Tony ride together to the Senator's grand white Greek Revival house. Jesse, the Ringing Bell Manager intercepts them about half a mile from their destination, where the tree lined lane leading to the front door starts. With him are a pair of unsmiling riders sporting rifles that are loosely aimed at the visiting pair.

Jesse greets the neighboring rancher. "Woody, you are not particularly welcomed, nor is that Irish scum. You definitively cannot come any further on this ranch unless you have a good reason; but you must hand me the rifles in your saddle scabbards and let me frisk you for handguns."

"Well Jesse," answers Tony, "you should ensure the Senator's safety by impounding your own guns. Last month the rumor was that you sought to have that young man, Fred arrested for shooting you. Both Woody and I know that the lad can't hit the broad side of the barn from the inside, so you must have shot yourself and sought to deflect the blame."

Jesse snarls.

Woody smiles, and then adds, "why don't you gentlemen keep us company to the Senator's front door. There we will leave our horses, and our rifles in their scabbards. As to handguns, you can check us as we go in."

With those words, Woody nudges Festus' horse forwards. Tony follows on Sorley. The Ringing Bell riders flank them closely up the lane to the hitching rail by the front door. Jesse hands his reins to one of his men and stands by the entrance. He checks both Woody and Tony for any handguns, and finding none, allows himself to stand by them as they knock. When the door is opened, Jesse listens carefully in case the Senator lets it be known that he wants his neighbor escorted off the property.

Upstairs, Gabrielle and William Howard Bell watch the pair come to the Greek revival house with some amusement. She smiles as she recalls that her husband guessed that the pair would visit. The Senator smiles, "As

I told you, if it is up to the predictable Woodrow Flynt, he will now grovel for a truce. In return, we will gag him."

The uniformed maid who opens the door looks at the two riders in their working attire, "Gentlemen, after you have removed your dirty boots and your manure-stained coats, you may step into the house. We are seeking to keep our hardwood floors clean." She then looks out at Jesse, and goes on, "Mr. Tortula, the Senator will not need you at this time, but would like you and a couple riders to remain available to escort these men off the premises after their short visit."

With those words, she turns past the two Walking Ys, and designates a short wooden bench. "Please wait here. The Senator will be with you as soon as he has time."

Senator Bell leaves the pair waiting a good half hour, without any further hospitality. A bell rings deep in the bowels of the house, and the maid comes back. "Senator William Howard Bell the Third will see you in his office, please follow me." She then leads them down a long hallway, around a corner, and shows them into the politician's office.

The office is quite grand, with built in bookshelves on two walls and windows looking to the front and to the south of the house. The Senator, impeccably dressed in a dark suit, smiles with cold calculating eyes. "Ah, Mr. Woodrow W. Flynt and I see you brought your foreman, Mr. Seamus Patrick O'Connor, to affect an unannounced visit. It is indeed an unexpected surprise. Mr. O'Connor, as this is your first time visiting me in this house, I would like to thank you for coming. To celebrate this rare event, I have asked my maid to bring all of us a fresh cup of coffee. I am assuming, Mr. O'Connor, that such a beverage would be enhanced by a dram of whiskey. Please sit."

With those words, he gestures to a pair of chairs facing his imposing flat-topped desk. The chairs are plush, restrain any movement, and with their soft seats, leave his guest a bit lower than they would expect. Tony grumbles, Woody smiles at the juvenile antics of the politician. The Senator goes around his desk and sits in his chair and looks down at the intruders. "What can I do for you gentlemen?"

Woody looks up, and cuts to the chase, "Senator, we have had some issues recently on the Walking Y and suspect that you may have some knowledge of the activities directed by the late Mr. John Keegan."

"Woodrow, regrettably, I cannot recall meeting this Mr. Keegan. As to being aware of his activities, I would have to be clairvoyant. So, what you are suggesting would be impossible. I have never had that man in my direct employ, and I would not hire any person to pursue any illegal or unethical activities. Furthermore, I can state that I have abided by our agreement except for political pursuits. I would still be appreciative if you would let me peruse your copy to make sure that I have not missed any other clause."

"Senator, amuse me for a moment. We know that even if Mr. John Keegan was sleeping in your bed, you would say that you have not worked with him. Thus, let's dispense with the posturing. We also fully expect that you have had a chance to destroy my copy of the December agreement which you signed, enabling us to let that rest. In short, you can dispense with your self-serving words. I did not come to discuss these issues."

William Bell looks on in mild interest as Woody then goes on, "More important, you are running for Governor, and I would like to focus on running my ranch in peace. Can we agree to stay out of each other's affairs through the election?"

"Mr. Woodrow W. Flynt, I would like nothing better. BUT, you and parts of your crew have done nothing of late except spread despicable rumors as to my activities. I WOULD APPRECIATE IF YOU CEASED SPREADING THESE DESPICABLE LIES. Do I make myself clear?"

"Again, Senator, for the sake of discussions, let's agree that you will not partake, instigate, or pay for any activities against the Walking Y, and in return, no one on the Walking Y will talk in any fashion that is uncomplimentary to either yourself, your wife, or the Ringing Bell Ranch. Can we agree verbally on such a course of action?"

The Senator looks incensed. "Mr. Flynt and Mr. O'Connor, there has been, is, and will be, no illegal activities directed at your ranch from any person or entity in my or my wife's control. So, such an agreement simply requires you and your crew to bridle their tongues. You must also not discuss any activities regarding this ranch or my wife or myself with Dr. Maxwell's wife, as she will then spread them. Do I make myself perfectly clear?"

"Yes Senator. We will both behave and vouch to that effect."

"One more important detail Mr. Flynt. You have hired a so-called governess by the name of Jennifer Hathaway, and she is living with you on the Walking Y. Please be advised that I have it from good authority that the woman in question is of doubtful morals and has been involved in more than one scandal and is reputed to be unstable and should probably be institutionalized. Her reputation is more along the lines of a loose woman working the night shift at The Prancing Mare. If you insist on retaining her, I will hold you accountable for all of her actions and any story she may weave that is slanderous to either my or my wife's reputation. Is that clear?"

Woody looks at the cold eyes facing him across the large desk, and replies, "Senator, while I disagree with your characterization of Miss Hathaway, I understand that we will be accountable."

"Then Mr. Flynt and Mr. O'Connor, what you propose is acceptable. However, be aware that should you not eliminate your slander with regards to my wife and myself along with any entity we operate, I will seek full recourse as allowed by law. Is that clear?"

At that moment, the maid brings in three cups of coffee and a bottle of excellent single malt whiskey. The Senator looks at her and states, "Please put mine on my desk, and these gentlemen are regrettably leaving now, so they will not have time for my hospitality, nor will that Irishman have time to drink the dram of whiskey you proposed to serve for him. Thus, please show them to the door, and have Jesse escort them to the property line."

***

Hardy, agitated, walks into the kitchen as the crew gathers for the hearty roast that was waiting on the stove, the baked potatoes in the oven, and the home canned vegetables that are warming with a garlic butter sauce. In addition, there is a nice round fresh baked country loaf of bread already on the table.

"Woody, as discussed, I picked up a few supplies at the general store in town. Mrs. Couchman laughed at me, and when I asked why, she suggested I purchase a copy of the *Hellenville Times*."

"Did you spend money on a newspaper? You know Hardy, we aren't rich enough to spend money on frivolities and she would do anything to get an extra nickel."

Hardy, steaming, tosses the newspaper on the table. "Look!"

"Local Ranch Hires Scandal Riven Governess:
The Walking Y ranch just outside of Hellenville, is rumored to have hired Miss Jennifer Hathaway as governess for five orphans the ranch acquired as free labor. Miss Hathaway's past includes her being at the center of the recent controversy in Washington, DC, which forced the Secretary of the Treasury to resign in disgrace. She is rumored to have entrapped him in a set of unspeakable scandals of a sexual nature. Prior to that, Miss Hathaway is also alleged from a very young age to have ensnared other men and even boys who were vulnerable to her disgraceful behavior ....

Her Uncle, Mr. John Keegan, a respected businessman from Butte with offices in Denver and Washington, took Miss Hathaway at a young age when her parents were shot. He was distraught by the shame she brought to the family, and recently killed himself leaving a note stating that he could no longer face the sordid activities of his niece. A long-time associate stated that Mr. John Keegan's greatest disappointment in life was that while he took in his niece, she spurned his best attempts to educate her in a Christian setting and she, from a young age enjoyed ensnaring young boys and leading them on a sordid path....

The table goes quiet. Jennifer sits at her chair white faced in shame. "Woody, they want to destroy you and the ranch, and I am now the weak point. I have no credibility in the world at large. I hate to say this, but I think I should leave. I cannot help you, and this will create problems in Hellenville for all of you."

Woody laughs, "Well, as I never gave a damn what people in town think, and as I have no intention of starting now. So, no, stay here, and the hell with them."

"Hear! Hear!" shout the others at the table.

Fred suddenly looks up, "I know how to outsmart them."

Woody turns to Fred, "all right Fred, how do we outsmart him?"

"Can we get to John Keegan's offices in Denver before they burn that down also? If we rifled through those papers, we might find something. All we have to do, is get some hint of a scandal to the Senator's opponent in the general election. We just need to make the Senator lose, without looking like we are behind the scandals."

Woody runs his hands over his face thinking. "Fred, you might be right. Jennifer, and I will leave in the early morning on the train."

Eric chimes in, "Not alone you don't. You need us orphans to do this with you, and you owe us big time for saving this place - again. No one will suspect us, and we all have a score to settle. Hardy and Tony can do the feed runs. Can't you Hardy?"

Hardy and Tony look at each other, but Woody thinks fast and before Tony and Hardy can answer cuts back in, "Well I was being hasty. That's not today's issue. Theoretically we have a truce with the Senator, and I would not want to be the first to violate it. Thus, I need to think about trying to find any hint of a scandal. That may or may not be the way to proceed…. Anyway, let's focus on dinner and our truce."

Here Woody smiles and looks around the table. "At least this means that we do not have to ride out on patrol tonight." He looks at Miss Hathaway and winks before continuing, "That also means that I can finally join you all in a game of poker! I want to win back some of those IOUs that are burning holes in your pockets.

Also, By Jeter Isely
Action Adventure in a Western Setting
The Walking Y – Book 1 in The Walking Y Saga – Audible narrated by Jason Markiewitz

Senator William Bell has Woody's Walking Y Ranch, once one of the finest in Montana, on the brink of bankruptcy when fate brings a young and ornery runaway to his door. Now, with the help of a drunken Irishman, a handful of orphaned teenagers, and a wild scheme they're ready to fight to keep the ranch. They're not the only ones willing to fight for it though. Senator Bell sees The Walking Y merged to his Ringing Bell Ranch as the perfect platform for his naked political ambitions. He and his hired guns are willing to do anything to take it. Even if that means murder.

The Buffalo Gun – Book 2 in The Walking Y Saga – Audible narrated by Jason Markiewitz

Senator Bell's iron-willed wife, Gabrielle, has buyer's remorse – but The Walking Y has an agreement and a possible confession about prior despicable actions that could destroy the Bell's lucrative political career. To keep his hands clean, Senator Bell hires the shadowy John Keegan to eliminate all on The Walking Y. The key is the deadly elusive accurate Buffalo Gun and his affinity for explosives. Meanwhile a related turncoat seeks to destroy the ranch from within. Woody, the owner of The Walking Y Ranch and Tony, his Irish foreman along with the five orphans must survive discord, flying bullets, and dynamite to survive.

The Legal Lackey (due in 2024) – Book 3 in The Walking Y Saga
The Governor's mansion beckons Gabrielle and Senator Bell. Both think they have destroyed all incriminating evidence that would foil their political greed. But as insurance the Senator has tasked the disreputable Malvin Wolf, Esquire with destroying The Walking Y once and for all. Guns, bullets, and knives are not enough to defend the ranch. Woody and his crew must outfox and attack. The deck is stacked against each Walking Y and the Senator has never lost a legal battle.

Travel Memoir
Naked Shorts – The Making of a Cowboy
After a childhood fraught with hardship and the loss of his parents, foster parents, and his chosen career, Jeter dreamed of escapades like the heroes in

the books and comics he loved. He sets out to see the world on his own grand adventure. From outrunning sandstorms to out thinking thugs, Jeter's journey brought him into a life that seemed straight out of one of his beloved adventure stories. Little did he realize that, on the far side of the world, he would discover the place he felt most at home – in the saddle of a horse.

Printed in Great Britain
by Amazon